INTOXICATE ME

UNDERBELLY CHRONICLES BOOK FIVE

TAMARA HOGAN

DEDICATION

2020 was a year in which a very solitary profession became even more so. Thanks to fellow writers, avid readers, and supportive family and friends!

As always, countless thanks to Mark—for holding down the fort, for herding the cats, and for the gift of time.

THE UNDERBELLY CHRONICLES

TASTE ME
CHASE ME
TOUCH ME
TEMPT ME
ENTHRALL ME
INTOXICATE ME

THE UNDERWORLD COUNCIL

Incubus: Elliott Sebastiani *
Second: Antonia Sebastiani

Siren: Claudette Fontaine
Second: Scarlett Fontaine

Were: Krispin Woolf
Second: Jacoby Woolf

Vampire: Valerian
Second: Wyland

Valkyrie: Alka Schlessinger
Second: Lorin Schlessinger

Humanity: (vacant)
Emeritus: REDACTED

Sec/Tech: Lukas Sebastiani
Second: Jack Kirkland

* President

CHAPTER ONE

It wasn't unusual for Jack Kirkland and Underworld Council President Elliott Sebastiani to work long hours together, sometimes at Elliott's home office. What *was* unusual? Being asked to provide bodyguard/driver service afterward. Jack was happy to serve—Elliott had a really bad habit of ditching his security detail—but... "Where's Adam?" *Damn it, am I going to have to fire yet another security guard?*

"His daughter had a hockey game."

"Elliott..."

Elliott reached into the entryway closet for their jackets. "I had every intention of staying in tonight, but then Lukas mentioned he and Scarlett were going out, and that Sasha was babysitting." A huge grin split his face. "She might need some help."

"Right," Jack said dryly. Elliott's daughter Sasha was fully grown and frighteningly capable. The man was besotted with his granddaughter. Two-month-old Coco Annika Fontaine had almost everyone wrapped around her tiny pinky finger.

Elliott handed him his jacket. "I'm not taking you out of your way, am I?"

Subtext: Do you have a date tonight? "Nope," he answered, slipping on his fleece jacket. He had a mountain of paperwork waiting for him at Sebastiani

Security. Lukas, Scarlett, and Coco lived right upstairs, in the building's top floor loft. "I'm ready when you are."

"Great." Elliott put on a beat-up navy pea coat. "'Bye, Claudette!" he called.

"Hold on, hold on!" His bondmate, Claudette Fontaine, hurried from the kitchen, carrying a 9x13 pan in a quilted fabric sling with handles. "Bring this leftover lasagna with you."

"That's a full pan, still warm from the oven," Elliott groused good-naturedly. "Why does my son eat better than I do?"

"Lukas forgets to eat, and you don't." She gave his stomach a tiny, loving pat. "There's another pan in the kitchen."

"Thank you."

A couple of years ago, Elliott's son Lukas had bonded with—married—Claudette's daughter Scarlett. Not long afterward, Elliott and Claudette, longtime Council colleagues and both widowed for years, had gone public with their own secret relationship.

Friends, family, lovers. Colleagues, bondmates, co-workers. So many relationships, so intertwined. After a decade spent in the Sebastiani family's orbit, Jack was still unraveling the skeins.

Elliott slipped his hands around Claudette's waist. "Are you sure you won't come along?"

Claudette glanced at her watch, then at the door to the office she and Elliott shared. "I'd love to, but I have a meeting starting in ten minutes."

Now he didn't feel quite so feeble. The Council's Siren First was working on a Saturday night, too.

Elliott took the pan. When he dipped his head to

kiss Claudette goodbye, Jack turned toward the door to give them some privacy. Elliott—all the Sebastianis—were incubi and succubi, a species that absorbed emotional energy for sustenance. When amorous, their bodies emitted intoxicating sex pheromones. Anyone standing nearby couldn't help but be impacted.

Anyone but *him*, because he took fast-acting pheromone intoxication meds almost every day. A human who spent as much time around sex demons as he did needed all the help he could get.

When Elliott and Claudette finally separated, her sleek, grayish-red bob was distinctly tousled. "Take good care of my bondmate now," she said to Jack.

He kissed her cheek. "Will do."

When they stepped into the penthouse lobby, the door to the other unit opened. Sasha Sebastiani appeared, wearing a lightweight down jacket, clingy black leggings, and black boots against the crisp November chill.

Sasha.

Great.

Not.

He steeled himself as her scent, a succulent mix of spice, jungle flowers, and earthy musk, saturated the lobby. Earth, air, water, fire…she was elemental, and her personality provided the spark. Today, her scent seemed more water-based than usual… Ah, her hair. Even wet, the short black and purple strands stood straight up from her head. The woman used enough hair product to withstand an F5 tornado.

"Hey!" Elliott crossed the lobby and hugged her. "I thought you'd be over at Lukas's place already. I was going to surprise you."

"I got hung up at the club." Sasha managed the Sebastiani family's entertainment interests. Both Crackhouse Coffee and Underbelly, a raucous nightclub, were located downstairs, on the ground floor. The Sebastiani Building sprawled over nearly a block of prime downtown Minneapolis real estate. "I just got out of the shower," she added, flicking a knowing blue gaze his way.

Damn it, she knew *exactly* where his thoughts would go—to her, naked, in the shower. To water, sluicing in slow motion over her lithe dancer's frame. To her hands, slicking soap over wet skin. Sasha was a succubus, a sex demon of staggering power, and she teased him for sport. The meds took the edge off, but…damn.

"Jack's giving me a ride over to Sebastiani Security," Elliott told Sasha, punching the elevator's call button. "Let's carpool."

Let's not. The last time Sasha had ridden in his car, her pheromones had hung around for days.

"Dad, if Jack gives us both a ride, then neither of us has a car," she said. "Someone would have to give us a ride home. There's no need to inconvenience anyone."

"It's no inconvenience," Jack said. As Council President, Elliott was supposed to ride with a trained bodyguard at all times. "Someone will give Elliott a ride home anyway."

The guilty, split-second glance Elliott shot his daughter confirmed his suspicions. Damn it, he *was* going to have to fire another bodyguard.

Adam Koivisto wasn't the first bodyguard who couldn't stand up to Elliott's charm offensive, and he probably wouldn't be the last. But every Sebastiani

Security operative knew leaving the President unguarded was a termination-level offense. "Just call downstairs when Lukas and Scarlett get back home," he said evenly. "Someone will drive you home, or wherever you'd like to go."

And with so many trained operatives in the building, it wouldn't have to be him.

As they rode the elevator down, her maddening scent spiced at the air. Thanks to the pheromone intoxication meds, his thoughts remained crisp and clear, but his cock had a mind of its own, twitching behind the zipper of his khakis.

Great.

Sasha inhaled subtly but deeply, her eyelids drifting to half-mast. One corner of her ripe mouth tipped upward, and her sharp-featured face turned voluptuous with pleasure. Incubi and succubi plucked emotions right out of the air, absorbing them for sustenance, emitting irresistible pheromones in response.

To her, his arousal was just an energy source.

Nothing personal.

Descending ten floors had never taken so long.

Elliott cleared his throat. "Where are Lukas and Scarlett going tonight?" he asked Sasha.

She blinked, then softly cleared her throat. "The Guthrie, I think."

As father and daughter talked about their day, Jack ignored his unruly body. Yes, he was attracted to her—hell, who wouldn't be?—but he'd decided Lukas's sister was off limits the day they'd met. His professional life was too entwined with the Sebastiani family to risk pursuing a personal relationship—and unlike them, and the rest of the Underworld Council, he was just a human being.

If he allowed himself to think about *their* history—about the crash that had marooned their paranormal ancestors on Earth several thousand years ago, and how successful they'd been sharing the planet with humanity while hiding their paranormal nature—his brains would scramble.

Nope, he was just a normal human man, trying to avoid the sexual web Sasha Sebastiani wove simply by…being.

Finally, the elevator stopped. "Wait here, please," he said. After clearing the elevator bay lobby—it was empty—he escorted Elliott and Sasha to the fire door leading to the underground parking ramp. "Hold here for a moment." He walked through the door first, scouring the wide expanse of concrete. No movement, no activity. No people, no headlights, no tail lights. With the sun setting and Underbelly not yet open for business, the ramp was half-empty. He retrieved Elliott and Sasha, then guided them toward his Volvo, parked halfway down the first row.

Sasha huffed out a visible breath. "Damn, it's cold."

"Coming outside with wet hair doesn't help." His phone, one of the Sebastiani Labs secure prototypes, vibrated in his front pants pocket. His father's ring tone. Jack absently reached for the phone, then glanced at the screen. An actual phone call. *Nice try, Dad.* He silenced the phone and slipped it back in his pocket. He was in no mood for his father's particular brand of emotional blackmail—

Thwipp.

"Get down!" Even as he dove for Elliott and Sasha, he knew he was too late. Blood bloomed from a bullet wound on the side of Elliott's head. The lasagna pan slipped from his grasp.

Thwipp. Thwipp.

He felt two hot stings as he tackled Elliott and Sasha to the concrete. As he rolled on top of Sasha, the pan hit the pavement, spattering them with red sauce.

Thwipp.

Sasha's piercing scream.

Oh, god. "Are you hit?"

"No!" She tried to scrabble out from under his body. "Dad. Daddy!" She squirmed, pushing at him. "Oh my god…"

His shoulder and back burned like hellfire, but he shoved her down, covering more of her body with his own. "I said stay down." Where the hell was the shooter? And why hadn't he grabbed his Glock from the Volvo's goddamn glove box before bringing Elliott downstairs? He lifted his head a stingy inch, then another. Damned if he'd give the guy another clean shot, especially when he couldn't return fire.

What the hell had he been thinking, looking at his phone? The split-second distraction had likely cost Elliott his life.

Seconds passed like eons, but there were no more gunshots, no squealing wheels of a getaway car, no hurried footsteps. The ramp was quiet as a tomb, except for Sasha's harsh, sobbing breaths. Shit, he had to be crushing her. "Are you okay?"

"Get. Off. Me." After a hard shove, she was free, crawling through the spilled lasagna to get to her father. Elliott lay crumpled on the pavement, his expression lax and an accusing pool of blood spreading under his head. "Daddy…" Her hands hovered helplessly, flitting over his frame like tiny, black-nailed birds.

Elliott's body would still be warm—his heart might still beat—but… "We need paramedics." Sasha's nose streamed blood, and there was a nasty scrape high on her right cheekbone. They needed paramedics, the police, a BOLO, not that he could tell Gideon anything about who they should be on the lookout for. Shit, he had to call Lukas. He couldn't let Lukas learn about his father's condition from a Code Red. And Claudette. He had to call Claudette. Tell her he'd broken his promise to keep her bondmate safe.

So many calls to make.

He tried to push himself upright, but his right arm wouldn't hold his weight. He tried again, but buckled to the concrete.

"Jack?"

"Can you reach my phone? It's in my right front pants pocket—"

"Quiet." Her hands came in for a landing, patting his arms, legs, and torso. "You've been hit."

He coughed, trying not to wince as she closed in on his right shoulder. His arm was dead weight, and breathing was becoming a serious problem. But Elliott was down. The President was down, and his assailant was getting away. "I need to call this in…" *Before I pass out…*

"Be quiet." She plucked a phone from her jacket pocket. "Just lay there and breathe."

"I'm trying." His lungs felt like they were clogged with lava.

"Try harder, damn it," she ordered. "Don't you pass out on me…"

He was vaguely aware of her dialing her phone.

"Just shut up and listen," she snapped to whoever answered. "This is the most urgent Code Red of your life." She provided her name, location, and a succinct overview of their situation: two Underworld Council members with gunshot wounds, critically injured and the gunman on the loose. "We need the police, and trauma paramedics. Tag Lukas Sebastiani, Commander Gideon Lupinsky, and Dr. Adnan Penn, MultiSpecies Trauma." She glanced down at him. "If Penn's not at the hospital, get him there, STAT." She must have put the phone on speaker, because she was still talking to someone when she climbed onto his back, put both hands against his shoulder, and applied pressure with her entire body weight. When she jammed her bony knee against his back wound, he couldn't help but groan.

"Sorry sorry sorry," she chanted. But she didn't move, didn't lighten up the pressure a single iota.

Lying on his stomach with his head turned to the side, all he could see was Sasha's right leg, kneeling on the hard, dirty concrete. "You're finally on top of me, and I'm not enjoying it one damn bit."

She didn't respond; she was too busy talking with the paramedics. It was probably for the better. What could he possibly say?

He'd failed them both.

The light faded to pinpricks, but pungent scents crashed over him: spilled motor oil, peppers and garlic from the lasagna, the fabric softener Sasha used on her yoga pants...

Sasha, succulent and salty, an elemental ocean bloom...

He inhaled as deeply as his drowning lungs would allow.

Inhaled again.

Then he closed his eyes, and let himself sink.

✳

In the private waiting room where Sasha sat with her family, it was hard to move, hard to breathe. The air was thick and ripe, viscous with adrenaline, confusion, sadness, grief… So many emotions, an inescapable yawning maw.

Through the door's glass-paned window, Memorial Hospital's emergency room lobby was utter chaos.

Because he was dead. The President was dead.

Her father—*their* father—was dead, and poor little Coco, a succubi/siren halfling, couldn't help but absorb everyone's staggering grief. She cried. She wailed. She sobbed uncontrollably without knowing why, her raw siren voice amplifying the emotion to heart-bursting.

"Oh, honey. I know." Scarlett paced the room with tears streaming down her face, trying to comfort her daughter. "I know you want your daddy, but he's so busy, and so, so sad…" she softly sang. Somehow, her voice suggested sunshine, Skittles, prancing ponies, and glitter on the breeze. Coco quieted, taking tiny, hiccupping breaths.

It took the edge off, just for a while.

"Thank you," Rafe murmured from the loveseat near the window. Her brother was sad but steady, his clay-flecked arms wrapped around his bondmate. Bailey had been at work, doing something with

Sebastiani Security's computer network, when the Code Red had come in. They'd been the first to arrive at the hospital, and had greeted her with a hug when she'd come out of her own exam room.

Bailey was Jack's best friend, and she was worried sick.

The buckles on Antonia's black bondage pants clanked as she approached the couch. "How are you doing?" her sister asked, handing her a cup of coffee before sitting beside her.

"I'm okay. Thanks." She took a quick sip, studying Antonia over the rim of the cup. Since taking a seat on the Council, Antonia had developed a primo game face, but beneath the surface, violent emotions roiled. Antonia had been upstairs, taking a shower in the penthouse apartment they shared, when an emotional blast had hit her broadside.

Her own memories were fuzzy—Jack's pain, his dawning horror and helplessness—but there'd been nothing from Dad. He'd simply...winked out, laughing one second and gone the next. Knowing he hadn't felt a single iota of pain brought an odd sense of relief, but...thank god the police had arrived before Antonia could get dressed and get downstairs. They'd stopped her at the parking ramp door, and hadn't let her see... Hadn't let her see...

The crappy coffee she'd just swallowed almost made a return trip.

Antonia's fingers touched her cheekbone. "How's your head doing? Need another ice pack?" The one Dr. Melvin had given her earlier lay warm and flaccid on the couch between them.

"I'm fine." *Liar.* Her nose and cheek throbbed, but she couldn't face another ice pack. She was absolutely freezing—her down jacket was definitely falling down on the job—but at least the color hid the worst of the bloodstains. She looked at her hand, the one holding the white mug. Even though she'd washed her hands over and over again, she still saw Jack's blood.

Ripples appeared on the surface of the coffee. Antonia took the cup from her shaking hand, then took a sip herself. When she wrinkled her nose, her tiny diamond piercing caught the light. "This is…really bad." But rather than set the cup down, she took another sip. Coffee was coffee, after all. "Look at all the uniforms out there."

On the other side of the glass window, every doctor, nurse, physician's assistant and phlebotomist not treating other patients hovered in the lobby. Blue-suited cops swarmed the place, and black-clad Sebastiani Security operatives fanned out, guarding the Sebastiani family and hustling Underworld Council members to a large conference room down the hall as they arrived. Wyland, a doctor and the Council's Vampire Second, stood outside her father's exam room, fangs flashing. This didn't deter Annabel Melvin, the Valkyrie MD who'd examined her earlier, from approaching him.

Sasha pushed to her feet, heading for the door. "Maybe she has information about Jack." There'd been no news about Jack's condition since he'd been whisked off to surgery over three hours ago.

Bailey stood as well, her face as pale as printer paper.

"He'll be fine," Sasha reassured her. Though Memorial Hospital usually catered exclusively to paranormal species, Bailey and Jack were exceptions. Both humans had been treated here before, by Adnan

Penn. She plucked at her black yoga pants, crusty with lasagna and Jack's dried blood, then stilled. "What do you and Jack do if you need blood?" Her throat went tight with panic. She wasn't a doctor, but paranormal species' blood couldn't possibly be compatible with—

"Hey." Bailey touched her forearm. "Don't worry about that. Adnan's got us covered."

Antonia joined them. "Memorial banks a small supply of human blood in case something like this happens."

She goggled at her sister. "How can you possibly know that?"

"Jack's a Council member, and Bailey's a key Sebastiani Security employee," Antonia said with a shrug. "It's a risk we decided to manage."

"You sound just like Lukas."

"Guilty as charged—and there he is, coming out of Dad's room."

They both inhaled, trying to get an emotional bead on their brother. "He's holding," Antonia murmured.

Lukas, still dressed for a theatre outing, had a quick conversation with Wyland and Dr. Melvin. After a terse nod, he went to talk to Chico Perez, one of Sebastiani Security's senior operatives. With Underworld Council members and members of the Sebastiani family scattered across the hospital's first floor, Chico had his hands full. Gideon Lupinsky, Commander of their covert police force, quickly joined them.

"Better late than never, gentlemen," Antonia muttered. "Present a united front…"

Antonia was right to worry. The lobby seethed with adrenaline, anger, and sheer helplessness. Everyone wanted to do something, *anything*. With the shooter still at large, jurisdictional pissing matches and rogue activity had to be nipped in the bud, and fast.

No one stopped Lukas as he strode toward the family waiting room. No one dared. Dressed head to toe in black, his big fists clenched and his expression ruthlessly controlled, her tall, hulking brother looked more like hired muscle than the owner of Sebastiani Security, much less the Underworld Council's Security and Technology First. When he joined them in the family room, the first thing he did was pull down the privacy shade on the door's glass window.

She hadn't even noticed there was a shade.

"Fuck," Lukas breathed out, sagging slightly. He reached for the roll of antacids he always carried in his pants pocket, popping three into his mouth before pulling Scarlett and Coco against him in a hug that sought as much comfort as it offered.

Whatever Scarlett whispered to him seemed to help. After a couple of minutes, Lukas kissed his daughter and bondmate, then came over to her. "How are you doing? Your cheek is really swelling up."

Her cheek, her nose, her elbow… Jack had shoved her under his body so quickly that she hadn't had time to break her fall. "I'm fine. How are you?"

"I'd feel a lot better if Krispin Woolf would stay in the goddamn conference room with everyone else." He looked at Antonia. "Did you notice him staring you down from the lobby?"

"Yes." Antonia didn't seem the least bit concerned she'd drawn the scrutiny of the Underworld Council's powerful WerePack Alpha.

"What's his problem?" she asked.

"Head games." Antonia rolled her eyes. "A feeble

attempt, at that."

Lukas, Scarlett, and Antonia—the Council members in the room—all exchanged a glance. When Rafe and Bailey joined in, she tried to bring her sluggish thoughts back online. "Okay, what am I missing?"

"He's trying to intimidate me," Antonia said.

Intimidation was the Alpha's modus operandi, but why focus on Antonia, today of all days— "Oh, I get it." The WerePack Alpha thought that Antonia—the newly-seated, supposedly immature, eighteen-year-old Incubus Second—would succeed her father as Underworld Council President. "Krispin doesn't know the details of our family's succession plan, does he?"

"Nope." Antonia's tiny smile was absolutely terrifying.

No wonder the place was crawling with cops and security. This was going to turn into a complete and utter shit show.

There was a quick tap at the door. Wyland poked his head in. "Claudette is ready to proceed."

Doctor, lawyer, historian, archivist... It was Wyland's responsibility to make sure the Sebastiani family's succession plan was duly executed, that Underworld Council leadership continuity was assured.

And suddenly, her father's death was real. She'd known this moment would come—that he'd die someday—but someday was supposed to be a goddamn century off. Her throat clogged, and her hands started to shake.

Holy crap, this is really happening.

Everyone started filing out. Wyland, exhibiting the

Regency-era manners he'd never let lapse with the passage of time, winged out his elbow. "May I escort you?"

She grabbed on. "Figured out I'm about ready to topple over, did you?"

"Annabel said you were shocky, and that you'd rejected pain medication."

"It makes my head fuzzy."

"And a broken nose doesn't?"

Nope. The pain helped her focus, and her bumps and bruises weren't worth mentioning, not when... "How is Jack doing?"

Wyland glanced at his watch. "He should be coming out of surgery soon." A muscle ticked in his jaw. "The sooner Gideon gets his hands on those bullets, the better."

Forensics. Ballistics. The hunt for the shooter was on, and the bullets were essential evidence. The President had been assassinated, and a Council member critically wounded. No doubt the bullets removed from Jack, and from her father, would eventually find their way to the Underworld Council's Archives. The bullets were important historical artifacts.

Would her father still be alive if he was just an ordinary man?

"Ready?"

Everyone else was gone. It was time to go. The hundred-foot walk across the ER lobby suddenly felt like the most important performance of her life. She pulled her body tall and straight, loosening her claw-like grip on Wyland's forearm. "Okay, let's do this."

The moment they left the family room, she felt weight of a hundred stares. The harsh fluorescent lights would illuminate every scrape and bruise, but she couldn't begrudge people their interest. Everyone present in the lobby knew she'd witnessed her father's death.

Today, she'd sacrifice decades of her life for a moment of anonymity.

Strength and grace, strength and grace... Thankfully the old ballet mantra was firmly locked in muscle memory, because moving through the thick sea of emotions took distinct physical effort. She absorbed the ebb and flow, inhaled the grief and empathy, and kept a neutral expression on her face even though her knee stung with each step. Just ahead, Lukas held the exam room door slightly ajar. Inside, Claudette sat on a chair beside the bed, holding her bondmate's hand.

His blood-stained hand.

The room whirled, an unexpected pirouette. Wyland stopped, gripping her tight. "Steady."

Lukas hurried over and took her other arm.

"I'm okay." But she didn't shake them off while she took two stabilizing breaths. "I'm okay. Let's go in."

As they entered the very white, very clean exam room—someone had obviously cleared away all evidence of how frantically the medical team had worked, trying to save her father's life—she focused on the most colorful thing she could see: Scarlett's outrageous red hair.

"After the leadership transition ceremony is over, we'll take some private time, as a family." Claudette's voice was steady, stable. Heartbreak bled from every pore, but her face was dry. Any tears she'd shed had been dashed aside, put away until later.

The Council's Siren First was ready for the drama

to come. If Claudette was ready, *she* had to be ready.

"I'll get the Council," Wyland said.

As he left, Claudette rose from the chair, approaching her. "Oh honey, your poor face." Claudette brushed a whisper-light kiss against her cheek, then gave her a head-to-toe inspection that missed nothing. "How are you doing?"

When Claudette held out her arms, Sasha fell into them, allowing herself to be comforted, until she caught sight of her father's hand poking out from under the crisp, white sheet that covered the rest of his body. "I'm a little banged up, but I'll recover." *Unlike Dad, so suck it up, Buttercup.* When she led Claudette back to the chair beside the bed, her father's bondmate immediately reached for his hand again.

Soon, the Medical Examiner would take him away, his body becoming a crime scene from which evidence must be gathered. He was beyond caring—the essential spark that made him "Dad" was gone, extinguished forever—yet—

The door opened. "Let's get this show on the road," Krispin Woolf snapped as he pushed into the room.

"Dad, show some respect." Jacoby Woolf, the WerePack Beta, looked mortified as he entered behind his father, his mobility scooter humming. He cast them all an apologetic glance.

"Respect? Members of the Underworld Council were herded into a conference room, then penned there like cattle." Krispin's lips thinned. "We've waited long enough."

"I'm sorry the President's death interrupted your busy Saturday night," Antonia said as the rest of the

Council filed into the room. "Your lap dance will have to wait."

Krispin stared at her.

Antonia stared back.

The hair on Sasha's arms prickled to attention.

Lukas moved so he stood next to their sister. Lorin Schlessinger, the strapping Valkyrie Second, took position at Antonia's other side.

Ready to fight.

Ready for anything.

Shit.

"And there's your brother, riding to the rescue." Krispin's mocking smile didn't reach his eyes. "He won't always be there to protect you, little girl." As he moved to the other side of her father's bed, he took in Antonia's bondage pants and biker boots. "Nice to see that you dressed for the occasion."

"This old thing?" Antonia said with a shrug. "Just a little something I threw on when I heard my father had been assassinated."

"Will you two stop it?" Jacoby snapped. "Now is not the time." He turned to Claudette. "On behalf of the WerePack, please accept our sincere condolences on the loss of your bondmate. It's a very sad day for us all."

Somewhere along the line, Jacoby had become adept at the polite, political lie. His father wasn't the least bit sorry.

"Thank you," Claudette said, regal as a queen. "Thank you all." She swallowed, hard. "I apologize for interrupting your evening plans."

"Oh, honey." Alka Schlessinger, the Valkyrie First, hugged Claudette from behind, not bothering to dash away her tears. "As if you had any control over this.

As if *anyone* had any control over this, other than the person who pulled the goddamn trigger."

Coco started fussing. Lukas took her from Scarlett, cradling her in the crook of his arm. "I think we're ready to proceed," he said to Wyland.

Damn right. Too many people in the room were holding onto their composure by the skins of their teeth.

Wyland set an ancient, leather-bound book and an accordion-pleated legal file folder on the bed, then picked up a sleek electronic tablet from the top of the pile. "Please gather round."

The Sebastianis assembled around Claudette, with Lukas standing at the head of the bed, closest to their father. While the other Council members found their spaces, Wyland gently touched her father's sheet-covered foot, as if including him in the proceedings.

She blinked away sudden tears.

"Some housekeeping first." Wyland tapped the screen. "This ceremony is being recorded, audio with no video. The recording will be entered into the Underworld Council record, and placed into the Archives for historical purposes. Incubi and succubi, sirens, Valkyries, werewolves, and vampires are all represented by at least one of their Council members. For the purposes of this gathering, we have a quorum." Wyland swept his ice-blue gaze around the room. "Two Council members are not present: Security and Technology Second Jack Kirkland, who is in surgery to repair life-threatening injuries he sustained during this attack on the President; and Valerian, the Vampire First."

No doubt Wyland had asked Valerian, nearly nine hundred years old and recently recovered from a bout of pneumonia, to stay home.

"Also present are President Sebastiani's son, Rafael Sebastiani; Rafe's bondmate, Bailey Brown; Elliott's daughter Sasha Sebastiani, who also sustained injuries during the attack, and President Sebastiani's granddaughter, Coco Annika Fontaine."

Too many heads swung her way, and Sasha huddled into her jacket. Compared to what happened to her father—what happened to Jack—her injuries weren't worth mentioning.

"Next item," Wyland said. "Allow me to read the pertinent sections of the Incubus/Succubus Underworld Council succession plan, which was updated approximately two years ago."

Krispin Woolf straightened. He wasn't tall, but he didn't need height to intimidate. Though he wore a beautifully cut suit, menace positively radiated from the man. The nasty scar bisecting his cheek rippled as his gaze flicked from Wyland, to Antonia, to Lukas, then back to Wyland again.

Oh, yes, he knew something was up. The tension in the room was suddenly thick as tar.

"As you may remember," Wyland began, "prior to Antonia Sebastiani being named the Incubus Second, her brother Lukas served in that role. Given Lukas's skills and professional interests—let me note for the record that Lukas Sebastiani is the founder and name partner of Sebastiani Security, a company specializing in protective security, threat assessment, and technological risk management—he recognized that recent technological advances, and changes in America's security posture, increased the risk that our existence might be exposed to humanity. After successfully lobbying the Council to create a Security and Technology seat with full voting rights to explicitly manage that risk, he chose Sebastiani Security's managing partner, Jack Kirkland, to be his Second."

Woolf's jaw tightened.

Yeah, that decision had *really* chapped Woolf's ass. Jack hadn't been the first human to serve on the Council—a rather famous scientist and science fiction writer, now deceased, had had that honor—but despite that, Woolf had mounted a massive legal challenge against Jack. To Woolf's surprise and dismay, there was nothing in the Council charter that prohibited a human from serving the Council in any capacity. There was nothing explicitly *authorizing* it, true, but nothing prohibiting it, either. The vote had been cast. Jack, a human, was in, and precedent set.

Krispin Woolf had a long memory, and he didn't like to lose.

"Two years ago," Wyland continued, "Lukas Sebastiani abdicated his seat as the Incubus Second to focus on security and technology issues. Elliott Sebastiani, in his capacity as Incubus First and using powers authorized by the Incubus and Succubus Charter, named his youngest daughter, Antonia, as Lukas's replacement." Wyland flicked an elegant finger across the screen. "Now, regarding the matter of succession."

The tension in the room became a physical weight. Lukas's linebacker frame somehow seemed larger as he handed Coco back to Scarlett, then blocked them with his body. Lorin shifted even closer to Antonia. Even Rafe, an avowed pacifist, stood next to Bailey with fists clenched, ready to fight if he had to.

There were very good reasons why she and Rafe

had opted out of anything having to do with the Council, and this completely unnecessary showdown illustrated most of them. She couldn't live a life where every statement, every movement, had to be politically calculated and assessed for risk. She refused to live a life where every action, every reaction, could be a matter of life and death.

Krispin flashed a cold smile at Antonia. "Time to stand on your own two feet, little girl."

Antonia looked at her thick-soled Doc Martens, then back at him. "Standing just fine, old man."

The hair on the back her neck snapped to attention. Coco started crying.

"Stop it!" Scarlett's powerful siren's voice rolled through the room, and everyone fell silent whether they wanted to or not. "Just…stop. This is not the time or the place."

Wyland cleared his throat. "Continuing on. The Incubus First, Elliott Sebastiani, was chosen Underworld Council President during the last election cycle. Ten years remain in his twenty-year term. As you know, the Council charter states that if the President dies in office, his or her Second will fill the position until the next scheduled election."

All heads swung to Antonia.

"Meaning a teenager with barely two years' Council experience is now our President," Krispin stated, sketching Antonia a mocking bow.

"If I may continue." Despite his phrasing, Wyland wasn't asking for permission.

As Wyland resumed reading aloud, Sasha watched Woolf all but lick his chops as he considered how he might take advantage of the situation. A piece of her wanted to see him try, because then she'd have the pleasure of watching her little sister carve Krispin Woolf's ass into rump roast. But it wasn't to be, because after consulting with the entire family, their father had added a clause to the Incubus/Succubus succession plan: that should he die within ten years of the document's signing, Lukas would be named the Incubus First, with Antonia remaining the Second.

Lukas would ascend to the presidency, not Antonia.

"What?" Krispin's face was as red as his necktie. He looked apoplectic, ready to stroke out. "Read that again."

Wyland did.

When Lukas and Antonia signed off on the plan, had either of them anticipated actually having to enact it? Their father obviously had, because he'd written the clause in the first place. Lukas had called it their Black Swan Clause, because black swans were supposedly as rare as…as rare as…

Tears clogged her nose, her throat.

"He can't do that!" Krispin shouted.

Chico and Gideon, waiting just outside the room, opened the door and slipped inside.

"He can. He did," Wyland informed him. "There's nothing in our Council charter prohibiting his approach."

Krispin's nose, cheeks, and mouth started to ripple. He clenched his fists. Clenched his jaw.

Holy shit, he was fighting a shift.

"Dad, calm down," Jacoby urged.

Everyone in the room stilled. If shifting in the boardroom was a major breach of Council protocol, doing so at the President's deathbed was… unimaginable.

"Show me the paperwork," Krispin half-growled, exposing lupine teeth. "The notarized, legally vetted copy."

Setting down his tablet, Wyland reached for the accordion-pleated file folder, withdrew a thick sheaf of paper, and handed it to Krispin. "The notarized succession plan is there, followed by the research which supports the legality of this action."

"Legal research performed by you," Krispin sneered, lips thinning.

Wyland went still. "Do you question my objectivity in this matter?"

Krispin didn't respond.

Smart man.

Everyone watched, silent, as Krispin flicked through the paperwork. When he lifted his head, alarm spiked the air.

The area around his mouth was…pulsing and rippling. Fangs sprouted, and his fingernails were lengthening into claws.

The WerePack Alpha was shifting, losing the fight.

"Dad, leave the room," Jacoby ordered. "Now."

Father and son, Alpha and Beta, stared each other down. Finally, with an inarticulate growl, Krispin threw the document to the floor and stalked out the door. Chico and Gideon followed.

The door closed quietly behind them.

Silence hung until Jacoby, with a hum of his scooter, picked up the paperwork and handed it back to Wyland. "I apologize for my father's inexcusable behavior."

Jacoby spent *way* too much time apologizing for his father's behavior.

"Let the record show that the WerePack Alpha,

Krispin Woolf, has left the room," Wyland said.

"What a fucking douche," Antonia muttered.

Wyland looked at the tablet and sighed.

No doubt he was thinking about the recording, but expecting decorum from Antonia, today of all days, was a pretty big ask. Hell, expecting decorum from *anyone* today was probably too much to expect. Wyland should be thankful Antonia hadn't called Krispin "The Shitlord," as she frequently did in private.

A silent giggle sneaked up. Amusement felt so...*wrong*, but the fact that she could feel amusement on this day was an unexpected gift.

"Shall we proceed?" Wyland said.

Claudette nodded, rising from her chair with Lukas's help.

Lukas held their father's hand as he recited the presidential oath of office. With a creak of old leather, Wyland opened the Tome, handed Lukas Valerian's favorite Mont Blanc pen, then pointed to a place on the yellowed parchment. After Lukas signed his name, Wyland carefully closed the book, murmured something, then kissed its cover.

Her brother was now President of the Underworld Council.

Wyland approached the head of the bed, then slowly pulled back the sheet to expose her father's face. He kissed both cheeks, then stepped back so each Council member and family member could do the same.

When it was her turn, grief crashed down like a demolished building. She wobbled, but Jacoby was there. She collapsed onto his lap, hard enough to make him wince. "Sorry."

"That's okay," he said. "Let me give you a lift." Right hand on the joystick, he steered the mobility scooter over to her father's bedside.

She didn't stand up. Instead, she drew strength from her old friend's familiar embrace, just for a moment.

"He looks...peaceful," Jacoby murmured. "You can do this."

An oil slick sloshed in her stomach as she looked anywhere but at her father. Everyone was watching. Everyone was waiting—except Wyland, who'd walked to the door to answer a soft knock. After a short conversation, he turned back to the room. "Jack's out of surgery," he reported. "Penn says he's stable."

Breath whooshed. Oh, thank the universe.

"One of the bullets broke his rib, just nicking a lung—an uncomplicated collapse, which should heal completely."

"And the shoulder wound?" Staunching the blood gushing from Jack's shoulder had taken every pound of pressure her body could produce.

Wyland paused before answering. "It was a through-and-through, missing the arteries but skimming very close to the brachial nerve cluster. We'll be able to better assess his condition once the swelling goes down."

It didn't take a genius to parse what Wyland *hadn't* said: possible nerve damage. But Jack was alive. He would survive, unlike her father.

Unlike her father.

It was time to say goodbye.

She pushed shakily to her feet, took a deep breath, and looked down. Though his beautiful gray hair was matted and bloody, his face and cheeks were clean.

Someone had pulled his hair down over his temple, covering most of the bullet wound.

Jacoby was right. He looked...peaceful.

"Jack's going to be okay, Dad," she whispered. "He's going to be okay." She kissed both stubble-roughened cheeks, then his cool lips. Then she lay down across his chest, hugging him.

Letting him take her weight, one final time.

As Claudette and Scarlett sang, "All that was...all that is...all that shall be..." in otherworldly siren harmony, Coco cried in accompaniment.

Sasha finally broke apart, and let the tears flow.

CHAPTER TWO

"You killed the wrong man."

There was nothing but silence from the other end of the phone line—which made sense, because what could the man say? Facts were facts: Jack Kirkland was alive, and someone else was dead. Ethan Covington hadn't fulfilled the contract. "You killed the wrong man," she repeated.

"Don't you think I know that?" Ethan snapped. "I know."

After several seconds of silence, muffled sobs whispered over the line.

Miranda DesJardins leaned back in her leather desk chair, exasperated. Her instrument of destruction—a former Sebastiani Security employee, a highly-trained badass—had just dissolved into tears.

Christ on a cracker.

She waited him out, tapping her French-tipped nail against the glossy cherrywood desk. The desk, the matching floor-to-ceiling bookshelves, and the executive desk accessories were well-traveled, moving from her San Francisco corner office, to a storage unit, then U-Hauled here...to the spare bedroom of this crappy South Minneapolis rental. The multi-line phone wasn't connected, and the laptop sitting next to it—top-of-the-line when she bought it almost ten years ago—was useless now. She'd been forced to dip into her dwindling savings to buy a new one.

So many unexpected expenses. Jack Kirkland had a lot to answer for.

"Ethan." Gripping the burner phone more tightly, she reached for what was left of her patience. "Ethan, calm down."

"Calm down? Are you serious?" His voice cracked, and an audible gulp clicked over the line. "Do you have any idea what we've done?"

"What *you've* done," she corrected. "And you haven't finished the job yet."

Silence stretched. No doubt he was trying to figure out how he'd pay his bills—and buy his pills—if he refused to fulfill the contract. No doubt he'd already spent her partial up-front payment. Vicodin was Covington's drug of choice, and fortunately for her, he chose it frequently.

Being fired from Sebastiani Security had left him underemployed and swimming in debt, with a burgeoning drug habit and his self-confidence in shambles. Yes, Ethan Covington was the perfect tool of Jack Kirkland's destruction—or he would be, if she could get him back on track. "Jack Kirkland fired you, ruined your life," she reminded him. "I thought you wanted payback."

"I do," he whispered. "I do."

"Good." God knew revenge was *her* motive. It was Kirkland's fault she'd gone to prison in the first place. Because of his completely inept defense, she'd lost her career, her family, and her pride, not to mention too much money and time. Too many of her best years had been spent behind bars.

She still had nightmares about prison, but she'd

also learned some very important lessons there: Watch your back. Stay under the radar. Don't get your own hands dirty if you can possibly avoid it. With his job history, skill set, addictions, and money problems, Ethan Covington had the perfect pair of dirty hands—if he'd stop crying and get with the goddamn program.

As Ethan collected himself, she looked down at this week's To-Do list. She still hadn't prepared job search notes for the meeting with her corrections officer, and she still had to go shopping for clothes. All of her designer business suits—the ones that had cost an arm, a leg, and the bulk of her childbearing years to collect—still fit, but they were *way* too dressy. With every push-up, pull-up, and ab crunch she'd done while incarcerated, she'd heard Grandmere's French-accented voice: "A DesJardins does not eat to excess. A DesJardins does not turn to fat. A DesJardins excels at everything they do."

Sorry, Grandmere. My clothes still fit, but I really dropped the ball on the last item. Kirkland's inept defense notwithstanding, a better criminal wouldn't have gotten caught in the first place. "Ethan?"

Pills rattled in a plastic bottle. "Give me a minute," he mumbled, setting down the burner phone she'd insisted he use for their communications.

"Ethan? *Ethan.*" Damn it, she was talking to thin air.

Maybe hiring an addict hadn't been the smartest choice.

While she waited for Ethan to finish anesthetizing himself, she updated her job hunting notes—jotting down dates, crossing off names, verifying that her receipts and other records were in order. She'd had a lot of casual networking meetings, both in person and over the phone, but no one had called back or followed up.

No one wanted a convicted felon on their payroll, especially one who'd screwed her previous employer over so badly.

"Okay, I'm back." There was a rustle as he settled in. "What's your name, anyway? It's really strange to speak with someone on the phone and not know their name."

Not strange enough to stop you from accepting a contract to kill someone. Money talks, I guess. "Call me Jane."

"As in Doe?" He gave a half-laugh. "Okay, if that's how you want to play it."

It didn't matter whether he believed her or not. "Ethan. A question."

"Yes?"

He sounded cautious. Good. "Were you high when you attempted to fulfill this contract?"

"What? No!"

"Then why did you miss?" Sebastiani Security didn't hire employees who couldn't hit the target.

"It was a very challenging shot," he said defensively. "The Sebastiani Building's parking ramp is crawling with video cameras, and the sole blind spot is narrow, and oddly shaped, requiring a contorted, sideways stance. Then, just when I took the shot, Mr. Sebastiani..." His voice wobbled, then steadied. "Mr. Sebastiani moved into my line of fire."

Elliott Sebastiani, the man who'd died, was CEO of a privately held company called Sebastiani Labs. In a delightful twist of coincidence, Elliott Sebastiani was also the same man Ethan had been fired for not effectively guarding—a psychological wound ,she wouldn't hesitate to poke. But not right now. No, right now she had to shore up Ethan's confidence, so he could get the job done. "We all make mistakes," she said matter-of-factly. "The survivors learn from them, and move on. Let's talk about next steps, because the sooner you finish the job, the sooner you get paid." She couldn't help but wince. Keeping one's hands clean was *really* expensive, but Ethan Covington *was* the perfect weapon.

Some scores could never be settled, but soon, Jack Kirkland would pay the ultimate price.

✳

Something dragged Jack from the depths of sleep.

A dark room. The squeak of soles against linoleum. Fabric brushing against fabric.

Shit, someone was in the room. When he tried to sit up, fiery pain radiated from his torso.

"Hey, you're awake."

He collapsed back against the mattress with a groan. "Damn it, Adnan." A week had passed since the shooting, but his shoulder still felt like it had taken a blow from Thor's hammer. "What time is it?"

Penn approached the bed, his e-tablet casting a ghostly glow. "It's about 6:00 a.m."

No wonder the room was so dark. The sun hadn't risen yet.

"Who did you think was here?" Adnan asked, setting the tablet on the bed.

"I don't know." Access to Memorial Hospital's

VIP floor was strictly limited, designed with Council member security in mind—but it was reassuring that he was alert enough to try to protect himself if he had to. "As soon as I fall asleep, someone wakes me up. And they're usually holding something sharp." Drawing blood, or forcing a nebulizer treatment on a man before he was properly awake, was cruel and unusual punishment.

Adnan grinned, rocking back on his heels. "You're getting testy. This is good."

"Why?"

"If you're complaining about interrupted sleep, not pain from gunshot wounds, it's a pretty good sign you're ready to blow this pop stand."

"You're releasing me?" His chest tube had been removed a couple of days ago—an experience he never wanted to repeat—and he'd exchanged IV pain medication for pills at the same time. The gunshot wounds themselves were sore, but healing. His right arm...was another story. The thing was numb, dead weight. No matter how hard he concentrated, no matter how hard he tried, it wouldn't move.

How was he supposed to write? Or use his computer or phone? His gun? Hell, how was he supposed to wipe his ass after taking a shit? Panic streaked through him. The prospect of not regaining use of his dominant hand—

Stop the hysterics. As long as he was alive, there was a chance the situation would improve. At least he *was* alive, unlike Elliott. And according to Lukas, Gideon, and Adnan—hell, according to everyone he'd spoken with—he had Sasha Sebastiani to thank.

Sasha had been the one who'd called in the Code Red, who'd applied pressure to his wounds after determining her father was beyond help. Despite her injuries—bumps, scrapes, and a broken nose—she'd provided essential information to the police. The forensic team hadn't found any fibers, footprints, or spent bullet casings where Sasha indicated she thought the shooter had been standing. Whoever the guy was, he'd found one of the parking lot's few video blind spots.

Bullets were all they had to work with, and there'd been no ballistics match.

They had nothing.

"Let's take a look at those wounds." Adnan turned on the overhead fluorescent light. After helping him sit upright, Adnan untied his hospital gown, plucked a pair of disposable gloves from the wall-mounted storage unit, and put them on with a snap. He peeled the tape and gauze from his wounds, then examined them, making annoying humming sounds Jack couldn't interpret. "The external wounds are healing well. The antibiotics are doing their job," Adnan said. "But due to the tissue damage, you still have some inflammation in your shoulder."

No shit. "You said inflammation could be the reason I can't move my arm and hand, right?" The 9mm bullet had cruised uncomfortably close to a bundle of nerves called the brachial plexus, which controlled arm and hand movement.

Adnan extended his hand. "Try to lift your arm and shake my hand."

He tried.

Failed.

Gritting his teeth, he tried, then tried again. No go. "Shit."

"It's early days yet," Adnan reassured him. "Give it

some time. Any sensation at all? Any tingling or burning?"

Actually... "I *do* feel a little bit. Of both." Was he imagining things? No. The sensation was there, and it hadn't been yesterday. "It feels like my arm fell asleep, and it's just starting to wake up."

"I suspect that's exactly what's happening," Adnan said, removing the gloves and throwing them in the wastebasket. "How's your overall pain level?"

"Manageable." *Barely.*

Adnan picked up his tablet again. "I hear you've been giving the nurses a lot of guff about taking pain medication."

"I don't want to take more than I need."

"Yeah, that's a good thing to be aware of," Adnan said, nodding, "but pain management is an important component of your recovery plan, and right now, I'm a better judge of what you need than you are." He poked Jack's abdomen with his index finger.

He instinctively clenched his muscles, half sitting up. When fiery pain shot through his body, he fell back to the bed. "Ow, damn it."

"See? You're stiff as a board. You're tensing your muscles against the pain, Superman, making things worse instead of better."

"But—"

Adnan poked his stomach again.

Another clench, another lurch. Between the bullet wound and the rib the bullet had broken, his back burned like the pits of hell. "Damn it! Okay."

"Good. I'll send a nurse in with some pain meds when I leave." Adnan tapped the tablet's screen. "I'd like to do a few more tests before we release you."

Release? "Okay."

"We'll schedule the EMG, the nerve conduction studies, and an MRI for today, and get outpatient physical and occupational therapy appointments set up before you go." Adnan glanced up. "We won't release you if your pain isn't adequately managed." Adnan locked gazes with him. "So take the goddamn pills."

"Okay, okay." He had to call Bailey. She'd agreed to stay with him for a few days after he got out of the hospital, just until he got his legs under him again. Thankfully his legs were in good working order. "How long until we know whether I'll need follow-up surgery on my shoulder?"

"Let's wait for the test results, and continue working with PT and OT," Adnan replied. "The tingling is a good sign."

Relief nearly swamped him. Not being able to use his arm and hand would be a challenge, sure, but he'd get by—especially if he knew it was likely a short-term problem.

Things were definitely looking up.

"One more thing," Adnan said.

"There's always a kicker somewhere," he muttered. "What is it?"

"I don't want you to take pheromone intoxication meds while you're taking pain medication."

"Not a problem." He'd be recovering at home, with no incubi or succubi in sight for the foreseeable future. "I just want to get out of here." Before Claudette came back to visit him. Before Sasha came back. They'd each stopped by the hospital several times, but thanks to the security cameras, he'd seen them coming. He'd feigned deep sleep every time they came in.

He wasn't ready to see them yet.

The only Sebastiani he'd spoken with since Elliott's death had been Lukas, and apologizing for his lapse of attention in the garage had been one of the hardest things he'd ever done. Lukas hadn't accepted his apology—or rather, he hadn't agreed an apology was necessary. "The gun had a suppressor on it, and Dad sustained a mortal wound. Despite being hit by the second and third bullets, you shoved Sasha to the ground before the fourth shot was fired." Lukas's eyes drilled into him. "Three seconds, Jack. It all happened in less than three seconds, and even with two gunshot wounds of your own, you saved my sister's life. So, no more of this apology bullshit. You aren't responsible for Dad's death. The fucking shooter is." Lukas had dragged a tired hand through his hair. "We—I—really need you back in the saddle at SebSec."

On that point, Lukas hadn't just been blowing smoke up his ass. With him in the hospital and Lukas busy with the Council, Bailey and Chico were doing their best to hold things together at work, but it wasn't a feasible long-term solution. At least Lukas didn't have to worry about Sebastiani Labs. Bailey had told him that Alka Schlessinger, who'd headed up Sebastiani Labs' Physical Sciences division for years, had stepped into the CEO suite.

Sebastiani Security, Sebastiani Labs, the Underworld Council…the aftershocks of Elliott's death would ripple through their culture for years to come, but nowhere more deeply than with his family. Lukas already looked like he carried the weight of the world on his shoulders.

I might have only one functioning shoulder, but my brain is working just fine. He was more than capable of riding a desk, and helping Lukas carry the load.

There was a knock at the door. He and Adnan both glanced at the security monitor. It was Bailey, flipping him the bird and flashing him an exaggerated cheeseball grin. "Come in," he called.

As Bailey entered, Adnan headed for the door. "Let me tag Neuro, get the ball rolling."

"Thanks." If an afternoon of probes, machines, needles, and electrodes was what it took to get out of here, he'd manage.

"Hey, Adnan," Bailey said, kissing his cheeks.

"Hey." He kissed her back. "How's the stomach doing?"

Bailey rolled her eyes. "It's fine. Just like it was the last time you asked."

"And just like the last time I asked, you're overdue for a follow-up appointment."

A couple of years ago, Adnan had repaired Bailey's ulcer, which had perforated after taking too many pheromone intoxication meds. Since he and Bailey were the only two people taking the experimental drug—hell, since they were his only human patients—Adnan kept very close tabs on their health.

"Damn it," Bailey muttered. "I'll make an appointment."

"See that you do." Adnan waved as he left, the hem of his white coat fluttering around his legs.

They watched as the door closed behind him. "He always looks like he's taken one too many bong hits," Bailey mused. "Who'd have thought we'd have a werewolf as our primary care physician?" She came to the bed, leaned over, and dropped a kiss onto each of his cheeks. "Ouch, you haven't shaved yet."

He hadn't taken a morning piss yet, not that anyone had asked.

"How are you doing today?"

"Better than yesterday." Even after Adnan's index finger treatment. "How about you? How are things going at work?"

"You know how it goes." Setting her bulging computer bag down on the visitor's chair, Bailey went over to look at the cards, flowers, and plants on the table next to the window. "Bad actors don't keep corporate office hours."

"Malicious incursion attempt overnight?"

"Yeah." She yawned. "I've been up since 2:00 a.m."

No wonder she looked so tired. Sebastiani Security's technology infrastructure was Bailey's baby, and it required round-the-clock care and feeding. He couldn't remember the last time he'd seen Bailey without that damned computer bag, which contained everything she needed to stop a hack in its tracks. Much like the President's 'nuclear football,' she was never without it.

Had he done her any favors nudging her into this job?

Failure sidled up, an old, familiar friend. Despite his best efforts—she'd been framed for the crime for which she'd been convicted—he hadn't been able to keep her out of prison. She'd served months instead of years, and in a minimum security facility, but she'd come out a convicted felon. She'd come out…changed. She'd parlayed the blot on her resume into a stunningly successful security consultancy, evaluating and exposing companies' security weaknesses from the inside, on the company's behalf, but when she'd grown tired of the punishing pace, he'd thrown her the same lifeline Lukas had once thrown him. She'd grabbed on, joining him on this wild ride.

And now he'd been shot. Elliott was dead. They'd all seen too much blood. "Do you ever miss your consultancy?"

She lifted her head from the exquisite orchid arrangement Claudette had sent. "What?"

"Do you ever regret accepting our job offer?" *Our.* Yes, he'd definitely allied himself with Lukas. With Sebastiani Security, and the Underworld Council. He belonged, yet he was different.

He was human.

"Are you serious?" she asked. "It's the perfect job. All technology, all the time. No management responsibilities, no boss breathing down my neck, an unlimited budget, an outrageous salary, and complete autonomy to use my entire skill set for good, not evil. What's to regret?"

"How about having to take pheromone intoxication meds? How about gunshot wounds? Hell, how about having to deal with Krispin Woolf?"

Bailey joined him on the bed, sitting cross-legged near his feet. "How about knowing that First Contact already happened and humanity just doesn't know it yet? Or that alien technology was discovered at a secret archaeological site? How about having a family again?" She caressed the fire opal bonding ring Rafe had given her. "Nope, I wouldn't change it for the world—though given your current accommodations, I can understand why you'd have second thoughts." She looked at him, too closely. "How are you doing? No bullshit."

"I'm a little sore." Okay, a *lot* sore. "Adnan said he's turfing me tomorrow."

"Releasing you? Awesome!" Her expression shifted from elation to concern. "How's your pain level? You were shot, and spent hours in surgery, little more than a week ago."

He shrugged, disguising a wince when his right shoulder didn't cooperate. "The pills help a lot," he admitted. "But what I really need is to get back to work." Because Bailey looked as exhausted as Lukas had. His friends needed his help.

"You'll come back to work when Adnan says you're ready, and not a minute before," Bailey scolded. "You're an Underworld Council member. If you need to stay in the hospital a bit longer, throw your weight around and say so."

"I'm ready to leave," he reassured her. "Thanks for offering to stay with me for a couple of days."

"Happy to help—and with your home office set-up, I can work there as easily as I can from The Bunker."

She could, but he knew she'd prefer not to. The Bunker, the equipment-stuffed computer room at Sebastiani Security, was her lair, her home base, her happy place. He'd do his best to make sure she got back there as soon as possible.

Her phone rang. "It's Cheyenne," she said, glancing at the screen. "I have to take this."

When Bailey and Cheyenne Winterbourne had a technology conversation, they lapsed into lingo few people could understand. "Go." He waved toward the door. "I'm going to take a nap." And take a piss.

Bailey scrambled off the bed and kissed his cheek. "Sleep tight." She snagged the strap of her computer bag, hefting a good twenty pounds like it was nothing, and waggled her fingers goodbye from the door. "Don't let the bedbugs bite."

The door closed, leaving him blessedly alone. There was no one to witness his slow shuffle to the bathroom, his decision to pee sitting rather than standing, or how goddamned shaky he was when he collapsed back onto the bed.

Damn it, he'd just woken up, and already needed a nap.

He stared balefully at the annoying fluorescent light Adnan hadn't turned off. It was a six-inch reach to the keypad integrated into the bed frame.

Six inches.

He tried moving his right arm, his right hand.

No movement—but for a supposedly numb limb, the thing burned like a son of a bitch. He rubbed his bicep, then tried again. No go.

"Damn it."

He tried again, and again, until his body shook. Until his wounds screamed. Until he was covered with sweat. "Shit." Six inches might as well be six thousand miles. Reaching across his body with his left hand, he turned off the light. He jabbed the button hard, just because he could.

Jabbed it again.

And again, and again, and again.

"Fuck!" he roared, grabbing the nearby water pitcher and hurling it across the room.

He couldn't appreciate the splat of water against the far wall, or the clatter of the plastic pitcher, because his broken rib was shanking him from the inside. "Fuck me," he gasped, slapping a hand against his chest—a completely useless action, because the broken rib was on his back. "That…was not the smartest move."

Lowering himself to the pillow, he waited for the pain to subside, for his breath to return. No nurse or guard came into the room. His temper tantrum had gone unobserved, for now. The nurse who brought his pain meds would find it, and someone else would have to clean it up.

Classy move, Kirkland.

He turned off the light with a shaking hand. Damn, he was as weak as a newborn kitten, but thankfully, Bailey would be the one to help him out at home. There'd be no need to hide his weakness, or put up a front. He could recover, and lick his wounds, in peace.

He'd be free of sex demons—free of Sebastianis— for just a little while.

✸

When Sasha got off the elevator, she headed straight for Bailey, who sat in a small room off the VIP floor's lobby with a phone clapped to her ear.

"Can you hang on a sec?" Bailey asked the person she was speaking with. "Thanks." She lowered the phone to her chest. "Jack's taking a nap."

Just like last night, dang it. She'd had zero luck trying to visit Jack in the evenings, so today she figured she'd try early morning. So much for *that* idea. She had to meet a delivery truck at Crackhouse Coffee's loading dock in about an hour.

"Ms. Sebastiani?" The guard sitting at the reception desk approached, extending an e-tablet and stylus her way. "If you could sign in, please?"

She complied, just like she had all the other times she'd stopped by to visit Jack and hadn't actually seen him. At this rate, he'd be out of the hospital before she saw him next.

Which was surely his plan.

Bailey put the phone to her ear again. "Cheyenne, can I call you back? Five minutes, tops."

A phone call with Sebastiani Labs' hotshot network architect at this time of day probably meant bad news.

Bailey hung up. "Malicious incursion attempt at Sebastiani Labs," she confirmed. "Our countermeasures held, but we have some shoring up to do."

Since meeting Bailey, Sasha had learned more than she ever wanted about hacks, cracks, exploits, and bad actors. "Do you have a minute to chat?" She hitched a thumb toward the corner of the main lobby, where a nubby-textured couch and a couple of chairs huddled around the room's most important feature: a high-end coffee pot.

Bailey eyed the comfortable furniture with suspicion. "Once I sit down, I won't want to get up again."

"I have to leave in a few minutes, too," Sasha said. "Come on. I'll make sure you're up and moving before I go." She picked up Bailey's heavy computer bag and started walking. Bailey shot to her feet and followed.

Bailey would follow the damn bag into an active volcano if she had to.

She set the bag down next to the couch. Bailey collapsed onto its nearest cushion, dragging her hands through her choppy blonde bob before massaging her own neck and shoulders. Bailey spent most of her waking hours at a keyboard, but refused to develop what she called a code monkey slouch.

"When did you sleep last?"

"A couple of days ago," Bailey admitted around a yawn. "I'd hoped to catch a nap this afternoon, but..."

But nothing. She'd call Rafe as soon as she left the hospital. Once she told him his bondmate hadn't slept in days, he'd take it from there. "How is Jack this morning?"

"He's still in some pain..." Bailey's phone blipped. She glanced at the screen, then responded with a blur of thumbs. "He's weaker than he wants to admit," she continued, a concerned look on her face. "I don't think he's strong enough to be released yet, but no one asked me."

"He's being released?"

Bailey nodded. "Probably tomorrow."

She'd washed too much of his blood off her hands barely a week ago. "What does Adnan say?"

"Adnan's the one who's releasing him."

After knee surgery, she'd felt shaky as a newborn fawn. She'd had plenty of family around to help her, but Jack lived alone. "Will he be all by himself? Home alone?"

"No, I volunteered to stay with him for a few days. He—" Bailey's phone rang, and her expression went needle sharp. "It's Lukas. I need to take this."

Sasha pushed to her feet, gesturing to the beverage station. "Want some coffee?"

Bailey blew her a kiss. "That would be awesome. Thanks."

She listened with half an ear while she filled two shiny white mugs with rich, dark roast. Something Lukas said made Bailey laugh—always a good thing—but if what she'd seen during the last couple of minutes was any indication, Jack might not get the best of Bailey's time and attention once they got home.

She considered her schedule over the next week or so, and took a deep, cleansing breath. "I don't believe I'm about to do this," she muttered.

When Bailey ended her phone call, Sasha handed her the coffee. Once Bailey's mouth was occupied, she blurted, "I'll stay with Jack. Once he gets home."

Bailey's eyebrows climbed, but she didn't stop sipping.

"You're so busy, and there's nothing on my schedule that I can't delegate." Flynn, Underbelly's night manager, could handle anything that came up at the club. "I have a backup, and you don't. Let me do this." As Bailey opened her mouth to respond, her phone blipped again. "See?" She waved at the phone. "Even the tech gods agree with me."

Bailey glanced at the phone, then silenced it without answering. "You and Jack argue all the time. Arguing is the last thing he needs right now."

Arguing was *exactly* what Jack needed right now. Physically uncomfortable, and not able to work or to use his dominant hand? Jack was going to be as crabby as hell, and whoever helped care for him would be a natural target for his frustration. The man had saved her life. The least she could do was fetch, carry, and shield Bailey from the worst of her best friend's temper. "I won't start any arguments," she promised. *But if Jack starts one, I'll sure as shit finish it.* "Seriously, you have so much going on at work right now, and you have to sleep sometime. Let me take care of Jack, just for a while."

Bailey eyed her as she sipped more coffee. "Okay," she finally said. "But let me know if he gets—"

"Don't worry about us. We'll be fine." Working up her most reassuring smile, she rose, then pointed at the wall clock. "And look, your time is up."

"Hmm?"

"You told Cheyenne you'd call her back in five minutes."

"Crap."

The ticking clock meant Bailey didn't have time to argue or reconsider—and she didn't either, not if she was going to be on time to meet the delivery truck from the blood bank. Underbelly's vampire clientele loved an authentic Bloody Mary, and last night they'd drained the club's supply dry. After that, she'd have to talk with Flynn about what needed to be handled at the club while she cared for Jack.

Bailey drained her mug then stood, rubbing her neck as she gathered her things.

Yes, a call to Rafe while driving to Underbelly would help set Bailey to rights. She'd recommend a massage, then a nap. What her brother and his bondmate did *between* those activities was entirely their business.

They went to the desk, signed out, and walked toward the elevator together. "Are you sure about this?" Bailey asked, pressing the call button. "About staying with Jack, I mean?"

"Sure." As the elevator doors opened, Sasha cast a

quick glance at Jack's closed door. "Don't worry, we'll be fine."

She avoided Bailey's gaze as they stepped inside. Jack would be fine—he'd get her very best effort—but how *she* ultimately fared remained to be seen.

CHAPTER THREE

"Take a right turn at the next light," Jack said curtly from the passenger seat. "Then another quick right."

"Okay." Flipping her blinker on, Sasha took the first turn. Jack was frustrated, in pain, on edge but in control. Adnan hadn't cleared him for driving, and he wasn't at all happy about it.

As they approached the second turn, her breath froze. An underground parking ramp. Jack's North Loop condo had an underground parking ramp.

Of course it did.

Get a grip. Winter was nipping at Minneapolis's heels, and parking ramps were a fact of city life. If she didn't get a handle on this...this...*thing*—and soon—she was going to be in a world of hurt.

"You okay?"

"Just cold." *Liar, liar, pants on fire.* Her shiver had nothing to do with the temperature. It was fear, damn it. She hadn't parked in the Sebastiani Building's parking ramp since the day her father died. The bullet hole had been expertly patched, and additional cameras installed. Whoever had scrubbed all that blood off the concrete should be nominated for sainthood.

Okay, time to nip this in the bud. She hit her right

blinker with more force than was necessary, glanced in the rear-view mirror, then turned.

Jack shifted his weight, reaching for his wallet with his left hand. His frustration spiked, filling the SUV.

"Need some help?"

"No. Thanks." He retrieved the wallet, flipped it open on his lap, and withdrew a silver plastic card. "Here's your key. It's coded for the parking ramp, the elevator, and my condo."

"You don't even want me here, and you got me my own key card?" She took the card from his hand. "Your mother raised you well."

His expression didn't change, but messy emotions lurked beneath the surface.

All righty then. I guess we'll cross 'Mom' off the list of light discussion topics.

"The card's Bailey's," he admitted.

"So that's why you wanted to swing by work before coming home." Despite her best efforts, she hadn't been able to talk him out of making a stop at Sebastiani Security between the hospital and here.

He shrugged. "I needed to pick up a few things, files and such, to be able to work from home for a few days."

Files and such? A few days? Adnan had told Jack to chill at home for at least a week, and she'd bet serious cash money that the surprisingly heavy box she'd carried from Sebastiani Security to the SUV held more than paperwork. But more importantly... "Do you realize you just shrugged with both shoulders?"

"Yeah." He rubbed his right shoulder with his left hand. "And my fingers started tingling earlier this morning."

"That's great news!"

His only response was a muscle ticking near his jawline.

He was in pain, and trying to hide it. *Some caretaker I am.* She needed to get him up to his condo and into bed.

She opened the car window, took the card from his hand, then waved it across the front of the control unit. The garage door hummed as it rose.

Even someone on foot would need a keycard to open this door. Would something like this have saved her father's life?

"Sasha? The door's open. We can go now."

"Yeah." And her teeth were chattering. The open garage door was yawning black hole, descending to… Parking places. Parking places.

It was the middle of the day. The sun was painfully bright. There was a cop car idling at the curb across the street. There was no reason to be afraid.

"Sasha?"

Okay, this is ridiculous. Suck it up, Buttercup. Tossing her sunglasses onto the dash, she took a shallow breath, eased her foot off the brake, and drove into the shadows.

As they descended, her eyes quickly adjusted to the light. Once they reached the second subterranean level, Jack pointed to an empty parking space right next to the door leading to the elevators. "That one's yours."

The parking ramp was clean and brightly lit, with security cameras no one bothered to hide. Relaxing slightly, she peeled her hands off the steering wheel, opened the door, and stepped out.

Jack had gotten out of the SUV and now stood at

her side, his gaze flitting over her bruised face. "I'm sorry," he said quietly. "I never considered you might be apprehensive about—"

"I'm *fine*," she snapped. How could a human read her so damn well? "Now that I'm down here, I'm fine," she amended, sighing. "Sorry. Ready to go upstairs?"

"Yeah."

It took two trips to get everything up to his top-floor condo, with her doing her best not to hover when Jack insisted on carrying too much of the load. He was sore and tired, and stubbornly trying to hide it.

Men.

"I want to use my key card this time," she said as they approached the elevator for the second trip. "Just to make sure it's working." Jack had insisted on carrying both of their duffel bags. His left arm was uninjured, sure, but he was starting to visibly tire, slouching slightly under the bags' weight.

"Go ahead."

No argument? Yeah, he was tired. "Abracadabra!" she said, waving her card before the slim control box. The red indicator light silently turned from red to green. The doors opened.

"After you," he said.

She stepped onto the elevator. He followed, pressing the button for the top floor before she could. Before the doors closed, she noticed the busy coffee bar on the other side of the lobby, with a scatter of indoor tables set up for customers who didn't want to brave the elements. "Nice set-up," she said as the elevator doors closed.

"You're not the only one who can get a decent cup

of coffee by going downstairs in your pajamas and slippers."

"Like you'd ever leave your condo without being fully dressed and groomed, ready to meet the day." What would Jack look like first thing in the morning, barely awake, with beard stubble, bedhead, and pillow creases on his face? A sudden heat simmered. *I guess I'll find out.*

The elevator stopped with a soft ping. They exited, walked down the carpeted hall, and stopped at the door to his unit. She took care of the key swipe, opening the door before Jack could. They stepped into a good-sized foyer.

He let the duffel bags slide down his arm to the tile floor as she toed off her wool-lined suede boots. "Let me take your coat," he offered.

Adnan had told her it was important that Jack use his arm, that he resume normal activities as his strength allowed. Setting her purse and the pharmacy bag holding Jack's pain meds on the long, slate peninsula separating the kitchen from the living room, she slipped it off and handed it to him. "Thanks." She crossed to the living room windows as he fumbled with the hangers. "Wow. What a view."

Jack's condo, a two-bedroom unit with clean, luxurious lines, overlooked the Mississippi River, and both Nicollet and Boom Islands. The trees along the river had already dropped their leaves, but hundreds of hardy Minnesotans were outside, walking, biking, and kayaking. Even in the late afternoon, the north- and east-facing windows made the most of the light. "I feel like I'm up in a tree house." But no tree house in creation exhibited such strong horizontal and vertical lines. Jack's leather furniture looked functional, comfortable—his decor was a sophisticated blend of dark wood, slate, and flashes of cool, brushed metal—but the focal point of the open concept living area was a huge fireplace made of gray slate slabs, large enough to form a wall. His home office was on its back side.

Anyone playing *House Hunters* Bingo would fill their card quite quickly—the open concept living area, slate countertops and stainless steel appliances in the kitchen—but what she'd seen of the office when she'd set a box there earlier, after their first trip upstairs, had reassured her. It looked lived-in, even a little…messy. "Your place is gorgeous." She'd never given much thought to what Jack's home might look like, but she wasn't surprised by what she saw. He had exquisite taste in cars, clothes, and women; why should home decor be any different? "And what an awesome location." His condo was only seven or eight blocks away from Sebastiani Security.

He picked up her duffel and set it on one of the bar stools lining the peninsula before going into the kitchen. "Sometimes I ride my bike to work."

"You're one of those?" When he bent to get something from under the kitchen sink, she bit back an offer to help. She was there to help with wound care, and to make sure he napped and took pain medication when he needed it. That was it. After a couple of muttered curses, he came up with a pretty brass watering can, which he set in the sink and filled at the faucet. A row of droopy-looking plants lined his kitchen window. The planter looked like a chemistry experiment, with clear, beaker-like cylinders that revealed the plant's roots.

"I didn't know you could grow plants."

"The plants do the hard part."

Yep—tired, in pain, and crabby along with it. "You know what I mean." She hadn't owned a live plant in ages. When she and Scarlett had lived together, Scarlett's cat Calamity had maimed or killed every plant anyone dared to bring into the house. "What are you growing?"

"Herbs." Jack used his left hand to pinch off a couple of dead leaves. "Oregano, basil, and rosemary."

So the copper-clad cookware hanging from the ceiling-mounted rack wasn't just for show.

Jack put the watering can back in the sink. "I imagine you'd like to get settled. Let me show you to your room."

Subtext: "I need you out of my hair for a while." Fair enough. God knew he'd had too little privacy to call his own lately. Before she could reach for her duffel, he picked it up and padded down the hallway. She followed, watching his glutes shift under a pair of well-worn khakis. Jack was the same height as Lukas, but built on leaner, more refined lines. He rocked a suit like no one's business.

Actually, the pants looked a little loose.

"This bathroom's yours." He gestured to the bathroom off the hallway.

She quickly poked her head inside. "Pretty." White with green accents, and with a gorgeous fern hanging near the window, the room felt restful and spa-like.

"And here's the guest room."

The walls were painted a subtle dove gray, but the queen-sized duvet was a riot of lime green, gray, and black lines against a white background. There was a desk, a wall-mounted flat screen TV, and a bedside table with a reading lamp. Despite Jack's hospitalization, the room was ready for guests.

How frequently did Jack have overnight guests? Guests who didn't share his bedroom, that is? Women hit on him at Underbelly all the time, and he wasn't a monk. Thankfully, he wouldn't feel up to overnight entertaining until well after she left. And speaking of which… "I think it's time for your next dose of pain medication." Jack's blue eyes were pinched with pain, and lines bracketed his mouth.

"I don't like taking pills," Jack muttered, setting her duffel bag on the bed.

"Why?"

"They make me feel woozy."

And control was his watchword. "Managing the pain is important for your recovery," she reminded him. If he was debating whether to take the pills or not, he definitely needed them. "There's no moral victory to win by toughing it out. Take the pills, then take a nap." She waved toward his bedroom. "Just forget I'm here."

"Yeah, right." Before she could respond to his tone, frustration spiked the air. "Could you open the pill bottle for me?" he asked. "I don't think I can do it myself just yet."

"Sure," she said briskly. "Let's go take care of that." Jack followed her from the guest room back to the kitchen. Once there, she scanned the tall, wooden cupboards. "Where can I find a small bowl?"

"There are some ramekins in the cupboard just behind you."

While she retrieved one of the small, white fluted crocks—his kitchen cupboards were military-neat— he removed the amber plastic bottle from the

pharmacy bag, then handed it to her. Opening the
bottle, she upended it into the ramekin. Pills clinked
against the crockery. "Here you go." She nudged it
across the dark gray slab. "Why don't you keep this in
your bedroom? We wouldn't want your guests to
think they're party favors."

"What kind of parties do you think I have?"

She lifted a brow. "One never knows."

Sighing, he reached for the crock with his good
hand. "I think I'll go to my bedroom. A nap sounds
good."

"Good." The fine lines fanning out from his eyes
seemed deeper, and his uncharacteristic slouch was
more pronounced. "You need the rest, Jack. You
were shot a little over a week ago, and you've been
flat on your back ever since." She waved at his torso.
"And your rib hurts from carrying all that stuff up
from the car, doesn't it?"

He drew himself up straight. "I'm fine."

Men.

"Where did you set that box you carried up?" he
asked.

"The one we picked up at Sebastiani Security?"
The box, originally used for printer paper, had been
heavier than she'd expected. "It's in your office, on
your desk."

"Good." He glanced into his office, as if to
double-check, then nodded. "Thanks."

What was in the damn thing, anyway? "Why don't
you take some medication, and then lie down for a
bit?" she asked. "There's nothing, and no one, that
needs your immediate attention—"

His cell phone rang.

"Surprise, surprise," she said, rolling her eyes.

Around Lukas, Jack, and Bailey, there was always a ringing phone.

Jack set the ramekin back on the counter, pulled his phone out of his pocket with the same hand, then glanced at the screen. An odd wave of anger drifted into the air. "It's my dad."

Had she ever heard Jack mention his family? She didn't think so. "Go." She shooed him toward his bedroom. "Talk to your dad, take your pills, then take a nap. I'll have some dinner ready when you wake up." It would be Vietnamese take-out, but whatever.

Jack glanced at his motionless right hand, then at the phone ringing in his left. His lips went flat with annoyance.

He couldn't get the pills without setting down the phone. *Some caretaker I am.* "Sorry." She plucked two pills from the ramekin and pressed them in his hand, alongside the ringing phone. "Go. Sleep tight. Don't let the bedbugs bite."

He stared at her, then turned and headed down the hallway. After a couple of seconds, the bedroom door closed.

Leaving her alone to snoop.

*

After closing the bedroom door, Jack hung up the phone without answering. His parents didn't know he'd been shot, and he was going to keep it that way.

The message his father had left a week ago, the one that had distracted him and gotten Elliott killed, still sat in his voice mail. He hadn't been able to listen to it, or to the other messages his father had left since. During his time in the hospital, he'd spent long minutes just staring at his phone. Staring at nothing. Replaying the scene in his head, over and over again, in a ruthless analytical loop.

The root cause of Elliott's death was inescapable: Guard distraction. *He'd* gotten distracted, on the job, and by a goddamn cell phone—something they covered on Day Fucking One of SebSec's new hire training.

Adding to the titanic sense of failure? The distraction itself could have been prevented. If he'd answered his dad's *first* phone call, which he'd also ignored, his father wouldn't have found it necessary to call again. There'd have been no second call, with its unique, rarely-heard ring tone, to distract him while guarding the President and his daughter.

If he'd answered his father's first phone call, Elliott might still be alive today.

And now that Elliott is dead, I still don't want to pick up the phone. Multiple phone calls and voice mails from a man who hated both probably meant bad news.

When the voice mail count increased by one, his hand tightened around the phone. Yeah, something was up, but he didn't have the energy to deal with it right now.

Would the guilt ever go away?

Setting the phone on the bedside table, he trudged to the bathroom to get some water to take the pills.

Sunlight flooded in through the skylights, casting a warm, beachy glow and heating the beige floor tiles. He was dying for a long, hot shower, but he couldn't bathe without asking Sasha to tape waterproof plastic wrap over his wounds first. Those soft, capable hands, touching his chest, stroking surgical tape onto his bare skin…

"Damn it." He hurt, he was helpless, and now he was half-hard.

Turning his back on the glassed-in shower, he strode to the sink and set down the pills. Without thinking, he reached for the water glass with his right hand—rather, his brain sent the order, but his arm didn't obey. Hot, stinging pain zinged from his shoulder to his fingertips. Without thinking, he slapped his left hand against his right shoulder, banging his bullet wound but good. He inhaled sharply, turning air into a razor blade that sliced him from the inside out.

Black dots swarmed in his peripheral vision. "Fuck, fuck, fuck."

Somehow, he managed to stay on his feet. No one saw him doubled over, eyes watering as he waited for the pain to recede and his critical thinking skills to come back online. No one saw how slowly and carefully he drew himself upright, or how long he leaned against the sink until he felt steadier. Using his left hand, he turned on the faucet, filled the water glass, turned the faucet off again, then took the goddamn Vicodin.

His pheromone intoxication medication, twenty yellowish-white tablets in a small Ziploc bag, sat next to his toothbrush holder. He glanced at his closed bedroom door, then back at the pills, considering. Adnan had told him not to mix them with pain medication, but maybe he could—

In the bedroom, his phone blipped. Lukas's ring tone, right on time. His painful bathroom slapstick routine must have gotten his friend's attention. Lukas's ability to discern other people's emotions at distance was unparalleled. God knew Sasha was no slouch herself.

Sasha knew he wanted her. She'd always known. She also knew he fought the attraction, but not why. She didn't need to know why.

Why the hell had he agreed with Bailey's suggestion that Sasha help him out for a few days? It was madness. Right about now, he'd empty his brokerage account for some goddamn privacy.

He picked up the phone. "Hey."

"Hey." Lukas's fingers clattered against a keyboard in a machine gun burst, then went quiet. "Just checking in. How are things going?"

He reached for his pillows with his right hand. "Damn it," he hissed as pain zapped down his arm. Maybe he should start wearing a sling as a reminder. "Can you hang on a sec?"

"Need more time to ditch my sister's carcass?"

"I'm putting you on speaker." He punched the buttons, a little harder than necessary. "This one-handed crap sucks the big one."

"I can tell."

What did his pain, his frustration, taste like to Lukas? "Sorry, man."

"No worries. How are things going?"

"Okay. We're settling in." What more was there to say? Lukas knew exactly how frustrated he was. He carefully propped his pillows against the headboard, sat, pivoted, then reclined with a sigh. Sasha had been right about the nap. "How are things going at work? With the Council?"

"I'm glad Alka has Sebastiani Labs under control,

because dealing with that on top of everything else would be the cherry on top of a massive shit sundae."

As Lukas brought him up to speed, he fought to stay focused. "Is there anything new on the investigation into your dad's death?"

"Not since we talked yesterday." There was a familiar-sounding thunk as Lukas propped his booted feet on his desk. "The shooter didn't use any gun currently in the system, but we know exactly where he stood—right in that video blind spot. There were no spent casings left at the scene."

"Sounds pro to me," Jack said.

"Yeah, but why? What's the motive?"

He could think of a dozen people who'd benefit from Elliott Sebastiani's death and plenty more who'd want his son and successor dead, too. *I have to talk to Chico.* If Lukas hadn't beefed up his own security detail, he and Chico would do it for him.

"Jack, you still there?"

"Yeah." But the damn drugs were hitting. He felt like he was melting into the mattress. "Does Krispin Woolf have an alibi?"

"That was the first thing Gideon checked," Lukas replied. "He was having a business dinner at Manny's Steakhouse when the shooting occurred."

Dinner at Manny's meant reservations, and a lot of interaction with attentive restaurant staff. No doubt the alibi had checked out. "Damn it."

"Yeah, we couldn't be that lucky," Lukas muttered.

Finding the WerePack Alpha guilty of assassinating the Underworld Council President would solve a number of Council problems in one fell swoop. Woolf had been a royal pain in their asses for a very long time, but no one had found any evidence to take him down.

Yet.

"Krispin Woolf was very annoyed to be asked for proof of his whereabouts by one of his own," Lukas said.

Commander Gideon Lupinsky, a were-shifter, had titanium gonads.

"So, how's the arm doing?"

His fingertips felt like he'd shoved his hand into a wasp's nest. His gunshot wounds throbbed, and they itched like hell. "It's there," he replied. "It's...sore."

"But you're getting some sensation and movement back. That's good news, right?"

"Yeah." Forming words and sentences was starting to feel like...work. The drugs were helping, another thing Sasha had been right about. "Lukas?"

"Yes?"

"What if I don't get full function back?"

Silence hummed over the line.

Shit, the man had lost his father, and he was complaining about a banged-up arm? "Sorry—"

"Jack, give yourself a fucking break. You were shot, twice, just over a week ago. Recovery takes time. Follow doctor's orders, and don't skimp on the physical therapy." Lukas paused. "And if you don't get full function back, you'll adapt."

His friend's brisk, matter-of-fact assessment was exactly what he needed. "You're a fine one to talk about recovery time," he groused. "When the shoe was on the other foot, it was impossible to keep you away from your desk." A couple of years ago, Lukas had nearly been killed by the same deranged man who'd killed Scarlett's sister Annika, and assaulted Krispin's daughter Andi. Stephen, the incubus at fault, had somehow escaped from their most secure psychiatric facility and was still at large. Krispin still blamed Lukas for allowing Stephen to escape.

"Do as I say, not as I do," Lukas stated.

Jack rolled his eyes. "Yes, boss."

"As long as you're in such a cooperative mood, please let Sasha help you."

He struggled to follow the conversation. The Vicodin was really kicking in. "Driving down into the parking ramp scared her shitless."

A pause. "How did she do?"

He'd known. "God, you're brutal." Lukas didn't deny the accusation. "After a little bit of hesitation, she did just fine," he admitted.

"Set the bar sky-high, and she'll kill herself trying to leap over it," Lukas said. "Sound familiar?"

Lukas knew him—*them*—too damn well.

"Helping you helps Sasha with her own healing process, you know."

Guilt was a finely honed weapon. Lukas didn't use very often, but when he did, his aim was true. "Don't expect too much," he cautioned. "We don't get along very well. We fight all the time."

Lukas's laugh was all too knowing. "Use your words, and you'll get along fine."

"Ha." If Lukas knew the words he wanted to use around his sister, and in which sexual positions, he'd… Hell, he'd do nothing. That was the problem. In the sex demon world, if it was consensual, it was game on. Sasha teased him all the time about how puritanical humans were about sex.

He scowled at his cock, still half-hard despite the painkillers swimming through his system.

Lukas laughed again. "I'll let you get some rest.

Talk to you later."

"Later." He hung up the phone, then collapsed back against the pillows. "'Use your words,'" he mimicked. "To say what? 'I want to fuck you?'"

Words weren't necessary. She already knew.

She knew, but she'd never tried to take advantage of the fact. Sure, she flirted and teased—she was a sex demon, after all—but consent was very deeply ingrained in their world, and he hadn't given his.

Their every interaction was a sexual sword dance, intricately choreographed and slightly dangerous. But they both knew the steps, and they'd both stuck to them.

Right now, I'm in no condition to dance.

He had no intention of becoming a notch on Sasha Sebastiani's bedpost. He'd plant himself in his bedroom, and keep the door closed. Focus on his PT, and take plenty of the naps Sasha herself had recommended.

Masturbate left-handed, once he could stay awake long enough to finish the job. Which—he gave a giant yawn—was not now.

He climbed under the covers fully clothed, and surrendered to sleep.

CHAPTER FOUR

"Sasha? Are you there?"

Flynn's voice brought Sasha's attention back to the phone. "Yeah," she said, leaning back against Jack's bed pillows. Trying to take a business call while Jack showered in the next room probably hadn't been the smartest idea. The bathroom door was open, so she could hear every distracting sound. Water hissed from dual showerheads, meandered down his spectacular frame, then hit the floor tiles with uneven splats... She cleared her throat. Now was not the time to fantasize about offering her hands as his washcloth. Flynn had a situation he wanted to discuss. Apparently last night's headliner had trashed Underbelly's largest dressing room after their performance.

"The cleaning staff found cocaine residue all over the place," he said.

She pressed her fingers to the bridge of her still-sore nose. "So much for the band's well-publicized sobriety."

"Didn't the lead singer just get out of rehab?"

"Yeah." Her eyes narrowed as the sound of the water falling to the shower's floor tiles became...more rhythmic.

Jack was no longer simply bathing.

She couldn't help but inhale, couldn't help but absorb the sharp sexual energy he emitted. As Flynn described the damage at the club, she couldn't do anything but try to ignore the delicious curl of sensation that slithered down her spine.

Somehow, within the next couple of minutes, she had to find enough self-control to dress Jack's wounds and get him started on his day. Then, and only then, she'd head to the guest bathroom, with its wonderful handheld shower nozzle.

She and Jack had the exact same problem, but they weren't doing anything about it—not together, at any rate. She'd never spent so much time alone in a bathroom in her life.

"Is there anything else I can do?" Flynn asked.

Flynn had been aces managing the situation, getting the band back to their tour bus and back on the road, but speaking to their business manager about reimbursement was her job. "I can take it from here. Thanks so much for handling things." Screw the band's rabid fan base. They'd never perform at Underbelly again. She glanced at the window. "You should have enough time to get home before the sun comes up." The sky was starting to brighten, but the sun hadn't popped over the horizon yet.

"Okay, Mom," Flynn said dryly. "I'll put on some VampScreen, just in case."

Flynn only lived a couple of blocks away from the club, but he rode a bicycle to work. The special sunscreen would buy him a little more time. "Wear a hat and mittens while you're at it."

Flynn laughed. "Talk to you later."

"'Bye." She tucked her phone into the pocket of her fleece jacket, then sighed at the bathroom door.

Leaving the room wouldn't help. Nothing would help. The sexual tension between she and Jack had always been explosive, and distracting herself was getting more difficult by the day. There was work, sure, and plenty of it, but during the time she'd stayed with Jack, she'd spent too much time either hate-watching HGTV, or reading—which didn't help, because her e-reader was loaded with erotica.

Lying on Jack's decadently soft bed wasn't helping in the least.

She got up and roamed around Jack's gray and blue bedroom, a color scheme no doubt chosen to showcase the exquisite mixed-media wall hanging dominating the room's west wall. A beautiful ocean scene with crashing waves, the textiles brought to mind not the relaxing, soft blues of the Caribbean, but of a scene more northerly, with sharp rocks and ridges lying just beneath the surface.

The scene seemed vaguely familiar, but she couldn't place it.

In the bathroom, the water splats got shorter, more erratic. She stilled, inhaling deeply and closing her eyes, savoring the snarl of sexual energy.

He came, silently and violently.

Locking her knees for support, she absorbed the blast. His plush orgasm suffused her, and she was half tempted to let her hand skim south. *No. Bad idea.* He'd be out of the bathroom soon, and he'd need her help to dress his wounds. To distract herself, she slipped open the top drawer of his bedside table and peeked in. There was a small white legal pad, a high-end mechanical pencil, some over-the-counter allergy tablets, and a box of condoms.

The good news? He had condoms. The bad news?

The box was half-empty, confirming he had a sex life.

The water turned off in the bathroom. She quietly closed the drawer, and was standing by the side of the bed when Jack padded from the bathroom into the bedroom a couple of minutes later, wearing low-slung flannel pajama bottoms and scrubbing at his damp hair with a towel. Though he couldn't possibly see her erect nipples through the thick layers of fleece, she crossed her arms over her chest.

Maybe Minnesota winters were good for something after all.

He had a beautiful body, built on leaner lines than Lukas. Anyone who'd spent much time with him knew Jack's tailored suits disguised some serious muscle, but seeing him wear little more than skin was a rare treat. With his broad shoulders, and beautifully defined chest, he was eye candy by any measure. The blond hair dusting his pecs darkened slightly as it traveled down his abdomen, then disappeared under his sagging waistband. The plaid flannel pajama pants should have looked very Ward Cleaver, but...didn't. The tissue-thin fabric draped faithfully over his penis—

"Where do you want me?"

Anywhere. Everywhere.

"Want me to sit on the bed again?" he asked.

"Yeah, that worked well yesterday." A bed, and so much beautiful, bare skin... Droplets of water lingered on his torso. She wanted to use her tongue as a towel.

Enough of that.

She climbed onto the bed behind him. After a good, private sniff—his soap reminded her of a deep, dark forest—she carefully dried, then removed, the plastic wrap she'd taped over his shoulder and back, and then started dealing with the soiled gauze. Thankfully she wasn't squeamish, because the bullet wounds were still pretty gory, particularly the exit wound on the front of his shoulder. "You're healing well," she said, setting the gauze on the towel she'd laid on the bedspread. Her hands hovered, hesitant to touch. Because she wanted to touch, very badly.

His breathing changed, growing slower. Deeper.

Damn it, he was drawing in her pheromones. She darted a quick glance at his lap. Yeah, there was a more prominent bump under the fabric than there'd been just a minute ago.

The man recovered quickly.

Talk about something, anything. "Did you play football when you were young?" Behind him, she rolled her eyes. Even trying to distract herself, she focused on his body—a complete Florence Nightingale fail.

"No. I didn't play basketball, either—which, given my height, is the typical follow-up question." A corner of his mouth tipped up. "Like any self-respecting NorCal boy, I surfed, and played Ultimate Frisbee."

And graduated from Stanford and Stanford Law while he was at it. "Frisbee? Seriously?" Though she teased him, she found the unexpected fact delightful. The Jack she knew was so damn serious all the time. "Did you have a college stoner phase I haven't heard about?"

"I plead the Fifth."

Grinning, she tore open the fresh gauze pads she'd need to dress his wounds. After graduating, Jack had practiced law at his family's firm in San Francisco before moving to the Twin Cities. "A surfer, hmm?" The turbulent water scene hanging on the wall adjacent to his bed made more sense now. "Have you ever surfed Mavericks?"

"You know it?" he asked.

"Yeah." The northern California surf break was world-famous—infamous—for its carnage. "Scarlett and I road-tripped there once."

"To Mavs? Why?"

"You know sirens; they love the water. Scarlett had a song in her head, and wanted some inspiration." Sasha picked up a fresh gauze pad, handling it around the edges. "The waves looked like mountains."

"They're amazing, aren't they?" Jack said. "Too much height for me, though. My home break is—was—just north of San Francisco." He paused. "It's been years since I surfed there. Since I surfed anywhere."

"So you brought a little bit of home with you to the heartland." She gestured to the wall hanging. "It's a beautiful piece." She tore a piece of surgical tape off the roll, positioned the fresh gauze pad over his back wound, then carefully taped it down. When she'd snooped around his place a couple of days ago, she hadn't seen a surfboard, but she *had* found a handgun sitting in the printer paper box she'd carried up from her car the day they arrived. She'd solved the mystery of what was in the box, but both the box and the gun had disappeared the very next day. "Have you ever thought about surfing Lake Superior?" she asked. A few crazy Minnesotans did, almost every year.

Jack shook his head. "I've watched some videos online, though. Those guys are nuts."

"And surfing a forty foot wave isn't?"

"Mavericks is cold, but Lake Superior?" He shivered. "That's some next-level crazy."

She finished dressing his shoulder wounds. "You're healing well," she said briskly, giving the tape around the last fresh gauze pad a completely unnecessary stroke. "Did Adnan say how long you needed the gauze?"

"Maybe another week." He slowly flexed the fingers of his right hand.

"Hey, look at that!" She grinned at him. "Better than yesterday."

"It's a start," he said with a sigh. "Never fear, you'll soon be able to get back to your own life."

"Don't worry about that." She patted his uninjured shoulder. "I'm keeping busy." And even with the gauze, even with the pain, so was he. Under her watchful eye, he balanced work and rest, and ate just enough to keep his big body fuelled. She caught him wincing occasionally, especially when he did his physical therapy exercises. Adnan had said that his fingers, hand, and arm might tingle quite painfully as he regained function. But Jack was right. Soon, he'd be able to manage on his own. Her job was nearly over. And speaking of which... "How's your pain level? Need a pill?"

"I took one before I took a shower."

"Only one?" Pain still showed in his face. "Are you sure you don't need the full dose?"

"Yes, I'm sure," he snapped. A heavy silence descended. "Sorry."

"About what?"

He looked at her, his blue eyes burning with an emotion his stony face didn't reflect. Pain was in the back seat, and frustration in the front. Frustration with his body. With this situation. With her.

Fair enough. She stood, gathering her supplies and

the discarded gauze and plastic wrap. "I'll leave you alone."

He reached for her forearm with his left hand. "Really. I'm sorry."

"For what?"

"For being a dick." He cast a disgusted look at his groin. "No pun intended."

"You're entitled to be a little crabby now and then," she said mildly. "I'll be out of your hair soon." Heat pumped from his body, and it was all she could do not to lean toward the warmth. "What's wrong? I can tell something is bothering you, but not what. Use some words."

His jaw tightened.

She touched his thigh. "You can't hurt my feelings, you know."

He looked at his lap again, then faced her. "Adnan told me I can't take pheromone intoxication meds and pain medication at the same time."

"So, you have an erection," she said, shrugging. Actually, he'd had a reassuring number of erections for a man whose body sported bullet wounds. "It's an autonomic physiological response," she continued, brisk as a nurse. "Don't worry, I won't take your hard-ons personally—"

"You damn well should."

She reared back. He'd never before acknowledged the outrageous sexual tension bubbling between them. "Are the pain meds loosening your tongue?"

"No," he said, exasperated. "I'm trying to have a frank discussion about this...this pheromone thing. About how important the pills are for me."

She sat beside him on the bed. "Okay."

"You remember the medication was developed

specifically for humans, to help neutralize the effect of incubus and succubus pheromones?"

"Yes." Incubi and succubi inhaled emotion as sustenance, and emitted pheromones in response. It was just her bad luck to crave the only man on the planet who took medication to neutralize their effect. The universe was truly perverse. "Do the meds really work that well?" she asked.

"Yeah, they do—and believe me, when one poor decision could negatively impact an entire culture, it's beneficial for me to have a clear head."

When she'd worked with Jack to coordinate event security for Scarlett's homecoming show at Underbelly a couple of years ago, Lukas had assured her that, taking the meds, Jack would have the clearest head in the house, but... "I thought you only took the meds when you worked large events."

His fingers flexed against his thigh. "I have the most powerful incubi and succubi on the planet as work colleagues, and I interact with them every day. I rely on the meds to remain objective, to stay free of influence, even from your family members."

Was he supposed to take the medicine so frequently?

"And then there's you."

"What about me?"

"Do you know how challenging it is for a lowly human to spend time around you? Around your pheromones? To question your own bodily responses?" He scowled at his groin. "Right now, I don't know which head I'm thinking with, or why."

He knew how important consent was in their culture. "Do you think I'd take advantage of any...befuddlement you might be feeling?"

"No, of course not. But—"

"But what? What's really bothering you?"

His emotions swung like a pendulum as he struggled to put his concerns into words. Or maybe the struggle was deciding what he'd share with her and what would remain private.

Again, fair enough.

"You addle my brain in the best of circumstances, and now is nowhere near the best of circumstances."

Men. "What's to think about? In the best and worst circumstances, we're two adults who want each other."

His jaw went tight. "It's not that simple, Sasha."

"It could be." When he jolted, she gave a shrug. "Why do humans have so many hang-ups about sex?"

"I don't have sexual hang-ups," he bit out.

Maybe not—according to the Underbelly grapevine, he was a generous, skilled, and inventive lover—but…*something* was going on. The emotions he was leaching had a dark, unpleasant residue.

"Of course I want you," he muttered. "Who wouldn't want you? But we're locked in a feedback loop. You're here, stuck in my condo with me. You can't help but inhale my—" he cast another disgusted look at his groin "—sexual energy. You get aroused—you can't help it—and emit pheromones in response that just make me want you more."

It took a couple of seconds to parse his words. "You think I wouldn't want you if you didn't want me first?" She couldn't hold back a snicker. "Oh, honey. Since we're being all mature and adult, finally talking about this…" She swung a leg over his lap, straddling him but still kneeling, and combed her fingers through his silky, damp hair. The position gave her extra height, putting them eye to eye. "I want to eat you alive. I always have. Pheromones have very little to do with it."

His breath hitched. His pupils dilated, nearly obscuring the navy blue of his irises. Time eddied and pulsed around them. Finally, his left hand rose, caressing her fleece-covered thigh before coming to rest on her hip.

It was all she could do not to lower herself onto his lap, to grind against the erotic heft of his erection—an erection she'd caused. His brain knew what his body wanted; why couldn't he just listen to it? The decision had to be his, but... "Kiss me, Jack," she murmured. "Please, just kiss me."

His head finally moved—toward her, thank the universe. She met him halfway.

Finally.

They dove at each other, frenzied and frantic, their lips crashing together so their tongues could tangle and dance. He tasted of toothpaste, of mint and man, and the scrape of his bristly cheeks hurt so good. When his erection nudged at her from below, she lowered herself down to his lap. Let him take her weight.

Their twin groans twined in the air.

He lifted his head and looked at her. His face was all hard planes, the skin of his cheeks drawn tight with arousal, but his expression was pure voluptuous pleasure. Though they were both breathing hard, the lines of pain formerly etching his expression were gone.

She'd always wondered what he looked like in the throes of passion. Now she knew.

She tasted him again, taking teasing little nibbles

around the plush perimeter of his mouth. A groan rumbled from his throat, and a split second later he took control, cupping her head with his left hand, holding her in place as he devoured her.

The grapevine was right, he had a very talented mouth. She couldn't wait until he— Their noses bumped. She reared back, hissing in pain.

"Shit. Are you okay?"

She gingerly touched her nose, blinking as her eyes watered up a storm. "Am I bleeding?"

"No. How's the bridge?"

"Okay." Damn it, she could feel him pulling back, pulling away. His expression was distant, analytical.

"Sasha, we can't..." He licked his lips, as if to remind himself of her taste. "We can't do this."

"I disagree. We can. We did, and very nicely." But on his side, the sparks they'd just shared were gone, doused by guilt and the dark smear of whatever it was that she'd sensed earlier. "Jack, it's okay," she said, exasperated. "Why do you deny yourself such simple pleasure?"

His jaw went tight. "There's nothing simple about it."

His emotions were a cauldron, roiling and swirling. He was physically aroused, but...confused. In pain, and...angry. Hotly, blazingly angry.

At her? At himself?

It didn't matter. She eased herself off his lap. Once her feet hit the carpet, she stepped away from the bed.

"What's wrong?"

You tell me, dude. Throttling back her frustration— after all, he'd revealed more about his thinking today than he had in all the years they'd known each other—she started gathering the supplies now scattered across the bed. The gauze wrappers crackled as she wadded them into a ball. "Do you play chess?"

"What?" He blinked. "Yes, but—"

"I want you, Jack, and you want me—but the next move is yours." Her casual pivot toward the bathroom took more effort than she'd ever admit. "Let me know if you want to play." She returned the supplies to the bathroom, throwing away the plastic wrap and used gauze pads. When she came back to the bedroom, he was still sitting where she'd left him, looking like she'd clobbered him upside the head.

And his breathing was labored. "What am I thinking, making your poor injured lung work so hard?"

"I'm okay." He gave his lap a final, disgusted glance, then gingerly moved toward the mountain of pillows. "I'm going to rest for a while."

"Good idea." She jerked her thumb toward the living room. "I'll see you in a bit."

As she left the bedroom, his cell phone rang. She closed the door on his ripe curse.

Whether he was swearing at the phone, or at the undeniable shift in their relationship, she couldn't be sure.

✳

Jack exited his bedroom with a reassuring bounce in his step. In the couple of days since Sasha had surprised him with her request for a kiss, his health, and his outlook, had taken a radical turn for the better. Funny how doing something as normal as running errands—walking to the doctor's office, going to physical therapy, getting a haircut—could make a guy feel halfway human again.

His recovery was going well. He'd cut way back on the pain meds, only taking them before he went to sleep. Soon, he'd be able to eliminate them altogether. And there'd been good news from Adnan this morning. Slowly but surely, his arm and hand function were improving. Adnan hadn't cleared him to drive yet, but told him he could resume normal activities as he felt able.

He felt like...playing chess.

Would he ever be able to look at a chessboard again without hearing Sasha's wicked euphemism echo in his head?

He wanted to have sex with her, and always had. Sasha was right—he wanted her, and she wanted him. Sasha had no relationship expectations; all she wanted was sexual pleasure. And when push came to shove, he *did* trust her. Why deny himself? Why deny her? She was perfect, really.

Knowing Sasha's two-toned hair and penchant for denim and leather would make his mother shit an elegant brick? Bonus.

"Hey, Sasha, I'm back!" he called down the hall. "Adnan said I—" Damn. Water was running in the guest bathroom. She was in the shower again.

He paused by the closed door, half-tempted to barge into the bathroom, snatch that detachable shower head out of her hand, and take care of her needs himself. Was the door locked?

He was almost touching the doorknob when his

phone chimed.

"What the hell am I doing?" he muttered, pivoting away and stalking to his office. He'd set the phone alarm to remind himself to dial into a conference call at Sebastiani Security, a call he'd now have to start with a hard-on. Dropping into his desk chair, he fired up his secure laptop and dialed into Lukas's meeting. When the software fired up, he saw Bailey, Chico, Gideon Lupinsky, and Antonia sitting around the long, oval table in Sebastiani Security's big corner conference room. Antonia wasn't on Sebastiani Security's payroll, but given her technical skills, Machiavellian political mindset, and her uncanny ability to connect disparate dots, she pretty much came and went as she pleased.

"Hey, Jack, turn on your webcam," she said.

So much for getting away with audio-only. He activated his camera with a sigh. "Hi, everyone." A chorus of return greetings peppered the line as Bailey bustled around the table, activating the in-room tech before sitting down at her own laptop. Throughout the meeting, his face would float in the upper left corner of the screen that covered most of the room's west wall. "Where's Lukas?" he asked.

"On his way." Bailey scowled at her pinging phone. After silencing it, she added, "His last meeting went long."

"Jack, did Sasha cut your hair?" Antonia asked, burrowing her chin into the neckline of her oversized sweater.

"Do you think I'd let your sister anywhere near my neck with a pair of scissors?" The pithy response came easily, automatically, but today, he slid an uncomfortable glance toward the door, hoping she hadn't overheard. "All kidding aside, we actually left the condo today." While he'd been getting his hair cut, Sasha had gone to the other side of the salon to get a manicure. Once they'd reached Memorial Hospital, she'd dropped him off at the curb, saying she needed to run a few errands during his appointment. He'd told her to go ahead, that he'd find his own way home. Instead of catching a taxi or a rideshare, he'd walked—slowly, yes, but he'd damn well walked. The chilly, bracing air had helped clear his head, but Sasha's actions in the bathroom right now were bringing the sexual tension back with a vengeance.

And in the meeting room less than a mile away, Antonia smiled knowingly. But instead of saying something snarky or embarrassing, her attention went to the conference room door.

Lukas walked in, his long, jean-clad legs making short work of the distance. "Sorry I'm late." After shaking hands with Gideon, he looked up at the wall. "Hey, Jack." Lukas's quick, searching glance was as thorough as a medical exam. "How are you doing?"

"Fine. And you?" Though freshly showered and shaved, Lukas looked tired enough to roll right back into bed.

Lukas answered with a grunt, pausing at the credenza to pump a cup of Crackhouse Blend from the air pot before sitting down in his oversized leather chair. "Thanks for coming today, everyone."

The business manners were strictly for Gideon's benefit; everyone else at the table spent as much time in this conference room as they did their own living rooms. Seeing Chico leaning against the brick wall behind Lukas's chair—literally at his back, even behind Sebastiani Security's locked doors—was reassuring.

"I wanted Gideon to update everyone on the parking ramp shootings," Lukas said.

Shootings, plural. He, too, was a victim. Should he even be here, listening to this? How might his presence compromise any future criminal case?

Stop thinking like a human. He was human, yes, but it wouldn't be the human courts rendering judgment in this case. The Underworld Council carried that painfully heavy burden, and compared to human courts, they had unusual latitude. But it was impossible for him to put his legal experience aside. With the Council's President assassinated and another Council member—him—nearly killed, and half the members of the Council related to Elliott either by blood or bond, no Council member would be entirely free of bias. He could help there, pointing it out if he saw it, but he had to push human rules of law to the back burner. Here, they simply did not apply.

As Gideon updated them on the status of the investigation, Jack sifted the information through both the prosecution's and the defense's perspectives. There were gaps and loopholes all over the place, the primary one being there was, as yet, no suspect to either prosecute or defend.

"What are we missing?" Lukas asked, staring at the ceiling. "The police work is solid, but the trail is going cold."

"Antonia has something she's been working on," Gideon said. "Some new analysis."

Every head turned Antonia's way.

He should have noticed she'd brought a top-flight laptop to the meeting rather than her usual e-tablet, and now she was connecting a joystick. Whatever they were about to see had taken some serious technological firepower to produce.

The image on his monitor flashed as Antonia shared her laptop screen.

"Antonia wrote some software that integrates the parking garage security videos with the crime scene data—the ballistics, the forensics, witness interviews, blueprints, and all the measurements—creating an integrated narrative of events," Gideon explained. "Layers of data can be stacked, viewed, or hidden on command." Gideon glanced over at Lukas. "This is the most realistic crime scene reconstruction app I've ever seen."

The daughter of the victim, working on the case? Accessing the crime scene data, and developing new technology to interface with that data?

This isn't the human legal system. This isn't the human legal system. This isn't the human legal system.

An instant message popped up on his screen:

[BBrown:] *You look ready to stroke out*

[BBrown:] *Are you okay watching this?*

It wasn't every day a man watched his own shooting, but he'd cope. In preparing the reconstruction, Antonia must have watched her father's assassination dozens—hundreds—of times.

He mouthed a curse. Typing with one hand was very slow going.

[JKirkland:] *I'm fine. But this case would be tossed out of a human courtroom so damn fast...*

Via the webcam, he saw Bailey's ironic smile.

[BBrown:] *We're not in Kansas anymore, Dorothy. Damn, my phone is blowing up*

[JKirkland:] *Is something wrong?*

[BBrown:] *Dude, something's always wrong*

Bailey glanced at her phone. Whatever she read there made one eyebrow cock up, Spock-like. She reached for her laptop.

"Jack?"

Everyone else was looking at him, waiting for him. "I'm fine," he assured Lukas. "Go ahead."

After another stare that stripped him bare, Lukas nodded at his sister, giving her the go-ahead.

Antonia started the program, displaying the Sebastiani Building's parking ramp. She oriented them first, explaining that she'd cobbled together all the parking ramp security videos, creating a three-dimensional representation of the crime scene. "We can examine the crime scene from any angle," she explained, demonstrating with the joystick. When she pressed a couple of keys, near-translucent measurement gridlines layered over the image. A digital clock appeared in the lower right corner.

"Ready?" she asked.

Breath whooshed through his suddenly constricted throat. "Yeah, go."

On-screen, the stairwell door opened, and the three of them entered the parking garage. Elliott was laughing, delighted with something Sasha had said, but he—on-screen Jack—hadn't joined in. He was scanning the ramp, assessing their surroundings.

Doing his job, which should have reassured him, but damn well didn't.

Because the man he was guarding was about to die.

There was another giggle from Sasha, walking at his left. Her head barely came up to his shoulder, and he outweighed her by at least a hundred pounds. It was easy to forget how physically small she was. In person, she was larger than life, filling up any room with sheer force of personality.

He could hear her now, pans clattering in the kitchen. At least she was out of the damn bathroom.

"Pause," Gideon said, glancing at Antonia. "Three-hundred-sixty degree pan, please?"

Gideon seemed as familiar with the program's capabilities as Antonia did—and if he felt the least bit intimidated asking an Underworld Council member to follow his instructions, it didn't show. The image on the screen did a slow twirl. "As you can see," Gideon pointed out, "all available angles show the garage is clear."

'All available angles' didn't matter when the shooter had taken aim from an angle the cameras didn't cover.

"The first shot is fired at 18:23:12," Gideon explained. "Antonia, enhance audio please. Do a full-speed playback, then repeat in slow motion."

His stomach rolled as Antonia clicked the keys. His left fist tightened, whitened.

"Full speed playback," Antonia said. "I'm starting about twenty seconds back."

Elliott laughing…Sasha laughing…him, scouring the corners… 18:23:09, 10, 11…and then, at 18:23:12, there was a barely-audible sound, the *thwipp* that shrieked in his nightmares…

Elliott's laughter went silent. His legs crumpled beneath him, and the lasagna pan fell from his hand. Both hit the concrete, hard. Red sauce and pasta went flying.

"Pause video," Gideon requested.

Antonia quickly obeyed, freezing the lasagna pan in mid-bounce.

"So, Jack's report was accurate. The weapon is clearly suppressed."

Chico glanced at Gideon. "9mm rounds, correct?"

Gideon nodded. "And if you look down, there's a shell casing on the floor. Antonia, replay in slow motion, please. Overlay bullet trajectory." Keys clacked as Antonia obeyed. They watched the sequence again, in painfully slow motion. The trajectory line appeared on the screen, confirming the shooter's location. "Whoever fired the shot was standing in that blind spot along the west wall," he said.

"Can you fast-forward, to immediately after the shooting?" Lukas asked. "I'd like to check something."

Antonia advanced the video a mere ten seconds, but when the picture stabilized, a lifetime had literally passed by. Elliott was dead, he was down, and Sasha was trying to push out from under Jack's body. He tried to watch objectively as she succeeded, as she crawled toward her father. As she realized his wound was fatal, and she screamed "Daddy!" Sobs wracking her tiny frame, she crawled back to him, grabbed her cell phone, and called in the Code Red. She climbed onto his back to staunch the bleeding, cursing at him, demanding he not die.

After a quick glance his way, Antonia fast-forwarded about four minutes, when two nondescript, mid-sized sedans—Gideon's teams—squealed into the parking ramp. One team started treating his injuries, and the other checked the area where Sasha indicated the shots had come from. Two cops approached the blind spot, weapons drawn, telling the shooter to come out with their hands up. No response. After a quick, silent two-count, one of the cops chanced a lightning-fast glance around the corner blocking their view. "Clear," she called.

"It's clear. No one there." Lukas clenched his hands into fists. "And the video didn't catch anyone leaving."

Lukas was right. "What the hell…"

Gideon and Antonia exchanged a look. With a couple of keyboard clicks, Antonia overlaid the crime scene with the Sebastiani Building's floor plans. Gideon reached for the basket of office supplies sitting in the middle of the conference room table, withdrawing a hand-held laser pointer. "Our best guess is that the shooter dropped in from here—" he jiggled a tiny, red light at the juncture between floors "—from above, through the ducting system."

Sure enough, an HVAC duct opened directly above the alcove. *Fuck.* Why had he never noticed that before? "Can you display the video from the service door?" The ducting system was accessible via a side street service entrance. There was a security camera installed above the door.

"Funny you should ask," Bailey said grimly. "Antonia, can I share my screen for a sec?"

"Sure."

Their hands moved in a familiar duet. With a

couple of keystrokes, Antonia's crime scene reconstruction blipped away, soon replaced by the image on Bailey's laptop screen. She was looking at the security feed he'd requested.

Every cell in his body went still.

"What's up?" Chico asked.

Bailey gestured to her phone. "Someone at SebSec just discovered an anomaly with that video feed. Watch."

The screen flashed, then displayed a familiar-looking span of nighttime city sidewalk, illuminated by a bright light mounted above the service door. The date and time stamp indicated the video had been taken at 22:30:02—10:30 p.m.—the night before the shooting occurred.

As the playback rolled, Jack scanned up, down, left, and right. There was a discarded water bottle lying on its side near the fire hydrant. A passing car splashed slush onto the sidewalk. No pedestrians, which didn't surprise him. The side street didn't receive much foot traffic. "I don't see anything unusual."

"Not yet." Bailey fast-forwarded several minutes. "Watch what happens at 22:40:34."

As they watched, the picture…blipped, and a woman who hadn't previously been there now stood on the sidewalk. Dressed for cold weather in a long down coat, winter boots, and a knit hat and mittens, she waited for her leashed German Shepard to finish peeing on the fire hydrant.

"Did you see it?" Bailey asked.

"No. Can you play it back?"

They all watched the video again.

"Ah. We didn't see either the woman or the dog

walk into the frame," Chico said.

Nope. They'd simply…materialized. "We didn't see the dog lift his leg, either," he added. "The video caught him mid-pee." Somehow, the time stamp now read 22:55:13. "The feed lost fifteen minutes."

Bailey nodded. "On a first, cursory run, no one noticed the missing time slice."

"Easy enough to miss," Lukas muttered.

The security guards on duty in the building that night wouldn't have noticed, either. Too subtle. "Jammed?" he asked Bailey.

"We're still analyzing, but it's likely. It also seems likely the shooter knew most of the third shift cleaning staff uses this door when they come to work."

And from there, it was easy to connect the dots. The night before Elliott died, the shooter, having observed employees' traffic patterns, jammed the video feed, then walked into the Sebastiani Building with a group of third shift workers. Once inside, he'd reversed the jam, crawled into the heat ducts, assumed his position, then simply…waited.

The shooting was pre-meditated, no question about it.

"He tailgated?" Lukas's head dropped to the back of his chair. "My father's killer waltzed in through a goddamn security door, and had the run of the goddamn building for nearly a day, because he tailgated?"

Bailey looked resigned. "People are always the weakest link."

"There was a below-zero wind chill that night," Chico noted. "It's no excuse, but the workers were probably heads-down, in a hurry to get inside, so they let basic security hygiene slide."

"Damn right that's no excuse," Jack snapped.

After penetrating the first line of defense at one of the Twin Cities' most heavily secured buildings—one where the Underworld Council president, two other Council members, and Sasha Sebastiani made their home—Elliott's killer had somehow gone undetected for nearly a day. "We need to check all the video feeds again," he said, "inside and out."

"On it." Bailey's fingers were already flying. "I'll acquire adjacent business's security videos through unofficial channels."

'Unofficial channels' meant hacking them. The hacked information would be inadmissible in human court, but as Bailey had said earlier, they weren't in Kansas anymore. The Underworld police force had no jurisdiction over human-owned businesses, so search warrants would be useless. Asking the other businesses for the video feeds directly would mean revealing why they wanted them. All things considered—all *risks* considered—Bailey's approach was the most expedient. Time was of the essence.

He looked at Gideon. "You searched the building in the aftermath of the shooting?"

"Yes, and it was clear. We didn't find a nest, but—" Gideon's lips flattened "—we didn't search the ductwork." He reached for his phone. "I'll get things started."

Lukas glanced at the room clock, then at him. "I have another meeting starting at the top of the hour. Can we watch the rest of the reconstruction video?"

Are you ready to watch yourself get shot? Ignoring his tingling hand, he gave a crisp nod. "Go ahead."

Taking control of the screen once again, Antonia

re-displayed the crime scene reconstruction video running on her laptop. The paused image they looked at now had caught Elliott milliseconds after the bullet hit, already dead but just starting to fall. Sasha was rolling her eyes, probably at him. Hadn't he made some sort of dismissive, smart-assed comment about cold weather and wet hair as he'd slipped his phone back in his pocket?

Gideon, finished sending text messages, set his phone on the conference room table. "As we play back, notice the timer at the bottom of the screen. The second and third shots come less than two seconds after the first, at 18:23:14."

Antonia glanced up, as if to say, "Fair warning," then hit play.

Jack watched as a yellow line zinged out from the blind spot, as a bullet hit his shoulder from behind. A fraction of a second later, another yellow line speared him in the center of his back, just to the right of his spine. Half-diving, half-falling, his left arm snaked out, dragging Sasha under him. The last shot smacked into the wall, but Sasha hit the floor hard—first her knee, then her face. He winced in sympathy. *Her poor nose.*

She started shoving against him, trying to scrabble out from under his body. She'd seen the pool of blood forming under her father's head.

"Dad! Daddy!"

Antonia paused the playback, then cut audio. "Sorry."

"It's tough viewing all around." Lukas touched his sister's forearm. "This is…amazing work."

"It is." Even if Sasha's screams flayed him alive.

"She won't accept a consulting fee," Gideon

grumbled.

"I don't want your fucking money."

He almost smiled. When Antonia was annoyed, she looked a lot like Sasha.

Antonia might not want the money, but her work—or *aspects* of her work—might be patentable. How did Sebastiani Labs protect their technology innovations? *There you go, thinking like a human again.* Patenting meant paperwork, and paperwork meant exposure. Sebastiani Labs protected their technology innovations by keeping them secret.

Chico straightened, pushing away from the wall. "Look at the trajectory of that last shot."

Antonia rewound, playing it back, and what he saw kicked him in the gut. If he hadn't pulled Sasha down with him, the bullet would have hit the base of her skull.

Kill shot.

Through the webcam, Lukas's gaze met his. "You saved my sister's life."

He couldn't respond. He was still trying to breathe again.

Gideon cleared his throat, breaking the heavy silence. He pushed to his feet and started pacing the room. "Elliott, Jack, and Sasha are walking toward Jack's car." Without him having to ask, Antonia highlighted the Volvo, parked down the row from their fallen bodies. "The video blind spot is to their front and left." Keys clacked as Antonia once again layered in the parking lot blueprints, then washed the triangular slice of space behind the support column, beyond the security cameras' sight lines, in translucent orange. "Overlay with dimensions, please?" Gideon requested.

As Antonia complied, Jack squinted at the screen. "The blind spot is barely three feet across."

"Pretty tight, space-wise," Chico said. "There's not a lot of room back there."

"And if our working theory is correct, the shooter dropped into the blind spot from the ductwork above."

When Antonia jiggled her mouse, an on-screen arrow fluttered around the opening to the ductwork. "Tighter yet fit," she observed, pursing her lips, "and whoever the shooter was managed to stay out of sight during the entire event. We haven't been able to discern the slightest glint of a barrel."

"He's aware of the blind spot, and knows how to position himself to stay out of sight," Jack said.

Lukas nodded. "And he probably dressed to blend."

But no one could blend into invisibility, and the security cameras hadn't caught anyone leaving the parking ramp after the shooting. "Is there any indication the shooter jammed the parking ramp videos after the event?" he asked Bailey.

"Nothing we've found, but we'll verify."

"So, how did he get away?"

Antonia's mouse jiggled over the ductwork again. "The same way he came."

He eyed the distance. "An eight-foot jump? Are you serious?"

"Yes. Given the evidence, or lack thereof, right now I don't see another solution."

Chico tipped his head to the side. "I could do it. Gideon could do it."

Gideon, a fellow were-shifter, nodded. "Most members of the WerePack could." He paused. "A lot of Valkyries could make the leap."

I couldn't, even at peak physical condition.

"There's one more thing I'd like to show you." Antonia panned along the edge of the outcropping that had shielded the shooter from view. She zoomed in, and sharpened. A darker smudge took form, barely visible against the gray.

Jack squinted at the screen. "Is that a hand?"

"Part of one," Gideon murmured. "Looks like he's picking up that spent casing we saw earlier."

They hadn't found any spent casings at the scene, so the other three must have dropped closer to his feet, out of camera range. "It looks like he's wearing tactical gloves." The thin, black gloves were popular in the security and target shooting markets. Sebastiani Security bought them by the case.

"Four shots, three hits, left to right, in less than three seconds." Gideon eyed the screen, hands on hips. "That's a pretty tough angle."

"Yeah." Jack imagined holding his Glock in his tingly right hand, imagined the contorted position he'd have to assume to take all four shots, yet stay hidden. In the conference room, Lukas, Chico, Gideon, and Antonia were twisting their upper bodies sideways, shooting arms extended, trying to position themselves so they could shoot, yet stay out of sight.

"Lukas and Jack would have trouble staying hidden," Bailey said. "They're both too broad across the shoulders."

Good to know I'm exceeding expectations somehow.

"I think I could do it," Gideon said.

"So could I," Antonia added.

"I could make the shot, but probably not stay hidden," Chico allowed, considering the space. "A left-handed shooter would have an easier angle."

Lukas cast a frustrated glance at the clock. "Debate that after I leave, please. Where does this leave us?"

Gideon's phone, sitting on the table, vibrated with an incoming text message. He glanced at it, nodded, then sat down. "Antonia's reconstruction—and this discussion—has given us some important information. We can surmise the guy is Chico-sized or smaller, and that he either already knew the layout of the building or knew how to find that information. The jammed security cameras indicate he researched employee movement patterns, and has technical know-how. He might shoot left-handed, he might wear tactical gloves, he's a very good shot, he used a suppressor, and he picked up his casings." Gideon paused, then looked at Lukas. "The list of people who'd benefit from your father's death is exhaustive, and we'll investigate all angles, but...this pings pro to me."

Lukas nodded grimly.

"Gideon, you keep saying 'guy,'" Antonia said. "Don't you think a woman could have done this? Or that we might be dealing with a team?"

"Well, sure," he allowed, shrugging. "I used the word 'guy' generically—"

"The word 'guy' implies the default person has a penis. As a data point, half of the population does not."

Gideon paused, then nodded. "Point taken."

Keyboard clacking, she redisplayed a wide-angle view of the crime scene, with three bodies down. "Another data point: There were two other people in the parking garage that day. How do we know Dad was the shooter's target?"

"Of course Elliott was the target," Jack said. "Who'd want to kill me or Sasha?"

"You're an Underworld Council member, and Sasha's a Sebastiani."

And the Sebastianis were their culture's most powerful family, but...why would someone want her dead?

Could Sasha be in danger?

"Chico, pull together a round-the-clock security detail for Jack's condo complex," Lukas ordered. Apparently he'd had the same thought. "Better safe than sorry."

"Speaking of which, how about a watch of your own?" Jack asked Lukas. "You're a bigger target than any of us now."

Lukas ignored his comment. "You'll cover Sasha?"

Sasha walked into his office carrying a lunch tray. "Cover me how?"

Heat crawled up his neck. Did her words sound as suggestive to everyone else as they did to him? How long had she been standing there?

"Hey, proof of life!" Bailey called from the conference room. "We were wondering whether he'd strangled you yet."

"Very funny." Sasha set the tray down on the desk—tomato soup, grilled cheese sandwiches, and potato chips were on the lunch menu today—then perched on the arm of his desk chair, slipping her arm around his shoulders so they'd both fit in the webcam's frame. Antonia, quick on the draw, had replaced the crime scene image with a picture of a grumpy-looking cat.

Sasha was fresh from the bath, her damp hair slicked back against her skull, and some strange alchemy had transformed soap and shampoo into an exotic bouquet. She hadn't bothered with make-up. Today, her facial bruises were a stark greenish-blue, the color of a tornado-warning sky.

"Thanks for getting back to me so quickly, Sasha," Gideon said. "Are you sure there's no problem closing down the Sebastiani Building's parking ramp for a couple of hours?"

Ah. Gideon's earlier text message exchange had been with Sasha, who managed the Sebastiani Building.

"Do what you need to," she said, massaging the tight muscles at the back of his neck. Yesterday, she'd informed him his neck was where he 'carried his stress.' "Flynn is looped in."

Stress or not, her touch felt fantastic. Since sharing that incendiary kiss a couple of days ago, she'd started touching him more and more frequently. Had she noticed how much he liked it?

Why *were* humans so puritanical about sex?

"Good progress, everyone." Lukas rose from his chair and headed for the door. "Please keep me informed."

"Will do." He waited until Lukas left the room. "Chico, can you hang on a minute?"

"Sure." On-screen, he watched everyone else gather their things and leave.

"Oops." Sasha suddenly stood. "I forgot your milk."

"I can get it—"

And she was out the door.

On-screen, Chico was closing the conference room door. "In your imagination, she's wearing a French maid's uniform, right?"

"Shut up." Without discussing it, they both turned off their webcams, darkening their screens and going to audio-only. The fact that Chico so automatically fell into their normal one-on-one meeting pattern was reassuring.

"How much of the re-enactment did she see?" Chico asked.

He glanced toward the door. "I was wondering the same thing."

"It looks like her bruises are fading."

"Yeah." But the little bump on the bridge of her nose was probably permanent, and would always remind him—and remind her—of what had happened that day. "We need to talk about Lukas's security situation."

"Damn right."

He saw Sasha leave the kitchen, carrying a large glass of milk. "Hang on a sec."

When she entered, she brought her maddening scent back with her. "Here's your milk."

"Thanks."

She set the milk on the tray, then snitched a potato chip. "So." With a little hop, she sat on his desk. "Have you given our recent conversation any more thought?"

She hadn't seen the crime scene reconstruction after all. "Which conversation is that?"

"The one where I asked why we weren't having sex."

There was a snort of laughter from the darkened screen. Jack hung up, ending the meeting.

"Have you given it any more thought?" She delicately licked salt off the potato chip, as was her habit. "Your recovery is going well. If you're not quite at full strength yet—" she glanced down at his lap, then winked "—I can do most of the work."

"No, you won't," he couldn't help but reply. God knew the hard-ons he managed in the shower were at full strength, as was the erection currently pitching a tent in his pants. Their gazes met, blue to blue. "Adnan's cleared me for everything but driving."

"But...?"

Of course they were going to sleep together—it was inevitable—but in one more day, maybe two, he'd be able to start taking his pheromone intoxication meds again. If they were going to sleep together, he wanted a little more protection first.

Sliding off the desk, she turned the office chair so he sat facing her, then she cupped his erection with her hand. "Want some help with this?"

He clenched his teeth. Her hand, and that gamine grin, were going to kill him. So was what he was about to do. "No." Covering her hand with his, he lifted it from his lap, then squeezed her fingers. "Not yet," he added.

"Are you okay?" She put her hand on his forehead, as if to check for a fever. "I don't know too many guys who'd turn down a blow job." She paused. "Actually, I don't know *any* guy who'd turn down a blow job."

"I don't doubt it." Any man who'd earned Sasha Sebastiani's intimate attentions would come running the minute she crooked her purple-nailed finger.

"Oh, I get it," she drawled. "You're wondering how many men I've blown."

"No." Well, maybe—but not in a judgmental way. Her former lovers, the ones he knew about at any rate, tended to be artists, chefs, and musicians.

Creative types—and paranormal, at that. How could a stodgy human lawyer possibly measure up? He looked up at her. "I don't like thinking with my dick."

She glanced at his crotch. His dick was definitely making its preferences known. "Why do you have to think at all? Why can't you just feel?"

Oh, I'm feeling, all right. "I'm not wired that way." He captured her hand again, bringing her knuckles to his mouth for a soft nibble. A luscious, and gratifying, burst of pheromones drifted his way. Closing his eyes, he let himself wallow, then reached for the one argument he knew she wouldn't fight. "You said the next move would be mine." Fuck, his throat was dry as dust. "I'm not quite ready to make it yet."

Two more days.

Two. More. Days.

Okay, maybe one.

"Damn you," she said good-naturedly, dropping a teasing, salty kiss onto his mouth before backing away. "It's your fault I'm spending so much quality time in the bathtub, you know."

Quality time masturbating. "You're killing me."

"Same goes." Another quick kiss. "Enjoy your lunch."

He stared at her swaying hips as she walked away. She made a saucy ninety-degree turn at the hallway, then disappeared from view.

After a couple of seconds, the guest bathroom door closed with a click.

* ping *

An instant message from Chico blipped onto his monitor.

[CPerez:]   *Working or sexing?*

Rolling his eyes, he reached for the keyboard.

[JKirkland:]   *I'm here*

[CPerez:]   *alone?*

[JKirkland:]   *Yes*

[CPerez:]   *I'm very sorry to hear that*

[JKirkland:]   *shut up*

[CPerez:]   *Call me*

Talking to Chico couldn't be avoided, and talking would be easier than typing one-handed. They had to discuss Lukas's security situation. As he reached for his desk phone, water started running in the bathtub.

One way or another, the woman was going to be the death of him.

But what a way to go.

CHAPTER FIVE

"One moment, please."

Frustration escalated, but Miranda shoved it back, shoved it down. Where was easygoing, easily-fooled Simone? The only explanation she'd gotten when she arrived for her appointment was that her former corrections officer had been reassigned—which didn't explain a damn thing. The new guy, Banner, showed every sign of being a world-class asshole.

He reminded her of Santa Claus from the classic *Rudolph the Red-Nosed Reindeer* Christmas cartoon. Bald, and almost as round as he was tall, Banner wore a beautiful gray suit, wire-rimmed glasses, and had a fussy gray mustache he clearly spent a lot of time grooming. If given only one word to describe the man, it would be "fussy." If given a second, it would be "dangerous." She hadn't missed the gun, holstered under his suit coat. He hadn't made the slightest effort to hide it.

He also hadn't bothered to familiarize himself with the details of her case. She'd been here for twenty minutes, and so far they'd spent every moment of their appointment time reviewing her history with the corrections system in nauseating detail. The man was a stone cold sadist, making her relive the worst experiences of her life over and over again.

Where the hell was he going with this?

Calm down. If there was one thing she'd learned during her time in the system, it was that respect for *her* time was not a priority.

Fuming, she sat with as neutral an expression as she could manage. The nondescript room was utterly utilitarian, with white walls, a rectangular table, two uncomfortable chairs, and overhead fluorescent light. There were no electronics in sight, not even a security camera, and so far, she hadn't seen Banner handle anything other than paper.

Did the corrections budget not run to computers?

"Ms. DesJardins."

His voice was raspy, like he was fighting off a cold. "Yes?"

"According to the prison psychologist, you still seem to have considerable resentment toward your lawyer—" he glanced at the document "—a Mr. Jack Kirkland."

Every nerve jerked to attention. Why did he want to talk about Kirkland? "Is that so surprising? He was my defense attorney, and I ended up in prison."

"You blame him for your incarceration?"

"No. I'm to blame." She didn't believe it, but she'd learned to say it. She'd been assured by Cynthia Roth Kirkland, co-owner of the law firm and Jack Kirkland's mother, that their son was the firm's most qualified lawyer for her particular case. Kirkland hadn't delivered, and she'd paid the price. "I did the crime, and I did the time."

Banner flipped another page, then scratched at a scab on his hand. "According to court transcripts, you assaulted Mr. Kirkland after the judge read the guilty verdict."

Carving a couple of fingernail grooves in Jack Kirkland's neck had been her last independent act before the bailiff hauled her away. "I was angry." *I still am.*

"He declined to press charges."

"Which I appreciate." In hindsight, losing control like that had been really stupid. Acting while in the grip of strong emotions rarely produced a good outcome. *Maybe I learned something in those therapy sessions after all.* "As you can see, I took advantage of therapy and anger management classes while I was incarcerated."

"So it seems." He flipped another page of the inches-thick document, then speared her with his shark-gray gaze. "Ms. DesJardins, any lingering resentment you might have toward Mr. Kirkland can't help but impact your ability to live a law-abiding and productive life."

Hiring a hit man to kill Jack Kirkland wasn't law-abiding, but it sure felt productive. She glanced pointedly at her watch. "Mr. Banner, we're running short on time." She opened her portfolio, withdrew her job search records, and passed them across the table. "I'd like to make sure we have an opportunity to discuss my job search. I have several promising leads."

"Thank you." He set her notes aside without looking at them. "Ms. DesJardins, why Minnesota?"

"What?"

"You were a lifelong California resident prior to your incarceration. Why relocate to Minneapolis after your release?"

Because Kirkland lives here, you doofus. Or maybe he wasn't such a doofus. He sure seemed interested in

Jack Kirkland. "I wanted a fresh start." She had no ties to California—no job, no lover, and her family had pretty much washed their hands of her. "I have some professional contacts both here and in New York City," she continued, trying not to watch as the man scratched his hand bloody. Did he have psoriasis or something? "I thought I'd explore job opportunities here first." The truth was, no one in Silicon Valley would take her call, and she wasn't having much better luck here in flyover country—but on the plus side, the cost of living was *so* much lower here than it was in California. Here in Minnesota, she could buy a four-bedroom home sitting on acres of property for the price of a San Jose crack den.

"Where were you the evening of Saturday, November 12th?"

Banner's question knocked the air from her lungs. She figured her name would come up at some point during the investigation into Jack's shooting, but...not *this* soon. "Let me check my planner." *Breathe. Breathe. Your alibi is so tight it squeaks.* Reaching into the leather briefcase sitting on the floor at her side, she pulled out her day planner and flipped to November 12th. "I was at Bachelor Farmer, having a networking dinner." Knowing Ethan's timeline for fulfilling the contract, she'd made a 5:00 p.m. reservation, then sent a text to her dinner companion to confirm. The receipt was in the back pocket of her planner—pre-dinner drinks and their meal, time-stamped 7:34 p.m. She'd paid for the meal with her credit card, and that was her distinctive signature at the bottom of the slip. She passed the receipt across the table.

He took it, gave it a quick glance, then set it aside.

That's it? "I'll need that back for my tax records."

He nodded. "Now, to your job search."

The abrupt change of subject flustered her. She'd been ready to deny knowing Jack Kirkland lived and worked in Minneapolis. To deny knowing he'd been shot, in a downtown Minneapolis parking garage, at approximately 6:25 p.m. on Saturday evening, November 12th. She'd rehearsed her denial, over and over.

This guy was anything but predictable.

She described her dinner with Annabel, an acquaintance of an acquaintance who worked as a financial analyst for a health care conglomerate, in more glowing terms than the event deserved. Annabel was on maternity leave, was thinking about making the leave permanent, and talked mostly about her baby.

Her lips tightened. Unlike Annabel, she couldn't afford to permanently quit working. She had to support herself somehow, and pay off Ethan Covington once he fulfilled the terms of the contract. Even with the blot on her resume, she honestly hadn't expected her job search to hit so many brick walls.

It really galled.

"Ms. DesJardins, are you familiar with a company called Sebastiani Security?"

Kirkland's current employer. Ethan Covington's former employer. "No."

"How about Sebastiani Labs?"

The company name sounded *vaguely* familiar, but... "No." She cast a puzzled look at Banner. "Who, or what, is a Sebastiani?"

He flipped the document closed. "We'll discuss

your job search in greater detail at our next meeting. Carry on, and remember that we'll need to consult the court if you want to relocate to New York City."

"Trying to get rid of me already?" she half-joked.

Banner rose, silently and wordlessly. His expression didn't change.

Their appointment was apparently over. She collected her purse, coat, and briefcase.

He escorted her from the room to the hallway. "I'll make a copy of your dinner receipt. Wait here, please." He disappeared behind one of the half-dozen doors lining the long hallway.

The walls were blindingly white, and very clean, and none of the doors had a sign or label. She looked up to the corners, where the walls met the ceiling. No security cameras here, either.

No security cameras at a government office? Since when?

A primitive warning skittered up her spine. Why had Mr. Banner asked to meet here, rather than at the corrections office where she'd previously met with Simone? She hadn't seen another living soul during the hour she'd been here.

Were they here alone?

Go. Leave, now.

She was turning toward the exit when Banner reappeared from a different door than he'd entered.

"Your receipt," he said, extending his hand.

Her self-reservation instincts were shrieking. "Thank you," she managed, plucking it from his pudgy fingers without touching him. She quickly stuffed it in her purse.

"Until next month, Ms. DesJardins."

She forced herself to nod. "Goodbye." She

escaped without shaking his hand, but felt his shark-like gaze follow her all the way out to her car. Throwing everything into the passenger seat, she got in the car, locked the doors behind her, then left the parking lot as quickly as the law allowed.

About a mile down the road, she pulled into a Target parking lot. "Hell," she breathed. Hands shaking, she reached into her purse for the burner phone. She had to talk to Ethan, had to cancel the contract. Had to make him back off, because a second attempt on Jack Kirkland's life would put *her* in the crosshairs.

Right now, self-preservation was more important than her need for revenge—at least until she figured out a better way to achieve it.

She'd probably have to pay Covington the whole damn fee just to keep him quiet, but if that's what it took to keep her out of prison, it would be worth it.

※

From his seat in the manufacturing plant's security office, Ethan monitored a dozen screens. Workers came and went out of the locker rooms. Vehicles entered and exited the parking lot. Pickles—thousands and thousands of pickles—whizzed by on a series of conveyor belts. Watching the pickles for too long gave him vertigo, and the sharp, briny smell made him nauseous, even on a good day.

Today was not a good day.

He needed food, and pills, before he jittered right

out of his chair. Where the hell was Bill? The other guard was supposed to relieve him ten minutes ago—

The guard office door opened. "Hey," Bill said, hitching up his pants in a way that made Ethan suspect he'd just dropped a satisfying deuce. "Welcome back."

"Thanks." He stood, removing his utility belt. The pepper spray, baton, and handcuffs were complete overkill, as were the uniforms, but the two-way radio really came in handy.

Bill dropped into the chair Ethan had just vacated. "How are you feeling? Did you end up going to the doctor?"

"Nah, it's just a bug." It sure as shit wasn't, but he couldn't tell a human what was wrong with him.

"Well, you've been out sick for days, and you look worse now than you did when you left."

After fucking up the Sebastiani Building contract, he'd gone on an epic, three-day bender, then had tried to come back to work as if nothing had happened. As if he hadn't killed the president.

It hadn't worked. Nausea, full-body jitters, sweating through his clothes... His boss had sent him home from work to shake off whatever bug he'd picked up.

It wasn't a bug, it was his body. Damn his Valkyrie physiology, and its overactive adrenal system. "Food, fight, and fuck" were the tried and true solutions, but no matter what he did, no matter what he tried, the imbalance was building. He could feel it.

"Are you limping?"

"Tough workout today." Resuming full-bore Krav Maga workouts when he was in the worst physical shape of his life probably hadn't been the smartest idea, but he had to do *something*. At SebSec, working out had been part of the job. He'd had all-hours access to their top-notch gym, and there'd always been teammates around for support and company. Now, he had to work out on his own—and ever since Kirkland had fired him, he'd really let things slide. Crawling through the Sebastiani Building's ductwork should have been the easiest part of the job, but he hadn't factored in his own muscle loss and weight gain. The belly hanging over his belt had almost been his downfall.

He could blame Kirkland for a lot of things, but he couldn't blame him for that.

And now, he had to get to the bathroom, *fast*, because his stomach was flopping like a fish on a hook, and saliva spurted under his tongue. "Gotta go," he blurted, quickly clocking out. "See you tomorrow." He hurried toward the door.

"Take care of those muscles, dude. Have a soak, take a sauna."

He managed a nod before leaving. Saliva flooded his mouth. *Hurry, hurry…* He scurried down the hall, as fast as his limp would allow. A vicious heat wave slammed into him like clockwork, simmering him from the inside out and slicking his skin with sweat. Weaving unsteadily, he made it to the men's room, dove into a stall, and heaved.

When his stomach was finally empty, he turned, then dropped onto the toilet seat. After he caught his breath, he reached for his Vicodin. The pills would glaze over the pain, blunt the rage. Make the nightmare go away, just for a while.

Sweat dripped as he stared at the tablets, then swallowed them dry. Relief—escape—were only five minutes away.

He stared blankly at the beige stall door, wondering, yet again, why he'd taken the Kirkland contract in the first place. Money, yeah—he had so many overdue bills, and the woman had offered him more money than he'd seen in a single place in his lifetime—but he couldn't deny that revenge was a factor. Money *and* revenge, in one fell swoop? Her offer had been irresistible.

But he never dreamed he'd *miss*, that he'd take out President Sebastiani instead of Jack Kirkland. His aim was just one more thing that had turned to shit since Kirkland fired him.

And now, President Sebastiani's death, and the search for his killer, was all anyone could talk about. At least here, in this human building, no one knew a thing—but out in the world? Out on the street? It seemed like every eye followed him. Judged him.

I deserve their judgment. Holy hell, I assassinated the president—the president I once protected.

Had John Wilkes Booth felt such hollow, aching grief after shooting Abraham Lincoln? Probably not. At least Booth had hit his intended target. He hadn't…and he'd already spent the down payment.

Amazing how quickly a guy could blow ten grand. Amazing how it wasn't enough.

You still have a job to do. Once he got paid, he'd buy himself a new life. Move someplace where it never snowed. Maybe Costa Rica, or the Dominican Republic. Live in a shack on the beach, off the grid. Yeah, with that kind of lifestyle, he could make ninety grand last a long, long time.

The men's room door opened. Someone wearing hard-soled shoes walked in, went to the urinal, and unzipped their pants. Fabric rustled.

"Ethan? Is that you?"

No use denying it. His black Sorel work boots were visible under the stall door. "Hey, Kirby," he called. Could he get away with staying in the stall? Probably not. *Might as well get this over with.* He flushed the toilet, then exited the stall. Kirby was standing at the urinal.

Kirby glanced over his shoulder. "Hi, Ethan. Feeling better?"

"Yeah, thanks." Thank god for urinal etiquette. A guy could only say so much to another guy when the other guy was holding his dick in his hand.

Kirby still managed to give him a thorough up and down before facing the wall again. "You've been away from work a lot recently. Is there something going on that I need to know about? Can I help?"

He'd taken almost a week of vacation time to prepare for the Kirkland job, and...yeah, he'd taken some sick time afterward, to deal with...to come to terms with—

"Ethan?"

Ethan walked to the sink, turned the water faucet on, then pumped soap into his palm. "Thanks for asking, but I'm fine."

No one can help.

"Okay." Kirby shook, tucked, zipped his pants. "I just wanted to make sure you realized that, as of yesterday, you're out of paid time off through the rest of the year." His boss joined him at the sinks, eyeballing him as he washed his hands. "Short-term disability's there if you need it."

"Do I really look that bad?" he half-joked.

Kirby didn't laugh. "You don't look well, Ethan."

Probably not, but tapping the human health system—tapping *any* health system—was out of the question. "I'll keep that in mind, Kirby." He grabbed a couple of paper towels, wiped his hands, then tossed the damp ball of paper into the wastebasket. "Thanks for your concern. See you tomorrow."

"Ethan—"

He slipped out the door, then made his way to the parking lot. Once in his truck, he battled rush hour traffic to the north metro, to his favorite gun range. Yeah, ammo was spendy, but he wouldn't get paid if he couldn't hit the damn target.

And he needed to get paid.

The burner phone rang as he pulled into the gun range, but he didn't answer. Listening to the woman bitch at him for missing Kirkland wouldn't help him get the job done. He needed a new plan, because yesterday afternoon, doing some reconnaissance on Kirkland's condo complex, he'd seen Sebastiani Security operatives posted at every entry and exit.

His former co-workers, now on high alert, would recognize him on sight. The job had just become a *lot* more difficult.

The burner rang again. "Damn it, lady." He opened the glove box, threw the phone inside, then closed the door. "And that solves that." He needed to think—think like the operative he used to be.

Dude. The operative you used to be didn't...use. He blinked, trying to focus.

What did he know, what did he remember, about Jack Kirkland? About his habits, his skills, his strengths and weaknesses? Kirkland managed day-to-day operations at Sebastiani Security, and hadn't gotten his job, or his position on the Underworld

Council, because he knew the boss. He was a lawyer, yes, but he more than held his own in the field, on the range, and in the cage. Yes, Kirkland was recovering from gunshot wounds right now, but it would be stupid to forget he kept himself in peak physical condition. He wouldn't be down for long.

Brawn, brain, and tight with the Sebastiani family. He'd interrupted a pretty cozy family scene the night of the shooting—Jack, walking with Elliott and Sasha Sebastiani, laughing and joking, the president carrying a pan of homemade lasagna to a destination he'd never reach.

He smelled peppers and garlic in his nightmares.

Think. Think.

Sasha. It would be difficult to catch Lukas Sebastiani flat-footed, but his sister? Sasha Sebastiani was five-foot-nothing, a hundred pounds soaking wet. She ran a nightclub, for fuck's sake. Hardly a physical threat.

Definitely some possibilities there.

He got out of the truck, grabbing his gun case from behind the seat. Yeah, Sasha Sebastiani was an angle worth considering. Everyone at Sebastiani Security suspected Kirkland had a soft spot for her, or wondered whether they might actually be lovers.

Lovers or not, Kirkland had already let one member of the Sebastiani family die on his watch. He'd be shattered to lose another.

CHAPTER SIX

Something dragged Jack from sleep. Opening his eyes in the dark, he waited. Listened.

A soft snuffle, barely audible, coming from the guest room.

Was Sasha crying?

He rolled out of bed and padded down the hall, pausing at the closed guest room door. Yes, she was sobbing, taking long, hitching breaths. Was she asleep or awake? Probably asleep, because the Sasha he knew would saw off a limb before exposing anything resembling vulnerability.

To me, anyway.

Opening her closed bedroom door felt like violating her privacy in some fundamental way, but what was he supposed to do? Roll over and go back to sleep when he knew she was in here, alone, crying her eyes out?

Nope, that wasn't happening.

When he opened the door and stepped across the threshold, he took a big, deep breath. The room smelled like her—jungle blooms, dark spice, and warm female skin—and her scent seemed concentrated, distilled, an airborne liqueur he craved more than oxygen. She hadn't pulled the blinds, so the moon spilled thin, milky light. Her body barely made a bump under the plush comforter, and most of her head was covered by the bedspread. All he could see of her was the black smudge of her hair against the pillowcase.

How could she even breathe?

Hell, how could *he*? Her pheromones were giving him a contact high, but he couldn't help but inhale. Under his pajama bottoms, his penis was shifting, stretching.

The bump beneath the blankets shifted, undulating as she rolled to face the wall. "Daddy…"

Her whisper was a blast of cold air, a solar plexus punch.

How many nights had she lain here, alone and crying, while he'd been too drugged up to hear? She'd been so busy caring for him, caring for everyone else, that her own mourning had dropped to the bottom of her priority list.

Well, I'm not drugged up now. Lifting the covers, he slipped into bed with her. She didn't wake, even when the mattress dipped. When he reached for her, touched her? Nothing but warm, bare skin.

He should have guessed that Sasha Sebastiani slept in the raw.

Some hazy portion of his brain told him to leave, now, but she turned and reached for him, sliding all that warm, bare skin against his, clinging to him like he was the only thing keeping her afloat. He tried to ignore the soft cushion of her breasts flattening against his chest, tried to ignore her stiffening nipples, his stiffening cock, the tears dripping onto his chest. Her scent shot straight to his brain stem, wine decanted specifically for his pleasure.

Where the hell was he supposed to put his hands?

At one time or another, every inch of her lithe dancer's frame had had a starring role in his most fevered dreams, dreams that found him waking up in a hot sweat with his dick in his hand. He'd admired her luscious body from afar—hell, who hadn't?—but to touch her? To hold her in his arms at last? Damn, it was all he could do not to— *No.* For fuck's sake, this wasn't about him. After all that had happened— her father was *dead*—the least he could do was comfort her without turning the experience into a letter to *Penthouse Forum.*

Her shoulder blades. Her shoulder blades should be safe enough.

He let his hands drop, and... *Not safe, not safe at all.* There was no give to her flesh, but that didn't matter. Her skin was satin-soft, and hot to the touch—

She shifted so she sat astride him, bringing their hips into diabolical alignment. He tried to move, tried to back away, but any movement just nudged his flannel-strangled cock closer to the humid vee between her legs.

Sasha didn't seem to mind. Her hands stroked his chest and abdomen, then cruised over his left hipbone to cup what she could reach of his ass. She flexed her fingers, humming her approval.

The sound slithered up his spine. "Sasha..."

"Hmm?"

She'd stopped crying, but she wasn't moving away. Neither was he, but... Did she even know who she was with? Was she awake, or had her succubus instincts taken over?

"Jack..."

Okay, that answered that, but—

Sliding both hands under his waistband, she

cupped his cock.

A strangled groan escaped. He slowly thrust between her hands, hissing at the friction. Eyes on hers, he flexed his hips and thrust again. And again.

What the hell am I doing? She's my best friend's sister. Lukas was his boss. For fuck's sake, Lukas was the *president.*

The pocket Venus grasping his cock with such authority would tell him his thoughts were patriarchal human bullshit. Hell, so would Lukas.

She decided. *She* chose.

And she'd chosen *him.*

Her lips were on the move, nuzzling through his chest hair toward his nipple, then licking it like a tasty treat. When she gave it a testing bite, savage pleasure zinged to his balls. Her scent seemed stronger, spicier—an essential, intoxicating brew.

"Jack?" His name bloomed hot and damp against his chest.

"Yes?"

"Make it go away."

The last wisps of his resistance floated away. Here in this dark, quiet cocoon, in this place out of time, he could give her the oblivion she sought—and if they slept together, maybe he'd finally find some relief from the insidious, grinding need he'd fought back for so long.

It was just sex, right? They were both consenting adults.

He could help her, and help himself.

He dragged her up his body, so their faces, their mouths, were even. Her lashes fluttered in the moonlight, hiding her expression. He stroked her cheek, then combed his fingers through her hair to cup the back of her head. Their gazes locked, then their heads both moved, meeting halfway.

Finally.

Her lips were slick and agile and urgent, like hot, slippery silk. Twin moans mingled when his tongue touched hers, as they dove into each other's mouths. Vibrated into each other.

"Mmm." She grabbed the back of his head, tugging at his hair to pull him closer. "More."

He complied, diving deeper. Oh, she was dark and lush, sweet and tart—as addictive as he'd always suspected she'd be, but he'd worry about that later. He clutched more tightly, dove deeper, suckling on her tongue. The gentle, testing kiss he'd envisioned quickly careened into carnal territory, all tongues and teeth and gnashing need. She was so small, but he wouldn't make the mistake of thinking she was weak. He hissed as her fingernails bit into his biceps. No, she was strong, and as hungry for him as he was for her.

He could dive into her mouth and drink for days.

She brought his left hand to her breast. Pressed it there. Her hands were fast, and busy, cruising down his chest, abdomen, then back under his waistband. She took his cock in a firm grip, stroking him from stem to stern. His eyes nearly crossed when she palmed his balls, as if testing their size and weight.

Doubt crept in. His tongue and cock were in fine working order, but he was nowhere near full strength. She was a succubus, a sex demon. Could a mere human satisfy her?

She dove under the blankets, pushed his pajama bottoms down, and took him into her mouth.

Oh, god. Wet, suckling heat…the rhythmic stroke

of her hand…the careful scrape of her tiny, white teeth. Any one sensation would be diabolical, but all three at the same time threatened to unman him. He half-wanted to slow her down, to give him a chance to reciprocate, but the little head was in control, and she had him halfway to liftoff. She slurped him down like a cherry Popsicle on a hot summer day, and her moan vibrated against the head of his cock.

She suddenly pulled away. Before he could miss her mouth, she popped up from under the covers, climbed on his body, and impaled herself on his cock.

He hissed through his teeth as she enveloped him in tight, clinging heat. She twisted her hips against his, somehow taking him deeper.

She opened her eyes, lifting the heavy curtain of her lashes. Her gaze had weight, promising him a tour through heaven and hell. Promising him he'd love every minute.

"Jack."

Her whisper stroked in dark, private places, but her slim, moon-bleached body writhed atop him with frank, open demand. She'd probably done things in bed that he'd never imagined, but—he gave his hips a gentle roll, surprising a groan from her—he'd do his best to hang on.

To do whatever she needed to make it go away.

His small thrust must have been the signal she'd been waiting for, because she rose to her knees then let herself slide. Again. Again. Caressing her breasts and body, he kept pace as she undulated, as she took them on a slow, gentle ride.

But slow and gentle didn't last for long. Her breasts shimmied as she increased speed, her rhythm fast and hard as she chased oblivion.

Did she know she was crying? As he reached to brush the tears away, she grabbed his hand, kissed it, then brought it to where their bodies were joined, where she stretched to take him.

Springy, silky hair. Delicate folds, drenched with need. He traced her intimate terrain, pressing the tiny kernel of nerves at the apex of her sex.

Her breath and rhythm hitched. She picked up speed, riding him harder.

He clenched his teeth—*do not come*—but his internal fault lines, lying coiled and dormant for so long, were slipping. Breaking apart. At the base of his spine, energy seethed and snarled.

Another hitch in her rhythm, then her eyes flew open wide. "Jack," she gasped.

As she shattered around him, the fault line snapped.

Gritting his teeth, he plunged one final time, hanging on for dear life as the world collapsed around them.

✳

Sweet, sweet relief.

Sasha snuggled against Jack's chest. His cock was still inside her, soft but substantial. She was tender between her legs, wonderfully so, and her muscles were as limp as boiled noodles. It was all she could do to keep still, to not wriggle and gear up for Round Two.

Her lips curled. They'd really given each other a

workout. He'd done exactly as she'd asked. He'd made it go away for a while.

His breathing had steadied out, and his heart thumped a steady beat. She turned her nose to his chest and almost purred. He smelled…fantastic, and looked even better, all blond and brawny, with his mussed-up hair and the scruff of beard on his chin and cheeks. *Like a tawny desert cat, temporarily at rest.* She combed her fingers upward through his chest hair, then traced his collarbone to his shoulders— Shit. The gauze pad. The gauze pad covering a freaking bullet hole in his right shoulder. "Oh, god." What the hell had she been thinking? She tried to scramble off his body, but he stopped her with a hand on her lower back. "Are you okay?" Shit, how long had she lain zoned out on top of him? "Jack, answer me."

The hand drifted lower, cupping her ass. "I'm fine."

His cock was hardening inside her. She swallowed a moan, then she sat upright. "Let me check your wounds."

His other arm wound around her waist, stopping her from climbing off his body. He tugged her down, giving her a lazy, tongue-twining kiss. "You did most of the work. All I did was lay here."

"Not true." Yes, he looked like a tawny desert cat, waiting for a chance to pounce.

She couldn't wait.

You'll have to. "Just let me take a quick look." He lifted his arm, giving tacit permission, but she caught him rolling his eyes as she climbed off his body and turned on the bedside lamp.

He recoiled, squinting against the sudden brightness.

"Sorry." Kneeling by his side, she examined the gauze. Dry and white, fresh as snow. Their activities hadn't injured him again.

"Satisfied?"

His voice was a rumble in the dark, asking two questions at once. Her reflexive shiver had nothing to do with the chilly room. "Mmm-hmm." She turned off the light, then scrambled back under the covers. His body radiated delicious heat. "You're like a sun-warmed rock," she said, snuggling up against him. "Or an oven-baked potato."

"Okay."

"I like baked potatoes."

He took her hand. Kissed it.

"Hey, you used your right hand."

He nodded, twining their fingers together. "Motion is coming back, but feeling and sensation? Not quite as quickly."

"How does it feel?"

"A little tingly, like it's asleep. An occasional painful zing." He looked at her, too closely. "How are you?"

Tipping onto her back, she stretched luxuriously. "I feel fantastic." Like a well-oiled machine.

"Really?"

"How can you doubt it?" If anything, the grapevine had understated his skill—or maybe they were very sexually compatible. She knew *he* was satisfied—she'd inhaled it for herself—but the lazy satiation was starting to mix with something else.

She sighed. *Humans.*

Shifting to her side, she propped her head up on an elbow so she could look at him. "What's with the guilt? Surely you don't feel guilty that we slept together?"

"No, but…"

"But what?"

"I came in here because you were crying in your sleep." He paused. "Calling for your father."

"And I woke you up. I'm sorry." *That* was the reason he'd come to her bedroom?

"Comforting you was the least I could do."

Every cell went still. "You slept with me to comfort me?"

"No, I slept with you because I wanted to." Staring at the ceiling, he gave a disgusted sigh. "And you were half-asleep."

"Not so asleep I didn't know exactly what I was doing." But what about him? Under the influence of pain meds, he couldn't consent.

How much medication had he taken before bed? *Had* he taken pain meds before bed?

"Sasha, I'm responsible for your dad's death," Jack said. "The least I can do is comfort you when you cry for him."

She sat up, letting the blankets pool at her waist. "What are you talking about? You're not responsible for Dad's death. His shooter is."

Jack didn't respond, but his scent—and his stubbornly crossed arms—made it clear he didn't agree.

"You are so exasperating sometimes," she muttered. "Why are we even arguing about this?"

"Habit? Misdirected sexual tension?" He glanced over at her. "It's kinda what we do."

Pain meds or not, he didn't seem impaired. She climbed onto his body again, straddling his tree-trunk thighs.

"What are you doing?"

The man might have questions, but his cock sure didn't. Warm life pulsed beneath the silky skin stretched over his hardness. "You're right about the sexual tension," she mused, cupping his penis between her hands. "I've wanted to have sex with you for years, and now that I have, I want to have sex with you again." She looked down at him. "How about you?"

She was going to get a straight answer out of him, once and for all.

He thought about it, longer than she thought most men could when their penis twitched between a willing woman's hands. Fourteen floors down, an ambulance wailed down the city street.

She started climbing off his body. "We don't have to—"

"Of course I want you," he said gruffly, stopping her with a hand on her hip. "You know that. You've always known that." His big body shifted against the mattress as he sighed. "But sleeping together—*continuing* to sleep together—would really complicate things."

"Maybe it would simplify them." Leaning down, she gave him a hot, silky kiss. "Why do humans have to make sex so damn complicated?"

"Because it is, damn it."

With a subtle shift of weight, she rose to her knees, then lowered herself onto his cock—slowly, so slowly. "Feels pretty easy to me." They both groaned when their groins kissed, when she bottomed out against his body. When he was fully engulfed in her slick, clinging heat.

She leaned forward to kiss him again.

He grabbed her head with both hands, bringing their mouths into perfect alignment.

And proceeded to eat her alive.

CHAPTER SEVEN

After climbing the single flight of stairs between Sebastiani Security's basement gym and the first floor lobby, Jack paused at the fire door, trying to steady his legs. He should have known better than to work out after his physical therapy appointment, to expend so much physical energy before he even started his first official day back in the office. Three miles on the treadmill, even at a walk, had definitely been a mistake.

Last night with Sasha had gone well, but this morning's workout had slapped him upside the head with a clue stick. He was nowhere close to fully recovered.

And if I don't start moving soon, I'll take root right here.

Walking through the lobby to the security door felt like slogging through freshly-poured concrete, but once there, he was able to lift his right hand to the biometric lock without an assist from his left.

Adnan was right. His shoulder was getting better, but it still hurt like a son of a bitch.

When he opened the heavy door, heads popped up from the cubicles and open bullpen.

"Hey, Jack!"

"Jack! Good to see you, man."

"Jack's back!"

"Hi, everyone." He gave the room a vague, communal wave, but focused on his office, twenty feet down the hall. If he slowed the slightest bit, his well-meaning colleagues would swarm like ants at a picnic. "I'll be out in a bit." Thanks to his typical meeting schedule, no one questioned him.

Once in his office, he turned on the light, closed the door, and collapsed into his oversized leather chair. *Shit, I'm out of shape.* Now that Adnan had given him the okay to drive, he could start putting in some serious gym time without inconveniencing Sasha.

Sasha. This morning, he'd woken in his own guest room, with Sasha curled around him like a sleek, exotic cat. It had taken more willpower than he wanted to admit to leave the bed and get ready for the day. After leaving a note on the pillow about his whereabouts, he'd walked the mile from his condo to Memorial Hospital for his doctor and physical therapy appointments.

Now that he had permission to drive, one of the reasons Sasha was staying with him was gone.

"Hell." At this time yesterday, he couldn't wait to get rid of her. Now that they'd slept together, he didn't want her to leave.

Pretty selfish, dude.

Yeah, maybe it was, but Sasha was right. He had to stop thinking like a puritanical human. Their relationship was sexual—strictly physical—and that was fine. Absolutely fine.

Wasn't it?

Shaking off the thought, he powered up his workstation, assessing what had shown up on his desk since the last time he'd been here. Something about his office made paperwork multiply like bacteria.

There was a quick tap at his door. Bailey came in, plopping her jean-clad butt in his visitor's chair. She was the only person other than Lukas who'd dare interrupt him when his door was closed, and she did so with impunity.

"You look wiped out," she said. "Maybe you should work from home today."

"Cut me some slack. I just came from PT." He didn't mention his ill-advised treadmill workout, the walks to and from his doctor's appointments, or last night's extra-curricular activities.

"That's not all you came from." She gave him a saucy wink.

Heat crept up his neck, but he kept his expression bland as white rice. Sasha was right—they were consenting adults, and their sex life was no one else's business. "Problem?"

"Not at all." Bailey eyed his torso, as if trying to assess his gunshot wounds through the fabric of his crisp blue work shirt. "I was going to ask how your recovery is going, but if you're feeling frisky enough to have sex...?"

Not discussing it. He reached for his computer mouse.

"Hey, you're using your right hand!"

"The swelling in my shoulder is going down," he said. "I was cleared to drive today." *Barely.* Convincing Adnan had taken all his powers of persuasion.

"I bet you're looking forward to having the Fortress of Solitude all to yourself again." She cocked a brow. "Or maybe not?"

Damned if she hadn't put her finger on the problem he hadn't let himself think about. He sure as shit wasn't ready to talk about it. "I—" His phone vibrated against his thigh. *Saved by the bell.* Plucking it from his front pocket left-handed, he glanced at the screen.

A San Francisco area code. It was his father, calling from his office at Kirkland & Kirkland.

Again.

Nope.

Ignoring the ball of anxiety forming in his stomach, he silenced the phone, then set it on his desk.

"Not answering a ringing phone?" Bailey's eyebrow climbed. "Did you have a personality transplant while you were in the hospital?"

Bailey often claimed she wouldn't recognize either him or Lukas without a phone clapped to one ear. He now had a better understanding of her annoyance with the distracting devices. Mindlessly glancing at a screen had stolen his focus at a critical moment, causing Elliott's death.

"What's wrong?"

She saw too much, but he wasn't ready to talk about Elliott, either. "It was my dad." He jerked his head toward the phone. "He was the one on the phone." An on-screen message informed him he'd missed a call. A second bubble blipped onto the screen.

"Voice mail," Bailey noted. "That's…interesting."

"Interesting, my ass."

"Are you going to listen to it?"

"I don't know yet." After his relationship with his parents turned to shit, radio silence had become business as usual—but he'd made sure Mrs. Whipple, his father's executive secretary, had his current phone number, just in case.

Shit, something must really be wrong.

"He hasn't tried calling you here at work? At your desk phone?"

"My parents don't know where I work," he admitted. "They don't even know where I live."

Her expression was half-admiring, half-horrified. "And I thought my relationship with *my* parents was fucked up."

A fucked-up family relationship was one of the things he and Bailey had in common. "We're a pair, aren't we?"

"Hey, friends are the family you choose." She glanced at the phone, then back at him. "But there has to be a reason he's calling you after all this time."

And calling not just once, but repeatedly. "Yeah, something must be wrong." He eyed the paperwork. "Damn it, I don't have the energy to deal with family drama right now."

Bailey gave a shrug. "You don't have to call him back."

He glared at her. "Stop being so goddamn neutral."

"You want my advice?" She rested her sweater-clad forearms on his desk. "The phone call clearly bothers you. Instead of having whatever's going on with your family looming as a question mark, wouldn't you rather know what you're dealing with? Once you have the information, you can assess for yourself what, if anything, you need to do."

She was right. He didn't have enough information to make an informed decision. Hell, at this point, he didn't even know whether a decision was necessary.

"Give it some thought," she advised, pulling her

own phone from the holder clipped to her hip pocket. "In the meantime, want me to fill you in on some of what's been going on around here while you've been gone?"

"Hell, yes." Reaching for a yellow legal pad, he lost himself in funding requests, staffing issues, and debriefs from the meetings she'd handled for him while he was in the hospital. After a half hour, he had a page full of notes, follow-up questions, and action items, written with his right hand. Damn, it felt good to be back in the saddle again. "Thanks for handling this stuff while I was gone. I know how much you loathe administrative work."

"Winnie was a huge help," she said, referring to one of Sebastiani Security's lieutenants. "And it's not like you were slacking somewhere, having fun in the sun." Bailey propped her black Chuck Taylors against the edge of his desk. "So, are you and Sasha a thing now?"

Were they? They certainly hadn't talked about it. He gave what he hoped was a sophisticated shrug. "Friends with benefits."

She snort-laughed. "Since when are you and Sasha friends? You fight all the time."

"We're friends," he said defensively. Sure, they fought, but he knew he could count on her in a pinch. That she was staying at his condo with him, helping with his wound care, spoke louder than words.

Did he want them to be—what had Bailey called it?—a *thing*? The sex was awesome, but...

"What's wrong?"

He looked at her, considering. Bailey was the only person alive who might actually be able to answer the question perking in his brain. "Do you still take pheromone intoxication meds?"

"No. After Adnan repaired my perforated ulcer, he recommended against it." She waved a hand. "And after Rafe and I sorted things out and got our shit together, there was no reason to risk taking them anymore."

The reminder of the risk was sobering. The medication was experimental, developed by Sebastiani Labs so humans—so *he*—wouldn't be unduly impacted by incubi and succubi pheromones while working in such close proximity with paranormals. He'd been taking the meds for years with no side effects when Bailey, frantic to avoid Rafe's sexual pull, had 'borrowed' medication from Jack's supply without his knowledge, and had taken too high a dose without medical supervision. Though Adnan wouldn't go so far as to say the meds had caused Bailey's ulcer to perforate, he didn't think they'd helped...

Crap. Adnan had cleared him to drive, but he *hadn't* cleared him to start taking pheromone intoxication meds again. He'd been so happy to get his car keys back that he hadn't even asked.

Not asking a question for which you don't want the answer was Lawyering 101, but...he was sleeping with a succubus. A sex demon. Wouldn't it be the height of stupidity to *not* take medication explicitly invented to reduce pheromone impact? He could clear the matter up with a phone call, but...

"Which side's winning?" Bailey asked, amused.

"Hmm?"

"Who's winning the argument you're having with yourself?"

"Shut up."

Bailey peered at him. "Why the question about

pheromone intoxication meds? Are you having problems? Did Adnan tell you to stop taking them, too?"

"No and no." Okay, his answer was…accurate, but not entirely truthful. Why was he lying to his best friend? Because now, he understood the gut-churning anxiety that had driven Bailey to take too many meds in the first place. His office chair creaked as he sat up straight. "Don't worry about the me and Sasha thing." Yeah, "thing" was as good a description for their relationship as any other, at least for right now. "Believe me, I'm not going to let myself be dragged around by the dick."

Bailey ticked items off on her fingers. "One, you might enjoy that. Two, I think you've been taking the meds for so long—and you've been avoiding this thing with Sasha for so long—that you've forgotten a key fact about how the meds, and how pheromones, work."

"What do you mean?"

"The meds make you less susceptible to pheromone intoxication—they help you with judgment—but they can't make you feel, or do, anything you don't already feel or want to do. Pheromones can't conjure sexual attraction out of thin air. They simply amplify what's already there." She aimed an angelic grin his way. "The attraction between you and Sasha has always been there. And that's the problem, isn't it?"

When he slumped back in the chair, he couldn't disguise a wince. His back wound burned. "There's no problem."

"If you say so."

"I do."

"Okay."

Why did she look so damned amused?

"In the meantime," she said, "you look ready to drop. Let me give you a ride home."

He hesitated. Would Sasha be there? Did he want her to be there? He mouthed a curse.

"Seriously, go home," she urged. "Go home, take a nap—either by yourself, or with company—and when you're ready, listen to your father's voice mail so you know what you're dealing with."

Bailey was right. He needed more information, and he couldn't get it without listening to his father's voice mails—including the one he'd left the day Elliott died.

But today was not that day, because waves of exhaustion were pounding him down. "Okay," he muttered. "I'll take you up on the ride."

"Good call." She went to the door. "I'll go get my coat. Meet me at the front door in five."

"Thanks."

He almost called her back. A slow walk home might give him time to figure out how to deal with Sasha once he got there. How was she feeling today? Had he helped her at all last night, or had he made things worse?

They'd explored each other's bodies to hell and back, but it was the baby-soft kiss she'd dropped on his sore right hand, not on his lips or his cock, that burned in his memory.

He'd helped her feel better, sure—but damned if she hadn't done most of the giving. That wouldn't happen again, not if he had anything to say about it.

After a slight hesitation, he unlocked his desk, grabbed some pheromone intoxication meds from the supply he kept at work, then slipped them into his front pocket along with his phone.

Just in case.

✸

As the coffeepot gurgled and hissed from the other side of Dad and Claudette's kitchen, Sasha stood on a step stool, studying the row of teapots displayed in the gap between the hickory cabinets and the ceiling. In a family of coffee addicts, her father alone enjoyed the occasional cup of tea, and he'd amassed an exquisite and eclectic collection over the years. Though some of the teapots rightfully belonged in a museum, he insisted they be used. To indulge him, the family had gotten into the habit of using the teapots to serve Crackhouse's signature coffee.

Should she use the Meissen, or the Limoges? The porcelain cat, with its upraised leg pouring spout? She reached for a colorful set depicting *Beauty and the Beast*'s Mrs. Potts and Chip. "God knows we need some comfort today."

Planning a memorial service was thirsty work.

There was already a gap in the teapot line-up, as obvious as a missing front tooth. The handmade teapot that usually sat there had a distinct starboard list, and the glaze, though gorgeous, was unevenly applied. The spout had fallen off and been reattached over and over again.

Rafe's first hand-thrown piece, made when he was a child, now held their father's ashes.

Mrs. Potts and Chip's cheerful, smiling faces unexpectedly blurred, but she dashed the wetness away. "No more crying today." Not here, anyway, and not now. She had to hold it together for Claudette.

Today was the first time most of the family had been in one location since Dad had died. Bailey was at work—something about installing a network security patch—but everyone else was here, and the details for public and private memorial services were coming together. The private service would take place in northern Minnesota next spring, after the snow melted, but the public service, the one for their people, would be held at Underbelly on New Year's Eve.

She'd initially been aghast at Lukas's suggestion—New Year's Eve was a night for partying, for celebration!—but his reasoning had been rock-solid. Closing the club for a private event on New Year's Eve wouldn't raise human eyebrows, and the venue—which their family owned and operated—was large enough to handle the crowd. His most persuasive argument? That they'd be able to reuse the event security plan she and Jack had put together for Scarlett's homecoming concert several years ago. If she hadn't found that point persuasive enough, Claudette's comment that she thought New Year's Eve was a perfect night to celebrate someone's life would have sealed the deal.

Holy bitchcakes, she and Flynn had a lot of work to do.

While the coffee finished brewing, she sent Flynn a quick text, asking if he could meet with her later that day. After a pause, she sent Jack a text saying he was on his own for dinner, but she'd be back by bedtime.

And immediately questioned it. The man was recovering from gunshot wounds. Was he strong enough to— "Stop it." If he was strong enough to have sex last night, he was strong enough to heat up a can of soup today.

Last night, he'd been *more* than strong enough.

Her body flushed with sudden heat. Jack was a classic overachiever, good at almost everything he did. Why should sex be any different? He'd completely fulfilled her request to make it all go away. With his help, she'd lost herself in sensation, wallowed in lush, erotic glory. Put her grief aside, just for a while. He'd been gone by the time she woke up that morning, but Mr. Consideration had left a note. There'd been no morning after chatter, uncomfortable or otherwise, but occasional twinges between her legs kept him hovering at the edge of her consciousness.

Suddenly, there was an arm around her waist. "How are you doing?" Antonia asked.

"I'm okay."

"Need some help?"

"Sure." Maybe Antonia wouldn't notice anything amiss. "Is Rafe back yet?" After she'd offered to make coffee, Rafe had gone down to the parking garage to get something from his Jeep.

"No." Antonia paused, studying her. "So."

"So…what?"

"How was it?"

"How was what?"

"Finally having sex with Jack?"

She should have known better than to think Antonia wouldn't notice. "How did you know I had sex with Jack? Maybe I had sex with someone else."

"When you're staying with him, at his place?" Her sister rolled her eyes. "Please."

Antonia clearly expected her to dish. They talked about their own sex lives, and everyone else's sex lives, all the time. But for reasons she wasn't quite ready to explore, she didn't want to talk about *this*—and thank the aurora, Antonia was experiencing a distinct sexual hangover of her own. "Have fun with Merrill last night?" she asked silkily. "I want all the details."

Antonia froze, then reached into a drawer for napkins.

Guilt belly-crawled, leaving a trail of slime in its wake. Using the relationship Antonia wasn't ready to talk about yet as a weapon against her was not cool. "I'm sorry. Yes, I slept with Jack." She touched her sister's shoulder. After a pause, forgiveness and understanding wafted toward her, thank the universe. Nothing cracked Antonia's hard shell faster than the unvarnished truth. "You know Merrill can stay overnight anytime, right?" she added. "Even when I'm there?"

Antonia nodded, then smirked. "Though I have to say, having the place to ourselves is pretty awesome." She grabbed a serving tray, then set the napkins on top of it. "How much longer do you think you'll be staying with Jack?"

"Until he doesn't need wound care, I would think." Jack could probably manage dressing his shoulder wounds well enough, but not the bullet hole in the middle of his back. "We're taking it day by day right now."

"Well, I'm happy his strength is returning," Antonia said, her voice as dry as winter air.

She let the suggestive comment slide as she transferred the freshly brewed coffee into the teapot. Antonia assembled the teacups, sugar, and cream.

"Sasha?"

"Hmm?"

"Have you seen Claudette cry yet?"

"No." And that was okay. She understood Claudette's need to bind some wounds privately, or as privately as one could when surrounded by her bondmate's rowdy incubi and succubi offspring. "Scarlett says she's doing well." Scarlett had spent long days with her mother, with Lukas visiting near-daily despite everything else he had going on. "Right now, I'm more concerned about her appetite." Always on the thin side, right now Claudette looked exceedingly frail and delicate, like a stiff wind would blow her over. What food might appeal? She opened the snack cabinet, then put a box of the shortbread cookies Claudette loved on the tray. "Maybe these will tempt her."

They rejoined the family in the living room. Where her own decor leaned toward Scandinavian modern, with bright colors and more than a dollop of kitsch, Dad and Claudette's home was all classic lines, rich colors, and lush textures. Thick carpets, framed paintings, antiques, and objets d'art combined to create a comfortable, gracious living space that spoke volumes about its occupants.

Sasha set the tray down on the piecrust table. Rafe had returned, and was setting a large cardboard box on the coffee table around which the well-stuffed couch, a loveseat, and a couple of upholstered chairs gathered.

"What is it?" Claudette asked.

Rafe started opening the box. "Do you remember the picture you took, of Coco napping on Dad's chest?"

Claudette's face lit. "You finished the sculpture."

"Yeah."

Claudette had commissioned it months ago, as a gift for Dad's next birthday—a birthday he wouldn't see.

Coco started fussing. "Yes, you know something's up, don't you?" Lukas murmured to the infant he held. With Lukas being so large, he, Scarlett, and Coco took up the entire couch. "Lots of emotions flying around here." When he cradled her tiny body closer, she immediately calmed.

Scarlett looked at the ceiling, exasperated. "How do you *do* that?"

Lukas shrugged. "I think she likes how I smell."

Pheromones could calm crying babies? Good to know.

"Dad used to do the same thing with all of you," Lukas added, stroking Coco's sprout of wild red hair. "Especially after Mom died."

Yes, he had, and his comforting scent still lingered, deep in her subconscious—but that didn't erase the stark reality that her father was dead.

Dead.

Both of her parents were dead.

Grief clogged her throat, a sudden landslide of mud and sticks and rocks. Her heart was going to crack apart, right there in her chest. When Lukas glanced her way, she held up a hand to keep him in his seat.

She had to buck up, because Claudette was smiling for the first time in days.

Claudette was trying to peek in the box. "Don't keep us in suspense."

"Okay, okay." When Rafe lifted a bubble-wrapped blob from the box, Antonia leapt in to help.

Rafe looked absolutely exhausted. How hard had he pushed himself to finish this piece, knowing Dad would never see it?

"Wow, this is heavy," Antonia said, lowering the sculpture to the coffee table and starting to unwrap it.

It was a horizontal piece, which made sense. The picture Claudette had snapped—the picture Rafe had used for inspiration—had been taken while Dad and Coco napped together on the couch.

"You used pewter," Claudette murmured. "Oh, it's the same color as his hair..."

Her father's hair had been a gorgeous, steely gray, just brushing his shoulders, and somehow, using hard metal, Rafe had captured its soft, silky flow. Dad's lanky, jean-clad body lay fully stretched out, utterly relaxed as he slept, his head comfortably propped on a couple of throw pillows. Coco napped on his bare chest with her knees pulled, frog-like, under her body, her little diapered butt sticking up in the air.

Tears sprang to her eyes. Yes, art could heal.

"It's so...alive," Claudette whispered. "Can I touch?"

"Of course."

Claudette stroked her finger over little Coco's body, then moved on to her bondmate's hair, long and loose, splayed across the pillow. She smiled through tears. "How utterly beautiful."

Rafe closed his eyes, then opened them again. "I'm glad you like it."

"Oh, honey, how could I not?" Claudette wrapped

her arms around him. "It's absolutely gorgeous."

Sasha had learned a long time ago that even world-renowned singers could need validation, and sometimes felt their talent was being judged every time they performed. Hell, back when Scarlett's band was still touring, Scarlett had thrown up before every performance. It made complete sense that her genius of a brother had a similar thing going on.

"It's beautiful. Perfect." Claudette kissed both of Rafe's cheeks. "You've caught the emotions perfectly. Would you help me find the right place to put it?"

She poured coffee as Rafe and Claudette wandered around the living room, eventually deciding to rearrange some things on the wall-length bookshelves so the sculpture could be displayed at eye level, under small accent lights. Grabbing the box of cookies from the tray, she collapsed onto the love seat. As soon as she opened the box, Antonia snatched a sleeve of shortbread, like an eagle on the hunt.

Coco gave a hungry squawk, then rooted around Lukas's chest with pursed lips.

Lukas laughed. "You're bound for disappointment there, honey."

"Looks like someone's hungry." Scarlett reached for the mint green baby blanket festooned with embroidered coffee beans. She draped it over her shoulder, adjusted her shirt, then reached for her daughter. Soon, the sound of contented suckling filled the room.

Rafe made his way back to the loveseat, plopping down beside her. "Here," she said, handing him the coffee she'd poured for him.

"Thanks." Cupping the mug in both hands, he sipped like she'd given him the water of life. Half a cup later, he came up for air. "Damn," he breathed. "I needed that."

With his blond hair scraped back into a ponytail, his cheekbones were more prominent than usual. Rafe clearly needed food, then sleep. "Dude, you need another cup of coffee like you need a hole in the—"

Head. Like you need a hole in the head.

Oh, my god.

"I can't believe I just said that." It was horrible, and so was she, because the tickle at the back of her throat meant a giggle fit threatened. She took a huge gulp of Rafe's coffee to try to wash it down. "Did Claudette hear what I said?"

"No." Rafe gestured toward the bookcase. "Look."

Across the living room, Claudette was shifting the sculpture this way and that, running her hands over every inch of its surface. "It's beautiful, Rafe. Perfect." She took his hand. The simple gold bonding ring he wore even when sculpting glowed against his skin. "Are you sleeping?"

"Are you?" he countered.

When Antonia snickered around her cookie, a hot flush heated her cheeks.

"That's what I thought," Rafe muttered.

"Seriously? *You're* going to give me shit about who I sleep with?" Before bonding with Bailey, her brother had had a reputation for hedonism, even among their kind.

Rafe cleared his throat, then reached for a cookie. "How is Jack's recovery going?"

Change of subject. Smart man. "He's improving."

Rafe inhaled, deeply and luxuriously. "If he's

strong enough to have sex, I'd say so."

She punched him in the bicep. "Shut up."

"*You* shut up," he mumbled through a mouthful of shortbread.

"You know there's no such thing as a secret in this family," Antonia piped up from behind the love seat.

"No couth, either." She tried to take the cookies away from Rafe, but he extended his arm overhead, holding the sleeve just out of her reach. "Damn it, Rafe—"

Antonia grabbed them from his hand, then ran.

"You little brat," he said, rising to follow her.

"Kids, stop fighting." Claudette rolled her eyes. "Oh, there's a blast from the past." Soon she was laughing through tears, telling stories about their childhoods, and about their father. So many stories about their father. They laughed, they smiled, they cried.

Finally, they cried.

Later, as they were leaving, Rafe sidled close. "Want some advice?"

"Rafe, I can handle my own sex life."

"I know, but...take it from someone who fell in love with a human. We incubi and succubi can get pretty lazy communicating about emotions because we can read them so easily. Humans need words." He grabbed his coat from the closet. "And sometimes, we interpret things wrong."

"Don't worry. My relationship with Jack is strictly sexual." And they'd had no problem communicating in bed. Zero. None. Nada.

Rafe laughed as he shrugged into his jacket. "You keep telling yourself that, honey."

"I will," she called, following him out to the lobby

where the penthouse elevators were located. When he pressed the call button, the doors opened immediately, thank the universe.

He kissed the top of her head, then stepped onto the elevator. "Tell Jack I said hi."

"I will."

"And that I admire his curve-breaking recuperative powers."

She flipped him off.

He sketched a mocking wave as the elevator doors closed, carrying him away.

Brothers could be so damn annoying. "Humans need words?" Using words would require she unsnarl her own tangled feelings first.

"Hell." With a quick pivot, she went to the penthouse unit across the lobby, the one she and Antonia shared, to pick up a few things. The fact that her feelings were all snarled up in the first place was a complication she simply wasn't ready to deal with.

CHAPTER EIGHT

At the end of a late-afternoon conference call, Lukas delivered an unexpected kick to the gut: "The family met earlier today. We decided to hold Dad's public memorial service on New Year's Eve, at Underbelly."

In his home office, Jack managed to stay silent, to stop himself from blurting an instinctive "No!" but he couldn't help the death grip he inflicted on his pen. "Did you consider other venues?" Venues where a Council member hadn't *died* because someone slipped through the cracks in his security plan?

Annika and Elliott. Two Council members, dead on his watch.

"Considered them, and ruled them out," Lukas said. "We own the building, and the businesses inside the building. Closing down the club to host a private New Year's Eve event is a no-brainer. Claudette wants to have a small gathering for the Council, friends, and family upstairs in the penthouse, immediately following the memorial service."

Leaning against the brick wall behind Lukas, Chico didn't appear to be concerned. Bailey was multi-tasking, her fingers quietly tapping at her laptop keyboard. No help there.

Okay, pull it together. "That's not a lot of time to

develop a new plan."

Lukas met his gaze through the webcam. "I'd like to re-purpose the security plan we used for Scarlett's homecoming show."

A sick shock ricocheted through his body. "You can't be serious."

Bailey looked up from her laptop screen.

"Jack, once and for all, stop blaming yourself for what happened that night," Lukas said, exasperated. "No one could have foreseen Stephen's actions. No one could have planned for them, or prevented them."

"That doesn't make Annika any less dead!"

Silence hummed across the line.

"Fuck," he whispered, dropping the pen.

Intellectually, he knew Lukas was right. No one had considered Stephen, a band mate Scarlett had safely traveled with for over a year, as a risk, much less a suspect in Annika's murder—especially when he'd staged the scene so it appeared he'd almost died himself. But after Stephen had nearly killed Lukas and Scarlett, Bailey had reminded them that, sadly, insiders had prime opportunity. It was true of technology hacks, of domestic partner homicides, of child sexual abuse.

Unfortunately, Stephen was now on the outside. Soon after his arrest, he'd escaped their most secure psychiatric facility. He was still in the wind.

"Jack." Lukas's gaze pinned him to the chair. "You know I'm right."

Yeah, he was. No matter how many security cameras they'd installed at Underbelly, or how many weapons they'd confiscated at the door, Annika had met Stephen of her own free will, and Stephen had killed her with his own bare hands.

The fact that he'd had no control over the outcome really stung.

A disgusted breath escaped. If Sasha was sitting here, she'd tell him to sac up. To put his ego, and his hurt little fee-fees, aside.

This wasn't about him.

The security plan *was* specifically tailored for the club, but... "I'd like to close Crackhouse Coffee for the full day New Year's Day." Having fewer people in the building would be helpful all the way around, and would give Sasha less to worry about. "And we should prohibit access to the Sebastiani Building's upper floors during the event itself." Annika had been killed in a fourth-floor recording studio while thousands partied below, on the main floor.

Lukas nodded. "Coordinate the details with Sasha."

"Will do." *Whenever I see her next.* She hadn't yet returned to the condo. "Chico, Bailey? I'd like to update our background checks on all Council members."

Chico straightened from his slouch against the wall. Bailey gave a curt, approving nod. Lukas scowled, but didn't object.

After Annika's death, Bailey had helmed the painful, warts-and-all review of what had happened at Underbelly that night. She'd called it a project post-mortem, but he...couldn't. The phrase cut too damn close to the bone. "Last time, we made too many assumptions about who was a risk and who wasn't," he reminded them. Stephen had flown completely under their radar. Annika had paid the ultimate price, and Lukas nearly so. Stephen had somehow electrocuted Lukas with a touch, temporarily stopping his heart and leaving him with a painful collection of burns. "We can't make the same mistake again."

Bailey was already taking notes. He'd bet serious cash money that Krispin Woolf was at the top of her priority list.

"As the new president, Lukas's physical security is paramount," he continued, "and we need heightened provisions for members of the Sebastiani family as well." Lukas looked annoyed, but didn't object. He couldn't, because he knew Jack was right. "Protection for Council members and their families, as always."

Bailey glanced up. "That's over a dozen people already."

Chico nodded as he tapped notes into his mini. "We're going to run into resource issues pretty fast."

And the resource issues would ripple through Sebastiani Security. Pulling Chico away from his current work meant other senior field operatives would have to be reassigned to cover.

"Winnie has a couple of projects coming to a close," Chico said. "She could probably tag in."

Winnie Otsego, a SebSec lieutenant, had been instrumental in capturing the hacker who'd tried to take down both Bailey and Sebastiani Labs the previous year. "That's good to know." He'd planned on reviewing project status earlier that day, but he'd had to go home and take a goddamn nap instead.

"If we get into resource trouble, we could probably move background checks on Council members' bondmates to the bottom of the list."

"While I agree with you in concept—" Krispin Woolf was a more serious threat to Lukas than, say, Valerian's bondmate Thane, or Wyland's bondmate

Tia Quinn "—I'd prefer to not get into resource trouble in the first place. I'll touch base with Winnie."

"Full runs on everyone?" Chico confirmed.

He nodded. "Check in with Sasha on event staffing, and add those employees' names to the list." He also wanted more security staffing. They'd learned the hard way that when hundreds of people with paranormal abilities gathered in one place, all bets were off. Without careful management, such gatherings could easily turn into an evolutionary game of Rock, Paper, Scissors. The werewolves had immense physical strength for their size, second only to the Valkyries, but both species were more susceptible to incubi and succubi pheromones than the vampires were. The vamps tended toward slender frames and less physical strength, but could influence others' thoughts. Both werewolves and vampires had fangs, but had conflicting rules about when they could be used.

But the sirens, the gentle sirens, could actually start a riot. They influenced emotions with their voices, emotions incubi and succubi couldn't help but absorb. The pheromones incubi and succubi produced in response could fill a room, resulting in unexpected behavior. Faeries, with their off-the-charts empathic abilities, were a very effective early warning system, and a fair number of Sebastiani Security's physical security specialists had at least some faerie blood.

This year, they'd all be working on New Year's Eve.

It was for scenarios like this that pheromone intoxication meds had been invented in the first place. If he took the meds, he—a human—would have the clearest head in the house.

His phone vibrated, buzzing like a mosquito on the top of his desk. His father again. As the meeting murmured on in the background, he stared at the screen. Would he leave another voice mail?

Yep.

Crap, Bailey was right. Time to find out what was going on.

He sat through the rest of the conference call, but the phone at his elbow was like a snake ready to strike. After taking a couple of action items—some things *were* returning to normal—the meeting ended. "Chico, see you in the gym tomorrow morning?" he called out before Lukas ended the call.

A pause. "Okay."

Chico might just as well have said, "It's your funeral," but the sooner he resumed daily workouts— *reasonable* daily workouts—the sooner he'd regain his strength. "Seven a.m. at the treadmills. Good night, everyone." He hung up before Bailey could tell him he was crazy.

An instant message appeared on his screen:

[BBrown:]   Are you crazy?

[JKirkland:] I'll take it easy

[BBrown:]   Make sure you do

He glanced at his phone. Sighed.

[JKirkland:] I have to return some phone calls. Gotta go

He closed the instant message window and

completely logged off before she could respond.

He stretched, fiddled with his pen. Made sure the pills he'd tucked into his pocket earlier were still there. Got up, adjusted the height of the flames in the gas fireplace, then sat down again. "Stop stalling." Snatching up the phone, he retrieved the list of voice messages his father had left him over the past two weeks. Taking a deep breath, he picked up his pen, ready to take notes. Retrieving the first message, he put the phone on speaker.

"Jack, it's Dad." A pause as his father cleared his throat. "Please call me at my office. It's a matter of some importance." At the end of the call, his father recited the date and time, as was his habit.

"Some things never change."

He retrieved the next message: "Jack, please call me when you receive this." Another recitation of the date and time, as if any cell phone wouldn't provide that information.

Jack glanced over to the bookshelf, to the outdated set of California Reporters he hadn't been able to leave behind when he moved to Minnesota. Everyone at Kirkland & Kirkland used online legal databases, of course, but his father was old school, happier using physical books, and had proudly given his son a set the day he'd passed the bar.

Was Mrs. Whipple still printing out his emails twice a day, and taking dictation to respond? Did Dad even have a cell phone?

The next message queued up: "Jack. I need to speak with you. Please return my call." Date and time.

How many messages would he have to listen to before his father provided some useful information? After almost a decade without contact, the fact that a 'matter of some importance' had arisen was a pretty safe assumption.

Jack retrieved the second-to-last message, the one his father had left when he'd been talking with Bailey in his office earlier today: "Jack, return my call." A heavy silence hummed over the phone line. "It's important."

No date and time.

He threw his pen across the room. "If you'd give me an idea what the *fuck* is going on, maybe I would!" The pen clattered against the floor, then skittered to a stop in front of the fireplace. "Damn it," he muttered, picking up another pen. He glanced at the yellow legal pad. When he'd started listening to the voice mails, he'd unthinkingly flipped to a new, blank page, scrawling the date and time at the top.

Just like his father had taught him.

With a shake of his head, he retrieved the last message, the one his father had left during the conference call.

"Jack, it's your fa—" There was a pause. "It's Dad. Since you haven't returned my previous calls, I'm forced to deliver this unpleasant news over the phone." His father sounded exhausted, his voice as rough as a mile of gravel road. "Your mother has breast cancer."

A harsh bark of laughter escaped. *I pity the cancer.*

An uncomfortable silence. "Given how we parted, I can understand why you haven't returned my calls. But for your mother's sake—for the firm's sake— please do." His father's voice cracked. "Please call."

He set the pen down on the legal pad, staring at the phone. On the fireplace mantel, the clock ticked the seconds away. Why had he never noticed how goddamn loud the clock was?

"Jack." Sasha stood just inside the door, holding a giant bag of cheese popcorn. "I'm so sorry. When are you leaving?"

He hadn't heard her approach the office. "Who says I am?"

"Seriously? Your mother has cancer."

When it came to his parents, he'd trained himself to feel nothing, but listening to his father's messages had ripped the Band-Aid off an old, festering wound. "Sasha, not everyone has a *Leave It to Beaver* family like yours."

She entered the room, scooped up his pen, and handed it to him. "I'm pretty sure Ward and June Cleaver weren't both killed in their own damn parking garage."

Oh, god. Sasha's mother had died in the exact same place, fighting off a robber, when Sasha was just a little girl. How in the world had *that* slipped his mind?

"I'd do anything to know my mom," she said wistfully. "Or to get just one more phone call from my dad, even if all he did was cuss me out."

Shame slammed into him. "I'm sorry. That was a really shitty thing to say."

"I'm sorry, too." She propped her hips against the desk. "We planned Dad's memorial service today, and my nerves are pretty raw." The bag crinkled as she reached for a kernel of popcorn. "Why don't you want to go home?"

"Minneapolis is home."

"Okay," she acknowledged, nodding. "Why don't you want to go to California? It sounds like your parents need you."

He opened his mouth, then closed it again. *Where*

should I even start?

"I've been told I'm a pretty good listener."

True. When she wasn't getting on his last damn nerve, she was one of the least judgmental people he'd ever met. Given some of the shenanigans that went down at Underbelly, a place sex demons went to blow off steam, she had to be. But...how could he make her understand? *Damn the torpedoes.* "My mother is...a difficult woman."

Amusement lit her face. "Bailey once told me that the reason mothers can push their kids' buttons so well is that their mothers installed them."

And Bailey would know, but... "Bailey's mom didn't do what mine did."

Sasha's brows rose. "I think we're going to need more popcorn."

He almost laughed.

"Come on." She extended her black-nailed hand. "Let's go to the living room. It's more comfortable there."

Taking it, he let her lead him from the office to the couch. "What smells so good?"

"Thanksgiving dinner."

Where had the time gone? The holiday had slipped by without notice. Taking her hand, he sat. "Who cooked?"

"Not me." Leather creaked as she plopped down on the cushion beside him. "Chadden sent Thanksgiving dinner to Claudette's house, and she sent everyone home with leftovers."

"It's nice to have a friend with a restaurant."

"Too true."

As she reached for the afghan draped over the back of the couch, the lamp illuminated her fading bruises, and a streak of dust on her cheekbone. She'd probably spent at least part of her day hefting boxes at the Sebastiani Building's loading dock. She was a lot stronger than she looked, strong and flexible, and her scent, an intoxicating blend of soap, hair products, and warm skin, wound around his brainstem.

She crossed her legs into a pretzel, then covered them with the afghan. Plucking a single kernel of orange popcorn from the bag she'd set between them, she examined it, then set it on her tongue. Her eyelids drifted closed as she slowly chewed. "I think I just came," she murmured. Opening her eyes again, she looked at him expectantly. "Okay, dude. Dish."

How was he supposed to string words together? To buy some time, he grabbed a handful of popcorn. "You realize this food has no nutritional value whatsoever."

"I know. Isn't it awesome?" She licked orange dust from her fingers with agile flicks of her tongue.

Averting his gaze, he popped a couple of kernels into his mouth. Cheesy, salty flavor exploded in his mouth, making his taste buds do a quick tango. "Mmm."

"Did you just moan?"

"No."

"Your secret's safe with me." She laughed. "Chadden would be horrified with my choice in appetizers."

Picking up the bag, he scanned the nutrition label. Every ingredient after corn had at least six syllables, undoubtedly cooked up in a lab somewhere. Calling the orange dust 'cheese' was a charitable interpretation at best. He eyed the fluorescent kernels staining his palm. "It would be rude to put these back in the bag."

"Definitely."

He ate what was in his hand. Chewed. With a curse, he took another handful.

"Hey, you're using your right hand."

"Adnan said I shouldn't baby it." His hand and shoulder were sore but definitely on the mend. Right now, it was the middle of his back that hurt the most. Physically, at any rate.

Damn it to hell.

"Tell me."

She knew *what* he was feeling, but not *why*. He'd have to find some words after all. "I haven't seen my parents in almost ten years."

"I know that much." She reached for more popcorn. "What happened?"

Just thinking about what his mother had done—and what his father hadn't—left a sour taste in his mouth. He glanced over, trying to imagine Sasha as a judge or juror he faced in court. How would she react? How would she rule?

She probably wouldn't react at all. The reason he'd cut off all contact with his parents would probably sound utterly ridiculous to her. *Why am I doing this?* Panicked, he started to rise. "I'll go check on the leftovers—"

"Nope." Quick as a whip, Sasha straddled his lap so she was facing him. Her fingertips skated up his chest, then to his cheekbones and temples, where they started a slow, comforting rub. "Breathe," she murmured, gaze locked to his. "Just breathe..."

He could no more stop his arms from wrapping around her than he could stop the world from turning. She was something solid to hang on to—solid and stable, when everything else was spinning.

"Jack, did your mother abuse you?"

"What?" He tried to straighten up, but the slouchy leather couch fought him. "No."

"Jack, look at me." Her expression was neutral, but her eyes blazed blue fire. "You can tell me, Jack. You can tell me anything."

"No, she didn't. No one abused me." He dropped what he hoped was a reassuring kiss on her lips. "But…"

"But what?"

He settled her more comfortably on his lap, searching for the right words. Would Sasha agree that his mother's behavior deserved being cut off by her son? It had been the right decision then, and he'd make the same decision again—but in retrospect, he could see how his own behavior had catalyzed his mother's actions.

Sasha was a sex demon, pretty much shock-proof. *Facts, nothing but the facts.* "When I was younger, I pretty much slept with anything that moved."

"Are you bisexual?"

He blinked. "No."

"Well, we'll leave that one to my fantasies, then."

"You've…fantasized about me? Sleeping with other men?"

"I've fantasized about you in…many ways." Her smile, her voice, dripped with sexual liquor. Then she laughed. "Oh, come on, Jack. You've never fantasized about watching two women have sex with each other? Maybe joining in? Why shouldn't women fantasize about the same thing?"

She was a sex demon; why leave it to fantasies?

She'd probably had more, and more varied, sexual experiences than he could possibly imagine. His face was on fire, but he stroked her temple, trying to match her casual cool. "So, you're saying that in your dreams, you've used me like a Ken doll?"

"Regularly, my friend—but let's get back to the subject at hand." Settling onto his lap, she reached for another piece of popcorn. "I believe you were talking about your youthful sexual exploits."

Somehow, he'd lost control of this entire conversation. "I've had a lot of sexual partners."

"Of course you have." Her gaze took a leisurely tour over his face and upper body. "As long as it was consensual…?"

"Of course it was."

"Safe?"

"Always." After discovering a lover had pricked holes in the condom she'd handed him—encouraged to do so by *his mother*—he'd always provided and used his own protection. Maybe he had his mother to thank that he'd emerged from young manhood with his sexual health intact—and if *that* wasn't a boner-killer, he didn't know what was. "Shit," he blurted. "We didn't use a condom last night." Or before dawn that morning.

"I have a contraceptive implant, and I tested negative for sexually transmitted infections at my last physical." She traced his jaw with her fingertip. "How about you?"

He released the breath he'd been holding. "Same—minus the implant, of course."

"Hmm." A thoughtful expression crossed her face. "I wonder if Sebastiani Labs could invent one."

"Invent what?"

"A contraceptive implant for men."

He nipped at her fingertip. "I'd volunteer as a test subject."

"Would you?"

"Of course." If such a thing had existed a decade ago, his mother's machinations would have been laughable.

Sasha shifted her weight, indirectly caressing his cock. "So, continue your story."

He jerked his focus back to the conversation. "After finishing college and law school, I took my place at Kirkland & Kirkland, my parents' law firm. As I mentioned, I...really enjoyed women, and they..."

"Really enjoyed you."

"I guess." He'd wallowed in variety, in the chase, in the dance of X and Y. "Legal associates work very long hours, and it was easier to date women who worked the same long hours I did." Smart, accomplished women, who wanted the same thing he did: Sex and companionship, with no commitment.

Or so he thought.

"Risky move, dating at work," she said.

"Tell me about it." But not for the reasons she might think. "After a while, I started to suspect that my mother might be...maneuvering certain women into my path, hoping I'd bite." And for a while, he had, with great relish. "But I didn't realize how far she'd go."

"To do what?"

"This is *so* embarrassing," he muttered, rubbing the back of his neck. "She figured a third-year associate might decide to stick around instead of talk to a headhunter, or that maybe talented paralegal might not push quite so hard for a salary increase, if she was sleeping with me."

"She offered the prodigal son as part of the benefits package?" Sasha lifted a brow. "I must say, that's a novel way of managing employees. What did you do when you found out?"

"I stopped dating. I buried myself in work. If I wanted sex, I'd—" he gave a shrug "—hit a bar in San Francisco, and have a one night stand my mother didn't know about. Then...I met someone."

"Someone special," she said softly.

"Yeah." Anna had been collateral damage in the final, messy battle he'd had with his mother, but she'd also provided him with an essential lethal weapon: information. "I met her in Union Square one Saturday. I bumped into her while she was feeding the pigeons." He gave a short laugh. "I scattered her papers all over the place."

Sasha grinned. "The classic 'meet cute'."

"I suppose," he allowed. "She was a high school social studies teacher, someone completely outside the legal world. Someone Mother hadn't put in my path."

"And you fell in love," Sasha murmured.

He shrugged his good shoulder.

"So what happened?"

"We dated for a while. Things were going well. Anna moved in with me, just before I took a new case. Bailey's case."

"She was accused of hacking a government database, right?"

The charges against Bailey were a lot more complicated than that, but...close enough. "And between her case and my existing workload, my long days got even longer. Mom was pissed off at me for taking Bailey's case without consulting her. Dad was pissed off at me because Mom was pissed off. Anna was pissed off because I was never home."

"Lots of anger."

"Yeah," he said, sighing. "One night I came home late—again—and it all boiled over. Anna said...she said..." He forced himself to continue. "She said, 'No wonder your mother offered me hazard pay to stay with you.'"

Sasha went still. "What?"

"My mother offered my lover money to stay in a relationship with me."

"That *bitch*," Sasha breathed. "Did Anna accept?"

"No, thank god—but Mom upped the ante, offering to pay Anna even more if she managed to drag me to the altar, or if she gave birth to my child."

"That's...the plot of a twisted novel," she marveled, laying her palm over his heart. "*The Barrister and the Baby Bounty.*"

He couldn't help but laugh. If only the payment plan his mother had offered Anna had occurred in a book instead of in real life. The story Anna told him had been utterly mortifying. "I later learned Mom had made the same offer to all the women I'd dated since law school." His mother had maneuvered so much prime pussy his way that he hadn't questioned his luck. *That's entirely on me.*

She looked at him, puzzled. "Does she actually want grandchildren?"

"I don't know." He couldn't imagine his mother dealing with drool, crying, and diaper changes. "Maybe it's a 'continue the family line' thing."

"No one's DNA is *that* special."

Sasha was a succubus. Hers probably was. "Mother would probably think about grandchildren in terms of business continuity," he mused. "She apparently thought me having a wife or child would tie me more tightly to the firm, and give her more control over my life."

"That's...pathological," she marveled.

He relaxed slightly. *It's not just me.* "With Mom, it's always about the firm." He caressed her hip with his tingling right hand. "My taking Bailey's case without consulting her was her last straw. Mine too, as it turned out." Their final confrontation, in his mother's corner office, had been loud and ugly. "We haven't had contact since the day I left the firm."

"Until your father's phone calls," Sasha noted. "Where was he when all this was happening?"

"Oblivious." He toyed with the soft hair at the nape of her neck. "He's the stereotypical absentminded professor, happiest when he's lost in his law books." His father's office, smelling of dusty paper and lemon drops, used to be his favorite place on earth. They'd spent many happy hours there, debating the finer points of the law. He...missed it. "My parents are oddly compatible," he said. "Dad's uncomfortable making any decision, and Mom's happy making them all."

"Maybe that's why he's been calling you. When someone is seriously ill, there are so many medical decisions to make." She paused. "Maybe he needs help."

He thought back to his father's final 'please.' To the uncharacteristic crack in his voice.

Shit, shit, shit.

"I have an odd question."

Her scent had deepened, darkened. He inhaled, drawing her in. "Yes?"

"How much was the bounty?"

Somehow, her tongue-in-cheek question turned years of shame to instant, scorching lust. His hands moved to her back, pulling her closer. "A million for marriage," he admitted. "Another million per child."

"That's...pretty kinky." She tilted her head sideways, as if assessing whether he was worth it.

Time slowed, thick and viscous. Finally, with a Mona Lisa smile, she nodded, then kissed him.

He sipped at her mouth, losing himself in her taste, in the flick of her slick, agile tongue, in the desire and pleasure she didn't bother to disguise. She was food, she was wine, she filled the empty, hungry places—

His cell phone vibrated, loud enough to hear it from his office. "Hell," he muttered against her mouth.

"That's really obnoxious," she said, shoving her hair away from her face.

Her hands were shaking. He'd made a sex demon shake. Maybe the day was pretty awesome, after all.

"Aren't you going to get that?"

He didn't want to, but... "Yeah."

Sasha climbed off his lap, then pulled her own cell phone from her jacket pocket. "I'll put the Gulfstream on standby."

He raked a hand through his hair. "I really don't have time for an unexpected trip to California."

"Make time," she stated. "You have a capable staff, and—" she lifted her cell phone "—you won't be completely out of touch."

He eyed her. "We need to work on the security

plan for your father's memorial service."

"I'll go with you." She smiled innocently. "We can multi-task."

Travel to California with Sasha? Suddenly things looked...sunnier.

She was right—as long as Chico had a handle on Lukas's physical security, he could really work from anywhere. He rose from the couch. "Okay, okay," he muttered to the phone. "I'm coming." Dropping a kiss on the top of her head, he hurried to his office, eyeing the phone.

Why did adulting have to be so goddamn hard?

Just before the call rolled to voice mail, he answered.

CHAPTER NINE

The drive north from San Francisco International Airport to Jack's family's home featured some of northern California's most scenic treasures, but since sliding behind the wheel of the SUV they'd rented, Jack had barely said a word. Once over the Golden Gate Bridge and past Sausalito, they'd veered east, over steep golden hills and through dense thickets of trees, to the Tiburon peninsula. Sasha shot a covert glance Jack's way. His expression was placid, but his emotions were as turbulent as the mighty Pacific Ocean.

It was exhausting.

Finally, he hit the blinker, then turned into a nearly hidden gravel driveway. Before long, the house came into view.

"Wow, some digs." The house was a stunning example of mid-century modern architecture, all juts and angles, tucked into the steep hillside overlooking San Francisco Bay. She could only imagine the killer view from the cantilevered deck. "Did you grow up here?"

"Yeah, I lived here until I went to college." Bypassing the concrete slab in front of the detached double garage, he parked under some oak trees. "The commute into the city can be a bitch and a half. Mom and Dad use a car service to get to work." Unfolding his long frame from behind the wheel, he stood and stretched. "Mom uses the commute time to do business with the east coast. Dad reads."

Money can't buy happiness, but it can sure grease the wheels. Take this trip, for instance. Yes, she and Jack would get plenty of work done while they were here in California, but summoning Daddy's private plane with a single phone call was the height of privilege.

Shit, the plane. Who owned it now? Was Lukas dealing with their father's estate along with everything else? Grabbing her purse, she got out of the car. She'd meant to call Lukas during the flight west, but the minute the Gulfstream reached cruising altitude, she and Jack had both fallen asleep.

Gravel crunched as she walked around the burly bumper, joining Jack by the driver's side door. They should have spent some of that time talking. Strategizing how they'd handle this visit.

"There's Dad," Jack murmured.

The silver-haired man standing by the French doors looked a lot like Jack, right down to the dress shirt and khaki pants they both wore. "Will your mom be here?"

"No, she'll be at the office all day." A muscle ticked in his cheek. "I thought it might be better to see Dad alone first so I can get some information about her health."

And after not seeing his parents for over a decade, it would be easier tackling them one at a time. *Yeah, we really should have talked about this.* His emotions were vacillating all over the place. She gestured to the back seat, to the lightweight coat he'd brought along. "Need that?"

"Nah."

"Okay." The simple question steadied him, as she'd hoped. She tipped her head up to the sky, to the mid-afternoon sun. "Mmm, it feels so warm here."

Jack gestured to the beat-up leather jacket she liked to wear when traveling. "You'll be glad for the jacket later." He glanced at the French doors, where his father waited.

"Ready?" she murmured.

"Damn the torpedoes."

Crossing the yard, they climbed several shallow stairs leading to the expansive back terrace. Two cushioned Adirondack chairs were perfectly positioned to catch the afternoon sun, and a black wrought iron table and matching chairs sat near a huge gas grill. Along the perimeter, empty rectangular planters sat ready to receive next spring's flowers.

And then, there was Jonathan Kirkland. Jack had four or five inches on his father height-wise, and was built on more muscular lines—or maybe that was a result of the punishing amount of time Jack put in at the gym—but if genes were any indication, Jack would have great teeth and a thick head of hair well into his sixties. Jonathan looked like he smiled more frequently than Jack did, with deep lines bracketing his mouth. Behind a pair of thick-lensed tortoiseshell glasses, jolly crinkles radiated from the outer corners of toasty brown eyes.

Brown eyes, not blue. Jack must have inherited his eye color from his mother.

"Hello," Jack's dad said.

His voice was a deep, smoky baritone, just like Jack's.

Silence lingered, because Jack didn't return his

father's greeting. His expression was smooth as ice, but underneath? Choppy whitecaps.

Oh boy. "Hello." She extended her hand. "I'm Jack's friend, Sasha Sebastiani."

Jack's father gave it a brisk shake. "Jonathan Kirkland. Very nice to meet you." Clearing his throat, he turned toward his son. "Jack. It's good to see you."

After a slight hesitation, Jack pulled his father into a rough hug. "Hi, Dad."

"Son." When Jonathan's voice cracked, Sasha locked her knees to steady herself. "I'm so glad you're home." He ran his hands over Jack's arms, shoulders, and back, as if cataloguing the changes a decade had wrought. "Where did all these muscles come from?"

If Jack's wince was anything to go by, he hadn't told his father about his gunshot wounds.

When Jonathan backed away, his eyes were gleaming. "Well. Please, come in." He opened the French door, gesturing inside with a welcoming hand. "Glenda has prepared all your favorite pastries."

She'd never seen Jack eat pastries.

"Glenda's still here?" Jack asked. "She hasn't retired?"

"Refuses to." Closing the door behind them, Jonathan ushered them into a great room that certainly deserved the name. The two-story room was a cathedral to art and craft, with its travertine masonry, bleached wood floors and ceilings, huge stone fireplace, and two vaguely Japanese-looking sliding panels that she assumed led to the other rooms on the main floor. Beautiful pieces of art graced the walls, including a narrow, intricate quilt that rippled down two full stories like a waterfall— but whoever had designed the space knew Mother

Nature was the star of the show. To the east, floor-to-ceiling windows framed a priceless water view.

"Oh," she breathed. The Kirklands' home sat high on the hills, overlooking downtown Tiburon and the broad expanse of the San Francisco Bay. Off to the right, white boats bobbed in the marina, and a large commuter ferry approached a big, wooden dock. Jack had mentioned the ferry, but when she'd suggested it might be fun to take it to his parents' house, he'd shut the idea down flat, muttering that a land getaway would be faster.

Jack and his father joined her by the windows, one man on each side, and they all looked out at the water. Sasha did her best to make small talk, asking questions about the town, the ferry, the boats, the shopping, until she suspected she sounded like a vacuous twit. Finally, she gave Jack a nudge with her elbow.

Jack cleared his throat. "So, how's work going?"

You haven't seen your father in a decade, your mother is fighting cancer, and you're asking about work?

"Fine," his father responded.

Silence.

Sasha mentally rolled her eyes. So much emotion, roiling in both men. So many words not yet said—but Jonathan had visibly relaxed, so maybe taking a circuitous conversational route was the way to go.

"The law hasn't changed very much, but the way it's practiced certainly has," Jonathan grumbled. "Too many damn computers, and too many crazies."

"Crazies?" she asked. "What do you mean?"

"Unhappy clients."

"Unhappy clients who've been deemed a potential risk to the company or its personnel," Jack finished.

His eyes narrowed. "Do we—do you—still have a private detective on staff?"

"Three now, and we've doubled the size of our security team. But I didn't ask you here to talk about our security issues."

Ooh, but he'd said the magic words. How much did Jonathan know about what Jack now did for a living? Jonathan's words were high-grade professional catnip, held just out of reach. She couldn't perceive even a whiff of manipulation from the man, but that didn't mean the father's words couldn't influence his son.

Jack had described his father as an absent-minded professor type, but she didn't see it.

Another uncomfortable silence descended.

Okay, enough of this. Time to change the dynamic. "Could you tell me where I might find a restroom?" she asked Jonathan. "I'd like to freshen up after the trip." Maybe they'd talk to each other if she left them alone.

"Certainly. Right this way." Jonathan opened a sliding panel on the south wall, exposing a hallway that, as she'd suspected, led to more of the house. "Just down the hall, the first room to the right."

"Thank you."

The small half-bath was a study in simplicity, harmony, and serenity—soft light, neutral colors, and natural bamboo—with a vase of tall-stemmed red sunflowers providing a pop of color. After using the facilities and dawdling over her hair and makeup, she left the bathroom, approaching the great room door. Male voices murmured—not loudly enough that she could hear what they were saying—but a quick inhale assured her that the emotional waters were relatively smooth. They didn't need her yet.

Good, because she was dying to see more of the house.

The Japanese decorating influence was even more evident here in the hallway. She took a minute to admire the black-framed woodblock geisha prints lining the walls, and the bonsai tree sitting on a heavily lacquered side table, but the two open doors down the hall beckoned. The first room, a bright, wood-floored space, held a treadmill, a yoga mat, Pilates equipment, and purple hand weights, but what most drew her attention was the mirrored wall, and the ballet *barre* installed at waist height.

Her feet were moving before she realized it. Grasping the *barre* lightly, she allowed herself one *plié*, one *relevé*, and a single, stingy pirouette before turning away and leaving the room. Given what Jack had said about his mother, Sasha wasn't inclined to form the slightest connection with Cynthia Roth Kirkland.

When she ducked her head into the second room, she couldn't help but smile. There were some differences, yes, but Jack's home office looked a lot like his father's. A huge partner's desk dominated the space, but given the partner's side was buried in a blizzard of papers and books, it was a safe guess that Jonathan didn't share the space with his wife. There was a distinct scent about the place—old paper, sun-baked dust, and furniture polish—but it smelled pleasantly musty rather than mildewed. If there was a computer, a digital tablet, or even a desk phone in the place, she didn't see it. Rows and rows of law books marched along the full wall of bookshelves, their jewel-toned spines standing straight and tall. A couple of interesting-looking *tchotchkes* broke up the books here and there, but it was an old family snapshot sitting on the shelf closest to the desk that snagged her attention. Jack as a lanky teenager, hugging his dad in front of a Christmas tree, with a tall, willowy blonde—unmistakably Jack's mother—standing several feet away, observing rather than participating.

She couldn't help but wince. Why did Jonathan display *this* picture? Did he not see how accurately it captured the family's fractured dynamic—

Anger.

Lava-red anger, boiling from Jack.

She ran toward the great room, hesitating in the hallway to listen at the door. Yep, Jack and his father were arguing, all right.

"Jack, your mother knows it was a mistake to fire you for taking Bailey Brown's case pro bono."

"She didn't fire me," Jack spat out. "I quit."

Ah, crap. Had they managed to talk about his mother's health before tumbling down *this* particular rat hole? She peeked around the door jamb. Father and son faced each other, hands on hips, both angry but making an effort to control it.

Talk about two peas in a pod.

"And she knows she made a mistake offering women money to, erm, date you," Jonathan added. He had the grace to look embarrassed about his wife's behavior. "The way she treated Anna was inexcusable."

Jack's brows rose. "You knew about that?"

There was a spurt of exasperation from Jonathan. "Jack, I know you think I'm completely under your mother's thumb—and there may be some truth to that—but do you think we don't talk to each other? That we don't have a partnership? Of course we do." Jonathan turned to stare at the ocean. "Jack, she's horrified by what happened between the two of you."

"Yeah, I can tell." Sarcasm dripped like acid. "She's horrified she got caught."

Jonathan swiped both hands through his hair. "She was looking for a way to apologize. You left before she could."

Jack's emotional pendulum took a wild, silent swing. "How fucking hard is it to say, 'I'm sorry?' Or, 'Son, I'm sorry I pimped you out to benefit the firm.' Or, 'I'm sorry I couldn't let you live your own goddamn life?' Three ways to apologize, right off the top of my head. But she didn't. She couldn't. She's constitutionally incapable of apologizing, of admitting that she was wrong." He turned away from his father, facing the water.

"You took off before she could try," Jonathan said tiredly. "Don't you think leaving the state was an extreme reaction on your part?"

"No."

She had to agree. How many chances was Jack supposed to give his mother to hurt him?

Jack faced his father again. "Dad, I didn't come here to re-litigate old battles. How's Mother?"

There was a long pause. "She just had her last chemotherapy treatment. Her treatment is going as planned."

"Dad, stop the objective lawyerly bullshit. How is she?" He paused. "You sounded really worried on the phone."

She narrowed her eyes. Jonathan *was* worried, but he didn't seem incapacitated by it. What the hell...?

"As you might imagine, she's not happy about losing her hair—" a wisp of a smile "—but the doctors caught the cancer early. They think she has a good chance for a full remission."

"Then why the hell did you call me?"

"Because this has gone on long enough!" The shout seemed to take the starch out of Jonathan's spine. He looked at the floor and sighed. "Jack, you're young yet, but someday you'll discover we never have as much time as we hope." Their gazes met. "There's nothing like a big health scare to bring what matters most into very sharp focus."

There was another wild emotional swing from Jack, but he didn't say a word about the shooting. About how, at this very moment, the gunshot wounds that had nearly killed him oozed under gauze, hidden under his tailored clothing.

"Jack, you're a lawyer," Jonathan continued, watching Jack carefully. "Despite our...estrangement, we have practical matters to discuss. The firm will be yours after your mother and I are gone."

"You brought me halfway across the country for an estate planning meeting?" Jack's voice was lacerating. "Fuck the firm. I don't want it."

"Then you can dissolve the company after we die, putting hundreds of people out of work."

Enough. She breezed back into the great room. "Mr. Kirkland, you have a lovely home," she said, drawing Jonathan's attention away from his son. "I couldn't help but notice the gorgeous woodblock prints in the hallway. Do you know their age?" As Jonathan discussed the prints' provenance, she slipped her hand into Jack's.

He grasped back. And slowly, slowly, his stress level drifted back down, like a balloon losing helium.

"Dad, if we want to see Mom during business hours, we'd better be on our way back to the city."

It was almost four o'clock. Why wouldn't they wait here at the house, until Cynthia came home from work?

But Jonathan was nodding, as if this was exactly what he'd expected his son to do. "Will you come back here afterward, then? We have plenty of room; you're welcome to stay."

"No, but thanks," Jack said. "I want to check on the house while we're here."

"What house?" she asked. Jack had told her he'd handle the California accommodations, but she assumed they'd stay in a hotel in San Francisco somewhere.

"I own some property just south of San Francisco, near Half Moon Bay."

Jack owned a house in California?

"You can use my office once you get to K&K," Jonathan was saying as they made their way to the door. "I'll let Chloe know to expect you."

"Chloe?"

"Mrs. Whipple."

Jack pursed his lips. "I think that's the first time I've heard her first name."

"Don't make the mistake of using it," Jonathan warned, humor warming his eyes. "Check things out while you're there, will you? Make sure we haven't slipped into the red, or that some black swan event isn't looming off on the horizon. An objective eye is always a plus."

Jonathan probably wouldn't appreciate what *her* objective eye saw. How could Jonathan just stand there, prattling on about the firm's finances, when his son was so upset? She understood, now, why Jack said he wanted a getaway car.

"Please give my apologies to Glenda." Jack's jaw was tight. "I'm sorry I missed her."

"Certainly."

So polite. Too polite.

Jonathan paused, his hand on the doorknob. "How long will you be here on the coast?"

"A couple of days," Jack said evenly. "We need to get back to Minnesota."

Back to Minnesota, not back home. As she'd just learned, Jack owned *two* homes—one in California, and one in Minneapolis.

Why did Jack still own property in California? If he ever wanted to move back and take his place at the family firm, he already had a place to live. The thought knocked her more than a little off balance.

The silence was dragging, so she dove into the breach. "It was nice to meet you, Jonathan," she said, kissing him on the cheek.

He quickly reciprocated, following up with a hug. "Nice to meet you, too, Sasha. Please come again." He glanced over at his son. "Any friend of Jack's is a friend of ours."

There was a slight pause before the first 'friend.' Yeah, he'd seen her holding Jack's hand, and had drawn his own conclusions.

"Goodbye, son," Jonathan murmured. "I'm glad to see you."

Jack gave a curt nod. After a slight hesitation, he pulled his father into another of those handshake-turned-half-hugs.

After the men separated, they stepped out onto the terrace. When Jonathan closed the French doors behind them, Jack's breath released with a whoosh. "Let's get the fuck out of here."

Her only response was a light touch at the back of his waist as they walked to the SUV. Jack jabbed a button on the key fob, unlocking the doors.

"Are you okay to drive?"

"Yeah." Jack glanced at his watch, then at the sky. The sun was diving for cover behind the horizon. "Traffic back to the city is going to be carnage."

He sounded as though he relished the battle. After a split-second assessment—out of his father's company, he was already less stressed out—she climbed into the passenger seat and buckled in. She'd leave him to it, because she had some thinking to do.

Jack hadn't completely ripped up his California roots after all—and now, with his mother ill, his father wanted to discuss the future of the family firm. When she suggested Jack return his father's phone calls, she'd never imagined *this*.

She glanced over to the driver's seat, where Jack was fastening his seat belt. What would it take to make him move back to the west coast? And if he did, where would that leave *them*?

As the car crept from the driveway, she turned on the heat. Was there even a 'them' for him to leave?

✳

In an epic case of good news/bad news, a familiar face sat behind the big, curved desk dominating K&K's outermost lobby. The good news? Security chief Charlie Jankowski was very good at his job. The bad news? Charlie Jankowski was very good at his job. There wasn't a chance in hell he'd get past that desk without his old friend busting his balls about the woman walking at his side.

Yep, Charlie had already locked eyes on her—but to be fair, so had everyone else. In this conservative environment, Sasha was a peacock among hens.

"Well, well, well." Charlie rose, expressionless, his linebacker frame accentuated by a tailored black suit. "The prodigal son returns."

"Shut up," he muttered. "It's good to see you, man."

"You, too. Your father called, told me you'd be stopping by." Charlie came out from behind the desk, pulling him into a half-hug. "I've missed my workout partner."

"You've obviously let yourself go since then," he said dryly. If Charlie had lost a single pound of muscle in the last decade, Jack couldn't see it—but the sidearm his old friend wore, in a harness under his suit coat, hadn't been part of the uniform when he'd left.

Hell. What other changes would he find once he got upstairs? "Charlie, I'd like you to meet my..." Shit, which relationship descriptor fit?

Sasha took charge. "Sasha Sebastiani," she said, offering Charlie her hand.

Decked out in denim and leather, with black-tipped fingernails and purple streaks in her aerodynamic hair, Sasha looked nothing like the women he'd dated in the past.

"Hello, Ms. Sebastiani," Charlie said, rolling the syllables around in his mouth as if tasting something exotic. "Very nice to meet you." He jerked his thumb at Jack. "What are you doing with this guy?"

Sasha considered, then flashed a gamine grin. "He's really good in bed."

Charlie roared with laughter. "Is he, now? That's good to hear." As he headed back behind the desk, he slapped Jack on the shoulder—the uninjured shoulder, thank god, because the man had hands the size of Christmas hams. "Kirkland, you gotta hang on to this one."

"I'll…take that under advisement."

Across the lobby, an unmarked door opened. Mrs. Whipple, his father's admin, sailed toward them like a sleek clipper ship, wearing a gray pantsuit, a silky white blouse, and a welcoming smile. Her hair was silver now, but she wore the same strand of signature pearls and knock-'em-dead red lipstick he remembered.

"Jack." She reached for a hug.

Another thing that hadn't changed? Her ability to convey a lot of information in very few words: *I'm glad you're here. I'm disappointed it took you so long. Is something wrong?* There was no way she'd missed that his return hug was…less than hearty. After a very long day, and too much use, his right arm wasn't quite cooperating. He kissed her cheek, hoping it compensated. "Hi, Mrs. Whipple."

"Hello." She turned toward Sasha. "And you are?"

"Mrs. Whipple, I'd like you to meet Sasha Sebastiani."

The women shook hands and exchanged pleasantries.

"Well." Mrs. Whipple gestured toward the unmarked door. "Shall we go upstairs?"

He hesitated. "Charlie, when do you get off shift?" He didn't want to just say hello and goodbye to someone who'd been a good friend so long ago.

"Now, as a matter of fact." Charlie glanced at the windows, wincing. It was full dark, and rush hour was in full swing. "I have to leave now to catch the start of my daughter's basketball game."

"You have a daughter?"

Charlie grinned. "Lindy. She's seven. A firecracker, just like my wife."

"Someone actually married you?"

"Hey, you're not the only one who's good in bed."

Sasha snorted out a laugh. Mrs. Whipple's eyebrow lifted, just the slightest bit—a sign of high amusement.

"We really need to catch up," he said to Charlie. Marriage, promotion, a daughter... So much had happened in his friend's life during the past decade, and he'd missed it all.

"How long are you in town?" Charlie asked.

"Just a day or two." And there were too many strangers milling around the lobby for him to rattle off his cell phone number aloud. Grabbing an appointment card and a pen from the sleek holder sitting on the top of the reception desk, he scribbled down the digits and handed the card to Charlie. "Call or text me. Anytime."

"I just might."

"I mean it." He shook Charlie's hand again. "It's good to see you."

"You, too." Charlie flashed Sasha his lady-killer smile. "Ms. Sebastiani, it was a pleasure."

"Likewise." She smiled back. "And please, call me Sasha."

"Will do."

They rode the private elevator to the top floor, to

K&K's executive offices. His mother and father each had their own large office suite at opposite ends of the long hallway, with a handful of junior partners' offices in between—private stalls to reward the firm's most productive workhorses. In the hushed quiet of the reception area, the carpet was plush, the wood was polished, and every light still burned bright. A whippet-thin receptionist nodded as they passed, but Mrs. Whipple didn't make introductions.

When they reached the hallway, she turned right, toward his father's office, instead of left, toward his mother's. *Bless you, Mrs. Whipple.* He wasn't ready to deal with his mother yet. Halfway down, a slim slice of light escaped from beneath his old office door. He was familiar with the routine: nearly 7:00 p.m. on a Friday night, with hours of work left to go.

Poor sap.

Nah, *poor* was the wrong word. The people boxed up in these skyscraper-view offices worked very long hours and had very nice bank accounts. It compensated—until, for some, it didn't. While he one hundred percent believed everyone was entitled to a vigorous legal defense, there'd come a point where defending unrepentant rich people accused of financial crimes started shriveling his soul.

I would have quit, sooner or later. The fight between him and his mother had catalyzed an action he would have taken regardless.

"Doing okay?" Sasha murmured.

"Yeah, why?"

"You're rubbing your hand. Do you need pain meds?"

Probably, but he needed pheromone intoxication meds even more. He'd taken a double dose when they'd detoured to the restrooms before entering K&K's main lobby, on the off-chance the experimental medication might provide some protection against his mother's particular brand of crazy. News of his arrival would reach his mother sooner or later. Emotional shrapnel was sure to fly.

Sasha touched his arm. "Jack?"

"I'm fine," he mouthed.

Passing her own neat desk, Mrs. Whipple led them to the double doors at the end of the hall. "Here we are."

Walking into his father's office felt like walking back in time. There was the partner's desk piled with papers, the thick, forest green carpet, walls of bookshelves, the built-in file cabinets... Everything looked exactly the same, right down to the crystal bowl of lemon drops sitting in easy reach. He looked around. "No computer?"

"Your father is still stubbornly analog," Mrs. Whipple said. "I'll go get you a laptop you can use."

She exited, leaving him to watch Sasha wander around in his father's office. She found the lemon drops, popping one into her mouth.

"Your father is a creature of habit, isn't he?" Sasha said, smiling. "This office looks a lot like the one he has at home."

When had she seen...? "Ah. You took a bit of a tour while Dad and I were talking."

"Yeah." She shrugged, unrepentant. "I wanted to give the two of you some time alone to talk."

For all the good it had done.

"Where's your mother?"

"Her office is at the other end of the hall. Separate work spaces suit them." He explained that his father was the legal genius, happiest with his sleeves rolled up and his nose buried in the law books, while his mother handled the firm's day-to-day business operations. With Mother's office so far away, Dad wouldn't accidentally wander in on an important meeting wearing rumpled khakis and a cardigan instead of the tailored suits she thought he should wear.

"Your parents' breakdown of responsibilities sounds really similar to how you and Lukas run Sebastiani Security," Sasha observed.

True, he *was* the public face of Sebastiani Security, but that was primarily because he was human and Lukas wasn't. It was…more than a little disturbing to think that his strengths, and his mother's, might run along similar tracks.

Mrs. Whipple swept back into the office holding a sleek black laptop, already booted up. "I've logged on using my account and password. You can get to any system I can."

Which meant he had full access.

"If you're going to be here for any period of time, we can arrange for you to get your own login credentials."

Would he even need them? He didn't know. "Thanks."

"Hard copies of our risk management materials are over there, in the leftmost file cabinet." She set the laptop down on one of the few empty areas of the desk. "Ms. Sebastiani, might I interest you in a cup of coffee or tea while Jack is working?"

"I'd love a cup of coffee, if you'd join me. And please, call me Sasha."

"And I'm Chloe," Mrs. Whipple replied, smiling.

"The break room is just down the hall."

Neither woman saw his jaw drop, because they were already headed out the door, chattering like old friends. "All righty then," he said to the empty office. There was no need to worry about what Sasha and Mrs. Whipple—Chloe—might be talking about.

Was there?

It was time to do what he came here to do.

Remembering his dad's joking comment about making sure the firm wasn't in the red, the first thing he did was check the balance sheet. In the red? Ha! Not even close. Not only was the firm on very solid financial footing, they'd paid out record bonuses last year. Mother was looking at real estate in both Palo Alto and San Jose, apparently considering opening satellite offices in Silicon Valley.

Smart move.

He dug deep and wide. No red flags. No open lawsuits, no settlements or payouts, no Human Resources trouble... He leaned back in the chair. Why had Dad wanted him to check things out? Maybe it was as simple as Dad had said, that Mother's illness had made them think about business continuity and estate planning. Or...maybe Dad thought that asking him to do some cursory research would pique his son's interest in returning to the firm.

Yeah, that clicked. "Nice try, Dad."

But unfortunately, his dad had a point. His parents weren't getting any younger. Hell, none of them were. Nothing like getting shot—or watching Elliott die— to drive home the point that tomorrow was promised to no one. He and Lukas needed to have a business continuity discussion of their own regarding Sebastiani Security, especially now that Lukas was

Underworld Council president.

He rubbed his aching hand. Professional hazards like bullet wounds aside, he'd probably outlive his parents. He would inherit their estate—their property, their belongings, and the company. What role would Kirkland & Kirkland play in his future? Did he have it in him to close down the firm? To put Charlie, or Mrs. Whipple, or that hungry-looking receptionist, out of work, and then simply walk away?

No. He couldn't do it.

That meant reestablishing at least limited contact with his parents.

Christ, did he have *that* in him? Earlier in the afternoon, Dad had apologized for Mother paying women to date him—an apology he was still waiting for his mother to make—but Dad *hadn't* mentioned the huge payout Mother had promised Anna if she managed to drag him to the altar, or that ridiculous baby bounty.

"A baby bounty, for fuck's sake." Sasha was right; it sounded like the plot of one of the romance novels Antonia gobbled like candy. Did Dad know the whole story?

There were still too many secrets in his family.

He leaned back in the old leather chair, rubbing his eyes. His own will was probably overdue for review. Written almost a decade ago, Bailey was his sole beneficiary, and...so much had changed since then. Lukas would take care of anything having to do with Sebastiani Security—unless he and Lukas died at the same time, which was a corner case he didn't have the energy to consider right now—but what about his personal estate? Property, investments, brokerage accounts? He didn't have kids, didn't know if he ever would. Little Coco didn't need the money. Neither, now, did Bailey.

Maybe I should just leave everything to charity and be done with it.

And speaking of being done with it... One last thing to check: The Crazies File.

The thick accordion file folder he retrieved from the bottom drawer of the file cabinet contained copies of any written communication sent to the firm containing the slightest hint of complaint, conflict, anger, or threat, and a record of any follow-up. Originals were kept by the security team—hell, maybe by Charlie—and would serve as supporting evidence should any client...escalate.

It couldn't hurt to take a look at things, as long as he was here.

Sitting back down at his father's desk, he paged through the thick file, neatly organized with the most recent communications first. Pissed-off clients, someone threatening a lawsuit, clients demanding another lawyer, another judge, another trial... He shook his head in amazement. Clients who'd threaten their lawyer *in writing* were their own worst enemies.

He'd traveled back a decade when his own name popped, on a complaint he'd never seen before. The client, Miranda DesJardins, demanded he be fired for his 'egregious mishandling' of her case.

DesJardins, DesJardins... ah, the Silicon Valley marketing executive. Intellectual property theft, and insider trading. DesJardins had shared confidential product information with a competitor. The competitor had beaten DesJardins' employer's company to market with a competing product, and DesJardins, who owned a tidy pile of the competitor's stock, had made a hefty profit she hadn't hidden nearly well enough. It was a textbook case—they had her cold—so his only recourse had been damage control, trying to reduce her sentence.

He'd done the best he could, but the judge had thrown the book at her.

Addressed to his mother, the letter had arrived at K&K a week after he'd quit. His mother's admin had responded, informing Ms. DesJardins that Mr. Kirkland no longer worked for the firm.

The bare-bones statement left a lot of room for interpretation—so much so that DesJardins probably thought her complaint had merit, that he'd been fired for cause.

He tossed the letter to the desk. "That's fucking fantastic."

"Jack."

Shit, his mother had come to him after all. He sat upright in the chair. "Mother."

She entered the room in her precise, deliberate way, taking five strides that left her standing in the center of the room. She didn't offer a kiss, a handshake, a smile… nothing that would lead him to suspect she might be happy to see her only son after ten years apart.

Nothing had changed.

"How are you?" she asked. She wore a cranberry knit jacket and skirt, a silk blouse, and businesslike black pumps that brought her close to six feet tall—no changes there—but her long, blonde hair was gone. On her head, she wore a mauve knit cap that looked soft and warm. She probably hated it.

She probably hated him, too, the son she hadn't been able to control. So be it. He rose to his feet, stepping out from behind his father's desk. He would be cordial, even polite—but he wouldn't be stupid. "I'm fine, thank you." Crossing the forest green carpet, he took her hand, shook it, then kissed her on the cheek.

She stiffened.

Nope, nothing had changed.

"You look…" A little thin, but healthier than he'd expected. A friend who'd just finished chemotherapy had told him that the current crop of anti-nausea medication could work wonders. "How are you feeling?"

"Quite well, thank you."

He waited for her to continue.

She didn't.

The silence stretched like a rubber band—until he snapped it. "Seriously? We haven't seen each other in over a decade, you have cancer, and we're going to stand here playing verbal power games?"

Her expression didn't change. "Our parting was…less than amicable."

"Ya think?"

His mother's lips went flat, but she didn't say anything. Sasha and Mrs. Whipple were coming down the hall, their conversation growing louder as they approached the office.

"Do you really think I could pull off purple hair?" Mrs. Whipple asked.

"Chloe, you'd *rock* purple hair. A few lilac-colored foils, blended with your natural silver, would be lovely."

The two women paused at the door.

"You don't think it would look, well, foolish? At my age?"

"No better reason to do it," Sasha said with a grin. "Jack, don't you think Chloe would look amazing with purple—oh." Sasha noticed his mother, standing in the middle of the room like a marble statue. "Hello." Her nostrils flared, ever so slightly.

What did she sense? Was his mother really as unfeeling as she seemed? Once he and Sasha got to the house—if they ever got to the house—he'd ask. His lover was a succubus. Why not take advantage of the unusual source of intel?

Mrs. Whipple's glance ping-ponged between the two women. "I'll be at my desk if you need anything."

"We'll be fine," he said. "Thanks for showing Sasha where the coffee is."

"Nice to meet you, Chloe," Sasha said warmly. "I hope to see you again soon."

"Likewise," Mrs. Whipple said. After a slight hesitation, she left.

The room went silent.

If Sasha hadn't initially noticed his mother, Mother had certainly noticed her. She took in Sasha's two-toned hair, cotton T-shirt, and tattered jeans with fastidious sniff. His mother probably had no idea that Sasha's leather coat, boots, and purse were as expensive as her own St. John knits.

"Jack, I see you're still taking in young, pretty strays." Her eagle eye wouldn't have missed Sasha's fading bruises. "New pro bono client?"

"New lover." He regretted the words as soon as he said them. His relationship with Sasha felt too new, too fragile and delicate, to be hurled at his mother as the latest weapon in their lifelong war. But Sasha walked over and slipped her hand into his, her allegiance clear. He gave her hand a grateful squeeze.

"Mother, this is Sasha Sebastiani."

His mother's eyes narrowed. "Any relation to Elliott Sebastiani?"

Sasha nodded. "He's my father."

Sasha spoke of Elliott as though he was still alive—and as far as humanity was concerned, he was—but his throbbing bullet wounds wouldn't let him forget Elliott was gone.

Sasha leaned against him, comforting without words.

"He sounds like a fascinating man." And the fact that Sasha was his daughter apparently made Sasha much more interesting. Provisional approval, and dollar signs, glowed as Mother came over, offering Sasha a handshake she hadn't offered him. "So, you're Jack's new girlfriend. We really should get to know each other better."

Sasha's fake smile exposed too many teeth. "Let's not."

His mother flinched. Silence hung for several uncomfortable seconds. "What did you say?"

"I said, let's not." She paused. "Ms. Kirkland, I know you're Jack's mother, and I know you're ill. I'm sorry about that." She eyeballed the chasm between mother and son—less than five feet, but it might just as well have been a mile. "But you have—pardon my French—one massively fucked-up family dynamic going on here, and I'm not going to play."

"What?"

"I'm not going to play," Sasha repeated. "Count me out."

She sounded like royalty, mildly displeased. He couldn't quite hide the smile.

"Not only am I not going to play, I'm ready to

leave now." When she glanced up at him, her eyes were blazing with an emotion he couldn't identify. "How about you?"

What had she absorbed? What had she interpreted? God, he wished they could talk. But...they really didn't need to. Not right now, anyway. Sasha was right; he could leave the field of play. He could choose to disengage.

With a nod, he did. "Let me put this file away first."

His mother turned to Sasha. "This is private family business. Who the hell do you think you are?"

"I'm your son's lover, and I think he's an extraordinary man. As for you and your husband?" Sasha shrugged. "Let's just say the jury's still out."

"Well, I never—"

"Never what? Never paid women to sleep with your son? Yeah, you did." His mother's cheeks turned hot pink. "Yes, he told me all about it," Sasha continued, "and why shouldn't he? The fault—the shame—is yours, not his. It was never his."

Not his. Never his.

"Jack," Mother bit out. "Say something."

Did she expect him to simply fall back in line? To fall back into their familiar, fucked up pattern?

"Jack?"

Yeah, apparently so. *Fuck that.* "Let's go." Lacing his fingers with Sasha's, they headed for the door. Once they reached it, he turned. "Keep your checkbook in your purse. Pregnant or not, she doesn't need your goddamn money."

Her eyelids flew wide.

They left the office, still holding hands. Mrs. Whipple wasn't at her desk, nor was the receptionist they'd passed earlier. By the time they got on the elevator, Sasha's shoulders were shaking. He couldn't blame her for being upset—

The second the doors closed, she burst into laughter. "Oh, my gawd." She sucked in a breath. "You evil, evil man! You let your mother think I might be pregnant!"

"Too evil?" Why was she laughing so hard?

"Just evil enough. She deserved it." She wrapped her arms around his waist. "With her for a mother, it's amazing you turned out to be so normal."

A lot of that was probably Bailey's doing. She often said they'd both been raised by wolves.

He studied her. "What did you inhale up there that upset you so much?"

"It took a few minutes to get past that hard, glossy shell, but once I did? Scarytown. Massive control issues. What's her deal?"

"I don't know."

"She loves you, in her way, but she's so...angry. Angry, and afraid, and ashamed."

"Ashamed of what?"

"The way she treated you, maybe?" Sasha shrugged. "I can tell *what* she's feeling, but not *why*. Until she changes her behavior, she's on her own."

Taking pheromone intoxication meds might have helped him handle the emotionally fraught meeting with his mother, to not get pulled into the crazy, but it had been Sasha's behavioral curveball— disengaging, choosing not to play the game on Mother's terms—that had really shut things down. Why hadn't he thrown one ten years ago?

I could probably use a shrink myself.

The elevator dinged as it reached the main lobby.

Though emptier now, several clients still waited in the sleek blue chairs. The black-suited woman who'd taken Charlie's place at the main reception desk nodded as they signed out.

"I'm starving," Sasha said as they walked across the lobby.

"I am, too. How about dinner here in the city? Ever been to The Stinking Rose?"

"No, but I've heard of it." She grinned. "Nothing says romance like garlic breath."

It was a relief to hear she still had romance on her mind. "I don't mind garlic breath if you don't." At the door leading to the parking ramp, he dropped what was supposed to be a quick kiss onto her lips, but she met him more than halfway, winding her arms around his neck.

When her hand cupped his ass, the security guard pointedly cleared her throat.

He took one step back. Sasha inhaled deeply and luxuriously before opening her eyes again. "I love garlic. Especially second-hand garlic." Her smile was sex personified.

"Good." It took both hands to open the door leading to the parking ramp, but he barely noticed the pain. Nothing—no odiferous, bulbed plant, no urgent phone call, no family drama—would keep him away from her mouth, her arms, or her body tonight.

Nothing.

CHAPTER TEN

It was after eleven by the time they got to Jack's house, a three-bedroom, two-bathroom rambler in El Granada, just north of Half Moon Bay. They'd closed the restaurant down, and traffic out of the city had been light. After the early morning flight and a day of drama, she should be exhausted, but...she wasn't. "That second cappuccino might have been overkill," she admitted, following Jack through a sturdily-furnished living room to the largest bedroom.

"I think you needed it." Jack set both duffels on the queen-sized bed. "You and Flynn were talking business on the phone almost the whole drive here."

"Yeah." And now her brain was humming. "Flynn had to kick some grabby assholes out of the club earlier tonight. He wanted to give me a heads up in case the media got wind of it."

"Why would the media be involved?"

"They're *famous* grabby assholes. Actors in town to make a movie." She drove her fingers through her hair with a sigh. "Flynn glamoured them, so their memories of the evening should be foggy at best." Thanks to her vamp-heavy staff, most humans who wandered into the club didn't stay very long and usually didn't return. "With me on the phone, you and the 280 could reunite, have a private moment," she teased.

He glanced at her questioningly.

"Seriously, though. Why do Californians say "the" before their highway numbers? It sounds really strange."

Jack stared at her like she'd sprouted antennae. "Let me give you a quick tour of the house."

At the restaurant, Jack explained that he'd bought the house soon after he'd started to work at Kirkland & Kirkland. He'd lived in it for a couple of years, and had rented it out since. It was functional and utilitarian, furnished with essentials and not much more, but when she opened the doors leading to the deck, a chilly night breeze carried the tang of the Pacific. "Can you see the ocean from here?"

"Yeah, and the sunsets are amazing."

Before they returned to Minnesota, she'd drink a cup of coffee looking at the ocean, at that little table tucked into the corner, just on principle.

"I'm sorry we missed the sunset tonight." When he wrapped his arms around her from behind, his body heat leached into hers. "That wasn't my plan."

"And what *was* your plan?"

"Romance, of course."

She shivered in warmth and delight. "The night's not over yet."

"Let me show you the rest of the place," he said, pulling her inside and closing the sliding glass door. "Pauline, the property manager, told me we were lucky to catch the house empty right now. An Australian technologist just ended a three-month stay, and some surfers will check in next week." He pointed out the gas fireplace, a small half-bathroom, and walked her through the kitchen. "It's nothing fancy, but it's got the basics." He explained that Pauline had stopped by earlier, to turn on the heat and stock the kitchen with a few essentials.

"As long as there's heat and coffee, I'm fine."

Pointing at the coffee maker on the counter by the stove, he peered into the refrigerator. "I think we can do a little better than that." Reaching inside, he withdrew a tray of fruit and cheese, and a bottle of white wine. "How about some wine and cheese by the fire?"

"Wonderful." Maybe more wine would counteract the caffeine zinging through her system. Sleep was hours away.

"There are some blankets and quilts in the hall closet if you'd like to make things a little more comfortable."

"I'm on it."

Not five minutes later, they were sitting in a nest of pillows and blankets on the floor by the fireplace, drinking wine and feeding each other bites of cheese. "So, I have a question," she said, leaning back against the warm stone hearth.

"Does it have to do with which item of your clothing I want to take off first?"

The rumble in his voice sent flame surging, but she battled it back. "Why didn't we wait at your parents' house for your mother to come home?"

Jack half-choked on his wine. "*That's* what you want to talk about?"

"What did *you* want to talk about?"

His gaze flicked to her lips. "I didn't want to talk at all."

Diving headfirst into desire was always tempting, but she'd learned the hard way that it only brought fleeting relief. Whether Jack realized it or not, he needed to unload. Debrief. "I can tell that what happened with your mother is bothering you." Retrieving her wine glass from the hearth, she settled in. "It bothered me, too."

He started to say something, then broke off with an odd half-laugh.

"What's so funny?"

"I was about to repeat something I've heard Lukas say dozens of times: 'There's no such thing as a secret in this family.' But I'm not family."

"Not *blood* family—a fact for which I'm grateful, being we're sleeping together," she said dryly. "But friends are the family we choose. You *are* family, in all the ways that count." When a muscle ticked along his scruff-roughened jaw, she covered it with her hand. "You and Bailey may be human, but you're ours now."

And you're mine. For now, anyway.

After a pause, he leaned into her touch, like a big, blond cat who'd decided to allow itself the comfort of touch. Turning his head, he pressed a kiss into her palm. "Thanks." He cleared his throat, then took a big sip of wine. "I apologize for how horribly Mother treated you at Dad's office today. It was inexcusable."

She couldn't discern a whiff of concern for himself, for how his mother had treated her son. Her heart ached for the boy, for the man. "There's no need for you to apologize," she said. "Any apology is hers to make, and frankly I'm not expecting one."

"Good, because it will never come. She never apologizes. Ever." He poured himself more wine, and topped off her half-full glass. "Back to your original question though, about why we didn't stay at the house and speak to her once she got home from work. There are several reasons. One, she works long hours, and has a very unpredictable schedule. If we'd waited for her at the house, we'd probably still be there." A theatrical shudder wracked his big frame. "No thanks."

Smiling, she pulled a soft, fuzzy blanket around her shoulders and leaned closer to the simmering fire. He was playing it for laughs now, but she couldn't forget how upset he'd been when they'd left Tiburon earlier in the day.

"Two, Dad wanted me to check some business files, some of which are only available at the office. And three…" He sighed. "I was pretty sure Mother and I would get into it, and I didn't want Dad to witness that. She's such a control freak."

Sasha hid her smile in her wine glass.

"What's so funny?"

"Are you sure you really want to know?"

"Of course."

"I was thinking, 'Like mother, like son.' Do you realize how much effort you've put into controlling outcomes today? For you, for your dad, for your mother? For me?"

"I—" That muscle in his jaw ticked again. "That's what I do."

"Yes, it is, and you're very good at it," she confirmed. "You've made a profession out of it. Hell, watching you and Lukas work is like watching a game of ten-dimensional chess." Shit, why had she even said anything? She took a fortifying sip of wine. "All I'm saying is that the need—the ability—to control outcomes is a trait you and your mother share. You use your skills for good rather than evil, but the skills are undeniably there."

Shock, anger, denial, recognition…he cycled through the emotions so quickly that the changes barely registered. His expression was smooth as a frozen lake.

She'd always found Jack's ruthless self-control utterly fucking hot—and regularly fantasized about making him lose it, with her, in bed—but learning why he'd developed the skill in the first place made her heart hurt. "It's okay to be angry," she ventured. "At her, I mean."

"I am. Believe me, I am. But I refuse to allow that anger control me. It's not productive." A self-mocking smile cracked the ice. "And if *that* statement doesn't prove your point, I don't know what would."

She gave a shrug. "The point I really wanted to make is that…you found the silver lining. You found the strength to turn childhood coping mechanisms into a lucrative profession." Setting her wine class next to the barely-touched cheese tray, she straddled him, resting her weight on his lap. Mmm, he was hard as a rock. "I can sense your anger sometimes," she admitted. "A few jagged edges, just beneath the surface."

"Really."

His rough voice burrowed into her. Letting the blanket fall, she looped her arms around his neck, careful to avoid his shoulder wound. "We all have those dark, jagged edges. If we're lucky, we find people who can live with our own particular variety." She recalled the conversation she'd overheard, Jonathan telling Jack that he and his wife talked, that they had a partnership. "Actually, your parents seem to have that part down."

"What do you mean?"

"He seems happy enough," she said with a shrug. "He clearly loves your mother, and probably has more awareness than you might think about why she behaves the way she does."

"God help him," Jack muttered against her lips.

"However dysfunctional their marriage might look from the outside, it seems to work for them." Even if it hadn't worked for their son. "Jack, protecting your dad isn't your job. Actually, for an absent-minded professor type, he seems to have a pretty good handle on things."

"Yeah, he does—but he still wants me to come back to the firm."

Her stomach churned. "I thought so."

"I'm not going to, of course. If Dad thinks asking me to check a few files and spreadsheets is enough to pull me back, he's sadly mistaken."

Jack talked a good game, but he was swimming in guilt. "If you've put returning to K&K behind you, why keep this house? Don't you think owning real estate within easy commuting distance to K&K gives your parents hope you might return someday?"

"Maybe," he allowed, shrugging, "but the house is also an excellent investment. Why sell when the rental market is so hot?"

"Can't argue with that." *Time to change the subject.* She stroked her cheek against his, letting the scrape of his stubble shrill into her. "Remember what I said earlier, about garlic breath being a turn-on? You smell, Jack." She paused. "You smell really, really good." He puffed a gust of breath into her face. She giggled, and huffed back. "What else do you need to do while we're here in California? Does our original plan to fly home the day after tomorrow still hold?"

"I'll need to take a quick trip back into the city tomorrow morning, but yeah—I should be able to finish up tomorrow, easy."

No wild bump of emotion. Whatever he was doing in the city tomorrow, it didn't sound as though he needed her company. "I'll stay here, then—confirm our return flight, then try to get some work done."

He stroked her cheek. "The wireless connection covers the deck."

"Good to hear." She and Jack could review the security plan for Dad's memorial service during the flight home. "I don't want to think about what my email in-box looks like," she muttered. "I swear, if you leave email unsupervised for too long, they pair off and mate, creating even more email."

"There's a visual I didn't need." Jack's gaze cruised her face, her upper body, her hips and legs. "I much prefer this one." He kissed her, a soft, gentle kiss that didn't stay that way very long. "Thanks for making this trip with me," he said against her mouth. "Having you along today really helped."

"Happy to do it." And she'd learned so much—about him, and about his family. "Know what else I'm happy to do?"

"What?"

Nipping his lower lip, she reached for his waistband.

"Sasha…"

Aah, the tension was back—the *good* kind of tension—but the hint of doubt he felt about whether she really wanted to do this had to go. "Sit back." She unbuttoned his khakis with a quick flick of the wrist. "Relax." As she unzipped his pants, she shifted off his lap, giving herself room to move. She spread the soft fabric apart, exposing his black cotton boxer-briefs and the erection they couldn't quite contain. Covering his hardness with her hand, she gave the head of his penis, peeking out from beneath the elastic waistband, a quick but thorough lick.

Breath hissed through his teeth.

"Mmm." His taste exploded on her tongue, salt and musk and man. "How can you doubt that I want this?" she whispered. "That I need it?"

Their gazes locked. The seconds hummed.

With a harsh groan, he shoved his pants and underwear down to his knees.

"Thank you," she breathed. To reward him, she swirled her tongue over his cock, from tip to base and back again. "Sit back and relax," she repeated, grasping him firmly in both hands. "You've had a long...hard...day, and I can do this all night long."

"Sasha..." His face was taut, lust battling with guilt and self-control.

Stop fighting yourself, damn it. She swallowed him down, taking him all the way to the back of her throat.

"Shit," he strangled out. After a pause, he flexed his hips, moving with small, testing thrusts.

Holding on, and finally surrendering to pleasure.

✳

"Yo. Dude."

Jack looked up. The surfer who'd approached him,

wet, shivering, and with a bloody scrape on his cheek, had clearly come up from the chilly water to check out the interloper who'd been watching the waves roll in at Mavericks. Even wearing a dry suit and flotation vest, the guy was *way* too scrawny to back up the attitude.

"Tourists usually sit up there," the guy said, pointing up at the rocky ridge overlooking the dark navy waves. "Not down here."

Jack stood, sighing. In his khakis, dress shirt, and jacket, he probably *did* look like a tourist. Had he and his friends been this annoying back in the day?

The guy backed up half a step, but darted a protective glance at all the gear other surfers on the water had ditched in the rocks. "Can I help you with something?"

"Nah, just watching the waves." *And thinking too much.* "Surf looks good today," he noted. The waves weren't big, but they were challenging. Sneaky.

The guy narrowed his eyes. "You surf?"

"Yeah."

"Here?"

"Yeah." On mellow days, anyway. "It's been awhile," he admitted. "I used to live nearby, but then I moved to the Midwest."

"Why the hell would you do that?"

"Work." Lukas's job offer had come at the perfect time, after he'd quit his job with K&K—and now, after a decade, he felt more at home with creatures of extra-planetary ancestry than he did with most humans. Hell, his lover was a succubus.

He'd missed Sasha during his day in the city, had thought about her while meeting with his rental property manager, and interrogating poor Glenda about his mother's health over lunch.

He missed her a lot more than he'd ever missed the woman he once thought he'd marry.

The guy yanked at the dry suit clinging to his crotch. The vulcanized rubber released with a soft sucking sound. "Ever compete at Titans?"

Titans of Mavericks, the big-wave surfing competition? Jack laughed. "Hell, no." Mavs might have been right in his backyard, but he'd never been good enough, or crazy enough, to surf on those rare days when the waves loomed so large, and broke so violently, that their crash registered on the Richter scale.

"Shit," the guy blurted. "Jonah just went down."

"Where?"

The surfer pointed to boiling white froth. A yellow and red board sliced into the air, fell back to the water, then danced solo on the waves.

Jack looked beyond the surfers bobbing in the line-up, assessing the incoming waves. "He has time." Time to surface, time to catch his breath, time to get clear of the next wave...if he was still conscious. The fight to the surface was a fight for survival, lungs on fire and ready to explode—and that was the *easy* scenario. He wouldn't wish a two-wave hold-down on his worst enemy.

Okay, maybe he'd wish one on the man who'd killed Elliott.

A Jet Ski towing a floating stretcher gunned toward the froth, ready to assist. "Come on, come on..." he muttered, scanning the water. The next wave was building, rising. "Hurry up, hurry up..." Off to the right, a dark head suddenly popped to the surface. "There he is," he said, pointing.

"Good eye."

The Jet Ski zoomed in. Pausing just long enough for Jonah to haul himself onto the stretcher, the driver gunned it.

And then they were clear.

"Yes!" The surfer offered his right hand for a fist bump, laughing when Jack was a little slow on the draw. "You *have* been gone for a long time."

"Yeah." He'd overworked his hand today.

"Well, welcome home, brah. Maybe we'll see you out there in the line-up soon."

"Maybe." *Liar.* "Take care."

The guy turned toward the rock-strewn path leading to the water, then disappeared, dry suit crackling.

Him, out there in the line-up? Nope, never again. Not even after he fully recovered—which, his aching body informed him as he sat back down, was probably weeks away. The painkillers he'd taken that morning had worn off hours ago.

He'd overdone it last night.

After that amazing blow job by the fire, he and Sasha had made love not once, not twice, but three times before tumbling into bed, exhausted. He'd gotten three hours of sleep, tops, and had woken up with every wound and body part screaming. Definitely worth it, but… Grimacing, he reached into his front pants pocket and pulled out the small Ziploc bag holding his meds. Ten painkillers, and…three pheromone intoxication tablets? Holding the clear plastic up to the dying light, he counted again. Yep. Only three pills, to last him through today, tonight, and tomorrow. "Way to go, genius." He should have thought about the rest of the trip yesterday, when he'd been popping the pills left and right.

Okay, time to think about rationing. He and Sasha had one more night here in California before flying back home to Minnesota tomorrow. His big, romantic plans for tonight involved steaks and vegetables on the grill, wine by the fire, and sex—and with sex on the agenda, he should probably take his pain level down a bit. Tomorrow, he and Sasha would spend hours cooped up together in an airborne aluminum tube. There would be no way to escape her pheromones.

Did he want to? He couldn't get last night out of his mind, the way Sasha had licked him like a lollypop, gobbling him down as if his dick was her favorite treat. No doubt about it, Sasha Sebastiani was the best lover he'd ever had, but...with all the pills he'd taken yesterday, there'd been moments when he felt like he'd been watching from a distance. Participating, rather than being fully engaged. Sure, he'd enjoyed the same mind-blowing physical sensations, and so had she. He'd enjoyed himself, but he'd never quite lost...control.

Control.

Ah, hell—Sasha was right. The minute she'd mentioned the personality traits he shared with his mother, he'd felt an unmistakable internal *click* of truth. Her follow-on observation, that he used his abilities for good instead of evil, was accurate, if overstated. During the time he'd worked at K&K, he and his mother had always butted heads, like two alpha rams trying to win at all costs. Even if the cost was their relationship.

Over lunch, Glenda had described his parents' last decade, the time he'd been gone, as 'relaxed' and 'fun'. For his part, he'd found the job of a lifetime in Minnesota. Severing ties had been the right call. Him quitting—him *leaving*—had been the best choice for everyone.

A white pelican swooped by, cawing. *Hell, even the bird agreed.*

But times, and plans, sometimes changed. His parents needed help—if not now, then eventually. He'd call his father tonight, and talk about next steps. It was time to re-engage, on terms they could all live with. One of his non-negotiable terms was that he'd do it long-distance, from Minnesota.

His parents were here, but his family was in Minneapolis.

Lukas had offered him so much more than a job: brotherhood, camaraderie, and a sense of belonging that had never been present in his own family. But...did that sense of brotherhood extend to his human business partner sleeping with his sister? Lukas *had* to know what was up—his sensory skills were unparalleled—but if it bothered him, he hadn't said anything.

Maybe Lukas was waiting for his bullet wounds to heal before inviting him down to the fighting cage.

And there he was, thinking like a human again. Sasha would call him out on his antiquated patriarchal bullshit, and rightfully so. The only reason he could see Lukas delivering an epic beat-down would be if Jack didn't treat his sister well.

Was he treating her well? Did he deserve to be in Sasha Sebastiani's bed? Right now, he felt like one of the few surfers left out in the line-up: paddling hard, racing the dark, racing the wave. Catching it, or not.

Success was a matter of effort, and luck.

Well, where Sasha was concerned, he didn't have to rely on luck or random chance, not when he had some tools to help even the odds. He eyed the pills again. Adnan had told him to not take both meds at the same time, but Adnan wasn't the one trying to keep his thoughts clear in such close proximity to the most lethal succubus on the planet.

This...this *thing* with Sasha was the wildest wave of his life, and he was hanging on by the skin of his teeth.

Out on the water, another surfer wiped out. After making sure the guy surfaced, Jack plucked a pain pill and a pheromone pill out of the bag, then popped them into his mouth.

The pills were survival tools—like a dry suit, or a flotation device.

And I need all the protection I can get.

✳

Snow crunched against Ethan's tires as he pulled out of Mystic Lake Casino and headed west. When he hit the county highway, he turned south, toward farm fields, rather than north toward the city lights of Shakopee. A glance in his rear-view mirror confirmed that the big Dodge Ram with the burned-out tail light was following him.

Desperate times called for desperate measures, but he wasn't desperate enough to make a drug buy in a parking lot crawling with cameras—not when there were so many remote gravel roads nearby. Sure, a remote location meant more physical risk, but he had a gun and he knew how to use it.

He'd learned the hard way that most of these guys carried.

He grabbed the can of Coke from the console cup holder and took a sip, savoring the whiskey's smooth, smoky kick. It was stupid to add drinking and driving to his lengthy list of sins, but he'd run out of Vicodin two days ago. If he didn't take the edge off, and fast, people could get hurt.

God, he needed to fight, to find some way to burn off the excess energy jittering through his system. The suburban gym he couldn't afford just wasn't cutting it anymore.

But today was payday. Today, he could buy more pills.

Just ahead was a side road, freshly plowed. He slowed, scanning the surroundings. The area was rural-residential, with a couple of houses on acreage, all set back from the unlit road.

No lights on in the houses. Perfect.

When he turned, the Ram followed. The guy had dropped back a little bit—probably making sure Ethan didn't have a partner waiting at the end of the road to jump him—which was smart. He'd been concerned about the same thing, which was why the dealer was following him instead of the other way around. He had the money, and money talked.

The road dead-ended in half a mile. He made a U-turn, positioning himself for a quick exit. As the Ram pulled up parallel, Ethan turned his headlights off but left the truck idling. He grabbed his weapon from the glove box, checked it, then slipped it into his jacket pocket.

The guy's headlights went dark. He, too, left his truck running. They both left their drivers' doors open, dome lights on, as they met on the road between the idling trucks.

"Hey," the guy said.

"Hey." The dude was about his size, wearing a navy blue down jacket, jeans tucked into Sorel boots, and a blue knit Timberwolves cap. One silver hoop earring, no facial hair, no tattoos that he could see… They were both so bundled up, he couldn't tell if the guy was carrying—but the pock-like scabs on his face screamed "meth."

"It's colder than the proverbial witch's tit out here," the guy muttered. He darted a wary glance toward the county highway, then scanned acres of snow-covered farm fields. "Are we going to do business here, or what?"

"Yeah." Their breath, their words, billowed ghostly white between them. Ethan handed him some folded bills. "You have what I want?"

The guy counted the money with quick flicks of his fingers. Nodded. He reached into his jacket pocket, then handed him a small plastic zip bag.

Holding it up to the light, Ethan made a quick count. *Ten pills short.* Anger surged, but he throttled it back. "The count is light."

"Is it?"

"Yes. Ten pills short."

"What are you going to do, call the police?"

Ethan stared at him. *I could snap this fucker's neck like a goddamn toothpick.* This guy had no fucking clue who—*what*—he was dealing with.

Under his jacket, his muscles twitched.

Control yourself. The last thing you need is to get hauled before the Council for killing a human.

He could do it, though. Kill him. Kill him, in so many ways…

The guy took a hasty half-step back.

Smart choice, asshole. "So, here's how this is gonna go down." Reaching into his jacket pocket, he pulled the gun. "You're either going to give me the pills I paid for, or give me my money back. Your choice."

"Sure, sure," the guy said, backing away. "I don't want no trouble."

Then why did you start it?

"I have more product in my truck. Let me correct your order."

"Hands where I can see them." No doubt the guy had a gun in his truck, too.

The man moved slowly and deliberately, a sign he'd discovered some self-preservation instincts. When he returned, he held two small plastic bags. One contained his familiar-looking pills. The other held a trio of small white rocks, surrounded by crystalline flakes that glittered in the light.

Meth. His brain lit up like a Christmas tree.

"On me," the dealer said. His cagey smile exposed a missing incisor. "An apology for the earlier trouble."

And a clever way to expand his customer base. It was tempting, so damn tempting, but… "No, thanks." He took the bag he'd paid for, leaving the other one dangling from the dealer's fingers.

The guy looked surprised, gesturing back toward his truck. "Can I interest you in anything else? Pills, rock, needles?"

The Ram was a goddamn rolling pharmacy. "Not tonight." It took monumental will to turn away, to turn toward his own vehicle.

"Well, you know how to contact me." The dealer gave a half-assed shrug. "No bullshit with the count from now on."

With a curt nod, Ethan returned to his truck, not taking the time to kick the snow off his boots before climbing in, closing the door, and driving away. When he reached the county highway, he turned north, back toward the city.

The Ram followed.

He hit the gas, putting some space between their vehicles, then reached for the can of Jack and Coke.

Suddenly, red and blue lights lit up the night behind him. "Shit." He checked the speedometer—he was driving just over the posted speed limit—then glanced in the rear-view mirror again. Behind the Ram, the squad car's lights bounced off the snow like spotlights at a rave.

"Shit, shit, shit." With booze, drugs, and a gun in the vehicle, he wouldn't get out of this with just a speeding ticket. He couldn't risk being booked into a human jail. The road ahead was flat and straight, but he'd have to chance it.

He opened the passenger window. As cold air filled the cab, he jettisoned the gun, the Coke can, and the plastic bag holding the pills. The gun and the pop can were heavy enough to land in the snow bank at the side of the road, but the plastic bag sailed backward, snatched by the wind.

Gone.

He checked the rear-view again. The Ram was pulling over, slowing to a stop. The squad car pulled in behind the truck. He hadn't been the cop's target after all...and now his drugs were gone. "Fuck!" His fist lashed out, cracking the in-dash display screen. He hit it again.

The screen flickered, faltered, then went dark.

Because of course.

"Fuuuuuck!" he roared, punching the dead thing again.

And again. And again.

When he jerked his attention back to the road, his knuckles were a bloody mess, but the jittery overload was gone. So, unfortunately, was most of his dash.

Two squad cars were screaming toward him, lights and sirens blaring. Backup for the drug bust, no doubt. He slowed and pulled to the side of the road, giving the squads ample room to pass. If there was honor among thieves, the guy wouldn't give the cops a description of his last customer.

Maybe, after the police left, he could go back. Search for the pills.

White pills against white snow? Good fucking luck.

I might be able to find the bag...

No fucking way.

He glanced in the rear-view mirror again. Okay, the pills were a total loss, but he might be able to find the gun in the snow bank... Nope. Too risky, and he had other weapons at home. He also had booze at home—no pills, and very little money, but plenty of booze. Enough to last until next payday if he was careful.

Maybe.

Speaking of paydays... He took the burner phone out of his inside jacket pocket. Looked at the screen. Nothing.

Nothing.

"God*damn* it!" He threw the phone at the ruined dash. It ricocheted, hitting the passenger door before clattering to the floor. "Damn it," he whispered, looking at his shaking hands as if they belonged to someone else.

When had he become a guy who'd crawl in the middle of a road, looking for spilled pills? Who'd threaten a drug dealer with a gun?

Someone who'd kill for money? Not just once, but twice?

"God, I need a drink." Hitting his blinker, he pulled back onto the road and headed for home.

CHAPTER ELEVEN

The Underworld Council's conferencing software took up every inch of his monitor's real estate. Jack clicked, dragged, and resized, trying to arrange documents, instant message conversations, and multiple video feeds into something usable.

Trying, and failing. "I need a bigger screen," he grumbled. He *had* one, at Sebastiani Security just down the street, but between the fresh snow, residual tiredness, and jet lag, he'd opted to dial into the Sunday night Council meeting from home.

So had almost everyone else. Only Alka, Lorin, and Willem Lund were physically present in Sebastiani Labs' boardroom. Bailey was still debugging a problem with the conferencing software's holographic view, so tonight, video feeds jostled for space along with everything else. Lukas, Scarlett, and Bailey had dialed in from Sebastiani Security's corner conference room, with Coco cradled in Scarlett's arms. Valerian and Wyland attended from their home overlooking the St. Croix River, on the Minnesota-Wisconsin border. Krispin and Jacoby Woolf, the WerePack Alpha and Beta, had each dialed in from their own home offices. Though the meeting software had positioned their video feeds side by side, the individual boxes emphasized the emerging divide between father and son. Antonia was sitting at Claudette's exquisite Louis XVI writing desk, alone. Apparently Claudette was sleeping, and Antonia hadn't had the heart to wake her.

Shame sneaked up on him. He hadn't talked to Claudette since Elliott died. He hadn't called, he hadn't stopped by the penthouse to offer his condolences... He hadn't apologized for letting her bondmate die.

Rubbing his stinging stomach, he scrawled "Contact Claudette" on a small sticky note, then considered the four-quadrant prioritizing grid he'd drawn on a legal pad. As the meeting progressed, he'd write tasks and action items on sticky notes, then place each sticky note on the grid based on a quick assessment of the task's importance vs. its urgency. The old school prioritizing approach was visual and tactile, and helped him keep a handle on his workload. After the meeting was over, he'd focus first on the tasks collected in the upper left quadrant of the grid, those he'd deemed both important and urgent, then work his way to the tasks in other grids as time allowed.

That was the theory, at any rate. Time never allowed.

He glanced over to the wall, to a large whiteboard festooned with hundreds of sticky notes. Sadly, any task he designated as Not Important/Not Urgent ended up there, in an action item graveyard, gone but not forgotten. Every now and then, he made himself look at the colorful sticky notes, fluttering like a Tibetan prayer flag. There were so many potential projects, so many ideas worth exploring, if only someone had the bandwidth.

He placed "Contact Claudette" in the Important/Urgent quadrant. He'd talk to Claudette tomorrow, right after his appointment with Adnan.

Casual chatter ceased the minute Krispin Woolf dialed in. Silence hung like a storm cloud. Fingers flew across keyboards as people continued their conversations online—or maybe, like him, they were just trying to get a little more work done before the meeting started. Jack looked at another yellow legal pad, scrawled with notes he'd taken on the plane earlier that day. He and Sasha had been home for about two hours. He'd returned a few phone calls, make a decent dent in his email backlog…anything to avoid thinking about the argument he and Sasha had gotten into as soon as the plane was airborne. He'd taken some pills. She noticed, and asked if he was in pain. "That looked like double your regular dose."

"What are you, my mother?" he'd snapped.

A black brow arched. "Your mother is one of a kind, thank the universe."

"These aren't pain pills," he'd responded. "They're pheromone intoxication meds."

She'd stared at him.

"Sasha, you can't begrudge me some protection."

"Protection from me, right?" She hadn't said another word, but her expression spoke volumes. As soon as the pilot turned off the seat belt sign, she'd walked to the tiny bedroom, closed the door, and stayed there until the flight crew announced their approach to Minneapolis.

She seemed to be back on an even keel by the time they'd landed, and they'd driven home without incident. Right now, she was in the kitchen, laughing as she talked to someone on the phone, but…he'd remember that disappointed look on her face for a long time to come.

"Okay, everyone, let's get going," Lukas said.

Willem started the recording, took roll call, then highlighted the first agenda item: sentencing Wyatt Cooper, the true perpetrator of the hack for which Bailey had been found guilty over a decade ago. Though Cooper was being sentenced for new crimes—attempting to hack Sebastiani Labs, and stalking Bailey, both using human accomplices—Jack was glad the fucker was finally going down. Learning Bailey's long-ago lover was an incubus and not human had been a nasty surprise, one that had nearly derailed Bailey and Rafe's fledgling relationship. On the positive side, Cooper being an incubus meant the Council had jurisdiction over his sentencing and punishment.

Wyland's recommendation flashed onto the screen: three guilty verdicts, one not-guilty verdict, fifteen years' incarceration and rehabilitation. Wyland explained his reasoning, citing specifics of Underworld law.

"I'm disappointed the cultural exposure charge isn't going to stick," Lukas muttered.

Jack shared Lukas's frustration, but agreed with Wyland's conclusion. Exhaustive forensic analysis, and hours of interviews with Cooper's human accomplice, a hacker named Owen Przybylski—aka SkoolHausRok—hadn't produced any evidence that Wyatt Cooper revealed their culture's existence to humanity. However, during his interview, Przybylski said he suspected Cooper was working for, or with, someone else. Cooper hadn't confirmed or denied this, even to reduce his sentence.

The investigative dead-end concerned him.

"We have no jurisdiction over Mr. Cooper's human accomplice," Wyland reminded them. "Mr. Przybylski provided valuable information during multiple interviews. After questioning, he was glamoured, then released."

With his memories selectively wiped, Przybylski would have no recollection of Wyatt Cooper, their work together, or having been questioned by a vampire lawyer.

"Any comments or feedback?" Lukas asked.

There was silence.

"Council members, it's time to vote," Willem said. "Please vote yes if you agree with the sentencing recommendation. Vote no if you disagree."

Jack clicked "Yes." So did everyone else—except for Wyland, who abstained.

"The sentencing recommendation is accepted," Lukas said.

And with that, the new Underworld Council president made his first official pronouncement. Lukas might be wearing jeans, a T-shirt, and steel-toed work boots instead of a suit, but his words rang with power and confidence.

Next, a review of ongoing projects. Bailey gave a short, pithy status report on her efforts to crack the encryption on the unusual tech unit Lorin had discovered several summers ago, at the northern Minnesota archaeological dig where their ancestors' spaceship had crashed. Buried in a box for almost three thousand years along with other artifacts they theorized belonged to the crew, the gadget looked utterly modern, and its red light still glowed. Though Bailey had figured out how to access its storage plane, she was still trying to make heads or tails of the thing.

Lorin grimly reported that there was still no sign of Paige Scott, the grad student who'd disappeared from the archaeological dig that summer.

Lips tight, Jack made a note to call Gideon Lupinsky. Just last year, Wyland's bondmate, investigative journalist Tia Quinn, had written a painful series about sex trafficking in the upper Midwest. If their police commander hadn't talked to Tia yet, it was worth following up.

Important/Urgent.

Wyland updated them on the archiving project, a multi-year effort to digitize the books and documents in their voluminous archives. Antonia was assisting him, freeing Bailey up to work on the tech unit.

"I have a question," Krispin said.

Of course you do. Jack couldn't remember the last time he'd attended an Underworld Council meeting where Krispin Woolf hadn't managed to pull them seriously off-topic. He glanced at the agenda. Crap. With discussions of old business over, new business was up next.

The cagey bastard had gotten better at choosing his moment.

"With Elliott's unfortunate death, the incubus/succubus succession plan requires an update," Krispin said. "What is the status of that work?"

Though it killed him to admit it, it was a very good question. With Lukas now the Incubus First, and Antonia the Second, was Rafe still the family's 'spare', waiting in the wings? God knew Sasha was more than capable of filling the position, but over the years, she'd made her lack of interest in Council matters very clear.

"Updates to the incubus/succubus succession plan require additional legal research," Wyland said. "That work is underway."

Lukas and Bailey exchanged a quick glance, one he hoped Krispin Woolf hadn't noticed. He opened up a private chat.

[JKirkland]: Mind your facial expression. You're on video. What's up?

It took several seconds for Bailey to respond.

[BBrown]:   Lukas wants me to take Rafe's place in the incubus/succubus line of succession

Holy crap. No wonder Wyland needed to perform additional legal research.

The idea was a complete curve ball, but…it made a strange sort of sense. Bailey, a human who'd received rare authorization to learn of the Council's existence as part of her critical work responsibilities, attended every Underworld Council meeting as Lukas's technology subject matter expert, so she was familiar with how the Council worked. As Rafe Sebastiani's bondmate, she'd married into the family business, as it were. During a recent hospitalization, Bailey's doctors had discovered she had a smidge of succubus heritage, which might satisfy Krispin Woolf, a species purist. Bailey wasn't likely to ever ascend to the top spot, but formally naming her to the line of succession meant Krispin Woolf would never again be able to challenge her right to sit at the table. It also let both Rafe and Sasha off the hook.

It was an idea without precedent. He appreciated

Wyland's caution. No doubt Lukas and Bailey had already discussed the idea at length.

[JKirkland]: Are you going to accept?

[BBrown]: I'm seriously considering it

[JKirkland]: Good. The idea has merit

[BBrown]: Yep

He might have recommended Bailey for the Sebastiani Security job in the first place, but she'd become indispensable on her own—

"Mr. Kirkland?" Willem's voice.

What had he missed?

[BBrown]: How's your health?

"I'm still a little sore, but recovering well, thanks." Lifting his right arm into video camera range, he flexed a slow fist. "I'll be returning to the office full time tomorrow."

"You apparently felt frisky enough to take a quick trip out to California," Krispin noted. "I'm surprised you wouldn't consider the search for Elliott's killer your top priority."

Fucker. "An urgent family issue arose."

"A romantic getaway with Sasha Sebastiani is an urgent family issue?" Krispin's eyes lit with malice. "I didn't realize things had gotten so serious between the two of you."

"Krispin, you're out of line." Lukas's voice was hard as stone. "Jack's personal relationships are his business, not yours. Not ours."

Well, that answered that.

"It's entirely our business if his relationship impacts his judgment," Krispin argued. "Look at him! He's distracted, and his focus is crap, but I guess I can understand why." Krispin's smile was slimy at the edges. "She's nearby, isn't she?"

Rage sluiced through him, a sudden, violent storm. "That's enough."

Krispin gave a knowing laugh. "With a succubus lover, there's no such thing as enough, is there?"

He shoved to his feet. "Would you care to repeat that?"

"What are you going to do, punch the air?"

Lukas rose more slowly, his massive frame looming.

In their separate video boxes, everyone snapped to attention.

"Mr. Woolf, you are out of order," Willem informed him. "I will mute your line if you persist."

Coco let out a piercing wail.

Scarlett cradled her daughter more closely, dropping a kiss on her forehead. "You're upsetting the baby."

"Why is there a baby at a Council meeting in the first place?" Krispin threw his hands up. "This isn't a goddamn daycare—"

Blip.

Willem had muted him. In his video box, Krispin's lips moved soundlessly.

Priceless.

But Coco's wail was like a teapot on the boil, high, loud, and sustained. Sound and emotion were dual blades, slicing everyone within earshot. Sitting in the same room as Coco, Bailey clapped her hands over her ears, casting a worried glance at the windows.

They'd hold. The bulletproof windows were more than a match for a shrieking siren infant. But little Coco Annika Fontaine was *very* annoyed, and everyone in earshot knew it.

"Mr. Sebastiani, I'm going to mute your line for a moment," Willem said.

Lukas nodded. "Give us a minute."

A minute? Good luck with that. Jack sat back down.

But Lukas was as good as his word. Little more than a minute had passed when an expression of blissed-out calm crept onto Bailey's face. Her hands dropped from her ears back to her keyboard.

[BBrown]: I know Scarlett isn't performing any more, but she could make a mint selling lullabies to calm pissed-off babies

[JKirkland]: Pissed-off people, period

He reached for a sticky note. Beyond babies, the concept had considerable promise as a crowd control approach. Hell, he'd seen the effect himself, when siren customers sang along to music Sasha played at Underbelly. He scribbled a note, then placed it in the lower left quadrant. Not Important/Not Urgent, and not his to pursue—but if Bailey didn't mention the idea to Scarlett, he would.

When Willem un-muted the Sebastiani Security conference room, Scarlett's calming hum saturated the line, washing the tension away. He could almost feel warm Caribbean beach sand under his feet, and cool waves lapping at his toes. A quick look around the virtual room confirmed that every meeting attendee had been transported to a happy place—even Krispin Woolf.

Well, that's interesting. He moved the sticky note to Important/Urgent.

Krispin's lips were moving, but they couldn't hear him speak. *We need to have Council meetings via conference call a lot more often.*

Lorin took advantage of the lull. "Krispin, making comments about other people's sex lives at Council meetings is getting to be a habit with you," she noted. "Over the years, you've made comments about Lukas and Scarlett, then Gabe and me, then Bailey and Rafe, then Wyland and Tia, and now Jack and Sasha. What's up with that?"

In his video box, Krispin's lips moved in blessed silence.

"Maybe he likes to watch," Antonia suggested. "Not that there's anything wrong with that, if everyone's on the same page…"

In his tight little box, Krispin was shouting, leaning in toward the video camera, and typing furiously. Words appeared in the meeting software's shared communication space:

[KWoolf:] Unmute me

Willem was studiously taking notes, not paying Krispin the least bit of attention.

[KWoolf:] UNMUTE ME

[KWoolf:] I SAID UNMUTE ME

Krispin's mouth started rippling, a precursor to a shift. A second later, his video box went gray.

He'd hung up.

"The WerePack Alpha has left the meeting," Willem stated.

"Good riddance," Antonia muttered. "Shit. I'm sorry, Jacoby."

Jacoby, the WerePack Beta, looked absolutely mortified. "I'd like to apologize for my father's behavior."

"I appreciate that, Jacoby," Lukas said, "but any apology is his to make." And they all knew better than to expect one.

Something really had to be done about Krispin Woolf. Jack had five follow-up meetings to schedule because no one trusted Krispin enough to discuss certain topics in his presence. He wrote another sticky note—have a lawyer-to-lawyer conversation with Wyland about the WerePack succession plan—and slapped it in the Important/Urgent quadrant.

What would the downstream impact be if Krispin was impeached? *Could* he be impeached? Could Jacoby ascend to the Alpha's seat if Krispin was still alive? Could Jacoby be challenged for the position? Krispin's own ascension to the Council had been bloody, a literal fight to the death. His face still bore the scars of that battle, scars he displayed proudly.

"Shall we finish up the agenda?" Willem suggested. "Mr. Sebastiani has another commitment at the top of the hour."

At 8:00 p.m.? Guilt trickled through him.

The last agenda item was a status report on the investigation into Elliott's death. There was silence, a weighty pause.

Jacoby noticed. "May I clear the air?"

Willem glanced at Lukas, who nodded. "Mr. Woolf

has the floor."

"I realize my father, and perhaps I, have to be considered possible suspects in Elliott's death." Jacoby spread his hands. "Ask me anything. I'm at your disposal. I'll gladly submit to questioning under vampire glamour. I'll assist with obtaining any information you require—" Jacoby took a deep breath "—even if that information implicates my father."

The fissure between father and son, long suspected, was now confirmed. Jacoby had just stated, for the record, that he'd ally with the Council, against his father, if required.

"That said," Jacoby continued, "I honestly don't think my father is responsible for Elliott's death. Dad obviously resented the fact that Elliott defeated him in the last presidential election, but…" Jacoby's gaze met Jack's. "If Dad wanted you dead, you'd see him coming."

Jacoby was right; subtlety wasn't Krispin Woof's style. But if not Krispin, who?

Lukas provided a status report on the investigation—ballistics, trace evidence, forensic video analysis—relaying the facts with bullet-point precision. "Bottom line, we're coming up empty," he said, looking grim. "It's time to broaden the search. Jacoby, I thank you for your very generous offer. If you could contact Commander Lupinsky—?"

"First thing tomorrow morning," Jacoby stated, nodding. "I'm happy to help."

[BBrown]: At least now we know Jacoby puts Council and culture above species.

[JKirkland]: I don't know that his father would make

the same choice.

And actions spoke louder than words. He grabbed another sticky note. "Jacoby - personal security." Important/Urgent. Krispin would find out about Jacoby's offer sooner or later, and when he did, he would *not* be happy.

Unhappy enough to try to eliminate the problem? Parent or not, Jack couldn't rule it out.

Parents. "I'd like to add a peripheral piece of information, if I may." He explained the nature of his trip to California, adding that his mother knew who Elliott was, but that she hadn't yet heard about his death. "The news isn't spreading. People are keeping their mouths shut."

"They'd damn well better," Lukas muttered. "Alka, have any Sebastiani Labs customers inquired about Dad?"

"Not yet." Alka looked tired. Trying to fill Elliott Sebastiani's large Italian loafers would do that to a person. "But it's just a matter of time until the human media discovers the news."

"Once that happens, we'll publish the news release Wyland's working on."

Wyland's news release would no doubt state that Elliott died of natural causes, perhaps from an unexpected stroke or heart attack. The real cause of death, a fatal gunshot wound, would generate too much attention.

"That ends the agenda," Willem said. "Is there anything else to discuss before we end the meeting?"

Scarlett looked at Lukas. "The memorial service…?"

"Yes, thanks," Lukas said. "The service will be

held at Underbelly, on New Year's Eve. You'll receive a formal invitation, but Claudette wanted to give everyone a heads up."

After a silent few seconds, Willem ended the meeting. People said goodbye, and video screens went dark as people logged out.

[LSebastiani]: Watch your six

It was a grim, but valid, reminder. Krispin was an obvious suspect, and they'd either clear the man or charge him. But Krispin hadn't killed Elliott, or shot at him and Sasha, who had?

[JKirkland]:   Will do. Sasha's, too.

[LSebastiani]:   So I understand

How should he respond to Lukas's wry comment? He wouldn't. His relationship with Sasha wasn't a topic he wanted to discuss over instant message.

[JKirkland]:   Another meeting at the top of the hour?

[LSebastiani]: With my daughter. I'm giving Coco a bath.

[JKirkland]: I'll let you go then. FYI, I'm officially coming back to work full-time tomorrow. I have an early appointment with Adnan, but I should be at my desk by noon at the latest.

[LSebastiani]: Good. I have a proposal I'd like to discuss with you.

He looked at the chat he'd had with Bailey earlier.

Yeah, her role change was a subject better discussed in person.

[JKirkland]:   *K*

[LSebastiani]: Good night, and say 'welcome home' to your… roomie

Punctuation could be amazingly expressive. Damn it, maybe Lukas wasn't as nonchalant about his relationship with Sasha as he'd thought.

[JKirkland]: Good night

He logged off, assessing the colorful sticky notes littering his grid before nudging the legal pad aside. Tomorrow was soon enough to sort them out. The sun had gone down hours ago, and his stomach was growling like a cement mixer. He wanted to clear the air with Sasha, to apologize about what had happened earlier, on the plane… Was that pizza?

Yes, that heavenly scent wafting into his office was sausage and onion pizza, his favorite. He also smelled Canadian bacon and pineapple.

A half-and-half pizza, with both of their favorites. As olive branches went, it was pretty damn good.

Who was he kidding? It was perfect.

✳

When Jack came out of his office, Sasha almost laughed. The expression on his face! He looked like he was having an orgasm. "Great timing," she said, setting the pizza box on the kitchen island.

"Bless you," he muttered, flipping the top off the box. "I'm absolutely starving." He grabbed a slice and took a bite, not waiting for the plates she'd turned to retrieve.

Starving, yes, and also in pain—but after the debacle on the Gulfstream earlier that morning, she wasn't going to ask him about it. "Sit down. Eat up." Setting the plates on the island side by side, she filled water glasses, grabbed the roll of paper towels, then climbed onto a stool.

She reached for a slice, bit in, and almost had an orgasm of her own. Thin crust, spicy tomato sauce, hearty Canadian bacon, sweet, juicy pineapple...the combination was ambrosial. After a *very* long day, almost all of it spent working, it really hit the spot.

She'd spent the entire flight home catching up on email and phone calls, but even more work had been waiting for her once the plane landed. She'd called Flynn, checked in with the coffee shop, and then had spoken with Claudette, who'd assured her she was 'fine.' After calling Antonia to confirm—yes, Claudette was tired, but otherwise seemed to be managing—she'd grabbed some earbuds, then curled up on Jack's leather couch while he attended a Council meeting in his office.

She should never have volunteered to choose the music for her father's memorial service. How the hell could anyone encapsulate someone's life with three stingy songs? It was an impossible task, one she'd found too painful to stick with. Eavesdropping on Jack's meeting had been far more entertaining.

"Does Krispin Woolf always act like such a shitwit

at Underworld Council meetings?"

Jack coughed, his body lurching. His slice of pizza fell to the kitchen island.

She leaped to her feet, hovering.

"I'm okay," he wheezed, bent double.

If he could speak, he could breathe, but she didn't budge an inch.

He clapped a hand to his chest, wincing as he coughed a few more times. Finally, he straightened up, clearing his throat. "Damn, that hurts."

His gunshot wounds. "I'm so sorry…"

"No worries." He picked up his glass of water, draining it. "Sit down. Please."

She obeyed, watching as he went to the refrigerator water dispenser and re-filled his glass. He sat again, picking up his fallen pizza. The stool squeaked slightly, protesting his weight.

"How much of the meeting did you overhear?" he asked.

"Most of it." Including Krispin's comments about the nature of their trip to California, and Jack's reaction, which probably explained the interesting red stain climbing his neck. "If you're worried about confidentiality, don't be. I grew up with Council matters—budgets, security, sentencing—discussed at the dinner table. Everyone in my family is either on the Council, or able to step in." She might not have an official role in the succession—and thanks to the plan Lukas had asked her about earlier, that happy state would continue—but she took pride in the fact that she could step in if she had to, and do a damn good job.

"I'm not worried about confidentiality," Jack said. "I'm just sorry you had to overhear Krispin being such an asshole."

"No skin off my nose." She was used to people speculating about her sex life, but did Jack realize how often people speculated about *his*?

"Has Lukas spoken to you about his idea for changes to the incubus/succubus line of succession?"

"Yes." She eyed the pizza box, then grabbed another slice. "Bailey has my full support."

Jack tore a paper towel off the roll, then wiped his mouth. "When did you speak with Lukas?"

"During the flight home, while I was sulking in the Gulfstream's bedroom." She'd spoken to Wyland, as well. Lukas had insisted. "I think it's a great idea, but as Wyland said, there's some research to do first." Damn it, it had to be done. "I'm sorry I was such a bitch on the plane earlier today," she said. "About your meds, I mean."

"You weren't a bitch. You were...concerned."

"I was a bitch, *and* I was concerned."

"If you insist."

His deadpan response, his complete lack of a denial, reassured her that at least *some* things hadn't changed. They could still joke and tease.

"Seriously, though—I'm sorry, too. I completely over-reacted to your question." He looked at his plate, then back to her. "I'm still trying to figure out why."

Wake up and smell the mother issues, dude. But she held her tongue. Jack had to work that one out for himself. "Well, it looks like we both have some thinking to do, because I'm usually not a flouncer."

"Really?" One corner of his mouth quirked up. "Because as flounces go, yours was world-class."

The smile, in the middle of apologies, made her go

all soft and gooey inside. *Keep it light...* "Thank you. I try." She sketched a mocking bow. "Come on, let's eat our pizza while it's still warm."

They chatted while they finished the pizza—about work, about plans for the memorial service, about their serious need for groceries. "I can swing by the grocery store on my way home from work tomorrow and pick up a few things," she offered.

Silence from Jack.

"Or not," she tacked on. Her offer only made sense if she'd still be staying here, with him. Sure, Jack was recovering nicely, but... "Am I overstaying my welcome?"

"No," he said quickly. "No, that's not the issue."

What is? His emotions were like a piñata, swinging all over the place.

"Did you hear what Lukas said at the end of the meeting, about us still being in danger?"

"Yeah."

"Until we know who killed your father—who shot at us—we need to take additional security precautions. I think solo grocery shopping is too risky."

"Seriously? Come on, do you really think we're in danger? Dad was clearly the killer's target."

Another wild emotional swing. "And I didn't protect him."

Oh, my. His self-recrimination was absolutely suffocating. "Jack, no one blames you." She touched his forearm. "Dad's death wasn't your fault."

He sat upright on the stool. "I'll ask Chico to coordinate a grocery delivery when I go back to work tomorrow."

"Oh, don't bother Chico—"

"I'll be talking with him anyway, about our security plan."

"We have a security plan?"

"Yes."

She'd been involved with Sebastiani Security operations often enough to realize that it made more sense, resource-wise, if she stayed here, with Jack.

Whether he wanted her here or not.

"Just jot down the groceries you want, and I'll pass the list along." He crumpled the paper towel, then dropped it on his now-empty plate. "I'm going back to work tomorrow. Full-time, I mean."

She nodded—an acknowledgment she'd heard him, not that she agreed. Jack had made it perfectly clear he didn't appreciate her input on how he managed his health.

"What are your plans for tomorrow?" he asked.

So he could tell the security team, of course. "I'll be at the Sebastiani Building all day long. I'm seeing Claudette in the morning, and then I'll be bouncing back and forth between Underbelly and Crackhouse for the rest of the day."

"Any evening plans?"

"I'll be at the club for a while." Flynn was scheduled to work the floor, but she'd…find something to do. Numb, she rose to her feet. "Is that all?"

"What's wrong?"

"I'm tired, that's all." *And I'm about to cry, damn it.* She tossed her napkin onto her plate. "I'm going to bed."

He reached for her. "Sasha—"

She turned away as the first tear spilled. "Good night," she choked out, heading to the guest bedroom. Jack was an adult who lived by himself. He was perfectly capable of cleaning up the mess in the kitchen.

Closing the bedroom door, she threw herself on the bed and had a good, therapeutic cry, one that cleansed away most of her anger but left sadness in its wake. "Damn it," she whispered, swiping tears from her face. "He warned me." He'd flat-out told her didn't want to feel dragged around by his dick. How could she blame him for taking a metric buttload of pheromone intoxication meds, even if it hurt her feelings? He was fulfilling his end of their bargain— that they have a casual, mutually-satisfying sexual relationship.

A band around her heart cranked tight. She couldn't blame him because her feelings were changing.

But one thing she *could* blame him for? Putting her duffel bag in his bedroom rather than the guest bedroom when they'd come home. Now, she'd have to leave the guest room to retrieve it.

Way to ruin a good flounce.

She rolled off the bed with a disgusted sigh. Retrieving it would give her a perfect opportunity to apologize, again. To try to smooth things out. To tell him she wanted to share his bed, share his life, on their original terms.

She'd manage any messy, emotional clean-up privately, after he'd moved on.

She paused at the door, hand on the knob. "Okay. I can do this." She took a fortifying breath. Opened the door.

And almost tripped on the duffel bag Jack had set on the floor.

✴

"So, Miranda." The man she'd met for a networking drink, a marketing executive for a Fortune Fifty company located in Minneapolis, set a heavy hand on her knee. "Want to get out of here?"

"No, thanks." She moved his hand. "Now, about the position we were discussing...?"

The trendy brewpub, with its corrugated steel walls and sky-high ceilings, was far too noisy to have a serious business discussion—something Bryce had probably known when he suggested the place—but the position he'd dangled was the most promising job lead she'd had in weeks. She leaned closer; it couldn't be helped. "About the executive position..."

But Bryce was talking about the Tesla he'd just ordered. "I won't take delivery for a couple of months yet, but..."

She let him blather on. What a waste of time.

"So, Miranda." Moist beer breath gusted against her cheek. He'd just finished his second flight. "There's a hotel right around the corner." The hand again, this time on her upper thigh.

She pushed it away. "Bryce, I'm only interested in business."

"How about...monkey business?"

"No."

The bearded bartender, who'd mixed her the best dirty martini she'd ever tasted, sidled closer. He cocked a questioning brow.

"I'm okay, thanks," she mouthed. In her purse,

one of her cell phones vibrated. "I have to get this," she told Bryce, turning away from him.

It was Ethan, of course. He'd called her five times during the last twenty-four hours, not that she'd answered. *She* called *him*, not the other way around. That was their arrangement.

What the hell did he want? Money, probably. She glanced back at Bryce and sighed. *Don't we all?* She hung up without answering.

"Go ahead and take that if you have to," he slurred.

As if I need your permission, asshole. "It's just my roommate." She dropped the phone back into her purse. "Now, to get back to the position we were discussing…" His hand crept under the hem of her skirt. "Stop. Touching. Me," she snarled, shoving it away.

The big bartender moved even closer, so only the width of the bar separated him from Bryce. He didn't say a word.

Bryce backed off.

Sipping her martini, she considered her next move. She wasn't about to let anyone feel her up so she could get a job interview, but she couldn't afford to burn bridges, either. "Bryce, how about we meet at your office next week to discuss this further?" It killed her to be polite to this jackhole, but if she didn't end this meeting now, she'd dump what was left of her drink in his overheated lap.

Her phone rang again.

Bryce licked his lips. "Maybe your roommate wants to join us."

Okay, we're done here. She looked him up and down, as if assessing his gym-toned body, designer suit, and two-hundred-dollar haircut. "Hmm. You *are* just his type. Let me—"

"Um." Bryce quickly slid off the bar stool. "Yeah, um, why don't you call my admin so we can discuss the job opening?" He downed what was left of his last beer. "I'll ask her to fit you in sometime."

Sometime meaning *never.* "Sure thing, Bryce."

Bryce was too buzzed to notice her sarcasm. He beat a hasty retreat, leaving her to pay the tab.

"Nicely played," the bartender said, his brown eyes dancing.

"Thank you." She drained her drink. "What a flaming asshole." And what an epic waste of time. But on the positive side, she'd leave with a receipt for the bar tab, evidence of a networking meeting for Mr. Banner. And as long as she was here... "I'd like another, please. The dirtiest martini you can possibly imagine."

The bartender grinned. "Coming right up."

When the phone vibrated again, she ignored it.

Ethan was becoming a liability, one she couldn't afford.

Well, every executive knew that, no matter how unpleasant, sometimes liabilities had to be eliminated.

She needed a gun—and thanks to her time in prison, she had a network for that, too.

CHAPTER TWELVE

Whether staffed by humans or paranormals, a doctor's office was one of Jack's least favorite places, and the workout Adnan was giving his arm wouldn't change his opinion anytime soon. Checking hand function, and his shoulder's range of motion, had sweat popping from every fricking pore.

"Take it slow," Adnan advised.

Damn right I'll take it slow. The exercise sequence he'd learned in physical therapy was easier now than it had been a week ago, but it still stung.

Adnan watched, tapping out a few notes on the tablet he held. "Your range of motion looks good."

"I see a lot of improvement, but..." He'd tried to assume a shooting stance holding his Glock earlier that morning. It...hadn't gone well.

"Don't push too hard," Adnan warned. "Nerve injuries are dicey. You've had a textbook recovery so far." Jack winced as Adnan poked around his bullet wounds. "They're healing well. Leave them open to the air for periods of time."

Was he supposed to walk around shirtless? Would Sasha even care?

What the hell had happened last night?

"How much pain medication are you taking?"

"I'm down to a tablet or two a day."

Adnan nodded, then handed him his shirt. "Well, as far as the road to recovery is concerned, you're on the Autobahn, my friend. When they wheeled you into the OR that night, I wasn't quite sure what your prognosis might be."

"Well, *now* you tell me."

"You're cleared for normal activities," Adnan said. "Desk work, sex, light exercise."

His face heated. He'd kinda jumped the gun on the sex.

"No weight lifting, no cage matches, no security ops," Adnan continued, updating his records. "Use your brain, okay? You don't want to have a setback."

He hadn't realized how much he'd taken functioning arms and hands for granted. "Can I ask you a question about pheromone meds?"

"Sure. You can start taking them again, by the way...if you haven't already."

Yeah, Adnan knew his patient well. "Do you think it's possible to build up a tolerance to the medication?" He described what he'd experienced in California—how the pills seemed to help regulate his emotions around humans, but didn't seem to work as well as they used to with incubi and succubi.

Adnan's eyes went sharp. "I'd say developing a tolerance is possible, yes. How much are you taking, and how often?"

Jack told him.

"Daily?" Adnan's eyes flew wide. "Jesus, Jack, that's over twice the maximum recommended daily dose. What ever happened to 'take as needed'?"

"You know what I do for a living. When *don't* I need them?"

Adnan flicked at his tablet. "How long have you

been taking high a dose?"

Since before they'd taken down Wyatt Cooper. "A couple of months," he said. *Liar.* Cooper had been in custody for almost a year.

"Let me do some quick checks here." While examining his eyes, ears, nose, and throat, Adnan explained the difference between tolerance, dependence, and addiction. "How do you feel when you don't take the meds? Any physical symptoms? Any anxiety?"

"I don't know. I haven't tried *not* taking them." Another lie. The way he'd felt at Mavericks, counting pills? Anxiety, definitely.

Shit.

"Sasha Sebastiani has been providing wound care, correct?"

Trust Adnan to cut to the chase. "Yes. She's staying with me at my place, and she went to California with me. Bottom line, it feels as though I'm taking more medication, but receiving less of a result."

"Living with a succubus, when you're used to living alone, might cause this type of change all on its own," Adnan mused. "You never get a break from the pheromones. Have you noticed this result around other incubi and succubi?"

No, damn it. "I haven't really been around other incubi and succubi recently. Once I go back to work, I can get a better feel for that."

"There's another possibility. Are you and Sasha Sebastiani sexually involved?"

After last night, who knew? But for the purposes of this discussion...? "Yes."

"Remember how the drugs work? They don't

create, remove, or eliminate emotions; they just help you exercise better judgment when you experience them." Adnan set the tablet down. "If you and Sasha are having a sexual relationship, it's possible the dosage you're taking isn't high enough to address the increased pheromone level."

"Fantastic," he muttered.

"Lay back on the exam table for a moment."

"Why?"

"Just do it." Adnan spent a minute or so pressing on his stomach.

Checking for an ulcer. Bailey had developed a bleeding ulcer after taking too much pheromone intoxication medication, trying to deal with her growing feelings for…feelings for…

Shit.

"Any tenderness or discomfort?"

"No." Not really.

Adnan helped him sit back up. "Well, we both know you're taking too much medication. While I don't see any negative impacts at this time, I want you to cut back to one pill a day, and to keep track of how you react around other incubi and succubi." Wise brown eyes met his. "You might speak with Bailey about her experiences taking the medication."

Bailey's experiences included emergency surgery, and discontinuing taking the medication altogether.

Hell.

"Anything else?" Adnan asked, handing him his shirt.

"I think that's it for now."

"Remember, sexual activity within reason."

"I heard you the first time."

"Dude, that was before I knew you had a live-in

succubus lover."

"Shut up."

Adnan gave him a gentle fist bump. "Later." With that, he was gone, off to his next appointment.

Jack got dressed, went to the lobby, and scheduled a follow-up appointment. As he left the clinic, he checked the time. Lukas wasn't expecting him at work for a couple of hours yet.

He had more than enough time to visit Claudette.

He drove to the Sebastiani Building on auto-pilot. Activity in the parking ramp looked like business as usual—cars in, cars out, people running errands, scurrying here and there—with humans oblivious to the fact that a man had been shot and killed there— that a bullet had missed Sasha's head by inches— barely two weeks earlier.

Sasha. Her tears last night had slayed him. An apology couldn't hurt.

There was no reason he couldn't talk to Sasha before visiting Claudette.

He took the private elevator to the first floor. When the doors opened, dissonant choral voices flooded the compartment. It took him a couple of seconds to recognize the song—"Hurt" by Nine Inch Nails—but he'd never imagined the song sounding like…this. Amplified by Underbelly's legendary sound system, dozens of voices gnashed and sliced.

Up on the stage, Sasha was dancing.

Wearing clingy black leggings and a sleeveless black T-shirt, with bare feet and a knee brace, she was a wisp in the dim light, but her anger and grief projected to where he stood, at the back of the house. He'd seen enough classical ballet to recognize some of her moves, but she connected them with violent, full-body jerks and swoops, sometimes simply stalking across the stage before starting to dance again, to choreography only she knew.

Suddenly, she stopped. Turned toward him, hands on hips. She stalked to the lip of the stage and stared.

Her gaze was a tractor beam, a physical touch. He couldn't break free. He...didn't want to. Shit, what had he been thinking, coming here without taking pheromone intoxication meds first?

Too late now.

Ignoring the stairs, she slipped off the edge of the stage, then padded across Underbelly's scarred wooden dance floor. As she drew closer, he could smell her pheromones, her frank sexual hunger. He could see it in the sway of her hips, hear it as fabric brushed between her thighs.

Feel it, below the belt.

When her bare toes bumped into his boots, every cell snapped to attention.

"Hi," she murmured.

"Hi."

Sweat glistened on her face and arms, and tears streaked her cheeks. Her pheromones had a piquant bite that gripped him by the dick and wouldn't let go. She was angry, sad, and definitely horny, but she probably needed comfort most of all. Would she accept it? From him, after last night?

He opened his arms. Silence stretched like an exercise band, taut and tight. Finally, she closed the distance, burrowing against his chest, wrapping her arms around his waist.

She was...so small. So sad. So careful—*too* damn careful, considering he wanted to tear off those flimsy leggings and fuck her against the bar, so hard the bottles rattled.

Stop. Comforting her didn't involve—

"Jack," she whispered. One hand dropped to his ass. Her fingers flexed, as if testing his muscles, his strength. Her other hand skated along his cheekbone, through his hair to the back of his head. She tugged, pulling their heads and groins together.

Hmm. Maybe it did.

"Are you sure…?" he murmured.

She bit his lower lip. Ground her hips against his cock. Her nipples were hard points beneath her thin T-shirt.

That answers that.

He picked her up and twirled her toward the bar. She was light as a soap bubble, but her legs were strong, twining around his waist and supporting her own weight. She writhed against his cock as if getting off was her top priority.

It was important. It was urgent. And he was the right man for the job.

He set her down on the edge of a barstool, letting it take her weight so he could hold her more tightly as they plundered each other's mouths. Behind the bar, backlit liquor bottles gleamed like jewels. The soaring music, and the muffled clang-bang from the kitchen, receded into the background. Her harsh breaths, her greedy moans, had his full attention.

Pheromones rippled like waves.

She pushed his hand between her legs, tossing her head back as he cupped her through the stretchy, humid fabric. "Not enough," she panted, pulling at her waistband. With a lift and a twist, she yanked the leggings down to her thighs, until they got caught on her knee brace. Before he could offer to remove the brace, she'd shifted her focus to the other leg, shimmying and tugging until the leg was bare.

She leaned back and spread her legs, offering herself.

He swallowed, hard. He was going to worship her like the goddess she was, slowly and with reverence.

Time floated away as he stroked and touched, caressing her damp folds. She was slick and hot, and she smelled like the sea: tangy, elemental, essential. Her pheromones bloomed, filling his head like sweet chloroform. He wanted to sip at her, drink her, eat her alive—

"Too slow," she gritted out, sitting up. There was a tug at his waist, a metallic clank, then a creak of leather as she yanked at his belt. The buttons at his fly quickly gave up the ghost. She pushed at his pants and boxer briefs down, out of the way. When his cock sprang free, she grasped with greedy hands, pulling him toward her. "In me," she demanded. "Now."

When the blunt tip of his cock kissed her core, he hissed in pleasure. He paused, fighting for control.

"Stop thinking so hard. Get inside me."

He obeyed, sliding all the way to the hilt.

"Fast." Her heels dug into his butt, spurring him on. "Hard."

Fast and hard meant quick and rough, but if the expression on her face was anything to go by, it was exactly what she wanted. He turned off his brain and listened to his body, obeying the drumbeat pounding with his pulse.

Perfect. Perfect. Perfect.

Mine, mine, mine.

She reached behind him, clutching his ass with

both hands. "Come for me," she urged, on the edge herself. "Now."

The diabolical tug was all it took. One, two, three more thrusts. A timeless pause, then release slammed into him like a lightning bolt. His knees buckled as he spilled inside her, as she shook apart in his arms. She grabbed on, helping him stay upright.

Finally, one of them found the strength to speak.

"Damn," she panted, stroking his ass. "That was just what I needed."

Her breath, warm against his neck, made him shiver. "Glad I could help."

"Sasha?" A male voice, calling from the kitchen.

"Shit," Sasha muttered, sitting up quickly. "Out here, Padrick," she called back. "Be cool," she murmured, wiping sweat from her brow. "He can't see anything unless he walks around to this side of the bar."

They were completely dressed from the waist up, but his pants were down around his ankles, and tails of his shirt barely covered his limp, wet dick. As Sasha tugged her T-shirt back down, he turned the barstool so Sasha's back was facing the kitchen, facing him. They were just two people talking, having a quick consult about something.

Just a quick consult, with their asses kissed by the breeze.

"Hey, Sasha—oh, there you are." Padrick, one of the managers at Crackhouse Coffee, popped his head around the kitchen door. "Do you mind if I turn the music down?" He waved back toward the kitchen. "I'm trying to do some paperwork, and it sounds like a funeral out here."

A thoughtful expression flitted across her face. "It

does, doesn't it? Sorry."

"I didn't mean to interrupt." Padrick took a step toward the bar. "I can take care of the music myself...."

"No worries." Sasha waved a careless hand, as if he hadn't ejaculated inside her not two minutes ago. "I got it."

"Want me to check the temp in here?" Padrick asked. "You look a little sweaty."

"I was dancing."

Her lips were red and puffy, and she had razor burn on her neck. It was all he could do to keep his hand away from his own sweat-soaked face.

"Okay." Humor glinted in the other man's eyes as he sauntered back toward the kitchen. "I'll leave you to it."

Padrick disappeared from view. "I think we got away with it," he whispered, wiping the sweat trickling down his temple.

"I don't think so." Sasha pointed to the wall behind him. Bit her lip. "I forgot about...."

The large mirror, reflecting their bare legs back to the room.

He closed his eyes. "That's just...great." He pulled up his pants. "At least my shirt tails are covering my ass."

Sasha giggled. "You sound so disgusted."

"I can't believe we did this here."

"Wouldn't be the first time," she said wryly.

True—at Underbelly, people all but copulated on the dance floor—but it was the first time it had happened to *him*. At least they hadn't lost control when there were other people around... Other people. Crap. "Where's Winnie?"

"In the kitchen, eating."

"Sasha—"

"Jack, she's right back there in the kitchen," Sasha said, exasperated.

"She's supposed to be your bodyguard."

"She is, and she's hungry. I told her I'd stay right here, in this room, while she caught a quick bite. Jack, the place is locked down tight."

"That didn't stop someone from jamming the security cameras and climbing through the freaking duct work."

Sasha looked to the ceiling above the bar, to the camera covered by a gray half dome. "And how many new cameras have you installed all around this building since Dad was shot?"

He pressed his fingers to the bridge of his nose. He'd forgotten all about the additional cameras. Where the hell was his brain?

"They're not on," she reassured him.

They weren't *scheduled* to be on, but Winnie could access any camera in the place, right from her phone. Had she?

Too late to worry about that, isn't it?

He knew he could count on Winnie's discretion, but how could he ever look her in the eye again? "I need to get going," he murmured, dropping a soft kiss onto her lips. "Claudette is expecting me upstairs, then I need to get back to work."

She nodded, sliding off the stool. Grabbing a couple of napkins from the bar, she matter-of-factly wiped her pussy, then pulled up her leggings, covering all that pale, delicious flesh.

"You're working tonight, right?" he asked.

She nodded. "Until Flynn tells me to get out of his

hair. I give him until ten p.m., tops."

So, she'd be home before bedtime. Good. They'd have a chance to talk, to clear the air about what had happened last night. It felt...*wrong* that they'd made love without first clearing the air about whatever had upset her last night, but Sasha didn't seem bothered.

Were they...okay? Would she share his bed tonight? Stepping closer, he chanced a silky goodbye kiss. "See you at home, then."

"Mmm." She patted his butt, then went behind the bar to turn down the music. "Later, gator." With a graceful pirouette, she headed toward the women's restroom.

Nope, she didn't seem bothered at all.

He made a pivot of his own, heading for the stairwell and the third-floor VIP restroom. It would be very poor form to pay a condolence call on Claudette without washing up first. Elliott would have laughed, telling him to leave his human hang-ups at the door.

Easier said than done.

Once in the restroom, he locked the door, stripped to the skin, then made quick use of the soap and a washcloth. After dressing again, he finger-combed his hair, turned away from the mirror, then pulled the small pill container from his pants pocket.

The pheromone meds had helped him manage a difficult conversation with his mother. Maybe they'd do the same with Claudette. "Better late than never," he muttered, swallowing two pills with a handful of water from the tap.

He should have taken them before walking into the building. He'd found Sasha drowning in grief, and what had he done? Wallowed in her pheromones like a pig in the mud, having sex with her in *public*, where anyone could have walked in. Just as she'd asked, just as she wanted, but…he'd shown *zero* finesse.

It wasn't the way he'd been taught to treat *any* woman, much less the woman he loved.

✳

Ethan shouldered into the bathroom stall, closed the door, then sat on the toilet. He pulled out the burner phone and dialed.

Waited.

No answer.

Why wasn't Jane picking up? They hadn't spoken in days. It was like she'd fallen off the face of the earth.

Unbuttoning his work shirt, he unclipped the flexible Neoprene flask from the harness holding it flat against his torso. The device, typically worn to carry alcohol into places or events where it wasn't allowed, worked just as advertised, but his T-shirt was clammy with sweat.

Well, beggars couldn't be choosers. Since throwing away his pills the other night, he'd had to make do with booze, but the good news? He was meeting a new dealer in a couple of hours, right after work. Setting the burner in his lap, he unscrewed the flask's small cap and sipped, grimacing at the cheap whiskey's harsh bite. Yeah, he needed drugs, but what he *really* needed was the payday for finishing the Kirkland job.

He had new information, damn it. A pizza had been delivered to Kirkland's place last night, paid for by a woman matching Sasha Sebastiani's physical description. He was ready, waiting for her instructions, but he was dead in the water if she wouldn't answer his calls.

Maybe it's a test. Maybe she wanted him to show some initiative.

I could do that. I used to, every day.

The burner suddenly vibrated.

The flask slipped, splashing whiskey all over his pants and work boots before hitting the floor with a splat. The unmistakable scent of liquor spread like the plague.

Door hinges squeaked as someone came into the bathroom. Hard-soled shoes clicked against the floor tile.

"Ethan, I recognize your boots." It was Kirby, of course. "Come on out of there."

He took a deep breath, then released it.

"Damn it, Ethan. We're not going to have this conversation through the stall door."

He shoved the burner in his front pants pocket, then fastened the buttons on his shirt. He didn't bother picking up the flask, or wiping up the booze. He'd been caught, dead to rights. There was no way to spin this.

When he came out of the bathroom stall, Kirby waited by the sink, jaw tight.

"What's going on, Ethan?" Kirby flicked a quick glance at Ethan's utility belt, at the baton and pepper spray all guards carried. "What's wrong?"

I'm addicted to painkillers, drowning in debt, drinking at work, and I killed the freaking president. What isn't wrong?

"I have no latitude here," Kirby told him, looking both disappointed and concerned. "Ansel Manufacturing has a zero-tolerance policy regarding drug and alcohol use on the premises. There's booze on your breath as we speak."

He didn't respond. He had no defense.

"Ethan, you need help. There are treatment options available through the company's benefits plan—"

"Thank you for your concern, but no." He *did* need help, but a human treatment approach wouldn't work. There was only one way out. "I think it's best if I quit, and resolve this on my own."

"Ethan—"

"Thanks, Kirby. I'm out of here." Quitting his job meant no regular paycheck, but maybe this was for the best. With no day job taking up his time, he could fulfill the Kirkland contract quickly. Get paid, then fly to some warm, Caribbean island. Dry out in style. Start over, someplace else.

Anyplace else.

"Ethan…"

He unbuckled his utility belt, handing it to Kirby. His employee badge quickly followed. "Seriously, man. Thanks."

He went to the locker room, then emptied the contents of his locker into the duffel bag he kept on the top shelf. There wasn't enough money in the world to wash Elliott Sebastiani's blood off his hands, but six figures for Kirkland's? He'd take it.

When he left the locker room, he almost bumped into Kirby, and a baffled-looking Bill was right behind him. Bill probably hadn't predicted that, not ten minutes after agreeing to cover him for a bathroom break, he'd have to escort Ethan from the building for the last time.

"Goodbye, Bill," he said.

"Goodbye."

They walked him right to the door, following procedure to the letter. There was a spring to his step as he crossed the parking lot.

Time to get this show on the road.

Once he got into his truck, he looked at the burner. She'd sent him a text message, something she'd told him she'd never do.

Your services are no longer required.

"What?" There had to be some mistake. He called her back.

No answer.

He tried again.

No answer.

He dialed a third time.

Nothing but a ring tone, mocking him.

He hurled the burner at the dash, not the least bit surprised when it disappeared into one of the fist-sized holes.

Because of course.

"Fuck my life," he whispered, reaching for the flask in the glove box as he left the parking lot. "Fuck it all to hell." As he drove home, anger simmered and sparked—anger at Jane, at Jack Kirkland, at the whole damn Sebastiani family, at the whole fucking world.

When he arrived at his apartment, he almost stepped on the piece of paper someone had slipped under the door. He picked it up, then entered the apartment, closing the door behind him. He set the duffel bag down, then read.

A rent increase. A big one. "What the hell…?" He read it again, blinking. Panic, and a red, red rage, swirled like a fiery tornado. His pulse pounded at his temples. His skin felt tight, too small, like a bratwurst sizzling on a grill, ready to burst.

His fist shot out, punching through the sheetrock. The impact rocketed up his arm, slicing the skin over his knuckles.

He hit the wall again, and again, and again.

His vision went hazy, then dark.

When he came back to himself, he was lying in the middle of his living room, shaky and spent. His knuckles were bleeding, and the wall sported half a dozen holes. But his vision was clear, and the noxious energy was gone.

Time to sac up, to show some initiative.

Money might be off the table, but he could still make Jack Kirkland pay.

*

Vehicles circled the Target parking lot like buzzards, ready to swoop on an open parking spot, but Miranda wasn't there to shop. Parked and idling in the outermost row, she cracked open her car door, tossed the burner phone into a huge snow bank, then closed the door with a snap.

She should have fired Ethan Covington a long time ago. Yes, he'd had all the right skills on paper, but he was just too unstable in the flesh. "Though the flesh was pretty damn fine," she mused, reaching into her purse for a lipstick. She hadn't had sex since before she went to prison, hadn't been hugged since the day she was sentenced.

Jack Kirkland had hugged her, just before he let the marshals take her away.

Big, brainy, and blond... She had a type, and Kirkland more than fit the bill. She'd spent too many years wallowing in that goodbye hug, too many nights fantasizing about—

A car horn blared.

Behind her, and slightly down the row, a salt-grimed sedan hovered with its turn signal blinking. The man behind the wheel tossed up his hands, as if to say, "What's the holdup, lady?"

So much for Minnesota Nice. "Happy Holidays," she muttered, throwing her lipstick back in her purse before backing out of the parking space.

The man flipped her off. She responded in kind. Pleasantries thus exchanged, she put the SUV into gear and left the crowded parking lot.

Leaving the phone, and Ethan Covington, behind.

Sometimes, to get a job done right, you had to do it yourself.

CHAPTER THIRTEEN

Snow crunched under Sasha's boots as she strode toward Sebastiani Security carrying a bulky cardboard box.

"Let me get the door for you." Winnie sidled around her. Before Sasha could say she could manage it herself, Winnie was opening the building's heavy, tempered glass door.

They entered, pausing to stomp snow off their boots.

"Feels good to get out of the wind," Winnie muttered.

"I should have worn a scarf." As she'd retrieved the box from the back of the coffee shop's delivery van, snowflakes had gleefully spat on her exposed neck, leaving her damp, chilled, and annoyed. Thankfully, the reception area was blissfully warm...which was the only thing the room had going for it.

The faerie designers Lukas hired had more than fulfilled his request that Sebastiani Security's lobby not feel the *least* bit receptive. The front door? Unmarked. The long, rectangular reception desk? Boring, completely bare, and never occupied. There were no chairs for waiting, and the walls, carpet, and window blinds were a chilly, industrial gray. Security cameras glared down from all four corners. Off to the right was a no-frills conference room, used for meeting people they couldn't or wouldn't allow through to Sebastiani Security's secure work area. To the left, an elevator and a stairwell provided authorized parties with access to the other floors of the building. Lukas and Scarlett's loft was on the top floor, and there was a gym in the basement.

Winnie veered left, toward the stairwell, then glanced back, hard-eyed. "You won't leave without me, right?" She slapped her hand against the security pad mounted next to the stairwell door. When the door clicked and beeped, she pulled it open. "Remember, we made a deal."

Earlier that morning, when Bailey had called saying SebSec was almost out of coffee, Sasha had jumped at the chance to deliver it herself. Winnie, on guard duty, had agreed, on two conditions: that *she* drive the delivery van, and that Sasha not leave Sebastiani Security without her. "Go work out." Sasha waved at the stairwell door. "I'll be on the first floor somewhere. Just text me when you're ready to leave."

Winnie didn't move.

"What?" she asked, exasperated. "I won't ditch you." She shifted the bulky box to the other arm. "I don't want Lukas to chew you out for losing me. I like you too much."

Winnie's penciled brow rose. "So, it's our friendship that's keeping you in check, not my badass bodyguard skills?"

She eyeballed Winnie's tall, muscular frame. "They're both factors." People in their culture lived, worked, and played together, forming a tangled knot of community. Lukas, her annoying older brother, was Winnie's boss, her best friend's bondmate, and their culture's top security wonk. And then was Jack. Friend, lover, colleague, nemesis… Jack ticked off too many of her own personal checkboxes.

Ticked off was right.

The steel security door leading to the first floor work area opened from the inside. "Sorry," Bailey said, slightly out of breath. "I meant to meet you by the front door."

"That desperate for coffee?"

"That, and you're carrying that bulky box."

"Perfect timing, then. Let's go."

"I won't be long," Winnie called from the stairwell.

"Take your time."

When Bailey hustled her through the security door, everything suddenly turned high-def. To the left, century-old exposed brick climbed the walls, framing entrances to the break room, a first aid room, Lukas's and Jack's offices, and conference rooms. To the right was a huge open work space, a high-tech playground where industrial chic reigned. People milled, keyboards clacked, and there was a trash-talking Nerf basketball game underway in the far back corner. Up ahead, Jack and Chico walked and talked, probably on their way to the large corner conference room at the end of the hall.

When had basic locomotion become so…sexy?

"Hey." Bailey waved a hand in front of her face.

She blinked, avoiding her friend's amused eyes. "I have coffee, and I can take it away if I want to."

They turned into the break room, where Sebastiani Security employees refreshed themselves with snacks and drinks around the clock. Deliveries from the blood bank kept the vampires happy, and almost everyone drank the occasional Diet Coke, but they all clamored for the magic elixir that was so delicious, and so addictive, that both the coffee and the business had been named after a place where people scored drugs. Sure enough, the deep drawer that held single-pot packets of Crackhouse Blend was empty. "What do you folks do, snort the grounds?"

"People are working some long hours."

Bailey grabbed a pouch from the box, started brewing a pot of coffee, then helped her fill the drawer. Soon, the rich, loamy scent of coffee filled the room. While Bailey filled her battered black DEF CON coffee mug, Sasha broke down the cardboard box, then slipped it against the wall behind the big blue recycling bin.

"Can you come back to The Bunker for a few minutes?" Bailey asked. "I have a question about your dad's memorial service."

She inhaled subtly. Bailey wasn't lying, but she wasn't telling the whole truth, either. "Sure." Invitations to The Bunker were rare, and she *did* have some time to kill while Winnie worked out.

They walked through the open work area, acknowledging the waves and 'heys.' After navigating a line of cubicles, they made it to the back wall, where yet another steel door with a biometric security pad stood guard. Bailey opened the door, and Sasha followed her inside.

The Bunker, Bailey's workspace, housed a good portion of Sebastiani Security's technology infrastructure. The servers, switches, and routers were secured behind yet another door, but even this room sported enough equipment to manage air traffic at

Minneapolis-St. Paul International. Computers covered every available surface, flat-screen monitors climbed the walls, and several rolling chairs provided the ability to quickly navigate between workstations. They headed for the corner, where a shabby futon, several comfortable chairs, and a beat-up table sat on a large, fringed area rug. Before becoming bondmates with Rafe, Bailey had practically lived here, sleeping on the futon more nights than not.

"So." Bailey plopped onto the futon. "How was your trip to California?"

Not the question I was expecting. I should have. "It was fine, though we weren't there very long." How much had Jack had told Bailey about the reason they'd gone? She took the chair directly across from the futon.

Setting her coffee mug on the table, Bailey picked up a bag of Cool Ranch Doritos. "How did Jack hold up?"

Bailey's question had layers. A glib answer wouldn't do. "Physically, he's recovering well," she said. "We went to Jack's parents' house in Tiburon—gorgeous place—and spent some time with his father." She hesitated. "Then we went to the law firm, where Jack had an argument with his mother."

"Business as usual, then, even fighting cancer." With a roll of her eyes, Bailey selected a chip. "Cynthia's a real piece of work."

"That's a polite way of putting it. She's…a formidable woman, but Jack held his own." She gave Bailey a quick run-down of their activities while in California. "We stayed at a house Jack owns, just south of San Francisco."

Bailey's brow lifted. "He brought you to the

house?"

"Why does everyone know about this house but me?"

"Why *would* you know about it? You and Jack haven't exactly spent a lot of time together outside of work." *Crunch.* "Until recently, that is."

Ah, there it was. Bailey wanted to grill her about her relationship with Jack. Fair enough, because she wanted to grill his best friend about the same subject. "Seriously, am I the only person who doesn't know Jack owns a house in California?"

Bailey kicked off her flats, then curled her legs beneath her. "Why does it annoy you so much?"

"I'm not annoyed." She grabbed Bailey's coffee cup from the table and took a slug. "I just think it's weird that it hasn't come up in casual conversation."

Bailey snort-laughed. "You and Jack don't have casual conversations. Too much sexual tension." She reached for another chip. "Do you remember the day Lukas told me about your culture? Just before Scarlett's homecoming show at Underbelly?"

"Sure." That afternoon, Sasha had walked into a pre-show meeting to find Lukas and Jack using a fricking PowerPoint presentation to bring Bailey up to speed, oblivious to the fact that Bailey was half in shock. She shook her head at the memory. "Men."

"You and Jack were striking sparks off each other even back then."

Her skin heated. Yeah, that day she'd flat-out taunted Jack about his physical reaction to her. As a succubus, she couldn't help but know he was attracted to her. The feeling had been mutual, and uncomfortable. To defend herself, she'd very shittily used the information against him.

"Damn," she whispered. *I started this.*

"What's wrong?"

"While we were in California, we had a huge fight about his pheromone intoxication meds." As she grabbed another chip, the comment Jack had made about needing some protection haunted her. "I think he takes too many pills, but given how much crap I've given him in the past, I can hardly blame him."

"Bullshit," Bailey scoffed. "He can try to trust you, for a start."

"I haven't given him much reason," she admitted.

"Maybe in the past," Bailey countered, shrugging. "How about now?"

Things had definitely changed between them. Their relationship had broadened and deepened, and not only because they were sleeping together. "He owns property in California. There's a law firm in San Francisco that has his family's name on the door. Aren't you concerned he'll move back to help his family?"

Bailey laughed out loud. "Hell, no."

"Even with his mother having breast cancer?"

"Nope. There's some…really bad blood between them."

She appreciated Bailey protecting Jack's confidences, but… "He told me about Anna," she ventured, "and why their relationship ended."

"Oh, thank the universe," Bailey breathed, leaning forward. "What the hell was his mother thinking, offering Jack's lovers money? It's positively batshit." She paused. "Not knowing why someone wants to be with you can be hell on your confidence. Cancer or not, I want to smack Cynthia silly for that reason alone."

Her own slapping hand was plenty itchy.

"So, why are you with him?" Bailey asked. "Is it just his admittedly luscious bod, or do you want something more?"

Annoyance spurted. "Why does everyone think I'm only interested in sexual relationships?"

"Because that's all you've been interested in in the past?"

"I like all my former lovers," she said defensively. "To this day, I'm friends with every single one."

Bailey gave a noncommittal hum. "Well, you've been living with Jack for a couple of weeks now. How are things going? How is he *really* doing? When I ask, all he says is, 'Fine,' or 'Okay.' Sometimes there's an expressive grunt."

"His bullet wounds are healing well, and he's getting mobility back in his arm and hand. He's almost off the painkillers, and he's sleeping through the night, but he still needs help with his dressings before and after bathing."

"Isn't his shower something else?"

She nodded. "I haven't used it yet."

"Girl, what's wrong with you?"

Seriously? "Bailey, the man is recovering from bullet wounds."

Bailey laughed. "I didn't mean 'Why haven't you had sex there yet.' But now that you mention it…"

"I'll put it on the agenda." Yesterday at Underbelly, Jack had demonstrated that he was well on the road to recovery. "But seriously, I'm worried about how many pheromone pills he's taking—especially after what happened to you."

Bailey's hand went to her stomach. "Well, I needed to have surgery because the pills perforated an ulcer I already had. Jack doesn't have an ulcer."

"Would he tell anyone if he did?" Yeah, Bailey looked concerned now. "He told me that the pills were important for his work," she continued. "That when he takes them, he's the person with the clearest thoughts in the room, able to respond to any emergency that arises."

"But he took pills while the two of you were out in California?"

"Yeah."

"Desperation sets in," Bailey muttered under her breath.

"What do you mean?"

"Nothing."

Nothing, my ass.

Bailey reached for the coffee mug. "Don't worry about Jack moving back to California. His self-preservation instincts are too strong."

It was a good reminder. Jack might be taking pheromone intoxication meds left and right, but he was an adult who knew how to take care of himself.

Bailey passed the mug back to her. "So, how long will you and Jack be roomies?"

"Probably not much longer." Jack *was* healing. She'd be able to move back home sooner rather than later.

Her cell vibrated with a text message from Winnie, who'd finished her workout. "Winnie's ready to leave. You had a question about Dad's memorial service?"

"Nope," Bailey said. "I just wanted some intel about your trip to California. Jack's been a pain in everyone's ass ever since you returned."

At least she wasn't the only one who felt out of sorts. "Well, back to work," she said, heaving herself to her feet. "No rest for the wicked."

Bailey stood too, taking her coffee mug back. "Speaking of rest and relaxation, you might see a group of us at Underbelly tonight." She took a long sip off the mug. "God knows we could all use a break."

Would Jack be there? She tried to control the bump of concern. *He's fine.* If Jack was strong enough to make love to her at Underbelly—standing up—he could certainly handle sitting there and having a drink with friends.

He was a grown man who didn't need a keeper— or wouldn't for very much longer. His wounds were healing nicely.

They headed for the door. Playing house with Jack was all well and good, but it would soon be time to get things back to normal. To *build* a new normal. Caring for Jack had been an oasis, time out of life.

But soon it would be time to get back to hers.

✳

A feeling of déjà vu floated over Jack as he exited the elevator near Underbelly's back bar. The music thumped, and the bass line rattled his ribs, but unlike yesterday afternoon, tonight the place was packed.

On Guilty Pleasures night, Sasha let her freak flag fly.

The crowd was usually more interested in dancing than raising hell, but he was relieved to see that undercover Sebastiani Security staff had formed several loose perimeters: one around the raised DJ booth, where Sasha stood, and the other around the big table next to the back bar, where the Sebastiani family, Council members, and their friends tended to congregate. Lukas and Scarlett were at home with the baby tonight, but Bailey and Rafe were at the table, chatting with Lorin and Gabe. Chico and Winnie, drinking dark beer, sat next to Chadden, who cradled a glass of blood-spiked red wine. Over at the bar itself, Flynn held court, pouring shots for Gabe's sister Glynna and Jenny Williams, the cop who'd helped saved Lukas's life the night Stephen had attacked him.

At the far end of the bar, Jacoby Woolf sat alone, sipping from a nearly-empty lowball. Waving to the people at the table, he approached the WerePack Beta. "Is this seat taken?" He tipped his head toward the empty barstool, which—as fate would have it— was the same one Sasha had sprawled upon when they'd made love yesterday.

"Please, have a seat." Jacoby caught Flynn's eye and gestured for a refill. "What can I get you?"

"A Diet Coke, please." He hadn't taken any painkillers since last night, but who knew what tonight might bring?

"A Diet Coke for my friend here," Jacoby said to Flynn.

He and Jacoby were not friends. Friendly colleagues, maybe, but sometimes even that was a stretch. He and Lukas—hell, everyone on the Council—disagreed with the WerePack too frequently for true friendship to develop.

"How goes your recovery?" Jacoby asked.

"Very well, thanks." Today was the first day he'd

left his wounds uncovered by gauze, open to the air. He didn't really need Sasha to care for them—for *him*—any longer.

"And the nerve damage in your shoulder?"

He didn't realize his health status was quite so widely known. "Getting better by the day. Adnan predicts a full recovery." To prove it, he used his right hand to lift the glass of Diet Coke Flynn had just delivered, then took a sip. "You look like a man with a lot on his mind," he said. "Can I help?"

"Actually, you might be one of the only people who can. Help, I mean." Jacoby took a healthy sip from his own glass. "I need a lawyer."

Hmm. "May I ask why?"

"Today, Gideon Lupinsky asked my father to present himself for questioning in the matter of the president's death, and in your shooting."

Wow. He hadn't realized that Gideon was at that point in his investigation. He didn't envy Gideon having to question his own Alpha about the president's shooting, but… "Doesn't your father have lawyers on staff?"

"He doesn't need the lawyer. I do."

He blinked. He was dying to ask some questions, but…was Jacoby drunk, or merely buzzed? How impaired was he? *Step carefully.* "Is your concern personal, or Council related?"

Jacoby laughed harshly. "Is there a difference?"

"Ain't that the truth." He sipped at his drink, thoughts racing. Fuck it, straight talk couldn't hurt. "Jacoby, you know where I sit, alliance-wise. Am I really the person you want to speak with?"

"I know exactly what I'm saying, and to whom— and Sasha has the music cranked up so damned loud that no one could possibly overhear our conversation."

Jack leaned closer anyway.

"For what it's worth, my father was with my sister and me the night you and Elliott were shot, but we both know he could have hired the job out." Jacoby's lips flattened into a tight, pale line. "What does that say about my father—as a leader, as a *man*—that I have no absolutely difficulty envisioning him putting out a hit on our president?"

Shock rippled through him. It took all the control he had to maintain a neutral expression.

"My father has never gotten over the fact that Elliott defeated him in our last presidential election," Jacoby added. "Dad's never been satisfied merely leading *his* people." He took a healthy slug of his scotch, then squared his shoulders. "For the good of our species—for the good of our culture—I need to discreetly explore some potential outcomes regarding the WerePack succession plan."

The schism between father and son ran deeper than he'd ever have imagined. "You might consult Wyland." As both a doctor and a lawyer, confidentiality was second nature to the man. As Council Archivist familiar with all species' succession plans, Wyland could probably answer Jacoby's questions off the top of his head.

"I need to do it sooner rather than later," Jacoby said. "Given Dad's mindset, and what he saw the Sebastianis do with *their* succession plan, he might try to write me out altogether." Tossing back what was left of his scotch, Jacoby gestured for a refill. "Maybe I should let him."

"Jacoby—"

"Hi, guys." Sasha sidled up between them. "Two of my favorite men, both within kissing distance." As good as her word, she kissed Jacoby on both cheeks, then him directly on the lips, before leaning against him and wrapping her arm around his waist. Tonight, she wore saggy, beat-up jeans with a thick belt, a black leather bikini top, and Doc Martens. Her scent, that lush mix of jungle flowers, hair products, and skin, drifted into his nose.

His annoyance at being interrupted quickly dissolved.

"Great tunes tonight," Jacoby said, grinning.

Sasha simply nodded, caressing Jack's neck. "And I feel like dancing." She looked at Jacoby, then at him as the music changed to something slow and throbbing. "Any takers?"

Jack rose to his feet, and took Sasha's hand. "Are you okay here?" he asked Jacoby. "Do you need a ride home?"

"I've got it covered."

Behind the bar, Flynn nodded, letting him know he'd make sure of it.

Jacoby waved them toward the dance floor. "Go dance."

Sasha kissed Jacoby's cheek again, then led Jack onto the dance floor—to the perimeter, where it was shadowy and dark. "I've queued up a long, slow-dance set to close out the night," she murmured, draping her arms around his neck. "I hope you can forgive me. Now I can finally get my hands on you."

"Forgive you for what?"

She tapped her nose. "You were annoyed that I interrupted your conversation with Jacoby."

He slid his hand down her bare back. "There

are…compensations. Why did you?"

"Jacoby seemed upset," she admitted. Then, she smiled. "I also noticed that he kept looking at someone down at the other end of the bar."

"I hadn't noticed." No surprise there; he'd taken a double dose of pheromone intoxication meds earlier.

"He was horny." She tapped her nose again. "The nose knows."

"I'll take your word for it." After a slight hesitation, he asked, "You and Jacoby seem close."

"Yes, we are." Instead of saying more, she pressed her body against his, swaying to the music.

She's going to make me ask. "You seem to know each other…intimately."

"We do. He's a good friend." A nostalgic smile crossed her face. "And yeah, we were lovers, many moons ago."

His arms tightened, pulling her closer. How could the man have ever let her go?

The smile dimmed slightly. "There's no reason for you to be jealous, you know. We were teenagers."

Jealousy was the least of what he was feeling. He opened his mouth to try to explain, but suddenly her lips were there, swallowing his words, sharing his air. When her tongue slipped into his mouth, he was a goner.

He moved them back into the shadows, pressing her against the wall with his larger body, blocking her from other people's view before diving into her mouth. It didn't matter that he'd taken pheromone intoxication meds before coming to the club—light, scent, and sound swirled around them, forming a dark, succulent whirlpool. He dove, over and over again. She clamped her hands on his ass then lifted a leg, bringing their groins closer together.

She was climbing him like a tree.

He gave her a boost, and she wrapped both legs around his waist. The wall took most of her weight, and a hungry groan escaped as her core met his cock. He couldn't feel her damp, inviting heat—there were too many layers of fabric between them—but if her rolling hips were any indication, she could feel his blunt, hard flesh just fine.

She was riding him like a pony, and if her speed was anything to go by, she was close to coming. He held on tight, urging her on, watching avidly as she writhed to the beat.

Faster, faster.

The music was too loud for him to hear the breathy little moan she made when she came, but he saw it in the movement of her lips. Felt it as her strong legs clutched him tight. She shook and quaked, then sagged against him, her head lolling back against the wall. Her sated expression, and the gleam of sweat dampening her hairline, made him feel foolishly proud.

Her slumberous gaze met his. "That was…"

"Amazing." Even with pheromone intoxication meds on board, he couldn't keep his hands off her. Something about the music, the lights, how she smelled and felt and *was*, made him want to huddle close, to never let her go. Watching her chase her own pleasure was the hottest thing he'd ever seen.

"Let's go upstairs," she murmured against his skin. "To my place."

"Great idea." Because once again, he'd forgotten all about the new security cameras, including the one directly overhead. Tomorrow, he'd pull, then erase, tonight's security tapes himself—and yesterday's while he was at it. Sasha might not mind who'd seen her in such an intimate, abandoned moment, but he did. "Is Antonia at home?"

"She's staying with Claudette. The place is empty." Dropping gracefully to her feet—some feat, given the chunky boots she wore—she kissed his jaw. "We can be as noisy as we want."

"I like how you think." He didn't want to be quiet. He wanted to fuck her in every room of the penthouse, then start over again. Something of his thoughts must have shown on his face, or maybe she could smell his lust, because she grabbed his hand, then broke trail through the throngs of dancers to the back bar.

As she had a quick word with Flynn, he noticed that Jacoby was no longer sitting at the bar. His scooter was gone. So were Jenny and Glynna.

Hmm.

"Flynn said he'd close up tonight," Sasha said. "Come on." She removed her key card from her back pocket, then led him past the bar and down the short hallway leading to the private elevator.

The doors opened almost immediately. He mouthed a quick 'thanks' to Flynn as they stepped into the mirrored box. "Did Flynn mention who'd taken Jacoby home?"

"Nope." As the elevator started its upward climb, her hands dropped to his belt.

And then there was no more thinking to do.

✳

Across the club, Ethan watched the elevator doors close, then whisk Jack and Sasha up and out of reach. He couldn't blame them for heading upstairs, for continuing the party in private. Whatever they'd done back there in the shadows must have produced some very high-test pheromones. Dancers thronged to the area, lingering, trying to catch a contact high.

At least someone's getting laid tonight.

He took a sip from his beer. Getting laid had been part of his plan for the night, as well—do some reconnaissance at Underbelly, then find someone else looking for a straight-up, friendly fuck—but he felt like shit. His hands were shaking, and he felt like bugs were crawling under his skin. The envelope he'd found on the driver's seat of his truck earlier that night hadn't helped.

What made that bitch think she could buy his silence with a measly thousand bucks? Hell, a grand wasn't enough to cover one month's rent, much less payment enough for…for…

Killing the president.

Killing the president.

I killed the president.

The thought was a vulture, circling overhead.

He couldn't even comfort himself that he'd stood on principle, that he'd turned down her blood money. No, he'd used it—to fill his gas tank, then to meet his dealer and make a huge buy. After popping two pills out in the truck, he'd come to Underbelly, then broke the last hundred dollar bill buying the beer he now held in his hand.

She'd bought him off, all right.

"Ethan?"

Chico Perez, his former lieutenant...just when the pills were hitting. It took some effort, but he straightened from the wall, blinking to focus. "Hi, Chico."

"How are you doing, man?" Chico shook his hand, then pulled him into a half-hug. "Haven't seen you in a while."

The pouch his dealer had given him, tucked into his inside jacket pocket, felt heavy as a freaking brick. "I'm fine, how about you?" He tried to suck in his gut. Perez had lost nothing of his physique since they'd last worked together. Nope, he looked exactly the same: jacked, shaved head gleaming, and riding that line between relaxed and alert. The diamond studs he wore in each ear glinted in the light.

Chico flashed a "just a minute" gesture toward someone sitting at the big table near the back bar. "What's up?" he asked. "Let me buy you another beer."

For a moment, Ethan actually considered it. Maybe he could pick Chico's brain about the search for the president's killer... *Nah.* Chico wouldn't discuss an open case in public, much less with someone SebSec had fired for cause.

Rightfully so. If they only knew then how low he'd go.

I killed the president.

"Are you okay, man?"

Such genuine interest. Chico's sharp werewolf nose couldn't miss the fact that Ethan's energy was dangerously out of whack. "It was a mistake to come here tonight," he mumbled.

Chico bent closer. "Sorry, I couldn't hear you."

Ethan drained his beer, then set the empty bottle on a nearby table. "I said, thanks for the offer, but—" he gestured vaguely at his own body "—I need to go blow off some steam."

"We're pretty evenly matched." Chico eyed him up and down. "Want to go out back?"

Perez would do it. He'd go outside with him right now, with no coat, and throw a few punches to help a former co-worker bleed off excess energy. "Thanks, but..." He looked at the dance floor, then winked. "I've got it covered."

Chico grinned. "Say no more."

If Chico thought there was sex on his agenda tonight, he wouldn't correct him. "It was good to see you," he said. "Really. Take care, man."

"Text me," Chico suggested. "Let's work out sometime."

It sounded like he actually meant it.

They bumped fists, just like old times. But it wasn't old times.

I killed the president.

Icy wind chased him as he made his way back to his truck, parked on a side street a couple blocks away. As he unlocked the vehicle, something fluttered under the driver's side windshield wiper.

A parking ticket.

He plucked the paper from beneath the wiper, crumpled it loosely, then tossed it to the curb. After starting the truck, he hit the blinker, then eased onto nearly empty, snow-dusted streets. The dashboard vents blew ice-cold air, but he didn't turn them off. The pills were hitting, glazing over the pain, but he had to stay awake long enough to make it home.

In the meantime, the itching was

driving…him…nuts. Keeping one hand on the wheel, he used the other to scratch his scalp and neck, so hard his fingernails came away bloody. Maybe he should have taken Chico up on his offer, after all.

He'd declined the fight, and fucking was out of the question. Food, then—and lots of it.

Tacos, burritos, nachos, quesadillas... Yeah, a run for the border sounded good. Once he got to Taco Bell, he'd order enough food to make even the most jaded drive-thru worker blink. Enough to get the rest of that bitch's money out of his wallet. Then he'd get home, climb into bed, and eat himself into a food coma. Enjoy oblivion, for just a little while.

It never seemed to last long enough. Tomorrow always came too soon.

CHAPTER FOURTEEN

When Jack reached Lukas and Scarlett's top-floor loft, Lukas opened the door before he could ring the bell. Bare-footed and bare-chested, wearing only faded jeans, he cradled Coco in one arm and gestured frantically with the other.

"Shh! She just fell asleep."

Jack nodded, entered, then quietly closed the door. After slipping off his shoes, he followed Lukas. The loft was a bright, open space, built for big men, with almost a half-court of hardwood floor, few permanent walls, and plenty of oversized furniture. Lukas hadn't shaved yet, and if he'd brushed his hair that morning, Jack couldn't tell. "You look wiped out."

"So do you."

He hadn't gotten a lot of sleep last night, and Lukas knew *exactly* what bedroom activity his early morning text message had interrupted. Slipping from Sasha's bed to have an early-morning meeting with her brother was one of the hardest things he'd recently done.

"How are things going downstairs this morning?" Lukas asked around a yawn.

"Second and third shifts were pretty quiet." He relayed a quick status report, then headed for the kitchen. "I need coffee."

"I think Scarlett made a pot before she left," Lukas said. "Can you bring me a cup?"

"Sure." In the stainless steel and hickory kitchen he knew as well as his own, he discovered a nearly full pot of Crackhouse Blend. "Bless you, Scarlett." He filled two oversized mugs with the lifesaving brew. When he got back to the living room, Lukas was half-lying on the slouchy leather couch. Coco, bundled in a mint green blanket decorated with dancing coffee beans, lay contentedly against his chest. Calamity, Scarlett's big, black cat, sat on the arm of the couch.

Watching his every move.

Jack watched back. The green-eyed menace hadn't nipped or scratched him in months, but why take unnecessary risks? He approached Lukas slowly and carefully, handed him a mug, then sat in the adjacent chair.

"Thanks, man."

"No problem."

They mainlined the dark, smooth brew in a comfortable silence. He'd slept like shit last night. Too many odd dreams.

"What's up?" Lukas asked. "Your emotions are bouncing all over the place."

There was no denying it; he didn't even try. "Is it true that faerie quilts catalyze dreams?"

"They can." A pause. "Ah. You slept at Sasha's place last night, didn't you?"

"Yes." After almost fucking her against a wall at Underbelly, in front of anybody who cared to watch. Clearly, the pheromone intoxication meds weren't working anymore.

A crack of laughter. "You poor bastard."

"What do you mean?"

Lukas explained that faerie artisans made the quilts after completing hours of in-depth, near-hypnotic interviews with the quilt's future owner. "My sister has always had...complex emotions and thought processes. Who knows what they pulled out of her head."

Jack thought about the quilt, a gorgeous mixture of purple, white, gray, and black swirls. *Heavy* on the black, but... "I think it suits her to a T."

"Right? They nailed it." Lukas looked down at his daughter. "Uh oh."

Coco's little body had tensed up. Her pale red eyebrows wrinkled as they drew together. The mint green blanket rose as she drew in a slow, deep breath.

"Ah, damn," Lukas breathed, cuddling Coco closer.

Calamity launched himself off the arm of the couch, slinking away to the bedroom.

"What's going on?"

"Cover your ears."

He obeyed, but after a pause, Lukas visibly relaxed. Whatever he'd expected hadn't materialized. "False alarm," he confirmed. "Her cries take some getting used to."

"Is she...hungry?" His nipples were tingling.

"You, too?" Lukas asked wearily.

"Yeah."

"Wyland will want to know. He's collecting data on how Coco's vocal abilities impact people of various species. We're learning new things every day." When a pair of tiny, pursed lips closed around Lukas's nipple, he looked down, nonplussed. "This is new."

Jack grinned. "Coco, I hate to tell you this, but

you're going to come up empty there."

Lukas gently nudged Coco's mouth away from his chest. "Scarlett nursed her before she left for the studio. Maybe I should feed her again." When she squawked, Lukas mouthed a filthy curse. "Today is Scarlett's first day back at work. I'm *not* going to call her about this. I am not."

"Didn't you help take care of your brother and sisters when they were young?"

"Yeah, but I've discovered there's a huge difference between helping out, with Dad's supervision, and being responsible for keeping a helpless infant alive."

"She doesn't seem helpless to me." His nipples still ached. "She'll be fine," he reassured Lukas. "Kids are pretty damn resilient."

"How do single parents do this? I outweigh her by well over two hundred pounds, but she's already kicking my ass." Lukas kissed her forehead. "Aren't you, sweetheart? Yes, you are."

As Lukas launched into baritone baby talk, Calamity sauntered back out of the bedroom. This time, the cat jumped onto the arm of *his* chair. Was that low, rumbly sound a purr or a growl?

"Shit, it's been ages since we had a face-to-face conversation." Lukas didn't bother covering another jaw-cracking yawn. "How are you?"

"Tired, but okay. You?"

"Same."

But not for long. Adding a newborn and the Council presidency on top of an already crushing workload was going to drive Lukas to his knees, if not to an early grave. They needed to make some changes, free up some of Lukas's time.

He could do some of Lukas's work if someone else did some of *his*, but right now, staffing was so tight it squeaked. Bailey was maxed out, already handling more administrative work than she wanted. Chico had leadership skills to burn, but he excelled at field work—and he'd made his total lack of interest in a management role excruciatingly clear during his very first job interview. Nope, Chico was a battlefield leader.

Winnie.

He sipped from his mug, feeling the hot, bracing brew sluice over his taste buds. Taking Winnie out of the field would hurt—she had great instincts, made good decisions under pressure, and could back things up with brawn if she had to—but SebSec had a number of operatives who could handle more responsibility if given the opportunity.

Would Winnie be interested in taking on a new role? He'd talk to her before bringing up the subject with Lukas. Elliott's death had wreaked so much havoc, rippling through so many lives in completely unexpected ways. Speaking of which… "How do you think Claudette is doing? Really?" His visit with her yesterday hadn't gone as he'd hoped. He'd wanted to apologize for not protecting Elliott, but she hadn't let him, serving up tea and sympathy instead.

"She's doing well, all things considered. Dad's cremains were delivered late yesterday afternoon, and Scarlett and I went to see her last night. Antonia's staying with her for the time being, and Alka was there, visiting." A muscle ticked in Lukas's jaw. "Alka said things are running smoothly at Sebastiani Labs, thank the universe."

"That's great news."

"Claudette mentioned that you'd stopped by for a short visit, emphasis on short. She's wondering how you are, too."

Shit. "I'm fine."

"Well, for my sake if not your own, please don't overdo it." Lukas eyed him over the rim of his mug. "If you go down, we'll *really* be up shit creek."

He sat up before realizing why he'd done it. Lukas had the same uncanny ability his father had had, framing an order or request as a personal favor, one you'd die to fulfill. And speaking of Elliott... "There's something I have to say to you."

Lukas straightened from his slouch. "No need."

"Damn it, let me say this." Because he was drowning in guilt. "I'm so sorry I didn't save your father. So, *so* sorry."

"There's no need for you to apologize."

"But—"

"Jack, I've watched the tapes dozens of times. I've put myself in your place, trying to extrapolate every possible outcome. That first bullet came out of nowhere. There was no warning, no tip-off. Neither of us could have prevented it. No one could have prevented it."

"You might have been able to sense something I couldn't—"

"Even if I did, I couldn't have *done* anything about it, so thank you for saving me from that." Lukas looked grim, yet resolute. "No one could have done anything about it, Jack. No one but the shooter." Coco shifted, grabbing a handful of Lukas's chest hair. He didn't even wince. "But despite your wounds, you saved my sister. Thank you for saving Sasha, Jack. Thank you for protecting my family." Lukas gazed down at his daughter. "We're forever in your debt."

"No, you're not. It was just…instinct." Save Sasha, or die trying.

"As I said, I watched the tapes. Despite all the desk work you've recently been forced to do—which is *also* my fault—you haven't lost any reaction time."

Jack rolled his stinging shoulder. "Well, I've got some time to make up now."

"No bullshit. How's your recovery going?" Lukas gestured to Jack's right hand, wrapped around the coffee mug. "You seem to be using your arm and hand almost normally."

"Almost," he said with a shrug. He told Lukas about his progress at physical therapy, and his lack thereof. "I'm not ready for the gun range yet." He wouldn't be until he could support the weight of his Glock a lot better than he could right now.

"Well, use your brain. Don't rush into anything you don't have to," Lukas advised. "I do have a Council thing I'd like to speak with you about."

"Shoot." A horrified heat stung his cheeks. "Damn, I'm sorry."

"Don't worry about it."

"But—"

"Jack, it's just a word." Lukas shoved an exasperated hand through his hair. "Let's talk about the main reason I called you. How would you feel about being named the Security and Technology First?"

"Are you shitting me?" he blurted.

"Nope. Given the diaper I changed just before you got here, I hope we've exceeded the morning's quotient of shit." Lukas stroked Coco's cheek. "As I'm sure you've already figured out, I need to shift some things around so I can do the most important things well."

But... "I'm human." It had taken every lick of political capital Lukas possessed to get a human named as the Sec/Tech *Second*, and Krispin Woolf had fought him every step of the way.

"With Dad's death, things have changed. You're the obvious person for the job." Lukas took another slug off his coffee cup. "Are you interested? It would mean a lot of changes at work..."

More changes than he'd originally planned. "I'd never imagined myself as the First," he mused. "Never wanted it."

Lukas snorted. "Tell me about it."

Yeah, Lukas hadn't wanted to be the Council president and Incubus First, either. One goddamn bullet—one brutal piece of metal—had changed the trajectory of dozens of lives.

"What would you think about Bailey as your Second?

Jack blinked. "I thought you'd asked her to be the Incubus/Succubus Second."

"I have."

"A human, holding two Council seats?"

"When naming Seconds, Firsts have complete latitude," Lukas reminded him. "Wyland verified this before Coco was born."

Skill-wise, Bailey *was* the best choice for the Sec/Tech Second seat. She already spent so much time at Council meetings as a technology subject matter expert that she had an assigned chair. But officially naming her as a Second—twice!—would seat another human on the Council without putting the matter to a vote. Politically, it was a brilliant move, but… "Krispin Woolf will blow a gasket."

"Let him," Lukas said bluntly. "If he's going to keep using our Council bylaws to postpone filling the Humanity seat, I'll use them to get another human at the table another way."

Most members of the Council were convinced that humanity would learn about their culture's existence sooner rather than later. Technology—smart phones—had changed the game, upped the risk. It was just a matter of time until someone from their culture went viral, doing something they didn't want humans to see. He and Lukas had convinced everyone except Krispin Woolf that having humans on the Council when that fateful day arrived might help smooth some rough waters. For some reason, Krispin kept throwing procedural wrenches in their plans.

There had to be a procedural way to stop him. He and Wyland were overdue for some ice cold legal scheming. Would Jacoby contact Wyland about his succession concerns? They'd be foolish not to factor them in.

"I'm confident that you're the right person for the job, but I'd like you to take some time, give it some thought."

"How much time?"

"As much as you need, of course, but I hope you'll make your decision sooner rather than later." Lukas freed his chest hair from Coco's fist. She fussed a little, then settled. "I understand you recently went to California to deal with some family issues. Is everything okay there?"

"No, but that's nothing new." He told Lukas about his mother's breast cancer—that her treatment was going well—but he didn't say anything about his dad pressuring him to take over at K&K. It was a non-issue—or it would be, once he spoke with his parents again.

"Do you need to go back? Take some time off?" Lukas paused. "Will your family factor in to your decision to take the First seat or not?"

"No," he said firmly. "I've made a long-term commitment here."

"Have you?"

They weren't talking about the Council anymore. Jack took a careful sip of coffee. "I've never known you to elbow into your sister's love life before." Not even when Sasha had dated that death metal guy, the one who carried a scythe and always smelled like weed.

"Believe me, I had this exact same conversation with Bailey when she and Rafe were getting all snarled up—and there wasn't a Council seat on the line then." Lukas shifted Coco to the other arm, then stroked her sprout of red hair. "I'd be shortsighted if I didn't consider all the ways that offering you this position might impact my family."

"Are you asking me about my intentions toward your sister?" Did he have any? Their relationship was serious, but—

Lukas laughed. "You poor bastard, you're still trying to figure it out."

He couldn't deny it. What *were* his intentions?

Where might the future take them?

"Well, just remember that when it ends, you'll still have to work together. You'll still have to deal with her."

Anger sparked. "What makes you so sure it'll

end?"

"You think it won't?"

What would their relationship *not* ending even look like? In Sasha's world—in the paranormal culture—people simply exchanged words to become bondmates. It was an oral contract between them, with no one else involved. Rafe, that lovesick fool, had offered to marry Bailey in a human church if she wanted, or to fly to Vegas and elope, but she'd chosen to bond in his culture's tradition instead. Even when he and Anna had gotten serious, he'd never considered what he wanted in a wedding ceremony.

Or in a marriage, for that matter.

Lukas's head jerked up.

"What?"

"Something's wrong with Sasha." Shoving to his feet, Lukas thrust his tiny daughter at Jack.

"Shit, let me set my coffee down first." Once he did, Lukas handed Coco off like a football. "What's wrong with Sasha?" Tucking Coco into the crook of one arm, he reached for his cell phone with the other.

"Support her head…"

"I know how to hold a fucking baby." *I think.* She was so small—small, and warm, and surprisingly solid. Yep, the football hold was the way to go. "What's wrong with Sasha?" he repeated.

"I don't know yet," Lukas snapped, reaching for his own phone. "But she's petrified."

Jack didn't doubt it. Lukas's ability to pluck emotions out of the air at distance was unrivaled.

Jack's phone rang. "It's Sasha." He passed Coco back to Lukas.

"Put it on speaker," Lukas ordered.

Jack obeyed. "Sasha? What's wrong?"

"Someone just shot at us. From the street."

His face went numb. "Are you hit?"

"No. Just scared." Her voice was shaky. "Winnie and I were...taking out the garbage."

The Sebastiani Building's Dumpster was in the loading dock. "Is Winnie okay?"

"Yes. She shoved me to the ground." Sasha's jagged breaths sliced him over the phone. "You SebSec folks are hell on my knees."

Better a banged-up knee than a bullet to the head. Again. *Fuck, fuck, fuck.* "Where are you now?"

"Crackhouse's back office," she said. "Winnie told me to stay put while she checks things out."

"Who's there with you?"

"Padrick's here, and Flynn's on his way. I couldn't leave if I wanted to."

She sounded crabby about it, which planed an edge off his worry.

"I heard something ping off the Dumpster, then Winnie pushed me down." Sasha took a steadying breath. "I think the bullet came from the street. I didn't see who might have shot at us."

Underbelly's loading dock cameras probably hadn't, either. They were aimed toward the Dumpster, not the street. Maybe they'd get lucky with the city's CCTV cameras, but he wasn't counting on it. The shooter was no doubt long gone, but there'd be a bullet for their crime scene team to retrieve.

Lukas gestured to the bedroom. "I'm going to get dressed. Back in a minute." He and Coco disappeared. Calamity trotted after them.

"Jack, when is this going to end?"

She sounded pissed off, not helpless or hopeless. Good. "We'll find the shooter." If Winnie was following procedure, she'd already called for backup. Once it arrived, they'd start working the scene. "Are you sitting down? Please sit down. Did you hurt your knee?" The Sebastiani Building, only blocks away, felt as far away as the Canadian border.

"Nah, I'm okay," she said. "I've done worse at dance class and kept right on going. I just…needed to bitch about something."

When Lukas came back out of the bedroom carrying Coco, he'd pulled on a black T-shirt and steel-toed work boots. "Let's go downstairs."

He nodded. They could better manage the emergency from the first floor, where the full power of Sebastiani Security could be put into play. "Stay on the phone with me," he said to Sasha. "I'm with Lukas at the loft. We're going downstairs."

Lukas detoured toward the couch, grabbing a pink and green diaper bag that had to weigh twice what his daughter did. Jack toed into his shoes. When they went into the hall, the elevator he'd taken upstairs to the loft was still there, waiting. He followed Lukas inside, and pressed the button for the first floor. "Hang on," he murmured to Sasha. "I'll be there in a couple of minutes."

Lukas gave him a side-eye. In an emergency, Jack usually coordinated operations from SebSec, and Lukas worked the scene. Sometimes Lukas could taste the emotions of a suspect before they dissolved, which came in handy, but…Lukas was president now. His days of responding to crime scenes were over. *I need to get over to Crackhouse, see Sasha for myself.* He pointed at the baby. "You have Coco."

Lukas opened his mouth, then gave a curt nod. "I'll issue a Code Red, then put a security wrap around Scarlett, Claudette, Rafe, Bailey, and Antonia."

The immediate members of his family, because this wasn't a random shooting.

He eyed the floor numbers as the elevator descended. *Hurry, hurry, hurry...*

"Here." Lukas's ever-present tube of antacids appeared in his peripheral vision.

"Thanks." He took the tube from Lukas, peeled off two chalky tablets, then handed it back. "Is Sasha still afraid?" he blurted.

Lukas's jaw clenched. "She's hanging in."

"What does Sasha taste like to you? Her baseline taste, I mean?" Why had he never asked before?

"Pomegranates," Lukas answered. "Thankfully, the flavor goes well with almonds."

His own baseline taste, the inoffensive almond—which Lukas had once told him was a key factor in offering him a partnership at Sebastiani Security. "I like almonds," he'd said. "They go with almost everything." To Lukas, when people were on an even emotional keel, their tastes were light, barely noticeable. When they turned deep and pungent, he couldn't help but pay attention.

Lukas thumbed an antacid into his own mouth, then tucked the tube back in his pants pocket. Yeah, Sasha was afraid.

"How good is Sasha at picking up emotions at distance, like you can?" he asked.

"Not particularly well at distance, but up close? She's lethal. So take a minute and calm down."

The elevator doors finally opened. Before he could dart away, Lukas stopped him with a hand on his uninjured shoulder. "Jack."

"What?" he snapped.

"She's okay. Pissed off, but okay. Calm down, get over there, and work the scene."

She's okay. Calm down. Work the scene. He gave what must have been a reassuring nod, because Lukas let him go. Their strides ate up the lobby carpet, and Jack opened the security door with a hand that shook. Once in the working area, Lukas turned into his office and Jack ducked into his. He exchanged his shoes for boots, then grabbed his coat and car keys.

He swore when he reached the parking lot. Snow, all over the car. It took precious time to swipe it away with his arms and bare hands, but he finally slid into the driver's seat.

It took three tries to get the key in the ignition. His hands were shaking, but he couldn't blame the snow.

It was open season on the Sebastiani family, and he'd never felt so damn helpless in his life.

※

She hadn't planned to use the gun today.

Miranda, parked a block and a half away and still jittering with adrenaline, watched as familiar-looking cars pulled into the Sebastiani Building's parking ramp. The Sig Sauer was in her tote bag, on the passenger seat. Sooner or later, she'd have to remove the silencer—correction, the *suppressor*—but right now she was shaking so badly she didn't trust herself to touch it. The supposedly light pistol was heavy as a brick, but she'd used it. She'd pulled the trigger.

And she'd gotten away with it.

She'd gone to the Sebastiani Building on

reconnaissance, just to scope things out. She'd driven around the block a couple of times, noting the location of the loading dock, the emergency exits, the fire escape snaking ten floors from the penthouses down to the alley. After figuring out the one-way streets, the parking gods had smiled upon her, producing an open space on a side street with clear sight lines to the back of the Sebastiani Building. Ignoring the payment kiosk—she'd only be a minute—she'd pulled on the black knit hat and scarf she'd picked up at Target, swaddling herself until only her eyes showed. Slinging the quilted Vera Bradley tote over her shoulder, she'd headed out into the snow.

And suddenly, there she was. Sasha Sebastiani, taking out the garbage.

Time had slowed to honey. *Reach into the bag. Grab the gun. Ready, aim, fire—right through the bag.*

Nothing to see here, folks.

It was louder than she'd expected, but no one looked twice—except for the tall, dark-skinned woman who'd shoved Sasha Sebastiani to the ground. But the woman hadn't come after her, hadn't pursued. Instead, she'd hustled Sasha into the building. And Miranda had just…kept on walking. In her ankle-length down jacket, knit hat, and yards of scarf, she was just another bundled-up, exasperated Minnesotan cursing the weather, trying to reach their destination without getting frostbite. After walking a couple of blocks, she'd doubled back, slowly making her way back to the car.

The snow was coming down faster now. The wind had picked up, turning the city streets into wind tunnels. The car engine was finally warming up, starting to pump heat instead of stingy cold air. As she held her hands in front of the vents, Jack's staid Volvo approached the Sebastiani Building ramp, then disappeared inside.

She glanced over at the bag, at the hole the bullet had punched through the quilted fabric. The people who'd told her not to get her own hands dirty had obviously never felt the solid heft of a gun in one's own hand. Felt the power, the potential, as it fired.

She liked it. She liked it a lot.

The hole in the bag was a small price to pay, but she should probably put in some practice time if she wanted to hit her target.

Tap tap tap. "Ma'am?" A man's voice, muffled but audible. "Could you open your window, please?"

A dark blue uniform. A badge. A leather utility belt, laden with equipment.

Cop.

She whipped a glance at the tote bag—the gun wasn't visible—then lowered her window with a hum. "Hello, Officer. Is there a problem?"

The cop leaned down, peering inside the car. "Ma'am, are you okay?"

"Yes. I'm fine. Why do you ask?"

"Well, you've been sitting here with your car running for a couple of minutes—"

"That's illegal now?" she snapped.

"No, ma'am," he said, flicking his Nordic blue eyes at her dashboard, with its lack of a paid parking receipt. "But there's a woman back here, waiting for your parking place." Sharp eyes scanned the interior of the car. "Your blinker is on, but you haven't moved."

Sure enough, her blinker was on, and there was a

lime green Kia waiting behind her. "Sorry." She gestured to her cell phone, tethered to a charger on her dash. "I just finished making a phone call."

He nodded. "Are you ready to move on?" Another pointed glance at the bare dashboard. "She's blocking traffic, and your time appears to be up."

Message received. "I'll be on my way."

He backed away from her window, tipping his snowflake-covered uniform hat. "Drive safely, now. We're supposed to get half a foot before this is over."

She forced a companionable smile. "Figures, doesn't it?"

"Right?" He knocked on the windowsill with a friendly knuckle. "You have a nice day, now."

She eased out of the parking spot, throwing an apologetic wave at the woman in the Kia. Instead of flipping her off, the woman waved back.

People were too damn nice here.

Traffic was slow-and-go, and she couldn't resist glancing at the Sebastiani Building as she passed. A trio of people stood at the loading dock door: the dark-skinned woman who'd covered Sasha, a stocky guy she guessed was Chico Perez, and big, blond Jack Kirkland.

The woman pointed across the street, indicating the place Miranda had been standing when she fired the gun.

Jack's gaze followed.

Safe behind the Lexus's tinted windows, Miranda sailed through their line of sight.

The delicious little zing felt like foreplay.

Traffic started to move, tires crunching through the snow. Once she reached the highway exit, she let herself smile. Seeing that righteous, worried scowl on

Jack's face had been worth the trip.

Ethan had been right. The most effective way to punish Jack was to threaten the Sebastiani family.

She'd practice until the gun felt light and right. And next time, she wouldn't miss.

＊

"Sasha, can you get the shallots?" Claudette called from where she was draining pasta at the kitchen sink. "Bottom shelf of the fridge."

"Sure."

Suddenly Claudette was at her side. "Okay, I saw that limp. I knew you were more hurt than you let on."

Damn it. "I'm not limping. I'm just…walking carefully." Her right knee *was* sore, yeah, but she wasn't hurt. "I'm fine, see?" Shallots in hand, she did a quick set of pirouettes to get back to the cutting board, disguising a wince as she picked up the chef's knife. "Want me to chop these?"

Claudette shot her an "I know you're lying" glance, but she didn't call her on it. "Please."

They worked in silence. Sasha chopped the shallots, and over at the stove top, Claudette tended to the garlic, sizzling in olive oil. Lukas's call, asking Claudette if they could use her dining room to provide everyone with a status update, had turned Claudette into the Energizer Bunny, and in the brisk way of someone who'd been entertaining on short notice for decades, she'd opened the refrigerator and freezer, then turned on the double oven. Sasha and

Antonia had spent a good portion of the afternoon working with Claudette, preparing enough appetizers to feed an army. Cooking, and bickering with Antonia, had helped keep her mind off Jack. But now, beneath the efficiency, Claudette was worried.

About me.

Sasha set down the knife. "Claudette, I'm a little banged up, but I'm fine. Really."

"You haven't fully recovered from the *last* time someone shot at you." Claudette pointed at Sasha's face. "That make-up is expertly applied, but it doesn't quite cover what's left of that black eye." When the oven timer buzzed, Claudette grabbed two hot pads. She removed two half-sheets from the lower oven— egg rolls and cream cheese puffs—and replaced them with two others laden with cheesy bread. "If your father were here, he'd know exactly how you were feeling. He'd know exactly how worried we—how worried *I*—should be."

Claudette's self-correction made Sasha's eyes sting. "Really, I'm fine," she said, giving Claudette a quick, one-armed hug before going back to the cutting board. *Getting there, anyway.* She looked at the wide-planked wooden floor, envisioning Jack working ten floors down. "I wish they'd hurry up." Now that he was in the building, she knew exactly how worried he was—and she wanted to comfort him as much as he wanted to comfort her.

What had they discovered in the loading dock?

Something hard glinted in Claudette's gaze. "This violence has to stop."

"Yeah."

Claudette tossed asparagus spears, carrot medallions, and broccoli florets into the sauté pan with practiced flicks of her wrist. "Where did Antonia go?"

She'd noticed one of her chicks was missing. "Next door, to take a bath."

"Good."

The Sebastiani siblings all had their own approach to self-care. Antonia took long, hot baths. Lukas sparred in SebSec's basement fighting cage. Rafe channeled everything into sculpting, and she usually danced. "With Antonia gone, she won't snitch all the cheesy bread."

Claudette grinned. "There's that."

She fought to stay focused on the shallots—the last thing they needed was a trip to the ER because she'd maimed herself with a chef's knife—but damn, it was a battle and a half. What was going on downstairs? The only thing keeping her from riding the elevator down to the first floor and finding out for herself was the promise she'd made to Winnie, who'd asked her to stay upstairs with Claudette and Antonia. "It will be easier to secure the facility if you all stay up here on ten." Sasha had been under security lockdown often enough to know that going rogue wouldn't help, but it didn't make staying in one place, away from the action, any less frustrating.

Downstairs, Jack was…seething. "I wish they'd hurry up," she murmured, staring at the floor.

"I know, honey." Claudette gave the sauté pan a shake. "I'm ready for those shallots."

Snap out of it. If Claudette could find the strength to decorate for Christmas—to wrap gifts, and to make her father's favorite vegetable concoction—she could focus long enough to scrape some shallots into a goddamn pan. Her hands were shaky, but she managed. Then she heard the front door open.

"They're here." She set down the cutting board and knife, then barreled through the swinging kitchen doors to meet everyone.

Lukas, Scarlett, and Coco came in first, carrying winter coats and laden with baby gear. Chico, Winnie, Bailey, and Rafe were next. Someone else had thought about food; Rafe was carrying four pizza boxes. "Good call," she said, taking the boxes so he could kick off his boots. Italian sausage, Vegetarian, Canadian bacon, and Hawaiian, covering most culinary bases. Claudette's menu additions would nicely cover the rest.

Now in his stocking feet, Rafe kissed her cheek, then took the boxes back. "I'll bring these into the dining room." He turned toward the living room, then paused. "It smells amazing in here."

Rafe wasn't talking about the cheesy bread. A large Christmas tree towered over in the corner, festooned with white fairy lights, silver strands of tinsel, and ornaments Claudette and their father had collected over the years. Cranberry candles glowed in squat glass jars, and gaily-wrapped gifts lay under the tree. Pine boughs draped over the fireplace mantel, and everyone's stockings hung from the clever decorative hooks Rafe had forged. Each pewter deer was unique, art in its own right.

"Look." Rafe pointed to the end of the mantel, to a riot of pink, green, and brown yarn.

"Oh my," she whispered. Claudette, with more exuberance than skill, had knit her new granddaughter a Christmas stocking. "When did she find the time? Hell, I haven't even started my Christmas shopping yet."

"Between work, planning Dad's memorial service, and watching over Jack, you've been a little busy."

Not to mention taking an unexpected trip to California.

"Speaking of watching over Jack…" Rafe leaned closer. "He's watching you right back."

I know. The last person through the door, Jack's gaze had warmth and weight, stroking like suede gloves. He kicked off his shoes, then came over to where they stood.

"How are you?" Jack asked, pulling her into his arms.

His jacket was damp from melted snow, but she didn't care. "I'm fine. How about you?" Wearing the same clothes as yesterday, short on sleep, and with fine lines bracketing his mouth, he looked completely wrung out.

He looked amazing.

Rafe's gaze bounced between them. "I'll, um, just go take care of these pizzas."

She hardly noticed when Rafe left. Jack's hands were on the move, patting her down for injuries. If his shoulder was sore, she couldn't tell. His face was expressionless, battened down tight, but his emotions roiled like a ship on rough seas. "Jack, I'm fine." She touched his cheek, looked into his eyes. "But I could use another hug."

The words were true, but Jack needed one even more than she did.

Standing stocking-footed in a mound of kicked-off boots, she simply held on, letting his chilly lips skate over her face and temples, then chase the chill away with his breath. His hands roved and patted and stroked. Slowly, gradually, the fear leached away. His touch morphed from clinical to caressing. She softened, he hardened. Her curves clung to his angles. The hand cupping her hip was a familiar, knowing weight, turning her knees to rubber. His face was expressive again, so expressive. Fear had planed away the rough edges, exposing something raw and delicate and new. She inhaled, trying to get a read on him. "Jack...?"

"Hey, can I sneak around you?" Chico asked, gesturing to the closet. He held Winnie's coat.

Behind Jack, the penthouse door opened. Antonia walked in and sniffed the air. "Jeez, will you two get a room? Your pheromones are stinking the place up."

Chico snickered.

Jack dropped a final, quick kiss onto her temple. As he stepped away, his hand cruised over her ass.

She barely controlled a shiver. *Work before play.* "Come on, Claudette is setting up in the dining room."

Chico's face lit up. "Did she make cheesy bread?"

"Of course she did."

Between the cheesy bread, pasta, and pizza, the dining room sideboard groaned with carbs, and the roasted vegetables and other appetizers were mounded in colorful bowls. Someone had set the table with the everyday mix-and-match Fiestaware, and coffee mugs huddled next to the coffee carafe. While everyone filled their plates, she and Claudette set out pitchers of ice water and bottles of wine, setting them next to the glasses on the long, cherry wood table where people could easily reach them. After taking some roasted vegetables and a slice of cheesy bread, she snagged the seat between Jack and Antonia.

With nearly a dozen people at the table—family members, bondmates, co-workers, and a baby—the room filled with raucous conversation. It felt more like a cocktail party than a meeting or debrief. Claudette was smiling, darting back and forth between the kitchen and dining room. With all her chicks safely in one place, she was in her element.

Until she made the last trip, carrying a tray of frosted brownies and lemon bars. Setting them on the sideboard, she paused, took a deep and visible breath, then approached her bondmate's empty chair.

With a bittersweet smile, Claudette sat, caressing the chair's smooth, wooden arms.

Love, loss, sadness, and steel... Sasha took shallow breaths until Claudette's misty grief shimmered away.

"Does everyone have enough food?" Claudette sipped some water, then cleared her throat. "Yes? Then let's begin."

Jack brought everyone up to date. Apparently the crime scene team had retrieved a 9mm slug from inside the Dumpster. "The Sebastiani Building's loading dock video caught Sasha and Winnie as they fell to the ground, but no sign of the shooter," he said.

"Our initial trajectory assessment has the shooter standing across the street, at sidewalk level," Winnie said. "I saw maybe half a dozen people on the sidewalk, but everyone was so damn bundled up." She stood, then went to the buffet. "Only a couple of people would've had an angle."

Sasha rubbed her sore knee. How had Winnie had time to notice who'd had an angle? She'd been too busy grinding *her* into the gravel. Under the table, Jack took her hand, lacing their fingers together.

"There was a short dude wearing a purple Vikings jacket. A woman in red, pushing a baby stroller." Winnie picked up an egg roll with a pair of serving tongs. "And someone in a long black coat."

"Any sign of a weapon?" Lukas asked.

"No."

"And you didn't find a bullet casing on the sidewalk."

"Nope, but we might have missed it in the snow. And we couldn't get footprints." Winnie gave a pragmatic shrug. "Too much snow."

A murmur from the nearby Pack 'n Play snagged everyone's attention. When Coco quieted, Lukas continued. "Any sense of Black Coat's height and weight?"

Winnie transferred two cream cheese wontons to her plate, then came back to the table. "About the same height as the woman with the stroller." She paused. "Weight is more challenging, because the coat was one those puffy sleeping bag coats that practically go down to the ankle."

"A woman, then," Antonia murmured.

Chico leaned in. "Why do you say that?"

"Dudes never wear those long down coats."

Sasha nodded. "Not unless they're standing on the sideline at Lambeau, wearing helmets, shoulder pads, and tight, shiny pants."

"It could have been a small man, wearing a woman's coat to throw us off track," Chico argued.

Antonia shrugged, clearly disagreeing. "Low odds."

Thankfully, Lukas halted further devil's advocacy. "Anything from CCTV?" he asked Bailey.

Did the City of Minneapolis realize how frequently

a world-class hacker covertly accessed their security cameras?

"We should have something to look at in a couple of hours," Bailey responded.

"Tomorrow morning is soon enough," Lukas said tiredly. "Everyone needs to get some sleep tonight."

And with that, the conversation about the crime scene just stopped dead, as if Lukas had activated some sort of Bat Signal that only Sebastiani Security workers could discern.

"Seriously?" Were they really not going to talk about this? She and Rafe were the only civilians at the table—the only two who didn't either have a seat on the Council, or work at Sebastiani Security—but that didn't mean she couldn't connect some pertinent fucking dots. "Am I just supposed to forget that Dad and Jack were shot with a 9mm, too?"

Lukas glanced at Claudette.

"Oh, come on. What's with the patriarchal bullshit?" Sasha snapped. "Claudette makes life and death decisions every day." At the end of the table, Claudette was steely, serene, and fighting a smile. "Use your nose. She's hurt, but she's holding." Jack's hand, his formerly immobile hand, was resting on the table between them. She covered it with hers. "We're all hurt, but we're holding."

Lukas inhaled, then sighed. "Sorry. You're right." He reached for his antacids, popping two into his mouth. "We retrieved four 9mm slugs from the first scene—one from Dad, two from Jack, and one from the parking ramp wall—and they all came from the same weapon. Ballistics is testing the bullet we recovered downstairs. Once they're done, we'll have more information." He crunched down on the antacids. "Ballistics aside, today's shooting presents three possibilities. One, the shooting was random. Two, Winnie was the target. Three? You were the target. Until we know which it is, you'll have multiple bodyguards around the clock."

"What?" she squawked. "Are you serious?"

"As a heart attack." Her brother pointed at her with his fork. "Do *not* push me on this."

At her side, Jack sat silently. If worry rippled off Lukas, Jack was battling rogue waves. She'd get no help there. He agreed with her brother.

Everyone at the table agreed with her brother.

Damn it.

"It's possible that you've been the target all along," Antonia mused. "You were the only person present at both scenes."

"The first time, Dad was the obvious target." She squeezed Jack's hand reassuringly. "And even if he wasn't, Jack's a higher value target than I'd ever be."

Antonia shrugged. "Depends on the shooter's motivation. And Jack wasn't the target today, was he?"

Nope.

"Have you pissed anyone off lately?" Lukas asked.

"Badly enough for someone to shoot at me? Twice?"

"You're kicking people out of Underbelly all the time," Antonia said, getting up to refill her coffee mug.

Jack shot her a pointed look. "Do the bouncers have a training issue I'm not aware of?"

Sebastiani Security trained Underbelly's bouncers very, very well. "No," she said. "But if it's possible, I like to handle things with a little less...bounce."

Jack looked at Lukas, exasperated.

"I'm not saying Sasha being the primary target of both shootings is the most probable scenario," Antonia chimed in, "but Lukas is right. At this point, it's not something we should rule out."

"What's with this 'we' shit?" Sasha muttered. "It's not you who'll be sitting under a security dragnet until this is over—"

"Yes, she will," Lukas stated. "Every Sebastiani and Council member in this room will be assigned around-the-clock security teams until we figure out what the hell is going on here."

After a short discussion about guard assignments, the meeting broke up, but no one seemed ready to leave. She, Antonia, and Rafe handled clean-up, leaving the beverages in the dining room but setting the kitchen to rights. When they came back out to the living room, she noticed Jack and Claudette sitting on the love seat, speaking quietly. Good, they needed to talk. Jack had been avoiding Claudette for far too long.

Claudette smiled, then gave Jack a hug. The naked relief on Jack's face was good to see, but difficult to watch.

He stood, then wandered over. "Are you ready to go?"

His low murmur stroked in sensitive places. "Yes. Your place or mine?"

"How about mine?" He stroked her cheek. "No offense, but I'd like to get away from your family for a while."

"No shit."

They were saying their goodbyes when the Code Red arrived. Lukas, Winnie, Chico, Bailey, and Jack all looked at their devices.

"What's up?" she asked him.

"DB in New Brighton."

A dead body. "One of ours?"

Jack and Lukas shared a grim look. "Looks like it."

Chico looked stunned, like he'd just taken a roundhouse kick. "What the hell happened?"

"We'll find out when we get there." Jack dropped a kiss on her temple—sweet, homey, and full of apologies. "Wait for me here?"

"I'll either be here, or at my place." She kissed him back. "Please be careful."

"Always."

As Jack, Lukas, and Chico trooped out the door, Winnie pulled Bailey aside for a private huddle, then came over.

"Bailey and I have to go back to the office," she said. "Do I have your word you'll stay here, on this floor, until Jack comes back?"

"Of course." She touched Winnie's arm. "Are you okay?" The other woman seemed shaken.

Winnie gave one curt nod, but didn't say anything else. As she and Bailey left, they trailed sadness, grief, and urgency in their wake.

She turned to Antonia. "What the hell?"

Antonia was already tapping at her mini-comp. "Let me see what I can find out."

If there was anything to find out, Antonia would find it. In the meantime, she'd try her best to keep Claudette occupied.

No one was leaving, so wine couldn't hurt.

CHAPTER FIFTEEN

Jack stared down at the body.

Ethan Covington was half-sitting, half-lying on the queen-sized bed, slightly slumped to the side, his brown eyes open and unseeing. Blood and brain matter spattered the pillows, and the back of his head was a pulpy mess. He was in full rigor, and had soiled his tighty-whities. The scent of feces was inescapable.

"An empty syringe, packets of pills, a bottle of Jack, and a bullet to the brain." Lead investigator Jenny Williams moved slowly and deliberately, touching nothing, ensuring her body cam supplemented the work already performed by the crime scene photographer and digital videographer. "Looks like he really wanted to die."

"Yeah." *Damn it, Ethan.* "You said the landlord called it in?"

Jenny nodded. "The landlord said he came to personally collect the December rent check, and to speak to Ethan about signing a new lease. When Ethan didn't answer, the landlord used his master to enter the residence."

"Why?"

"Ethan's truck is out in the parking lot, so the landlord figured Ethan was dodging him because he didn't have the rent," Jenny explained. "He went out to the truck to see if Ethan had fallen asleep in the cab or something. Ethan wasn't in the truck, but the landlord noticed a lot of dashboard damage. He wondered whether Ethan had been injured in a car accident."

Jack skimmed Ethan's face and upper body. "I don't see any impact injuries."

"Check out his right hand."

Ethan's scarred knuckles looked like they'd seen a lot of action, with nicks and cuts both healed and fresh. "You think he punched his own dashboard?"

Jenny jerked a thumb toward the living room, where they'd noticed holes in the wall near the door. "It's a possibility. The truck doesn't have any exterior damage." She leaned closer, peering at but not touching Ethan's scuffed-up hand. "We'll bring the truck in, check it out, but he's a Valkyrie. I'd guess something, or someone, pissed him off royally."

The Ethan he knew—the Ethan he'd *known*—rarely lost his temper.

Jenny straightened. "So, the landlord knocks on the door, calls Ethan's name, and uses his master when there's no response. He comes in, finds this, tosses his cookies just inside the bathroom door, then calls it in."

"The landlord's one of ours?"

"Yeah, incubus."

"That simplifies things." The landlord had known to call *their* police force, not the MPD. The vampire detective currently questioning him probably wouldn't have to wipe the guy's memories afterward.

"Did Lukas—erm, President Sebastiani—sense anything we can use?" Jenny asked.

"Not this time. The only emotional residue he

tasted belongs to the landlord."

"Well, that helps establish the timeline."

"Yep." Jenny had worked with Lukas often enough to understand that the *absence* of taste meant Ethan had been dead for at least twelve hours, because otherwise Lukas would have picked something up. If anyone else had been in the apartment helping Ethan *get* dead, their trail had also gone cold.

Jenny withdrew a temperature gauge from her kit, then bent over Ethan's body.

They'd have to wait for the ME to determine the official cause, manner, and mechanism of death, but to him, it looked like Ethan had bled out from a self-inflicted gunshot wound. The liquor and drugs might have been enough to kill him on their own, but Ethan hadn't left death to chance. He'd used the Glock to seal the deal.

Jenny was right; Ethan had really wanted to die.

Jenny straightened, then read her gauge. "Estimated TOD is sixteen to twenty-four hours ago. ME to confirm." She logged the information for the record, then took in the body, the spatter, the position of the gun, and the items lying on the bed. "So, he's lying in bed, watching TV, propped up against his pillows. Eating some Taco Bell, drinking his Jack, swallowing some pills, shooting up. Before he's completely incapacitated ..." She pantomimed putting a gun in her mouth, pulling the trigger, then letting gravity do its thing with body, arm, hand, and weapon.

He nodded. "Looks plausible to me."

"Nasty exit wound," she noted.

They'd probably find the bullet in the pillows or

mattress. "Do you mind if I turn down the TV?" Ethan had been watching porn when he died. Jack could tune out the writhing bodies easily enough, but the moans, groans, and *boom-chicka-wow* soundtrack made it tough to concentrate.

"Go ahead." Jenny didn't seem to have the same problem; she was busily cataloguing the items on and around the bed. "He didn't bother to hide his fixings," she mused, examining the aluminum foil, white powder, and lighter sitting on the bedside table next to a serviceable lamp. She pointed at a rubber exercise band lying on the bed next to his left thigh. "He probably used that to tie off."

"Heroin?" he guessed.

"The lab will confirm, but it looks like it to me. Burner phone, iPhone... We might be able to get a line on his dealer, but..." She shrugged.

Yeah, probably not. Burner phones, bought with cash and used to call *other* burner phones, were usually investigative dead ends. "The iPhone might cough up something useful."

"Yeah." Jenny opened the bedside table drawer with her gloved hand. "Pen and paper. Coins totaling sixty-one cents. Box of condoms, unopened. A couple of Milky Way bars. No sex toys, but..." She gestured toward a bottle of hand lotion sitting by the lamp, and dozens of soiled, wadded-up tissues on the floor next to the bed. "Indications of compulsive masturbation are present at the scene."

Yeah, the dead had no privacy.

"We've got some empty flimsies down here on the floor." Jenny crouched to get a closer look. "Three small, clear, zip-top bags."

The kind dealers used to distribute pills. Hell, his

own pheromone intoxication meds arrived from the lab packaged the same way.

"Nine loose pills here on the carpet—Vicodin, Percocet, and Oxy. Looks like he bought himself a party pack." Jenny stood. "We'll have to wait for tox to confirm which meds he actually took."

Was Ethan's dealer human, or one of their own? What were the legal ramifications either way? The Underworld Council had no jurisdiction over humans.

He eyed the Glock, a newer model he'd considered buying himself. Ethan hadn't upgraded his cell phone, but he'd upgraded his weapon.

It was a 9mm.

Jack thought back to the last time he'd seen Ethan, the day he'd fired him. Ethan had behaved professionally enough for a guy losing a job he loved—he hadn't tried to argue; he'd known the firing was justified—but Ethan's life circumstances had clearly taken a turn for the worse between then and now.

Could Ethan be their shooter? Had Ethan blamed him, or Sebastiani Security, for firing him? If so, why kill Elliott? It didn't make sense.

Chico appeared in the doorway, grimacing as he took in the bed, the body, the blood. "What a mess."

He knew Chico's comment was more about the sad situation than the condition of the scene, but...Ethan's first-floor unit looked like a landfill. Out in the kitchen, the garbage stank, the sink was full of dirty dishes, and a blizzard of bills, papers, and snail mail covered the island separating the kitchen from the living room. There were empty pop cans, liquor bottles, candy wrappers, and fast food bags on the floor throughout the apartment. Ethan had confined his dirty laundry to the bedroom, tossing it toward the open closet, but the bathroom hadn't been cleaned in ages, and the towels reeked of mildew. One of the bathroom walls sported a fist-sized hole, a match for those near the front door.

"He was a Valkyrie," Jenny reminded them.

And between the food wrappers, the holes in the wall, and the semen-stained tissues, the evidence was piling up. "Food, fight, fuck" was a familiar Valkyrie mantra, describing the methods they used to manage their species' hyperactive adrenal systems. Signs of a Valkyrie spinning out of control were all over the place.

Why?

"How are things going out there?" he asked Chico.

"The landlord has been interviewed and sent on his way. The crime scene team is ready to start in here when Jenny gives the word." Chico took one careful step into the room, avoiding crumpled fast food bags. "Well, the fast food explains his weight gain."

Ethan *had* gained weight. His formerly flat belly bulged over his underwear's elastic waistband like a hairy inner tube.

"Remember what a neat freak he used to be at work? His desk was always clean, and he hand-washed Mr. Sebastiani's Town Car every day, whether it needed it or not."

Jenny's head snapped up. "That's right, he used to work for Sebastiani Security."

"He used to be one of the President's bodyguards," he confirmed. "We—I—fired him, slightly more than a year ago."

"Why?"

"Elliott gave him the slip one too many times."

The final nail in Ethan's coffin? The day Elliott decided to join a street protest in downtown Minneapolis. The march had been peaceful, but Elliott had turned off his phone. He'd been off the grid, incommunicado, for over two hours. He'd returned safely, but the shouting match he'd had with his son afterward had been one for the ages. Anyone who'd heard Lukas threaten to chip his father like a dog still talked about it.

Now that *he* was president, Lukas really needed bodyguards, too.

Good luck convincing him of that.

Jenny snapped off her gloves, then reached into her cross-body bag for a digital tablet. "Can you forward me a copy of Ethan's employee file?"

"Is tomorrow morning soon enough?"

"Sure."

"Aren't you out of the office tomorrow morning?" Chico asked.

His appointment with Adnan. He was *so* ready to be done with doctor appointments.

"I can take care of it," Chico offered.

Delegate. "Thanks."

Chico cast a bleak look at the body on the bed. "I talked to him at Underbelly last night."

Jenny paused her tapping. "He was there? I didn't see him."

That's right; Jenny had been sitting at the bar. "I didn't see him, either," he said. After speaking with Jacoby, he hadn't had eyes for anyone but Sasha. "Was he alone?"

"Yeah," Chico answered. "We talked for maybe a minute, tops, around midnight. He said he had to leave. I thought he was meeting someone. You know, a date. I *hoped* he was meeting someone, because he looked jittery even then." He glanced at the silent porn, the pile of tissues on the floor, then scrubbed his palm against the back of his neck. "I offered to go out to the alley with him—you know, to throw a couple of punches. He said no."

Jenny touched Chico's arm, commiserating. "So, we know he was alive as of midnight last night."

Twenty-two hours ago. Damn it, why had Ethan killed himself? Why last night?

Jenny made another careful circuit of the room, stopping in front of the open closet. "Shirts, pants, shoes, boots. Gym clothes, sweatpants, sweatshirts, folded. A half-dozen dark suits in dry-cleaning bags, hanging here at the back."

The suits had been his uniform when he'd guarded Elliott.

Jenny rose on tip-toe, peering at the upper shelves. "More workout gear, shorts and flip flops, stored away for winter. Tactical gloves, and some righteous dust bunnies. Five gun cases, closed. Three boxes of ammo." She dropped to a crouch, examining a mound of navy blue fabric at the top of the laundry pile. "Looks like a uniform. Do either of you know where he worked?"

Chico shook his head.

"I don't, either." Sadly, he hadn't given Ethan much thought after firing him, a stain he'd carry on his conscience for a long time to come. "He never asked me for a job referral. You?" he asked Chico.

"Nope."

"He probably knew better." Rising, Jenny tapped her screen. "Alka or Lorin might know where he worked."

"*I* should know," Chico bit out. "Damn it, he was a member of my team. I should know." His voice thickened. "I should have known he was in trouble. I should have yanked him into that goddamn alley last night whether he wanted to go or not."

It didn't surprise him that Chico blamed himself, but... "Look around, Chico. Things have been going downhill for Ethan for a long time."

"He could have reached out."

"But he didn't."

"But—"

"Chico." Lukas's big frame filled the bedroom doorway. "Sparring in the alley wouldn't have helped. He was too far gone." A cheek muscle ticked as he studied the scene, the spatter, his former employee lying dead on the bed. "A 9mm Glock?"

"Yes."

Lukas glanced over at him. "Gee, what a coincidence."

"It might be," Jack pointed out, trying to ignore a familiar tingle—one Lukas apparently shared. "Jenny found five gun cases in the closet. We need to wait for Ballistics to finish their testing."

Jenny's eyes narrowed. "You think there might be a connection to President Sebastiani's death?" She reached for her cell phone. "I'll tag Gideon."

"Don't bother him. He's on vacation." Their overworked police commander was in northern Minnesota right now, freezing his ass off ice fishing.

"You don't want me to inform my boss? Please."

Of course Jenny wanted to contact her boss. In Gideon's place, he'd be livid if she didn't.

Jenny's thumbs flew as she sent a secure text. With a possible connection to Elliott's case, Jack was pretty sure Gideon would start packing up the minute he received it.

"Jenny? Mr. Sebastiani?" someone called from the other room. "We found something."

Jenny let the crime scene techs into the bedroom to start their work, reminding them to be on the lookout for drugs and sharps. "Check the fast food bags. He might have a stash somewhere."

They went to the kitchen, exchanging the scent of shit and semen for smelly garbage and spoiled food. Every dish sat unwashed, and used paper plates filled the garbage can to overflowing. The appliances and countertops hadn't been wiped in ages, and Jack's disposable booties stuck to the linoleum with each step he took.

"It looks like the deceased was having some financial trouble," the tech said, indicating some envelopes and papers she'd pulled from the pile on the kitchen island. Wearing a face mask and a hooded Tyvek coverall, very little of the woman was visible, but her coffee-brown eyes had seen it all and then some. "Lots of overdue bills here, and the landlord said he was habitually late with his rent." She extended a piece of paper. "And then there's this."

"A termination notice from Ansel Manufacturing, Inc.," Jenny noted, not touching it. "He was fired two days ago."

Chico turned and left the kitchen.

Lukas stopped Jack from following. "Give him a minute."

The tech's gaze bounced between them. She cleared her throat. "I'll start bagging and tagging here."

"Thanks, Eva," Jenny said. "We'll get out of your

way."

They moved to the only area of the apartment where crime scene techs weren't working, a carpeted area in front of the bathroom. From there, Jack could see the techs working in the bedroom, smell the landlord's vomit on the bathroom floor. Chico stood in front of the living room window, staring out into the dark.

"We'll interview Ethan's boss, pull his financials," Jenny said, "but I think we can guess what might have led Ethan to self-terminate at this time."

One of the techs bagged and tagged one of the three Taco Bell bags lying on the bed. "He completely slipped off my radar," Jack said.

"He slipped off everyone's radar." Lukas rubbed his eyes. "Believe me, there's plenty of blame to go around."

Did Ethan have a family? Friends? Questions swarmed like wasps at a hive.

Jenny's phone pinged with an incoming message. "Guys, we still have a lot of work to do here. The ME won't be able to start the autopsy for hours yet, and Ballistics won't get their hands on all these weapons until tomorrow morning at the earliest. Why don't you go home and get some sleep?"

Jenny was too polite to mention it, but Lukas looked tired enough to audition for *The Walking Dead*—and he, wearing wrinkled, second-day clothes, probably didn't look much better. Still, he hesitated.

"Go," Jenny urged. "We'll take good care of him."

And the crime scene team would probably relax, and work more efficiently, after he and Lukas cleared out. "Okay."

He was…tired. Utterly exhausted, body and soul.

Jack took a final look at Ethan Covington before moving to the living room to remove his Tyvek shoe covers. Maybe he shouldn't complain about doctor appointments. At least he was alive to have them—unlike Ethan, who'd spend what was left of the night on a cold, hard slab instead of snuggled up to a warm, sleeping woman.

He didn't give a damn *how* whacked-out his dreams might be tonight. Once he climbed into Sasha's bed, he wasn't moving until the sun rose.

He looked around. "Where's Chico?"

"He left."

"Damn it, I wanted to talk to him."

"Give him some space." Lukas tapped his nose. "He'll be okay."

"If you say so."

Lukas handed him his coat. They left the apartment, walking side-by-side down the carpeted hall.

"We have 9mms coming out of our ears," Lukas muttered.

The possibility that Ethan could be Elliott's killer had clearly occurred to Lukas. "Yeah, we're on the same page there."

"I don't believe in coincidences."

I don't either. "We'll let ballistics rule it in or out, and take it from there." They reached the empty lobby. "Why would Ethan shoot your father? Someone he practically worshipped?"

"Maybe he was disappointed Dad didn't fight for him to keep his job when we decided to fire him."

"*I* fired him."

"And I agreed with your decision," Lukas said. "At this point we can't rule anything out."

"But I fired him over a year ago. Why wait so long to retaliate?"

"You saw the condition of his apartment, and all those weapons. Maybe things just...built up." Lukas's jaw went tight. "I wish I could have picked up something more useful at the scene."

Lukas was blaming himself, too. Yeah, there was plenty of blame to go around.

They exited the building and walked out into the snow. Across the parking lot, a tow truck was loading a newer-model F-150 onto a trailer. "That must be Ethan's truck," Lukas said, stuffing his bare hands into his coat pockets.

"Nice ride." It didn't have any exterior damage that he could see. "Ethan always took really good care of his vehicles."

Lukas suddenly chuckled. "Remember how much shit he used to give you about your car?"

"Yeah." Ethan thought his decade-old Volvo was a yawn on wheels—a crime against bachelorhood—and he hadn't kept his opinions to himself. If there was laughter in the SebSec break room, Ethan was usually in the thick of it. Now, that laughter was forever silent, gone from the world.

They stood, watching, until the tow truck pulled out of the parking lot.

Lukas turned toward him. "You realize we have another problem."

"Yeah."

If Ethan had died last night, he couldn't have shot at Sasha this morning.

Sasha was still in danger, and he had no idea why.

✸

Early the next afternoon, Jack turned the Volvo into the Sebastiani Building parking ramp. Why had he even mentioned that odd little stomach twinge to Adnan? Damn it, why had he opened his big fucking mouth?

The ballistics report he'd just read, confirming the 9mm Glock Ethan had used to kill himself had likely been the same weapon used to both shoot him and kill Elliott, faded into the background. He now had a far more urgent problem.

Adnan had ordered him to stop taking pheromone intoxication meds.

The quick arm and shoulder check he'd been expecting at his doctor appointment that morning had turned into a three-hour tour through the endoscopy lab, then back to the exam room, where Adnan had informed him he was the proud father of a bouncing baby ulcer.

No doubt Adnan had been on the phone the minute Jack left, reporting his symptoms to Sebastiani Labs. Damn it, he needed those pills to do his job, to— "Shit." He stomped on the brake. Wheels squealed as the Volvo lurched to a stop, inches from the rear bumper of an SUV he hadn't seen.

"Shit," he breathed. He gave the driver an apologetic wave. The driver waved back. When the SUV pulled away, he eased his jittering foot off the brake, moving forward at a more sedate pace.

No more pills. How was he supposed to do his fricking job? The medication had been developed especially for *him*, the Council's only human member and Sebastiani Security's first human hire, so he could work with incubi and succubi. In this business, a couple-second delay could cost someone their life.

If he couldn't take the pills, he couldn't guard Sasha—and God only knew what the lack of meds would mean to their fledgling relationship.

Did Adnan realize he'd just shattered the foundation of his patient's life?

He parked, got out of the car, and looked down. Would he ever be able to park in this ramp and not see Elliott's blood staining the concrete? Not see the bullet hole in the wall, hidden behind a fresh patch?

He drew in a slow, steadying breath, then another—not that it would make the upcoming conversation any easier. He glanced at the ceiling. Sasha had probably already picked up on his mood.

He took the stairs up to the main level, then badged into Underbelly. The club's main floor was dim and quiet, but up on the second and third floors, workers were deep-cleaning the tables and chairs bellying up to the balcony rails. Something metallic crashed in the kitchen. Flynn, checking bottles at the back bar, didn't even blink.

"Are you looking for Sasha?" Flynn pointed at the one-way windows up on three, overlooking the dance floor. "She hasn't left her office all afternoon."

It looked like Sasha had kept the promise she'd made to Winnie, that she'd stay put while Winnie attended an important meeting at SebSec. With two more security doors between Sasha's office and the rest of the building, she was as safe as she could be without a guard's physical presence. "Do you have a minute?" he asked Flynn. Flynn had worked the back bar the night Ethan had died. He might have noticed something, anything...

"I didn't see him in person," Flynn said, "but Sasha and I pulled the security tapes for the detectives first thing this morning."

Sasha hadn't stirred when he'd kissed her goodbye at first light. She must have woken up soon after, then hit the ground running.

"Ethan bought a Summit at the front bar at 10:33 p.m., then took up position against the west wall." The box cutter flashed as Flynn broke down a cardboard box. "He didn't speak with anyone other than Chico Perez. They had a short conversation around eleven, then Ethan left."

"Just one beer?"

"Yeah."

Jack considered the timeline in context with the ME's preliminary autopsy report. Ethan had been at Underbelly for a half-hour, tops. The single beer wouldn't have contributed much to Ethan's whopping .224 blood alcohol level, but it had kicked things off. The Taco Bell that Ethan had eaten— purchased on his way home from Underbelly, according to the receipts they'd found in the fast food bags—hadn't absorbed much of the booze. The ME had confirmed the heroin, but had to wait for further tox results before confirming the presence of other drugs.

Jack fully expected they'd find them. Why *wouldn't* Ethan have taken the other drugs they'd found on-scene? He'd gorged on everything else he had on hand.

"We copied you on the security files," Flynn said. "Did you receive them?"

"I haven't had a chance to check e-mail since this morning." One more thing he had to get to yet today. Left unattended, e-mail had a habit of multiplying like rabbits. "Thanks." With a wave, he headed for the stairwell, badging at the door. When he reached the third floor, he sighed.

Make that *one* security door between Sasha and everybody else. Her office door was wide open. He heard her voice, and the murmur of music, before he saw her.

"You want Andrew Zimmern to make you cheese curds. In your dressing room."

Sasha must be negotiating a gig rider. Though Underbelly's world-class amenities always exceeded technical specs, band members' personal requests could be…entertaining. During her performing days, Scarlett's rider had required that a particular brand of toilet bowl cleaner, and a new pair of women's size medium rubber gloves, be present in the dressing room's bathroom when she arrived. Scarlett puked before every performance and insisted on cleaning the toilet herself.

When he tapped on the door jamb, Sasha smiled and waved him in. Extending one black-nailed forefinger, she indicated she'd just be a minute. He nodded, closed the door, then sat on the lime green velour love seat. Clearly, Zimmern was out of the question…or was he? The size and breadth of Sasha's social and professional networks never stopped surprising him.

"Cheese curds sound awesome!" she chirped, rolling her eyes. Wearing faded jeans, scaled-down leather shit-kickers, and a vintage Blondie T-shirt, sitting at her cluttered L-shaped desk, she looked alert, adorable, and in complete control of her domain. Her two-toned hair stood on end, and the thick black kohl rimming her eyes gave them a hard-edged pop—all the better to glare at the contract she held in one hand. Her workhorse of a laptop sat open behind her, a spreadsheet glowing on the screen.

A wily expression crossed her face. "I know how much you and the band value authenticity. What do you think about having an actual Minnesota State Fair worker make the cheese curds?"

Somehow, Sasha made this suggestion sound like the sexiest idea anyone ever had—or maybe it was the pheromones. The room smelled like her, a luscious combination of jungle blooms, spice, and sex—a sneak attack that left him dizzy, hungry, and hard. He shifted on the couch, trying to disguise what was happening behind his fly, but Sasha, still talking on the phone, managed to skim his frame with a hot, knowing gaze that promised monkey business.

His fingers twitched against his thighs. His pulse pounded hard enough to hammer nails.

When she inhaled, her eyelids went to half-mast. Her expression was stark, saturated with erotic intent.

He blinked, fighting the undertow. She was drawing him into a sexual feedback loop, in the middle of contract negotiations.

How nice to be able to do one's job drowning in pheromones. He…could not.

It was a struggle, but he managed to kick free. Shoving to his feet, he stalked to the office door, yanked it open, and strode into the hallway.

Sasha's gaze drilled into his back from behind. Yeah, she knew something was up.

He stood in the hallway, gulping big breaths of

fresh air until his thoughts started to clear—proof positive he couldn't guard her effectively without taking the pills. Sasha had taken care of him after he was shot, and now he had to return the favor.

She'd be safer if he tapped out, if he assigned someone else to…guard her body.

Winnie was the short-term solution to the problem, of course. Great skills, and no inconvenient erections—no jealous rage strokes on *his* part because a bodyguard *had* an inconvenient erection—but logistics were going to be a challenge.

He reconsidered, then shook his head. It had to be done.

How should he start this conversation? He scowled at his fly. *Fuck it, she's a sex demon.* Sasha saw men with inconvenient erections all the damn time.

He turned back to the office.

"Yes, the worker could certainly wear their State Fair uniform," she was saying. "Yes, and the paper hat."

Wearing the paper hat apparently sealed the deal, because she wrapped up the call quickly after that. "How the hell are you going to manage that?" he asked, sitting back down on the couch.

"Padrick worked at the State Fair back in the day, and he's already on the schedule to work at Underbelly that night. He'll go for it." The sizzle was gone from her gaze, and her voice had turned into a deep freeze.

Yeah, she knew something was up.

She scribbled a note on the contract, set it down, then pointedly glanced at the space he'd left between them. "What's wrong?"

"We have to talk."

Her nose twitched, then her face went smooth as a sheet of ice. "Say no more."

"I haven't said anything yet—"

"You don't have to," she snapped. "I can smell it on you."

"Smell what?"

She inhaled deeply again, wrinkling her nose as if the office suddenly smelled like an outhouse. "You're breaking up with me. You reek of it."

What the hell—

"That's just great," she bit out. "That's just fucking fantastic."

She'd obviously drawn the wrong conclusion from whatever mess of emotions he was leaching.

Say something. Fix this.

He...didn't.

Sasha had inhaled the decision his conscious mind wouldn't let him make. The realization was a sucker punch, a huge, vicious wave holding him down.

His soul was screaming for air, but he kept his mouth shut. Tried to preserve what little oxygen remained in his lungs. Breaking up, at least temporarily, *was* the best solution. Winnie could do a better job protecting Sasha without him bumbling around, complicating the job.

She threw the pen to the desk. "You chickenshit."

He finally took a breath. "Sasha, I can't protect you."

"That's reason enough to break up with me?"

Don't say anything. Don't say anything. "I'm sorry." Hopefully he could fix it, fix this, after they caught who'd shot at her. After she was safe. And if not? *She'll still be alive to hate me.* He slowly rose from the couch, trying not to stumble. "Winnie will be your new permanent guard."

"Fine."

Her response flayed him open. He almost welcomed the pain. "Are you ready to go?"

"Go where? Back to your place?" She barked a humorless laugh. "You've got to be kidding. I have a little more work to do here—" she waved toward the spreadsheet "—and then I have a staff meeting. Winnie's due back in an hour. When she gets here, she can take me back to your place to pack my things."

"Okay." Gazing into her kohl-rimmed eyes felt like looking down the barrel of a gun. He was the target in her cross-hairs.

"I'd appreciate it if you made yourself scarce while I clear out."

They stared at each other until her desk phone rang. Once, twice. "I have to take this," she finally said.

He cleared the lump from his throat. "I'll take up position at the stop of the stairwell until Winnie relieves me."

"Fine."

The phone rang again. She punched a button, putting the call on speaker. "Blake! Hi, there!"

"Well, hello there, cupcake." The guy's southern drawl was thick as thieves. "How you doin' up there in the Great White North?"

He waited for her to chew the guy out for calling her cupcake, but it didn't happen. With a delighted laugh, Sasha turned away from him, giving him her back.

Numb, he walked away.

Walked out of her office.

Walked out of her life.

✳

Miranda followed the young woman in charge of the condo's sales office down the carpeted hallway. The brunette's discreet brass nametag, pinned to her trim black suit, identified her as "Claire."

Claire was about to have a very bad day—a firing offense kind of day—but it couldn't be helped.

They paused in front of the entrance to Jack's top-floor condo. "Are you, like, sure I can't come inside and help you?" Claire asked. Her heavily-mascaraed gaze took in Miranda's uniform and leather utility belt. Loaded down with a baton, Taser, radio, handcuffs, pepper spray, and her gun, the belt was damn heavy. "I'm not supposed to let anyone—"

"Claire, as I told you downstairs, all I need is for you to open the door so I can execute this search warrant." Which was as fake as the police uniform she wore, but Claire didn't know that. "Remember, this is a confidential investigation." She lifted her hand, resting it on her gun. "You're subject to arrest if you tell anyone I was here."

Claire gulped, then swiped the master key through the lock on Jack's door. There was a chime and a click.

"Open it, please." No sense leaving fingerprints behind.

Claire obeyed. "I appreciate that you came to the office. That you didn't just, like, break the lock and force your way in."

There was no need, not when the condo association's least-experienced employee had access to the master key. "No worries." Miranda flicked a quick glance at the discreet camera peering down from the ceiling near the elevator. Her disguise—the uniform, the heavy make-up, the itchy, short-haired wig—should be enough to get in, get out, and be gone without anyone recognizing her. "Thanks again, Claire," she said, shouldering into the condo. "The Minneapolis Police Department thanks you for your cooperation. And remember—"

"I can't tell anyone." Claire mimicked locking her lips with a twist of her French-manicured fingertips. "I'll just, like, go back downstairs to the office."

If Claire worked in *her* office, those extraneous 'likes' would be quickly coached away. *But you don't have an office any more, do you?* "Thank you," she repeated, closing the door.

Screw being a business executive. Playing cops and robbers was a *lot* more fun.

Figuring out the best way to break into Jack's condo had been oddly satisfying, giving her brain both a logical and a creative workout. She'd staked out the condo's sales office, identified the weakest link—and last night, she'd tailed Jack to Ethan Covington's apartment without being made. Watching from the parking lot across the street, it hadn't taken long to connect the dots, especially when they'd wheeled out a body bag.

Ethan was dead, and she needed information.

She pulled her cell from her front pocket. The GPS tracker she'd slapped on Jack's car while he was at a doctor appointment earlier that day showed he was still at the Sebastiani Building. "No doubt fucking

Sasha Sebastiani, up in the penthouse Daddy's money bought," she muttered, staring at the glowing red dot.

Forget that skank. It was time to get to work, to look for any information tying her to Ethan Covington.

Pulling on some disposable gloves, she locked the door, then headed right to Jack's sleek, classy home office. The bookshelves were packed, and a white board fluttered with colorful sticky notes, but his desk was clear and clean, and his laptop was powered down. There were no papers lying about, and the desk drawers and file cabinets were locked up tight. "Damn." Jack didn't practice law in Minnesota, but he hadn't slacked off on confidentiality habits one bit. She tapped her lip, considering. If her goal was to get in and out of Jack's condo undiscovered, breaking the desk and file cabinet locks would be stupid.

Maybe if she searched the rest of the condo, she'd find the keys to the desk.

Tastefully decorated, the space smelled like fresh herbs—probably due to the plants sitting on the kitchen windowsill—but signs of cohabitation, of a woman's presence, were all over the place. Sasha's clothing, shoes, duffel bag, and device chargers were strewn carelessly about the guest bedroom, but the wispy panties on the floor next to Jack's king-sized bed, and the fur-lined handcuffs lying on the bedside table, made it clear where they spent most of their time.

She went to the master bathroom, an outrageously sensual space that had wet and dry areas she'd only seen in magazines. Over in the glassed-in shower enclosure, Sasha's high-end shampoo and conditioner cozied up to Jack's utilitarian body wash. "Just moved right in, didn't you?" Sasha had her own sink, with a toothbrush sitting in a holder. Jewelry, make-up, and hair care products were scattered about the counter top. "What a slob—ooh, Le Mer," she breathed, picking up the heavy white and pink jar from the vanity top. The viciously expensive French moisturizer had been a daily part of her beauty routine before she went to prison, but she damn well couldn't afford it now. She opened the jar and inhaled. The familiar, delicate scent danced into her nose, taunting her, igniting a sudden, seething anger.

That bitch had everything Miranda wanted—money, makeup, and man.

Closing the jar, she jammed it into her jacket pocket.

She found Sasha's huge make-up bag under the sink and started shopping, adding an Urban Decay eye pencil, a bottle of black nail polish, and two tubes of lipstick—one red, and the other an interesting shade of purple—to her take. She considered taking Jack's toothbrush, but contented herself taking a good long sniff. Sasha wouldn't miss the make-up—she had half a Sephora store in that fricking bag—but a man as fastidious about personal hygiene as Jack would miss his minty-fresh toothbrush in a hot second. She opened the cabinet beneath Jack's sink. Maybe he had an extra tube of toothpaste she could take—

Condoms. A box of condoms, on the bottom shelf.

Just in case the jumbo-sized box she'd seen sitting on Jack's bedside table wasn't enough.

Because they were fucking so damn often.

Her pulse bubbled behind her eyes, boiled at her

temples. Anger seethed like lava—hot, red, rising.

Her phone blipped. Jack was on the move; she'd have to work fast.

"Fuck being discreet." She pulled the baton from her belt and started swinging.

CHAPTER SIXTEEN

Sasha glanced away from Jack's flexing thigh as he braked for the turn into his condo's parking ramp. The short drive from Underbelly had taken forever, and was made in complete silence. He'd even changed his breathing, the bastard—trying not to inhale too deeply, as if she had body odor or cooties or something.

It wasn't her fault Winnie wasn't available.

A hum as Jack lowered his car window. Cold air flooded the front seat as he swiped his badge and waited for the gate to open. With another annoying flex of his thigh, he eased off the brake, then pulled into the shadows.

"I have some new information about your father's case," he said.

She slipped off her sunglasses, sliding them into an outside pocket of her purse. "Our case, you mean?" Jack reaching for her, protecting her with his body as they fell, was something she'd never forget.

Navigating the route to his parking place seemed to take an outsized portion of his attention as he explained what ballistics testing had confirmed: that the gun Ethan Covington had used to kill himself was likely the same gun that had killed her father.

"Ethan killed Dad? And shot you?"

"It appears so."

She turned toward him. "But why?"

"That's the million-dollar question."

And the only guy who could answer it had killed himself. "Something doesn't make sense," she muttered, facing front again. "Ethan liked Dad a lot. We all spent time with him, our whole family. He worked with Lukas, he ate at our family's table. No one sensed anything threatening, or dangerous, or...well, *off.* Why would he kill Dad?"

"We might never know," Jack said. "His apartment had a lot of signs of a Valkyrie in decline—lots of fast food bags, fist-sized holes in the wall, drugs and booze, and indications of compulsive masturbation."

"Food, fight, fuck." Damn it, what had tipped Ethan over the edge?

"Taking all the evidence into consideration, it appears Ethan died within an hour or two after leaving Underbelly."

"Did Ethan buy the drugs at Underbelly?" If he did, it needed to be nipped in the bud, fast.

"Not that we've discovered. Gideon and Jenny are working the dealer angle. But—" Jack glanced over at her "—we have a timeline problem."

"What is it?"

Jack eased the Volvo into his reserved spot. "If Ethan died late Tuesday night, he couldn't have shot at you Wednesday morning." His wrist flexed on the gearshift as he put the car into park. "The person who shot at you is still at large."

"Even *I* know time of death estimates are just that—estimates. How solid is the timeline?"

"Lukas came up empty at Ethan's apartment."

Which meant Ethan had been dead at least twelve

hours by the time Lukas and Jack arrived at the scene. When live ammo whizzed into Underbelly's loading dock, Ethan was dead.

Well.

Jack's breathing was less controlled now, his emotions surging and spiking. He was afraid, afraid for her. More than that, now that she wasn't royally pissed off at him she could sense the stain of guilt and shame, and a crushing sense of failure. As a Type-A perfectionist who rarely failed, Jack didn't know what to do with his unruly emotions.

Swirling in that roiling maelstrom? He loved her.

The doofus loved her.

If he loved her, why had he let her break up with him without a fight? And why had she jumped to conclusions? If only she'd *talked* to him. If only she'd used her words. "I need some air."

He grabbed her arm. "Sasha, let me go first—"

"I know that," she snapped, yanking it out of his grasp. "Jack, I've been under guard in some way, shape or form since the day I was born." The same would be true long after he left.

What a mess.

Jack got out of the car and looked around. "Okay, let's get to the elevator."

She grabbed her purse, got out of the car, and walked to the elevator, hyper-aware of how Jack assessed the angles, positioning his body to take a first hit. She was never so happy to get behind the closed doors of an elevator in her life.

And there, she smelled...sorrow, and the regret under the shame. Not a hint of emotion showed in his face. His profile was stone, like an Easter Island monolith.

What the hell was going on? Something didn't add up.

Well, explanations were his to provide. She'd give him a reasonable amount of time to sort out his thoughts, but it was up to him to figure out what was going on in his oversized brain.

The elevator finally reached the top floor. "Stay in the elevator until I clear the hall," he said as the doors opened.

"I know." It was hard to be annoyed with him when he positioned his body so it filled most of the gap.

Shouldering out of the elevator, he looked up and down the hall, then gestured for her to follow. The gray commercial carpeting swallowed their footsteps as they approached the door to his unit.

Jack unlocked the door, gesturing for her to go ahead. She walked in, set her purse on a barstool, then paused. "Was the cleaning service here today?"

"No. What's wrong?"

"I smell something." There was an odd emotional energy in the condo—female, angry—or maybe it was just her. "Do you have another lover I don't know about?" she joked.

Bad call, because Jack took her seriously. "No! Don't you know I—"

"Love me? Yes, I know. I wondered if *you* did."

He didn't respond, just stood there with a muscle ticking in his jaw. Literally biting back words.

"Nothing more to say?" Apparently he was beyond such immature baiting. She...was not. "You seem to have your head up your ass in a major way right now."

Jack looked around, as if searching for his sanity.

"Sasha, someone's trying to *kill* you."

"We don't know that. Maybe it was a stray bullet."

"In the middle of a weekday morning?" he scoffed. "Please."

"Why would someone want to kill me? I run a nightclub and a coffee shop."

"You're your father's daughter, a member of a powerful family, and you manage a lucrative chunk of the Sebastiani family's holdings."

"So, Lukas thinks this is financial?"

Jack hesitated. "We don't know."

"Well, let me know when you do." Wheeling around, she headed toward the guest room. "I'm packing up."

After a pause—so many feelings flitting across his face, so many words left unsaid—he moved toward the door. "I'll be right outside, here in the hall."

She needed more distance than that. "Can you…just go downstairs or something?" Fourteen floors weren't enough to completely buffer his unruly emotions, but it would be better than nothing. "I'll text you when I'm ready to go."

"Promise?"

"Yes."

Silence hung as they stared at each other. Finally, with a nod, he did as she asked. When the door closed behind him, the click sounded solid. Final.

"Damn it," she whispered around the lump in her throat.

Stiffening her spine, she went to the guest room to pack.

✴

The lobby's coffee kiosk was doing brisk business for a late weekday afternoon. After paying for his brew, Jack carried his cup to the only empty table he could find. He shrugged out of his jacket, sat down, and pulled out his phone. *Might as well try to get some work done.* Anything to stop him from thinking about Sasha, upstairs, packing to leave.

"Damn it." He'd made a huge mistake with her, but now wasn't the right time to figure out what to do about it. With a weary sigh, he checked his email, returned a few phone calls, and after scrolling around their calendars a bit, found a half-hour to speak with Winnie about a possible change in role... "Damn it." Any plans for Winnie were dependent upon *him* accepting the Security and Technology First chair. If he couldn't take pheromone intoxication meds, if he didn't have the clearest head in the room, was he the right choice for the job?

He canceled the unsent meeting request, searching Lukas's calendar instead. He had to talk to Lukas first. The stakes were too damn high.

Information about his doctor appointment, and the need to pause the R&D on the pheromone intoxication meds, had no doubt reached Lukas—and he *had* to be having second thoughts about making the offer. Risk assessment was the man's business, and a game-changing risk had just shown up.

With a couple of taps of his stylus, he booked an urgent meeting with Lukas first thing tomorrow morning.

By this time tomorrow, he might be emptying out

his office.

As soon as he hit 'Send', his phone vibrated with an incoming call from Gideon. He hesitated, then answered. He wasn't out of a job yet. "Hey, Gideon."

"Hey," Gideon said. "Jenny and I are at Ethan Covington's apartment. We found something. Can you talk?"

At the nearest tables, young mothers with strollers were deep in conversation. The guy with the laptop wore ear buds, bopping to music only he could hear. "Go ahead."

"Jenny found a manila envelope, tucked above a ceiling tile in Covington's bedroom."

The hair on the back of his neck prickled. "What's in it?"

"We don't know yet," Gideon said. "It's addressed to Lukas Sebastiani or Jack Kirkland."

"Open it."

"Jack, the lab has to process the envelope for fingerprints and trace."

"So, be careful. The important evidence is inside the envelope." He was sure of it.

Gideon sighed. "Okay. Give us a minute to set up here, and then I'll patch you in. I'm putting you on speaker." There was some rustling on Gideon's side of the call.

At the next table, one of the babies wailed. A split-second later, the other joined in sympathetic infant harmony. Time for his own ear buds. As he reached into his jacket pocket, his hand brushed against a small zippered bag.

Pheromone intoxication meds.

It took real force of will to pull his hand away, ever so slightly.

Adnan's warning about ulcers flitted through his mind. How much could taking one pill hurt? Just one tiny pill, to get through this shit show of a day.

The plastic bag was suddenly in his hand.

He stared at it, then glanced at the ceiling, imagining Sasha packing. Last night, he would have taken a pill—hell, two or three—without thinking twice.

Without thinking twice.

When had taking the pills become such an unthinking habit?

Not this time. He shoved the bag back into his jacket pocket. Grabbing his ear buds, he untangled them, popped them into his ears, then turned the phone on its side. There was a quiet ping as Gideon's body cam came online, allowing Jack to see the scene from Gideon's perspective. Jenny was with him, wearing a mask, disposable gloves, and protective eyewear. A legal-sized manila envelope lay on a sterile plastic tarp they'd draped over Ethan's kitchen island.

Gideon moved closer to the envelope. "Do you recognize the handwriting?"

Spiky cursive marched across the surface—Lukas's name, then his, scrawled in fine point black ink. "Yes, that's Ethan's handwriting."

"Thanks." Straightening, Gideon looked at Jenny, who was removing a sterile blade from its packaging. "Ready?"

She stepped into position. "You're sure the envelope is clear?"

"I didn't smell chemicals, explosives, or metals," Gideon confirmed.

Jenny shot him a look. "Your werewolf nose is a lot faster than calling the bomb squad."

Hell, he hadn't even considered that Ethan might have put something lethal in the envelope. Before he could object, Gideon's gloved hands entered the frame. Using the slightest amount of pressure at the sides, he held the envelope steady as Jenny ran the blade along its bottom edge. Neither touched the sealed flap, where fingerprints or DNA might reside.

When Jenny straightened and stepped back, Gideon carefully slid the envelope's contents onto the sterile drape. "Five pages, stapled. It looks like a Sebastiani Security case file."

Ethan had stolen a case file? A Sebastiani Security case file out in the wild was an unthinkable breach, a firing offense. "Which case? Let me see." Even their most garden-variety case would reveal to whoever picked it up that paranormal species walked the earth.

"Give me a minute." Gideon slid the envelope to the edge of the tarp, then positioned the document so it would stay on the sterile surface. There was a pause as he read the first page. "It's *formatted* like a Sebastiani Security case file, but it isn't one of yours. Ethan wrote it." He flipped to the second page. "It looks like a confession," he said. "A confession for making a contract hit."

I knew it. "Who offered the contract?"

"A woman Ethan refers to as 'Jane Doe.'"

"Well, that's no help. Physical description?"

"None provided. They never met in person. They communicated using burner phones."

Damn it. "What did—"

"Jack, can you hold off on the questions for a second? Let me finish reading this."

He tried to read along, but Gideon's body camera was too far away from the document. He leaned back in the chair. So, Antonia had been half-right. Their shooter had been a man—Ethan—but he'd been hired by a woman.

A woman who called herself Jane Doe.

Why would this Jane Doe want Elliott Sebastiani dead?

Jealousy? Had she and Elliott had an affair? Jack ruled the idea out as soon as it entered his mind. How many times had he heard members of the Sebastiani family complain about how impossible it was to keep a secret in a family of incubi and succubi? Maybe Jane Doe was a woman from Elliott's past, upset that after so many years alone, he'd finally taken a bondmate.

Gideon abruptly looked up from the papers. "Jack, where are you?"

"At my condo." Had they finally caught a break? "What did you find?"

"Jack, Elliott wasn't the target. You were."

Reality took a quick one-eighty. "What? Who'd want me dead?"

Something hard jabbed into his ribs from behind. "Hang up," a woman said quietly. "Now."

The smooth alto voice tugged at his memory. Whoever she was, she had a gun.

"I said, hang up."

He could easily overpower most women, but an armed woman, in a public place, with a dozen or so civilians in the vicinity? Nope.

"Jack?" Gideon's voice, through his ear bud.

Ear buds. The woman wouldn't be able to hear Gideon's side of the conversation. "Gideon, I need to go. I have a slight situation here."

"Do you need assistance?"

Thankfully, Gideon had recognized the Sebastiani

Security code phrase. "Yes. Call me back later, at my condo?"

On the video feed, he watched Jenny whip off her gloves, then grab her phone.

"Confirming location, you're currently at your condo?" Gideon said.

"Yes." He didn't bother telling Gideon he was in the lobby. With Jenny pinging his phone, they'd be able to pinpoint his location to within a foot or two. Whether he'd be dead or alive when backup arrived was another question entirely.

"Do you need a Code Red?"

"Yes—"

The woman yanked the buds out of his ears. Reaching around him, she ended the call herself, then clamped a hand on his stinging shoulder. "Stand up. We're going upstairs."

As he rose, the voice finally clicked: Miranda DesJardins. What the *hell*... Talk about a blast from the past. "Ms. DesJardins," he said, nodding as he turned. Her hair was shorter, and darker—maybe a wig?—but he recognized her. "Out of prison, I see." He hadn't thought about her in years, but the timing was probably right.

As revenge motives went, not keeping a client out of prison was a good one.

Instead of a designer suit, Miranda wore a blue MPD uniform he suspected wasn't hers. The shirt patches were right, but he didn't see a badge. Command insignia glinted on her shirt collar, but he didn't see a name tag. Her leather duty belt was half-empty, but she held the most convincing piece of equipment: a 9mm Sig.

With the pleasant smile on her face and her hand

resting so familiarly on his shoulder, they probably looked like they were good friends.

She stepped closer, giving his shoulder a vicious squeeze. "Let's move to the elevator."

Upstairs, where Sasha was. "No," he said evenly. "If you're going to shoot me, you're going to have to do it here."

"Okay," she agreed. "And after I do, I'll take out everyone else in this lobby, starting with those annoying babies at the next table." She beamed a smile at the children's mothers, who smiled back. "Which will it be?"

She had an oddly distant look in her eyes, as though she had very little to lose no matter what she did, but she was doing a damn good job of hiding her drawn weapon. "Okay, okay." He took a chance, stepping away from her long enough to put on his jacket, pick up his messenger bag, and press a button on his phone before tucking it in his front pants pocket.

One decision at a time. Damage control—containment—was the immediate goal. As long as he stayed alive, he could protect Sasha.

They pivoted toward the elevator.

"Hey!" one of the mothers called out.

He turned back. "Yes?"

Miranda dug the barrel of the gun into his ribs again, hard enough to bruise.

The woman pointed at the paper cup he'd left on the table. "Don't forget your coffee."

He picked it up. "Thanks." Throwing the hot liquid at Miranda might buy him enough time to—

"Honey?" Miranda said sweetly, grabbing the cup from his hand. "We're running late."

She wrapped her coffee-holding arm around his waist, pulling him against her body, against the gun, as they walked toward the elevator. They probably looked like a couple who couldn't keep their hands off each other long enough to get upstairs.

Once they reached the elevator, she threw the coffee in the garbage can, pushed the elevator call button, then snuggled back against him. The tip of the gun barrel dug into his midsection, where he was still sore.

"What do you want?" he asked.

Her only answer was a vacant, frightening smile.

The elevator doors finally opened. "Let's go," she ordered.

One decision at a time.

He stepped onto the elevator. As the doors closed, he fought the instinct to look up, toward Sasha.

One decision at a time. One decision at a time.

The elevator started to climb. It was all he could do to control himself, to not let fear get the best of him. He could hear his own harsh breathing, feel his heart pounding a primal warning. If only he could give Sasha a heads up, a warning of some kind...

Maybe he could. What had Lukas said? Sasha's emotional interpretation skills were unmatched, especially at close range.

They rose one more floor. Another.

Closer.

One decision at a time.

One second at a time.

Abandoning control, he opened the floodgates, sending a violent gush of emotion her way.

Hoping she could make sense of it.

Hoping it was enough.

CHAPTER SEVENTEEN

Sasha winced, trying to block out the deafening roar inside her head. *Damn, he really wants me gone.*

She jammed the phone charger into her bulging duffel bag. "I'm packing as fast as I can." She eyed the pile of fleece jackets, yoga pants, fuzzy socks, and underwear still piled on the guest room bed. They'd never fit in the bag, and she still had some things in the master bedroom and bathroom. How had so much of her casual winter wardrobe ended up here at Jack's?

She found an empty gym bag at the bottom of Jack's walk-in closet, then walked around, gathering her things. When she plucked yesterday's panties from the floor, she avoided looking at the strip of condoms, and the foolish fur-lined handcuffs, lying on Jack's bedside table, evidence of the previous night's fun—

"What *is* that?" She smelled it again, stronger this time. "Someone's been here."

She inhaled, trying to sort the tangled emotional skeins. In the background were the other residents of the condo—a subtle hum, fragile filaments most humans couldn't perceive. In the foreground, two entities battled for her attention. One was all edgy anger, hot lust, and jealousy—definitely female. The other, bold and insistent, was Jack. He was angry, yes, and afraid. Afraid of what? The fear was there, controlled, tamped down, but dominating it all was his demand that she get the hell out of his condo.

"I'm trying, I'm trying," she muttered, heading for the bathroom. Something wasn't adding up…

She stopped dead at the threshold. "Whoa."

The bathroom was *trashed*. The big mirror looked like someone had taken a bat to it, leaving sharp, reflective shards scattered across the granite countertop and tile floor. The gorgeous vessel sinks were smashed beyond recognition. Drawers were tipped upside down, cabinets pulled off their hinges… She took one careful step into the room, avoiding the shrapnel. Thankfully, the plumbing was still intact—there'd be no water mess to deal with—but most of her makeup was swimming in the toilet bowl. Over in the shower area, where the tempered glass walls had cracked but not shattered, someone had scrawled, *Die bitch* in what looked like matte purple lipstick.

My lipstick, damn it.

She needed to get Jack up here, now. Would he even pick up the phone when she called?

As she left the bedroom, the condo's front door opened. "Sasha?" Jack called. "Are you here?"

"Yeah," she called back, walking down the hall toward the living room. "I'm glad you're here. I have something to—"

Over by the door, a woman dressed in blue held a gun to Jack's head.

Sasha didn't move, didn't speak. Didn't bother to ask, "Officer, is there a problem here?" The woman's emotions were a familiar, toxic brew—and she was wearing matte purple lipstick.

The woman pushed Jack from behind, giving his right arm a vicious twist. "Get inside."

He obeyed. When the cop closed the door, her gun hand jiggled.

Emotionally unstable, uncomfortable with her weapon, wearing purple lipstick on duty… *Police officer, my ass.* If this woman was a cop, she'd eat her knee brace.

What the hell did she want?

"Sit down," the woman ordered, shoving Jack toward the couch.

He sat. *Good.* That meant the gun wasn't pointed directly at his head.

When Sasha went to join him, the woman stopped her. "Not you, bitch. You come here."

A bump of fear-laced anger from Jack. She wished she could comfort him. "Are you the person responsible for the artwork in the bathroom?" He looked puzzled. "Someone trashed the master bathroom and wrote "Die, bitch" on the shower wall," she explained. "Using my brand-new lipstick."

"It's nice, isn't it?" the woman said.

"I don't think it quite works with your skin tone."

The cop stopped preening. "I should have written 'Die, cunt' instead."

"You should have." In their culture, "cunt" was the highest of compliments.

The woman's emotions were a weaving, drunken brawl—anger, confusion, resentment, jealousy—and yeah, the gun looked too heavy for her hand. She glanced over to the couch, where Jack sat tense but poised, ready to take advantage of any opening.

She'd have to create one.

"Officer...what's your name?" she asked, injecting subtle sexual liquor into her voice. "I don't see a badge."

The woman didn't respond, just stared. *Good, good.* Her pupils were starting to dilate.

"This is Miranda DesJardins," Jack answered from the couch. "She's a former client—"

"Shut up," the woman said. "One more sound out of you, and I'll splatter her brains all over the carpet."

There was a bolt of panic from Jack, though he appeared outwardly calm. He was more afraid for her than he was for himself. Bad call, because the woman wanted them both dead.

Stay put, Jack. Give me some room to work. "Miranda? Miranda, look at me." Her voice was plush and inviting, a hot toddy with a kick you didn't notice until it was too late. "Can you tell me what's wrong?"

"Him. You. Everything." When Miranda gestured toward the couch, her gun hand wobbled. "He just won't die."

The woman's flat, matter-of-fact tone was more frightening than yelling would be. She was unstable, and in deep, deep pain. *Keep her talking. Distract her with conversation...* "Why do you want him to die?"

"It's his fault I was found guilty, that I was sent to prison," Miranda said. "I used to be a Silicon Valley executive, but now I can't get an interview for even a mid-level position."

"That has to be difficult." She was certain Jack had done his best for his client.

"As if you care," the woman scoffed.

"I do, Miranda." She took a tiny step closer. "I do care."

Miranda took a step of her own, unable to resist

the pheromones' magnetic sexual pull. Her pupils were turning into wide, black pools, and her eyelids were starting to droop.

So was the hand holding the gun.

Jack shifted, moving closer to the edge of the couch. His face was like stone, but his emotions were a maelstrom. He'd realized what she was trying to do: flood the room with pheromones. If he hadn't figured it out, the erection he was sporting was a pretty good tip-off.

Would Jack ever trust naked, honest desire again? She shoved the thought away. Right now, their top priority was getting out of here alive.

Time to turn up the heat.

She stepped closer, locking eyes with the other woman. "Miranda? What did you mean earlier, when you said Jack just wouldn't die?"

Miranda blinked, then cleared her throat. "I'm sorry about your father. He was never the target, you know."

Her stomach clenched tight. "What do you mean?"

"That day in the parking ramp? Ethan missed the target." Miranda shrugged casually. "Instead of hitting Jack, he hit your father."

She almost lunged for the woman's throat. *You sociopathic fucking bitch.*

Breathe. Breathe.

Control yourself, damn it.

She dropped into the familiar mental exercise Dad had taught her, sending the primitive emotion on a journey from the brain stem, to the mid-brain, to the pre-frontal cortex—home of logic and rational thought.

In a couple of heartbeats, she felt calmer, sharper, but Miranda was having trouble with her balance. *Distract her, keep her talking.* "So, Jack was the target all along?"

"Yes. Ethan missed, so I had to fire him." Miranda aimed a scathing glace at Jack. "One more man who couldn't get the job done."

The woman sounded so casual, as though reciting a grocery list rather than confessing to a contract hit.

"If you fired Ethan, who shot at me in Underbelly's loading dock?"

"I did." Miranda's negligent shrug knocked her slightly off-balance. The gun bobbled, then steadied. She took a step back. "If you want a job done right, you have to do it yourself."

Sasha eyed the space between them. The other woman's emotions were a whirling gyre, and she was growing dizzier and hornier by the second. *Draw her back into range.* "I can understand your frustration with Jack, but—" her voice was whiskey-smooth "—why kill *me*?"

"Because everything's so goddamn easy for you! You're rich and thin and successful and beautiful. You have a family that loves you. And now—" Miranda took two steps toward her "—you have *him*."

Not anymore.

"Jack and I were supposed to get married, you know," Miranda continued. "After the trial was over."

"You two dated?"

"Not…exactly."

Over on the couch, Jack mouthed a curse.

Understanding came in a flash: Cynthia.

"His mother said he was really attracted to me, that he was ready to settle down. That he couldn't date a client, of course, but that after I was exonerated, the coast would be clear." Miranda's expression went stony. "Yeah, that…didn't happen." She swallowed, then pointed the gun at Jack. "When they hauled me away in handcuffs, you acted like you didn't care."

"I did, Miranda." Jack said softly.

The gun bobbled again. "I told you to shut up!"

Panic burst in her chest. "Miranda? Miranda, look at me…" Soon, Miranda's attention, and the barrel of her gun, were back where she wanted them. "I'm so sorry." And she was. "Jack's mother had no right to say that to you, to make commitments on Jack's behalf."

Jealousy had had years to ferment, to turn pathological. Cynthia Roth Kirkland had a hell of a lot to answer for.

"When I was released from prison, I discovered Jack had moved on—to Minnesota, to a new job, and…" Miranda aimed the gun. "To you."

Fear spurted. The woman knew enough about weapons to aim for her torso, and at such close range, she probably wouldn't miss. "I don't have him, you know," she blurted. "He dumped me just this afternoon."

The gun wavered.

Now!

She kicked Miranda's hand, sending the gun flying. Before the other woman could react, Jack was…there, driving her down to the carpet. He flipped Miranda onto her stomach, then straddled her.

"Get off me!" Miranda yelled, trying to buck Jack off with her body. It was futile; he had the weight, height, and strength advantage. That didn't stop him from grabbing the nightstick from her utility belt and flinging it out of reach before twisting her arms behind her back.

"Get the cuffs from the bedroom," he ordered.

"Doesn't she have a pair on that belt?"

"Nope."

Gun, nightstick, pepper spray. Yeah, offensive weapons had been her priority.

"Don't forget the key."

Sasha ran to the bedroom, retrieved the handcuffs and key from the bedside table, then came back. Jack made short work of cuffing Miranda, but he kept her pinned on the floor. Whether due to intelligence or exhaustion, the woman stopped fighting.

"Can you reach in my front pocket and get my phone?" he asked.

"Um, sure." Studiously ignoring his erection, she snaked her hand into his pocket and plucked out the phone. A glowing red light made her heart skip a beat. "How long have you been recording?"

"Since she forced me onto the elevator at gunpoint."

His voice was full of self-recrimination, but she wanted to dance a jig. "Jack, you recorded her confession!"

He gave a curt nod, explaining that he'd been on the phone with Gideon and Jenny when Miranda had gotten the jump on him, and that Ethan's written confession had been found at his apartment. "I managed to issue a Code Red before she made me hang up the phone."

"I should have taken it away from you," Miranda muttered into the carpet.

Jack ignored her. "Between Ethan's written

confession and this recording, there should be more than enough evidence to convict her for Elliott's death."

Even if she hadn't personally pulled the trigger, Miranda DesJardins was responsible for killing both Ethan and her father, and for severely injuring Jack. Jack might argue that charging her for Ethan's death was a stretch, but...

Jack's eyelids fluttered. His big body tipped slightly sideways.

"Whoa." Woozy from all the pheromones, no doubt. As she steadied him, she noticed the blood blooming on his shoulder, bright red against his snowy white Oxford shirt. "Jack, you're bleeding."

He glanced at his shirt, then the door, where loud footfalls pounded down the hallway. "I think our back-up's here. Tell them the scene's secure before you open the door."

"I know how this works."

When she opened the door, Lukas, Chico, and Winnie stood there with their weapons drawn. "We caught the Code Red while we were at work," Lukas said. "Gideon and Jenny are a couple of minutes behind us." Her brother scanned the room, taking in the gun, the nightstick, and the handcuffed woman lying on the floor. Winnie and Chico entered the condo, then fanned out. Lukas stood still, gathering the room's emotional energy using his nose and his taste buds.

What did Miranda's emotions taste like? Between the pheromones and the fighting, what kind of fucked-up emotional residue had she and Jack left behind?

Lukas reached for his antacids. Popping two into

his mouth, he walked to the center of the room. "What happened here?" He looked down at Miranda, lying still and silent on the floor. "Who is this?"

"This is Miranda DesJardins, a former client of mine," Jack replied. "And this—" he handed the phone to Lukas "—is her confession."

"To what?"

"Hiring Ethan Covington to kill me."

"And he missed," Miranda said, disgusted. "Men are a perpetual disappointment to me."

Winnie came back from the bedroom. Chico followed close behind. "The bathroom's trashed," he noted.

Miranda laughed. "Damn right—ow!" She squirmed. "Get your knee out of my kidney, asshole."

Jack didn't comply. "Ethan killed your father by mistake. I was the target all along." His guilt flooded the room, but he kept his eyes on Lukas. "I'm so damn sorry."

Lukas's fingers tightened around the phone. "It's not your fault."

Winnie took it from his hand. "I'll just take this into evidence," she said matter-of-factly. "Is there any reason to keep recording?"

Jack shook his head. "We have everything we need."

"Except for a damn ambulance," Sasha snapped. "Jack's bleeding."

"My scab re-opened. It's nothing." When Chico stepped closer to check, Jack waved him off. "All I need is a gauze pad."

Morons. "Three weeks out of surgery, and he dove onto the floor to take her down. Can't you see he's lightheaded and white around the mouth? He needs to go to the hospital and get checked out."

"I'm more impacted by the pheromones you whipped up."

She knew this was going to be an issue. "She had a gun pointed at your head! I used the tools I had available to me—"

"Fight later," Lukas bit out. "Explain."

"Sasha whipped up some pheromones to distract Miranda," Jack said. "Once she was woozy enough, Sasha kicked the gun away."

Chico waved his hand in front of his nose. "So that's why it smells like an orgy in here."

"Charles." Winnie's voice was tempered steel. "Please relieve Jack."

New voices at the door. Gideon and Jenny had arrived.

Jack rose slowly. Chico kneeled, taking his place. "I haven't frisked her yet," Jack cautioned.

"Got it." Chico looked at Miranda's wrists, then back at Jack. "Nice cuffs, dude."

There was a pulse of embarrassment from Jack, but he didn't let it show. "As Sasha mentioned earlier, we had to use the tools we had at hand."

Chico winked at her as Jack walked away, joining Lukas and Gideon in conversation near the door. Winnie was on evidence collection detail, taking pictures of the scene and securing Miranda's weapons. Chico and Jenny took Miranda into custody without incident, nearly carrying her out the door. Across the room, Jack and Lukas were in quiet conversation. Jack had his hand on Lukas's shoulder, offering comfort.

Somehow, he'd known Lukas needed it.

Speaking of need, the blood stain on Jack's

shoulder was growing larger, and now Jack was leaning oh-so-casually against the wall. "Morons," she muttered, approaching the men. "Lukas, Jack needs to go to the hospital."

"No ambulance," he grumbled.

At least he hadn't flat-out refused treatment.

"I'll take you," Lukas said. "Do you want to ride along?" he asked her.

Yes. No. Maybe. Did Jack even want her there?

Jack said nothing, answering her question.

"Sasha, I'd like to get your statement sooner rather than later," Winnie said.

Thank you. "Let's do it now."

Lukas was surprised by her answer, but his expression didn't change. "Okay." He and Winnie exchanged a glance. "Someone will call you with an update."

"Okay."

Jack stood there, silent and pale—but beneath the smooth surface, he was a hot, confused mess.

Okay, if that's how you want to play it. She turned toward Winnie. "Ready when you are." Jack had made it more than clear that he didn't want her—in his condo or in his life. When he returned from the hospital, he'd find she'd cleared out, that she'd followed his wishes.

The next move, if one ever came, was his.

*

Bailey breezed into SebSec's corner conference

room carrying a laptop under one arm and an odd, triangular box under the other. "Hey, Jack." She set the items down next to him, then headed for the credenza to get coffee. "You're here early."

Jack had wanted the room—any room—to himself for a bit. Almost everyone who worked at Sebastiani Security had found a reason to stop by his office that morning. Apparently him checking into the hospital for a couple of days had caused some concern. "What's in the box?"

"It's a Charlie Brown Christmas Tree." There was a hiss from the air pot as Bailey pumped coffee into a mug. "Want a cup?"

"No, thanks." Along with pheromone intoxication meds, Adnan had put coffee on the forbidden list—at least until his stomach stopped stinging.

She came over to the table, set down her mug, and started opening the box. "Christmas is only a couple of weeks away, and no one's put up any decorations."

Along one side, the white box said, "This tree needs you! One tree for you to love." He was not aware a tree needed love. "Do you need some help?"

"Nope."

In less than a minute, she had the thing set up, screwing a short, green bough into a simple wooden base and hanging a single, shiny red ball near the top. He was about to say the tree hardly qualified as decor when everyone else started filing in for the meeting.

Chico, grunting a hello, grabbed a cup of coffee, then took up his usual place leaning against the brick wall. Gideon and Jenny, who'd been in the building to meet with Sebastiani Security's faerie profilers, hit the coffee pot, then took the chairs closest to the door. Antonia, eyes glued to her phone, squealed with delight when she saw the tree. Winnie came in, sat, then fired up her tablet. Wyland entered, carrying two leather bags. One, a trim, black Tumi, no doubt held his computer gear. The other, shapeless and battered by centuries of use, held the old law books Wyland usually found himself consulting during most of their meetings— Crap. The Council meeting. His hospital stay had completely fucked up his sense of time.

Wyland had been the doctor to examine his shoulder the night Miranda had been arrested, and he still wasn't sure whether he'd fallen into such a deep sleep naturally or whether he'd gotten a pharmaceutical assist. When he'd arrived home almost two days later, the meeting he'd scheduled with Lukas to discuss his reservations about Council changes had come and gone.

And so had Sasha. She'd moved out of his condo, just as he'd asked. He hadn't heard from her, or about her, since.

He was half-rising from his chair to catch Lukas in his office when Lukas walked in. Focused, holding a tablet, and wearing what Jack had come to call 'presidential casual'—black dress pants, black shoes and belt, and a dark gray dress shirt, open at the neck—Lukas nodded hello to the room, then sat down. "Thanks for being here, everyone."

Lukas's wardrobe was one more reminder that his friend really needed help, but Jack wasn't sure *he* was the right solution.

"Let's get going," Lukas said.

Gideon brought everyone up to speed on police activity. They'd interviewed Ethan's boss at Ansel Manufacturing, who confirmed he'd fired Ethan. "He was caught drinking on the job. He told the manager he wasn't interested in pursuing treatment."

Wyland's jaw went tight.

Jack shared Wyland's frustration. Ethan had known not to expose his species' physiology to human doctors, but why hadn't he sought help from their own? Damn it, how many times had he heard Council members refer to 'the secret they would all die to protect?' This time, someone literally *had*.

Gideon moved on to Miranda's interrogation. "Ms. DesJardins made a full confession, corroborating Ethan Covington's. She confirmed the burner we found in Ethan's truck dash was the one she called when they needed to communicate. The other burner was the one he used to contact his dealer."

"The dealer used his own cell phone to do business," Jenny added, shaking her head. "We sent Shakopee PD an anonymous tip."

"I'm still waiting for a return call from Ms. DesJardins' corrections officer," Gideon said. He glanced at Bailey, then at Jack. "It turns out he's no stranger."

Jack sat up straight in the chair. "Andrew Banner? Are you serious?"

"Serious as a heart attack."

Bailey's lips went thin. "Small fucking world."

"Too small." He and Andrew Banner had spoken more times than Jack wanted to remember during the time Banner had been Bailey's corrections officer. Bailey and Banner had had regular check-ins as she completed the terms of her probation. Even though they'd kept their dealings with Banner well away from Sebastiani Security's paranormal doings, Jack had come away from each conversation with hackles raised. "Does Miranda—Ms. DesJardins—have a lawyer?"

"Yes," Wyland said. "Me."

Every head swiveled toward the end of the table.

"Ms. DesJardins is human."

It took a couple of seconds for Wyland's meaning to sink in. Miranda was human, which meant they didn't have jurisdiction. The paranormal legal system was explicit about how it treated humans.

Miranda would never be tried, much less sentenced. The woman who'd killed Elliott—who'd killed their culture's president—was going to walk.

Fuck.

Miranda didn't know she was being represented by the Vampire Second, the world's most experienced legal mind. She also didn't know Wyland's final service for his human client would be to wipe all memory of her crime, and all interaction with their paranormal culture, forever from her mind.

"The faerie psychologist observing our interviews states Ms. DesJardins has been truthful throughout our questioning, with one exception," Gideon said. "Ms. DesJardins claims to have had a romantic relationship with Jack in the past."

Jack didn't mention the expectations his mother might have planted in Miranda's mind. "Ms. DesJardins had a romantic interest in me, which was not reciprocated. I was her lawyer. Period."

"Understood," Gideon said. "The profiler suspected it was wish fulfillment. Ms. DesJardins seems unusually interested in your relationship with Sasha Sebastiani."

Everyone who'd heard the recording he'd made that night knew he and Sasha had broken up.

Actually, they'd heard Sasha say, "He dumped me." Lukas hadn't said anything yet. Antonia hadn't done anything…yet.

He eyed her. Antonia wouldn't waste energy punishing someone so pathetic. She and Lukas knew exactly how miserable and confused he was.

Gideon cleared his throat. "Ms. DesJardins stated that, due to his addictions, she no longer considered Ethan Covington a reliable employee, so she decided to handle the job herself. Her intention the night of your conflict was to kill Sasha, then you."

"Why kill Sasha?"

"Jealousy, of course—and because she knew it would hurt you," Antonia answered.

Gideon nodded. "Thankfully, she wasn't very familiar with firearms."

"And Sasha has a killer kick." At such close range, Miranda wouldn't have needed familiarity with her weapon. Sasha flooding the room with pheromones had impaired Miranda's ability to aim, much less fire.

"Oh—we found a tracker on your Volvo," Gideon mentioned.

"What?"

"Ms. DesJardins tagged your car in the Memorial Hospital parking ramp, during your appointment with Dr. Penn."

If Miranda tagged his car while he was at Memorial, she'd known exactly when he left the hospital, and that he'd driven from there to Underbelly, where he'd waited several hours for Sasha to finish her work.

Plenty of time to trash his condo.

"We took the tracker into evidence," Jenny said. "Your car's clear."

Chico levered away from the brick wall. "This isn't the first time someone's tagged one of our vehicles. We need to schedule regular sweeps."

Jack exchanged a glance with Bailey, whose car had also been tagged in the past. "Good idea."

"Winnie and I will work out the details."

He nodded.

"Anything else on the case?" Lukas asked.

"That's it for now," Gideon answered. "We're picking the interrogation up again in a couple of hours." He and Jenny stood, and gathered their belongings. "Let us know if you need anything."

Chico and Winnie also stood, knowing the next portion of the meeting was Council-oriented. Jack took advantage of the opening. "Lukas, I need a minute of your time."

"Now?"

"Yes."

"All right."

The other Council members stayed in the room. He followed Lukas down the hall.

Lukas turned into Jack's office rather than continuing to his own, dropping into the larger of Jack's two visitor's chairs.

It was a clever move on Lukas's part, but right now, the last thing he felt was a sense of control. As he rounded his desk, he refused to look at the framed photograph on the wall, of Mavericks on a calm day. Bailey had once told him she thought the photograph captured his personality in a nutshell: placid and controlled, power tightly leashed, until the right, rare conditions arose. Then, navy blue waves lurched to the sky then crashed down, crushing the unfortunate target. "You're a protector," she'd said. "You hold your strength in reserve until it's needed."

Bailey thought he was a protector? *Yeah, right. Tell that to Elliott.* He sat at his desk, wincing as his muscles protested. *Tell that to Sasha, who'd protected herself from Miranda just fine.*

When he looked at Lukas, he found his friend looking right back, with too much knowledge in his eyes. But Lukas didn't speak. He didn't ask a question to break the ice, or to make it easier for him.

Fair enough. It was *his* responsibility to put his roiling, unruly doubts into words. "We need to do something about your security," he said.

"That's what you pulled us out of a meeting to discuss?"

No, but it was a start. "There are too many things we haven't talked about," he groused. "There's never enough time."

"True, time's at a premium." Lukas folded his arms over his stomach. "So let's cut to the chase and talk about you taking the Sec/Tech First seat, not my supposed security needs."

"Supposed? Lukas, your father died right in front of me." Oddly, this was an easier place to start the conversation. "Think of the impact to the culture, to Sebastiani Security and to your family, if you were killed or incapacitated because you refused to take reasonable precautions."

"You must not have noticed Dad's armored Town Car sitting out there in the parking lot." Lukas groused. "Chico and Winnie have assigned me a driver and provisional security detail."

"Why provisional?"

"They want to clear the team members with you."

A bark of laughter escaped. "I don't think I'm the

best judge of that."

"Hmm?"

"Lukas, one of my previous hires literally killed your father."

"Ethan went off the rails—"

"After I fired him—"

"It was the right decision, the only responsible decision to make, and I agreed with you." Lukas's gaze drilled into him. "Jack, you couldn't have foreseen what Ethan would do. No one could." He paused. "Dad's death wasn't your fault. Stop beating yourself up."

"That's easier said than fucking done," he snapped. "The President didn't die on your watch."

"He would have."

The words clapped him back in his chair. "What?"

"I said, he would have."

"No." Jack shook his head. "You could have—"

"Done what?" Lukas leaned forward, intent. "Jack, I've watched the tapes hundreds of times. There was nothing there to find, no edge for anyone to work with."

"How about recognizing Ethan's taste?"

Lukas shook his head. "Ethan was a regular at Underbelly. Even if I'd remembered his baseline taste, I wouldn't have thought there was anything odd about sensing it in the club's parking ramp. I certainly wouldn't have initiated a search of the ramp, much less the HVAC ducts, before escorting Dad and Sasha to a car."

"You would have been carrying your goddamn weapon—"

"And done what with it? When? Dad was hit with no notice. You were hit, twice—and even severely wounded, you protected the other principal." A muscle ticked in Lukas's jaw. "You saved my sister's life."

Sasha, crawling toward him, then staunching the blood from his wound. "I'd say she saved mine."

"Maybe you saved each other's."

Jack didn't respond.

Knowing amusement flashed across Lukas's face. "Well, can I just say…now that the shoe's on *my* foot, I understand why Dad ditched his guards all the time. What a pain in the ass."

"It helps that you live where you work. Most of your dad's security risk was due to his commute to Sebastiani Labs."

"And yet, he died at home." Lukas eyed him across the desk. "FYI, I won't be confined to this building."

"No one expects that."

"Scarlett does."

"She said that?"

"No," Lukas admitted. "But she's so afraid."

"Can you blame her? The last president was *assassinated.*"

"Dad wasn't the target!"

"You're right, but that doesn't make him any less dead."

Lukas closed his eyes. Swore.

"Lukas, everything's changed, so damn quickly. Give Scarlett some time to get used to the new normal."

Lukas tipped his head back to stare at the ceiling, as if reassuring himself that Scarlett and Coco were safe. "Time always seems to be in such short supply. And speaking of which…" Lukas's gaze pinned him to his chair. "I want to announce that you'll be taking the Sec/Tech First seat at the next Council meeting."

The next Council meeting was scheduled for the end of the month. "I'm no longer certain I'm the right person for the job."

"Because of the pheromone medication thing?"

"Adnan told you?"

"Of course he did."

Jack scowled. "So much for medical privacy."

"When the Underworld Council's only human representative is taking an experimental medication, developed specifically for him, by the president's own company, medical privacy flies out the window—and you consented to that condition when you started taking the meds." Lukas scraped a tired hand through his hair. "Sebastiani Pharma's director was *not* pleased to hear about your ulcer."

"Well, it's not a *bleeding* ulcer—"

"Yet," Lukas interrupted, "but according to Adnan, you're well on your way. Dr. Billings agrees that we need to put the program on hold."

"What?" Panic set in. "Can't the meds be—I don't know—improved, or modified somehow?"

"Jack, one hundred percent of patients who took the drug developed ulcers. It's going to take some time."

"How much time?"

"Dr. Billings estimates two years."

Jack sagged back in the chair. Until this moment, he hadn't realized how much he'd counted on a quick fix from the brainiacs at Sebastiani Labs. He'd resigned himself to taking a break from the meds long enough for the ulcer to simmer down, but he assumed there'd be *something*, some new-and-improved version, waiting in the wings.

There wouldn't be.

He forced himself to speak, to turn down the job of a lifetime. "Lukas—President Sebastiani—I must decline your offer of Council promotion."

"Fuck the formality, Jack. Tell me why."

"Without the meds, I'm simply not qualified."

Lukas made a slashing motion with his hand. "Bullshit. Do you think you need the meds?"

"Are you kidding me? The whole reason the medication was developed was to help me, a mere human, keep a clear head when working with incubi and succubi. I work with incubi and succubi every damn day."

"You might have benefited from the boost when you were first getting used to our culture, but you've more than gotten up the learning curve. Believe me, your mental acuity off the meds is not a problem. Current discussion notwithstanding."

Why couldn't Lukas see the truth when it slapped him upside the head? "That drunken dive I made at Miranda? It was sheer dumb luck it worked. Sasha's pheromones rendered me completely ineffective."

"It looked like teamwork to me."

"I—"

"Do you think Bailey is any less competent because *she* can't take the meds anymore?"

Silence. "No."

Lukas lifted a brow. "You're a special case, then?"

"No, of course not." Lukas was making his reservations sound ridiculous. They weren't.

"Jack, you're fully capable of interacting with us, of making intelligent decisions, without taking the meds. So, what's the *real* problem you were trying to solve by taking so many pills? This is about Sasha."

"I'm not discussing my relationship with your sister with you."

Lukas eyed him. "You don't appear to *have* a relationship with my sister at the moment."

True.

"I can tell what's going on between you without either of you saying a word," Lukas continued. "She loves you, you love her. So, what's the problem? You know she'd never use her pheromones to manipulate you, right?"

Trust Lukas to cleave right to the heart of it. "How the hell am I supposed to know that? And why haven't I heard about this ability before? Is the ability to produce pheromones at will a characteristic all members of your species share?" The night Miranda attacked them in his condo was the first time he'd seen or heard of it.

I hope. Did succubi ever…fake it?

"It doesn't surprise me you haven't run up against this before," Lukas mused. "Very few members of our species exhibit this ability."

"How many of your species?" He was pretty sure he knew the answer.

"Me, Rafe, and Sasha," Lukas admitted. "We're not sure yet about Antonia."

Evolution had favored the Sebastiani line. It made no sense to him that this ability would pass Antonia by.

"The ability seems to run stronger in Sasha than it does in Rafe or me," Lukas said, "but using it takes a toll. The energy drain is enormous."

His stomach jumped. "Is Sasha okay?"

"We couldn't wake her up for over a day after she

returned home from your condo."

He pushed to his feet. "Did she see a doctor?"

Lukas waved him back into the chair. "Throttle back. She's fine—or she will be, if she follows Wyland's instructions."

He sat back down. "Wyland examined her? He didn't say anything." Nope, the taciturn vamp had just walked into the corner conference room, said hello, then took his books out of that ratty bag as if nothing was wrong. "Why didn't he say anything?"

"Not so concerned about *her* medical privacy, are you?" Lukas shifted in the chair, reaching for his antacids. "Wyland said she'll be fine, told her she needs to rest, and replenish her energy. She's sleeping a lot, and eating everything in sight."

"Who's taking care of her?" *I should be taking care of her.*

"Claudette's on the job. The last I heard, Sasha had just woken up from a nap. She and Antonia are watching a holiday baking marathon and stuffing themselves with Christmas cookies."

The Sasha he knew didn't nap, not even after Olympic bouts of sexual activity. She never slept eight hours straight, much less twenty-four. She must have been utterly exhausted—which, now that he thought about it, wasn't at all surprising. When Miranda attacked, Sasha had wielded her pheromones like a battle-axe, a blunt weapon she'd used to save their lives.

Sasha's natural pheromones, the ones she produced when it was just the two of them, were soft and plush, with occasional sharp edges he'd come to crave. Whenever they made love, Sasha came away from the experience recharged, not depleted.

He drew a shaky breath. Rubbed his stinging stomach. "I'm a fucking idiot."

"Finally, we agree." Lukas's tone was drier than winter air. "But Sasha's also called me twice today to see if you're okay." Lukas inhaled, then subtly moved his tongue behind closed lips. "Jack, you're not okay."

He didn't bother denying it. Physically, he was well on the road to recovery—Wyland had assured him that tackling Miranda hadn't done any lasting damage—but emotionally? 'Not okay' was an understatement.

He'd fucked up the best thing in his life, and he didn't know how to fix it.

There was a vibration against his thigh. Reaching into his front pants pocket, he pulled out his phone, then looked at the screen. "A text from my father."

"Do you need to respond?"

"It's not an emergency, but I suppose I do." Because there was more than one fucked-up situation in his life. His mother's interaction with Miranda—the mistaken impression she'd left in the woman's mind—had nearly gotten Sasha killed. He glanced at the screen again. "My parents want me to fly home for Christmas."

"Maybe you should."

"That's the *last* thing I thought you'd say." Lukas knew exactly how fraught his relationship with his parents was.

"Given what Miranda said on that recording—" Lukas's voice went hard as flint "—you have some things to straighten out with your mother." He jerked a thumb toward the monitors taking up too much space on his desk. "Getting away from all this for a while might help clear your head. Clarify your thoughts about your future."

His future at Sebastiani Security. His future as an Underworld Council member. His future with Sasha, if she could ever forgive him for being such a fucking idiot. But skipping off to the west coast right now would create so many other problems…

Stop it. Lukas is right to be concerned about business continuity. "Let me run an idea by you first."

As he laid out his idea about a change of role for Winnie, a spurt of his old energy returned. Lukas didn't look entirely happy, which meant he was on the right track.

"Damn it, go ahead," Lukas muttered. "If Winnie agrees, she can have a trial run while you're gone."

"You really want me to go to California, don't you?"

"What I really want is for you to be healthy and happy. I want you to make decisions you can live with."

"Okay, I'll go." Yes, he'd go home for Christmas, and set his mother straight once and for all. "I could pull Miranda DesJardins' case files while I'm there. Wyland might find them useful."

Lukas shook his head. "You're such a workaholic."

"Look who's talking."

"Take the Gulfstream."

"I won't turn it down, but…"

"What?"

"Claudette invited me to spend Christmas Day with your family." Not that he'd even thought about Christmas gifts yet. What the hell would he get Sasha for Christmas?

Would she even care?

"Dude, give my sister a chance to miss you."

His head snapped up. "How did you know I was thinking about Sasha?"

Lukas made an obnoxious kissing sound. "Do you really want to know what your special brand of lovesickness tastes like?"

"Fuck you."

His muttered response must have reassured Lukas. "Meet with Winnie, then get out of here. I'll tell Sasha where you are, and that you're okay." Lukas pushed out of the chair, came around the desk, then pointed at Jack's center desk drawer. "Give me the rest of your meds."

Jack shot him a look, but went over to the Mavericks print to retrieve the tiny key he kept along the top of its frame. "Don't quite trust me?"

"No sense tempting fate." Lukas watched as he opened the desk drawer. "Jack, I really need you to come back with some clarity. Too much is riding on your decision."

Lukas—his friend, his boss, the president—was right. He handed Lukas the last remaining zippered bag, which also included the loose pills he'd discovered in his jacket pocket the day of Miranda's attack. "It looks like I'm going cold turkey."

"Dr. Billings said it's safe to do, but please call her if you have questions or concerns." Lukas pocketed the pills. "Your right arm seems to be recovering well."

"Hmm?"

"You used your right hand to reach for your phone, and to get these pills."

And he hadn't even thought about it. He made a careful fist. "No pain."

At least one thing was looking up.

Lukas went to the door. "Let us know when you'll be back."

Would he get his mental shit together before the next Council meeting? Who knew? "I'll be home by New Year's Eve at the latest." He wouldn't miss Elliott's memorial service for the world. "Please give…everyone my regrets about Christmas."

"Will do."

After Lukas left, he sat down at his desk again, the place where he spent most waking hours. He activated his monitors, keyed his password, then swore. After several days away, his unread email count was well into the triple digits.

"Screw it." He set an 'out of office' auto-response for incoming email, powered down, then called the private airport. Once the Gulfstream was booked, he texted his travel plans to key Sebastiani Security employees, then called Winnie. "Can you come to my office when you get a sec?" he asked.

"Regarding your travel plans? You didn't provide a return date."

"I know."

A pause. "I should be clear in about ten minutes."

"That's perfect. Thanks." He hung up.

Ten minutes was just enough time to let his father know he was coming home for Christmas.

"I can't believe I'm doing this." But Lukas was right; he had to see his parents, and tackle some painful subjects they'd all ignored far too long. And he had some work to do, too, even if he didn't crack open his laptop while he was away. He had to answer some questions for himself before he could answer them for Lukas. He had to think, to make some decisions…decisions that could impact the rest of his life.

Putting half a continent between him and Sasha couldn't hurt.

Ten minutes were now eight. Time was ticking down.

"Okay. Let's do this."

He picked up the phone and dialed.

CHAPTER EIGHTEEN

"Yowsah, Yowsah, Yowsah," Sasha sang as she approached Underbelly's back bar. An old school Chic song always filled the dance floor, and tonight was no exception.

Flynn was mixing greyhounds with his usual flourish. He had an audience—a trio of regulars who, according to the grapevine, had made a bet between them: Who'd be the first to tempt the hot vampire mixologist into their bed? As far as she knew, no one had won—not that Flynn would say anything if one had.

"Hey." Flynn garnished the last of the drinks with a curl of lemon, then served them. "I didn't think you were working tonight."

"I'm not on the schedule, but I wanted some company." Two days' rest was plenty. Wyland wouldn't agree, but if she spent any more time in her bedroom, she'd go bananacakes.

"Mission accomplished."

The club was hopping for a weeknight. The dance floor was packed, and the tables lining the second and third floor balconies were full. On the first floor, the sleek banquettes were crammed with people taking advantage of the appetizer menu. Chicken wings seemed to be popular tonight. The smell made her stomach growl.

Rafe, Bailey, Lorin, her bondmate Gabe Lupinsky, Winnie, and Chico were sitting at the back table, along with Gabe's sisters Gwen and Glynna. Jacoby's mobility scooter was tucked away behind the bar, but the man himself was nowhere in sight.

"He's in the bathroom," Flynn murmured.

She glanced at the hallway leading to the restrooms. At least Jacoby was sober enough to make the trip on foot. She was worried about Jacoby.

"He had company," Flynn added.

"Who?"

Flynn winked, then poured her a Diet Coke.

Flynn was right. None of her business.

He set her cola on a coaster. "Are you still trying to convince Lukas to open the bar the day of your father's memorial service?"

"No, I gave up." Lukas had shot the idea down as a security risk. Winnie and Chico had agreed with him. And Jack? She had no idea what Jack's opinion might be. Jack was in California, spending Christmas with his family.

He hadn't told her he was leaving.

Jack's travel plans were none of her business, either.

His absence left her coordinating the memorial service's security plan with Winnie and Chico, and it felt...very odd. She and Jack often argued during the process, but she'd long ago realized the zing of conflict was part of the fun.

Better get used to it. "We're also shutting the kitchen down for the day," she said.

"Crackhouse will be closed, too?"

"Yeah." Shutting down the shared kitchen meant

food smells wouldn't waft into the room during the memorial service. There'd be no clanging pans, no food prep, no clean-up, and every employee could attend the service as a guest rather than a worker. Afterward, a small group of family and friends would gather upstairs at Claudette's, where they'd enjoy appetizers and desserts catered by Chadden's restaurant.

Sipping the icy soda, she assessed the club. The dance floor was packed, yes, but the room had an odd, sad vibe. People at the banquettes and tables spoke to their friends behind raised hands. "What's everyone talking about?"

"Ethan Covington."

She wasn't surprised that news about Ethan's death had hit the grapevine.

"Is it true he committed suicide?" Flynn asked.

"Yes."

Flynn sighed. "Given how erratically he behaved the last few times he was here, I can't say I'm surprised to hear the news." He picked up a damp rag, then ran it over the already-spotless bar. "Ethan was a troubled guy, that's for sure."

The faerie psychologist evaluating Miranda DesJardins suspected Ethan's grasp on stability had gotten decidedly worse after meeting her. "I just wish someone could have helped him," she said.

Old knowledge flashed across Flynn's face. "Sometimes, there's nothing we can do." A subtle motion from a customer at the end of the bar caught his attention—a lift of a finger, a nod in return. "We're selling a lot of shots tonight," he said, reaching for a bottle of scotch. "People toasting a lost friend."

It was difficult to nod, to keep a straight face. To stop herself from shrieking, *That 'lost friend' killed my father.* But she managed.

Ethan's role in her father's death clearly hadn't hit the grapevine yet—which was good, because Lukas had ordered that all details about the investigation remain confidential—but... She rubbed her throbbing temples. When she'd come downstairs, she hadn't anticipated watching so many people toast her father's killer.

"Hey, I think Bailey's trying to get your attention."

Sure enough, Bailey was waving from the table. "Do you need anything from me?" she asked Flynn.

"Nope, we're under control here. Go enjoy yourself."

She joined the group at the table, saying hello and making sure everyone had drinks before dropping into the empty chair next to her brother's bondmate.

"Hey," Bailey said. "How are you doing?"

The greeting sounded casual enough, but everyone at the table except Gabe's sisters knew she'd spent the last two days flat on her back, recovering her strength after the battle with Miranda. "I'm fine. A little tired," she admitted, because Rafe, sitting on Bailey's other side, would no doubt notice she was wearing more makeup than usual. She took a healthy swallow of her Diet Coke. "It looks like the news of Ethan's death has hit the grapevine."

"Yeah."

Glynna Lupinsky, sitting on her other side, leaned closer. "I feel terrible. Why didn't I—why didn't anyone—notice how troubled Ethan was?"

"He fell off everyone's radar," she murmured. And Dad had paid the ultimate price. Maybe that's what stung the most. If someone—if *she*—had noticed what was going on with Ethan, would her father still be alive? They'd never know, because she hadn't. "I got to know him a little, when he was Dad's driver," she said to Glynna, who was leaching genuine grief. "He was…nice. Dad really liked him." The words left a bitter aftertaste, maybe because they were true.

Glynna lifted her shot glass. "To Ethan."

Shit, she's waiting for me to join her. She managed a companionable sip of Diet Coke.

Gwen Lupinsky, sitting on Glynna's other side, tapped her sister on the shoulder to get her attention. They were soon engaged in animated conversation, their fingers flashing as they used American Sign Language.

Sasha swiveled back toward Bailey with relief. Bailey knew the whole sordid story, so there was no need to pretend or perform.

"You're right, you know," Bailey murmured. "Ethan *was* nice. He was polite."

"Ethan was a lot of things." *Including a killer.*

"He was a great co-worker, but in hindsight? He was too empathetic to be a good bodyguard." Bailey took a sip of her red wine. "Jack's kicking himself for not noticing Ethan was in over his head, for not supervising him more closely."

She could see why Jack would feel that way.

"But there were no complaints." Bailey gave a shrug. "Your dad liked him. You said it yourself, everyone liked Ethan."

"And Dad had no reason to complain. He was getting exactly what he wanted from the relationship—freedom." *Damn it, Dad.*

"By the time Jack realized there were serious gaps

in Elliott's security coverage, Ethan had already screwed up so badly that Jack had no choice but to fire him." Her fingers tightened on the glass. "Jack is certain him firing Ethan was the catalyst for this whole, sad sequence of events. That him firing Ethan made Ethan susceptible to outside influence."

"This isn't Jack's fault." But she could see how Mr. Responsibility would think it was. Damn, he'd had been drowning in guilt and shame—she'd read *that* much correctly—but she'd mistaken the reason why. "None of this is his fault."

"Oh, he knows that in his head," Bailey reassured her. "But in his heart? That's another matter entirely."

And Jack's heart was no longer in her keeping. Had it ever been? "Have you heard from him since he went to California?"

"No. Complete radio silence, at Lukas's request." Bailey explained that, in addition to Lukas wanting Jack to take an actual vacation, Jack's absence was a trial run. Jack might soon be shifting some of his operational responsibilities to Winnie.

She read between the lines. If Jack ascended to the Council's Sec/Tech First chair, he'd have to delegate some of his Sebastiani Security work to someone else. Lukas's proposal was a smart one; Jack was the right person for the job. Jack delegating work to Winnie while he was on vacation must mean he was seriously considering accepting the position.

Getting over Jack would be so much easier if he pulled up stakes and moved back to California, but their people—and her brother—desperately needed him.

I need him, her heart whimpered.

You want *him,* her brain responded.

Both were true, damn it—but as the great philosopher Mick Jagger once said, "You can't always get what you want."

What a mess.

"Well, Jack said he'd be back in time to attend the next Council meeting," Bailey said. She bit her lip. Worry eddied around her. "I wish I knew how his detox was going."

"What detox?"

"Adnan told Jack he had to stop taking pheromone intoxication meds." Bailey looked at her. "He didn't tell you he was brewing an ulcer, did he?"

"No." Apparently Jack's body hadn't been in her keeping, either. Had their relationship really been so superficial? Tendrils of worry sprouted, growing like kudzu. "How's his stomach?" Bailey's ulcer had perforated, requiring emergency surgery.

"He'll be fine," Bailey reassured her. "He turned over all his pills before he left for California. Sebastiani Labs is suspending the program."

"Good." Not having the meds would make him feel like Samson without his hair, or a soldier without a weapon, but... "Shit, that's it," she blurted. The final puzzle piece clicked into place.

"What's it?"

"That's why he broke up with me. Without the pills, he'd feel too vulnerable." She shot Bailey a knowing glance. "That's also why he took the pills at times other than when he was at work."

"When the two of you were alone?"

"Yeah."

Bailey glanced pointedly at Rafe. "Gee, *that* sounds familiar." In an ill-fated attempt to regain a sense of control when she was falling in love with Rafe, Bailey had done the same thing. They'd worked through it, had found their way to each other, but Sasha doubted she and Jack could do the same. Now that he couldn't take pheromone intoxication meds, Jack probably considered what she'd done to Miranda in his condo a deal-breaker.

His safety net was gone.

Well, Jack feeling he *needed* a safety net—him not trusting her—was a deal-breaker, too, damn it. She'd rather live without him than live like that. It would hurt, yes—but she'd get through it. With the help of her family, and the friends sitting that that table, she'd get over him.

Eventually.

She caught Flynn's eye, beckoning him to the table. "Could we have a round for the table, please?"

"Sure. Another Diet Coke for you?"

"I'll have a shot of Macallan."

Flynn nodded approvingly. After checking what others wanted to drink, he headed back to the bar. As he reached for the whiskey, the opening notes of Robyn's "Dancing with Myself" pumped from the club's sound system. She couldn't help but laugh.

When the universe spoke, it made sense to listen.

Tonight was the first night of the rest of her life, and it was up to her to find a way to live it well.

She leapt to her feet, grabbed Bailey's hand, and headed for the dance floor.

✳

"You're positive you won't move back to California?"

Jack stared at his mother, curled up in the chair closest to the fireplace, sipping a steaming cup of green tea. Chemotherapy might have ravaged her body, but today she was a cashmere-clad Terminator who just...kept...coming. "Yes, Mother, I'm sure," he said for what felt like the tenth time. "I like my job very much."

If I'm still capable of doing it once I get home. Since arriving, he'd unconsciously reached for his meds more than once—a sure sign he'd gotten too used to taking them. The good news? As Adnan had predicted, he hadn't experienced physical withdrawal symptoms.

"Jack, I don't understand." His mom reached for the sound system remote, silencing Mariah Carey before she could tell anyone what she wanted for Christmas. "I don't understand. How can you work for someone else's family firm when your own family so desperately needs your help?"

"You'll be back in the saddle in no time." He glanced at his dad, placidly sipping red wine in the chair next to his mother. No help there, but he hadn't expected any. "It's not like I'm leaving you high and dry," he said. "I agreed to take a seat on K&K's board." That was the compromise he'd made with his parents. He'd serve in an advisory capacity, and help guide the practice into the future, but he wouldn't accept an executive position or be involved in day-to-day operations.

"I don't understand why you'd work for a company where you have no ownership stake. You used to have more ambition." His mother's gaze went razor-sharp. "Unless you're using this job with Elliott Sebastiani's son as a stepping stone to an executive position at Sebastiani Labs. Now *that* I could understand."

Grief sucker-punched him, but his mother was too busy planning the next decade of his life to notice. As his parents talked, he pretended to sip his eggnog, trying to regain his equilibrium. What would his mother say if she knew he'd worked with Elliott Sebastiani for ages, and knew him on a first-name basis? That Lukas, Elliott's son, was the leader of Earth's paranormal species? That her *own* son held a seat on their ruling council, and had for years?

As usual, his parents were in their own little world, not paying him the slightest bit of attention. Having so much emotional privacy felt…strange. He'd really gotten used to having incubi and succubi being up in his business all the time. Thankfully, with his family, all he had to do was listen, and keep his mouth shut.

Elliott's death clearly hadn't hit the human media yet, because his mother was speaking about him as though he was alive. "He'd be stupid not to hire Jack," she was saying to his dad.

Nice to know, but it was time to nip this in the bud. "Mom? Mom. I'm not interested in working at Sebastiani Labs."

"No?"

"No. I'm really happy where I'm at."

"Working for the son."

For the President, actually. "Yes. I'm up for a promotion," he added, sipping at his eggnog.

"Did you hear that, Cynthia? A promotion." His dad raised his glass in a toast. "More responsibility?"

"Definitely." If he accepted the Sec/Tech First

chair, his decisions would impact an entire culture. "I really love the work, and I'm good at it."

His dad eyed him approvingly. "The perks are already pretty great if you have a private plane at your disposal."

Taking the Gulfstream made him feel uncomfortable. He'd spent too much of the flight to California remembering, gazing at the plane's tiny bedroom door like a lovesick fool. "It sure saves time."

Glenda came out of the kitchen carrying more eggnog. "Another mug?"

"I'd love one," he said, smiling.

"Are you sure you won't try the wine?" his father asked. "It's a gorgeous pinot noir from Oregon…"

"No, thanks." During the time he'd been in California, he'd lain off both booze and caffeine, and his stomach felt better for it. "Glenda, isn't it about time for you to leave?" Glenda's son and his husband were hosting the family's Christmas celebration later that evening, but she'd insisted on working a half-day anyway.

"After this, I'm on my way." Leaning closer, she refilled his mug. "When are you going back to Minnesota?"

"Tomorrow." Though he'd managed a couple of solo outings while he'd been here—lunch with Chloe, and a Sharks game with Charlie—spending three weeks with his parents was two weeks too long. He was more than ready to go home.

After Glenda made her goodbyes, he walked her out to her car. On his way back to the house, he steeled himself for the conversation to come—one he'd put off until the end of his stay.

His mother had to butt out of his love life, once and for all.

When he came back into the house, Mannheim Steamroller drifted from the speakers, and his parents were having a quiet conversation. He sat back down, picking up the eggnog he'd set on the hearth. "We need to talk about a former client."

His mother lifted a penciled brow. "I thought you weren't going to get involved in day-to-day operations."

Somehow, she managed to look surprised, bored, and satisfied at the same time. Jack brushed his annoyance aside. "This is a risk management issue."

His parents exchanged a glance. "Chloe told me you'd asked to see the risk file," his father said. "Do we have a problem?"

"Yes." It was all he could do to not rub the bullet wound in his shoulder. "Miranda DesJardins."

His mother was suddenly very interested in her cup of tea. She took a careful sip, then another. "Can you refresh my memory? Chemo, you know." She touched her cashmere knit cap, mauve today to match the rest of her ensemble. "My brain isn't working quite as well as it used to."

Oh, your brain is working just fine. He let her get away with it, because it served his purposes to be the one who laid out the facts. "She was a marketing executive for a Silicon Valley technology company, charged with intellectual property theft and insider trading." He paused. "Her case was my last before leaving California."

"Which you lost, correct?"

"I see your memory is miraculously improving." Did she remember receiving Miranda's letter, and responding in a manner that led the woman to believe her anger was justified?

"Why bring this up now?" his mother asked.

"Ms. DesJardins was released from prison earlier this year. She followed me to Minneapolis."

A ghost of a smile. "Still pining after you after all these years, even though you lost her case?"

Anger, simmering for years, came to a boil. How could such a smart person be so *wrong*? Slowly, deliberately, he set the mug back on the hearth. It was either that or hurl it across the room. "First off. Stalking is a crime, not a compliment. Second, the prosecutor had an open-and-shut case and you know it. DesJardins was found guilty on every count because she *was* guilty on every count."

"You failed to make a deal—"

"Believe me, I tried. No go." It hadn't helped that DesJardins hadn't shown the slightest hint of remorse. "I did my best." On this, his conscience was clear. "I did the best I could for my client."

"She could have been so much more than a client." His mother glanced over at his father, who—surprise, surprise—sat silently on the sidelines while they duked it out. "She wanted to be so much more."

"*You* wanted her to be so much more," Jack accused. "You encouraged her. You led her to believe I was interested in a personal relationship."

His mother half-shrugged, acknowledging his point. "She looked like a perfect match on paper—advanced degree, a challenging career, a philanthropic family. Once I met her, she looked even better."

"Better for what?"

"Procreation," she stated baldly. "Miranda was attractive, healthy, and her biological clock was ticking. She told me she wanted to start a family sooner rather than later."

He stared at her. "You wanted grandchildren, and I wasn't getting the job done?"

"Not quickly enough."

"News flash. Your timeline isn't a factor in my reproductive choices." *Dear jumping Jesus.* "I can't believe you led her to believe—"

"Jack, I was just trying to…expedite matters. To move things along."

"Like you did with Anna?" His mother looked startled. "Yeah, I know about that." An uncomfortable thought crossed his mind: if his mother *hadn't* interfered in his relationship with Anna, they might have gotten married and had a child or two by now. He might never have left California, or accepted Lukas's first job offer. He might never have met Sasha, much less come to love her.

Was loving and losing worse than never having loved at all?

He set *that* uncomfortable thought aside. "Mother, your track record is horrible. Your interference actually chased away my fiancée, a woman who might have given you what you wanted. Your next choice, Miranda DesJardins, is a convicted felon—"

"You were supposed to win the case! Or at least plead it down to house arrest, then probation. It was her first arrest, for a white-collar crime. As a non-violent offender—"

"Non-violent?" He shoved to his feet. "Mom, she pulled a gun on us!"

"A…gun?"

"Yes. On Sasha and me."

"Is everyone okay?" his father asked.

He speaks. "Yes," he said, sitting back down. "DesJardins was arrested before she could do any real damage." Other than to his relationship with Sasha.

No, that wasn't fair. He'd done most of *that* damage himself.

"Speaking of which," his mother ventured, "how are things going with Elliott Sebastiani's daughter?"

"None of your business," he bit out. "If you want me to take that board seat, you'll butt out of my personal life, from this day forward."

She looked at him, as if assessing whether he meant it or not. Something in his face must have convinced her, because she finally gave a slow nod.

Not enough. "Say it out loud."

"An oral contract? Seriously?"

Was she offended or impressed? At this point, he didn't give a shit. "Yes, an oral contract, and I'll resign from the board the first time it's violated."

"I—"

"Try me."

"Cynthia," his father broke in. "This isn't some random lawyer sitting across a negotiating table. It's our son, and I want him back in our lives. Agree with his terms, then butt out."

The fire crackled and popped, punctuating the silence. Finally, she straightened in her chair. "State your terms," she said.

His thoughts raced as he reached for his cell phone, then hit 'record.' "Repeat after me: I, Cynthia Roth Kirkland, do solemnly swear I will remain completely uninvolved in my son's personal relationships, from this date forward."

More silence. No doubt she was probing his hasty statement for loopholes. Probably finding them. *Shit.*

"Mother—"

"I suppose your terms are reasonable." She repeated his statement, exactly as he had. "Good luck dealing with your punk rock lover." A spark of humor glinted. "I bet she's a handful."

He didn't correct her mistaken impression that he and Sasha were still involved. Instead, he stated his name and the date for the record, then asked his father to do the same. The contract was dodgy as hell, but it couldn't hurt to have a witness. He saved the file, then emailed everyone a copy.

And that was that.

"There's something really strange about the Sebastiani family," his mother mused. "I can't put my finger on it."

"Cynthia, butt out," his father ordered. "Would you like more tea?"

"Actually, I think I'm in the mood for a nap." Rising from the chair, she looked at his father. "Would you like to join me?"

His father blinked then pushed to his feet, quickly enough to send the wine sloshing. "Certainly." He looked questioningly at Jack.

"Go ahead," he said, waving in the general direction of their bedroom. "I have some work to do. Upstairs," he added. His childhood bedroom, now a well-appointed guest room, was located as far away from the master suite as the floor plan allowed. He couldn't remember ever overhearing his parents having sex when he was young, but... Headphones. That's what headphones were for. "See you later."

Before disappearing into the hallway leading to their bedroom, his dad winked at him.

Yep, definitely time to go upstairs.

He stood, flexing the fingers of his right hand. Yes, he did have some work to do—email to read, text messages to return—and…yes, he'd review the document Lukas had sent via encrypted channels late last night: an updated version of the Security and Technology Council charter, naming him, Jack Kirkland, as the Sec/Tech First, and Bailey Brown as the Second.

Had Lukas sent the draft on the off-chance Jack might take the job, or had his friend known what his decision would be before Jack was aware of making one? Because, yes—he was going to accept the position, and do the job well, regardless of the mess he'd made with Sasha.

"This calls for a toast." He picked up his dad's wine glass, then took a small sip. Smooth, jammy, with a final, peppery kick... "Yeah, that's nice." Leaving the glass behind, he headed upstairs.

He wanted the job on its own terms, but he'd be lying if he didn't admit that accepting it kept him in Sasha's orbit. He wanted the job, *and* the woman— and if he couldn't have both, he'd move heaven and earth to make things right between them. To let her know that their breakup was his fault, not hers.

The fault had never been hers.

He owed her that much, and more.

CHAPTER NINETEEN

From her seat in the front row, Sasha watched the siren choir as they swayed on Underbelly's flower-laden stage. Her father might well be the first world leader to have an a cappella version of a Depeche Mode song performed at his memorial service, but Eric Whitacre's dissonant arrangement of "Enjoy the Silence" was oddly perfect.

She steeled herself for the high note she knew was coming, the one she found so shatteringly beautiful even when sung by a human. When sung by Scarlett, a grief-stricken siren, considered the voice of her generation?

It was an arrow to the heart, piercing and cathartic. Gasps, sobs, and the emotions of nearly two thousand people rippled through the room. Sasha opened herself to the collective pain, absorbing it. Welcoming it.

Such a staggering loss *should* hurt.

Lukas, sitting down the row, reached for more antacids. She glanced over to the cameras, discreetly live-streaming the service to thousands who couldn't attend in person. What did a culture's collective mourning taste like? Lukas had assured everyone he could handle the emotional load—and as far as she could tell, he was—but maybe the live-stream had been a mistake.

Jack, sitting in the front row across the aisle, noticed Lukas's movement. His gaze skipped to her, and he lifted a questioning brow.

Jack's emotional mix was turbulent, complex. It was tempting to try to sort through all the skeins, but now was not the time or place. She reassured him with a subtle nod, then focused on the stage again.

No more trying to interpret Jack's feelings. The man could speak for himself.

The last notes of the song echoed through the performance space, then faded away. Having lanced the grief, now healing could begin. She saw gentle smiles as the choir filed off the stage, then took their seats. When Scarlett handed Lukas their daughter, his pleasure flooded the row.

Up on stage, Wyland, seated stage left with Valerian, helped Val to his feet. Both vampires approached the linen-draped table holding the Tome, her father's cremains, and a slender, white candle that had burned throughout the service. Wyland stayed close as Valerian, resplendent in his white ceremonial robes, picked up a pen, leaned over the ancient book, then recorded her father's death. Once Val finished, Wyland closed the book with great care, then stepped back.

"We now consign Elliott Sebastiani to the Fade," Valerian said. "May one so beloved never fade from our memories." Cupping the flame with a shaky hand, he blew out the candle, caressed the teapot holding the cremains, then raised both hands to the sky. "All that was, all that is, all that shall be."

"All that was, all that is, all that shall be," the crowd repeated.

When Coco babbled a loud stream of baby nonsense, laughter rippled through the room.

The brightness of Valerian's smile rivaled the sun. "Let us go in peace."

The stage lights dimmed and the floor lights brightened, subtle signals that the service was over. People rose to their feet. Hundreds of conversations started, jacking the noise level from one to ten in an instant. Sasha tried to ignore Jack, but his height made it impossible. They'd managed to greet each other earlier, carefully and politely. They'd inquired after each other's Christmases, and then he'd told her he was taking the Sec/Tech First chair—news she'd already heard from Lukas and Bailey.

Jack wasn't moving back to California, but where did that leave *them*? His emotions were all over the place, bouncing like a pinball on a hot machine.

"Let's clear the room as quickly as possible." Lukas's voice came through the tiny earpiece she and about two dozen other people were wearing. With every Council member in the building, the memorial service was a maximum-security event.

But of course, clearing the room was easier said than done. There was a crush around Claudette. Calm and serene, she looked resplendent in a perfect white pantsuit, stylish kitten heels, and an exquisite platinum necklace that flashed in the light. No one but family knew that its center stone had been crafted using some of her bondmate's cremains.

Lukas, Scarlett, and Coco stood with Claudette, contributing to the slowdown. She'd bet serious folding money that most of the people surrounding Claudette were as interested in eyeballing their new president as they were in offering sympathies to the

Siren First. Holding his tiny daughter, Lukas looked almost approachable. She couldn't begrudge people wanting—needing—some reassurance.

Three Council members and a baby? Irresistible.

Rafe, Bailey, and Antonia worked the room, accepting condolences while hustling people along. She did the same, gently herding people away from the stage and toward coat check. At the table near the back bar, she saw that Wyland had convinced Valerian to take a seat—or maybe Val's partner Thane had.

"Sasha, come in," she heard Flynn say via her earpiece.

She activated outgoing audio. "Flynn, what's up?"

"Valerian asked for some brandy snifters. He said he brought a special vintage from home."

Flynn's anticipation was evident. Any liquor a 900-year-old vampire called 'a special vintage' would be special indeed. Council members who'd seen Valerian set a bottle on the table were already making their way over to join him. Plainclothes security guards fanned out around the table, forming a gauntlet.

Lukas sighed, then gave a subtle nod.

Smart man. "Go ahead," she said to Flynn.

Already behind the back bar, Flynn reached for a tray. "If you'd said no, people would have started swigging right from the bottle."

"Save one for me."

"Will do."

The lure of rare brandy wasn't enough to draw Jack to the back table. Instead, he approached Claudette. In a beautiful gray suit and sky blue tie, he looked downright jumpable. Their gazes snagged for a moment. Jack smiled, then leaned over to say something to Claudette.

"Hey, Sasha."

Jacoby was using his mobility scooter today. "Hi there. Thanks for coming." She hugged him, then they kissed each other's cheeks. "You're coming upstairs, right?"

"I don't think so." Jacoby indicated his father, standing alone, surrounded by his personal security guards. "Dad hasn't stirred any shit yet today, and I'd like to keep it that way. I think it's best if we take our leave."

Jacoby's reason was bullshit. Alpha and Beta, father and son, had arrived at the memorial service separately, and if they'd exchanged a single word during the ceremony, she hadn't seen it. Jacoby carried a new weight, a soul-deep pain she could sense and absorb but not interpret. She took his hand in hers. "What's going on, Jacoby?"

He looked around the room, where almost a hundred people still milled, then smiled. "How about dinner sometime next week?"

His facial expression didn't match his emotions. Somewhere along the line, her old friend had become an astute politician. "If you don't call me to confirm a date, I'll just show up on your doorstep." Her words were both a warning and a promise. "I don't care what kind of sexual shenanigans I interrupt."

"Shenanigans?" His expression went faux-innocent. "*Moi?*"

"Yes, you." There, his energy was better. "You and your guest tied up a bathroom at Underbelly for a long time the other night." She still didn't know who he'd been with. "Who's the lucky lady?"

"A gentleman never tells."

Interesting. Well, she'd find out sooner or later—probably sooner, because she and Jacoby were having dinner together next week, come hell or high water. "What does your schedule look like?" she asked. "I'm open—"

Coco let loose an air-raid wail.

Jacoby winced, clapping his hands over his ears.

Krispin Woolf had approached the group surrounding Claudette, probably to offer his condolences. "She really doesn't like my dad," Jacoby said.

Coco's self-preservation instincts were already top-notch. She shrieked like a banshee every time Krispin came near.

"Is no one capable of silencing that child?" The WerePack Alpha sounded as though he'd be happy to do the job himself.

She wasn't the only one to hear it. Lukas handed Coco to Scarlett, then blocked them with his body. Jack shifted to stand at Lukas's left, and Winnie flanked Lukas on his right. Behind the barrier created by their bodies, Chico hustled Scarlett, Coco, and Claudette away. Krispin's own guards moved in. A half-dozen Sebastiani Security guards formed a line in front of Lukas and Jack.

It happened lightning-fast, a choreographed dance.

Everyone went still, waiting.

Watching.

Tension seethed and pulsed.

Impasse.

"Okay, everyone," Jack said, calm and controlled. "Let's stand down."

The cool authority in his voice was *totally* fucking hot.

Still, no one moved.

"Oh, for fuck's sake," she heard Scarlett mutter from behind the front bar, where Chico had hustled his charges. She stood, righteously pissed off. "All guards, fall back."

Her powerful voice rolled through the room. The guards moved like marionettes, taking jerky steps backwards whether they wanted to or not, leaving Jack staring Krispin down. Lukas's attention was split; her brother was more pissed off at Scarlett for leaving safe cover than he was concerned about Krispin Woolf. But Jack? He was completely focused on the WerePack Alpha—not starting anything, but clearly ready to finish it.

Yeah, *totally* hot.

At her side, Jacoby cleared his throat, shifting in his chair. Yeah, she must be leaching pheromones something fierce.

Finally, Krispin took a mocking half-step back. "I'll take my leave. Until next time, gentlemen."

She wasn't the only one to hear the threat.

Krispin headed for coat check, his guards following. "Keep that baby away from me," he said over his shoulder.

Coco flat-out chortled.

Woolf's cheeks went red. Sasha couldn't hear what he muttered to his closest guard, but she understood his feelings just fine. Coco needed a security detail.

"I'm so sorry," Jacoby murmured.

"It's not your fault." Something about Jacoby's energy was *really* off. "Dinner," she reminded him. "This coming week."

"I won't forget." They kissed each other's cheeks again. "Talk to you soon," he said. Jacoby turned his scooter and set it in motion. He departed with a quiet electric hum.

Sasha's cell phone vibrated. Plucking it from her pocket, she read Chadden's text message. They were ready for guests upstairs.

Sasha brightened the floor lights even more. Soon, the cavernous space was empty except for family, Council members, and close friends. She took a sharp-eyed look around. Having served no food, and no beverages other than Val's brandy, clean-up was negligible. The third-shift crew would take care of the chairs, clear the stage, and sweep the floors. Flynn would handle the snifters. She'd already told the crew chief to leave the flowers on the stage; she'd take care of those personally.

Tomorrow.

"Sasha, I'll get the front doors," Flynn said in her earpiece.

"Thanks."

"I'll secure the second and third floors," Jack said.

He'd ditched his suit coat, loosened his tie, and rolled up his shirt sleeves. When had suit porn become her personal catnip? More importantly, when could she get a couple of minutes alone with him? Sure, they needed to talk, but right now, she just wanted to jump him.

Antonia sidled up next to her. "Have you talked to him yet?"

"No, not yet."

"What are you so afraid of?"

She shot her sister a dirty look. "I'm not afraid."
Am I?

They watched as Jack disappeared into the stairwell leading upstairs. "Can't you tell?" Antonia asked. "He wants you something fierce."

True, but… "Sometimes wanting isn't enough."

Antonia grinned. "It's a damn good start."

Speaking of which… "Where's Merrill?"

The grin dissolved. "Upstairs, at our apartment. She'd had more than enough attention for a while."

She winced, commiserating. The Sebastianis were used to a complete lack of privacy—it was all they'd ever known—but newcomers could find the lack of anonymity disconcerting. The fact that Antonia's lover had sat with the family at the president's memorial service was probably already blazing up the grapevine. She squeezed Antonia's hand. "Will she join us at Claudette's?"

"Yeah."

"Good." At the back table, Thane poured amber liquid from an ornate Rémy Martin decanter. "Have you tasted the brandy yet?"

"No." Antonia wrinkled her nose. "Flynn said it was Louis XIII cognac, bottled in 1874."

No wonder Flynn was so excited. "We'd better make sure they save him a sample."

"Let's save one for Jack, too."

With his stomach problems, should Jack even be drinking? She bit back a response and followed Antonia to the back table. Jack was an adult, old enough to know whether he should drink or not. He was also adult enough to speak with her about…how had Antonia put it? Wanting her something fierce.

Was wanting—was *sex*—enough? It always had been in the past.

She sidled into the space between Val and Thane, wrapping an arm around each man's shoulders. "Any hooch left?"

"Hooch?" Val reared back in his chair, horrified by her lack of couth. "Oh, my dear…"

As Val rhapsodized about the cognac, the second floor lights flicked off. She couldn't see Jack, but he was up there, moving in the shadows. His spiky impatience pricked her nostrils.

Antonia sensed it, too. Standing on Val's other side, she mouthed, "He wants to talk to you."

Or maybe he just wants to get the hell out of here, away from me. Maybe he's as tired as I am, and wants to go home to his bed. Gads, what a long day—and I didn't spend half of it on an airplane.

Stop it. Didn't you learn your lesson the first time? Stop trying to interpret Jack's feelings.

Antonia was right; they needed to talk. They had to use their words—clear the air, once and for all—then, painful though it might be, negotiate the parameters of their new normal.

Maybe tonight, maybe tomorrow, but it had to be done, and soon. Their culture would pay the price if they failed.

CHAPTER TWENTY

With Claudette's guest list limited to family, Council members, and a couple dozen close friends, security needs were nil, so Jack accepted a flute of champagne from the server. Stepping into a space between the Christmas tree and the hearth where he could watch the room, he took a small, testing sip.

Nope, the bubbles didn't wash away the nasty aftertaste of the situation Krispin had started downstairs, but somehow, Claudette and the Sebastianis seemed to have set the unpleasantness aside. Scattered across the penthouse's spacious living room and dining room, the family members appeared relaxed—eating, drinking, and chatting with their guests. Antonia and her girlfriend were deep in conversation next to the swinging doors leading to the kitchen. Rafe stood behind a makeshift bar in the dining room, helping Flynn serve Valerian's rare brandy to a dazzled crowd. Over on the couch, Scarlett breastfed Coco, laughing with Krispin's daughter, Andi Woolf, and Wyland's bondmate, Tia Quinn. Lukas and Wyland had taken up a spot near the closed door leading to Elliott and Claudette's home office.

He should probably join them, but right now he was more interested in what was happening on the loveseat. Chadden, out of the kitchen and now a guest, held a fork up to Sasha's mouth, trying to feed her a bite of his Chocolate Raspberry Bombe.

Surely she recognized Chadden's tried-and-true seduction move? The dessert was delicious, but...she needed vegetables. Something healthy. Under the expertly-applied makeup, she looked utterly exhausted.

Claudette was suddenly at his side. "Jack, why are you hiding behind the Christmas tree?"

He set his champagne flute on the mantel, nestling it among some fragrant pine boughs, then kissed Claudette's cheek. "Just trying to stay out of the way."

"There *are* a lot of large men here tonight, aren't there?" Looping her arm through the crook of his elbow, she assessed the room. "So many people, here to celebrate Elliott's life. I'm so glad you made it back in time for the service."

"I wouldn't have missed it for the world." Over on the loveseat, Sasha had opened her mouth, accepting Chadden's offering.

Did he think the woman couldn't feed herself?

Sasha brought her hand up to Chadden's wrist as her lips closed over the fork tines. There was eye-rolling bliss as she chewed, tasted, swallowed.

His mouth went dry. Blood rushed to his groin. Thankfully, he'd put his suit coat back on before coming upstairs.

Over by the kitchen door, Antonia gave him a mocking, knowing look. He turned his back on the brat. "Thanks again for letting me say a few words at the service," he said to Claudette. The memorial service's program hadn't specified who'd speak, just that there would be speakers. He hadn't prepared anything, had just spoken from the heart about how Elliott had supported him, a human, in so many ways. He'd closed by thanking the Sebastiani family for sharing their father—with him, and with the world.

"Your words were beautiful. It's important that the people of our culture get to know you, especially with a job change coming your way."

Trust Claudette to consider the political ramifications, even at her bondmate's memorial service. "It's not a done deal yet," he cautioned. "Krispin's going to put up one hell of a fight."

Her expression went hard. "Let him. Even if Jacoby votes with his father against the proposal, the 'yeas' will prevail."

"Well, the next council meeting should be interesting," he said. Krispin would be even more of an asshole than usual, testing for any possible weakness.

Testing me *for weakness.*

Would he be able to handle it? How long had it been since he'd attended a Council meeting without taking pheromone intoxication meds first?

And why had he started taking meds before Council meetings in the first place? He really didn't need them there. Elliott, Lukas, and Antonia were the only Council members whose pheromones he had to manage, and he trusted them not to—

He trusted them.

Over on the loveseat, Sasha took the fork and plate from Chadden, then started eating the cake with obvious relish.

Don't you trust Sasha, too?

Of course I do.

How had he let everything get so fucked up?

"Jack?" Claudette waved a hand in front of his face.

"I'm sorry, could you repeat that?"

"I asked how your Christmas was."

"Good," he said. "Quiet, with just the three of us." Probably very different than the Sebastiani family's celebration, which tended toward noise and rowdiness. "And yours?"

Claudette laughed. "You know how it goes. Coco received more gifts than everyone else combined. How are your parents? Your mother?"

He'd just finished filling Claudette in on his mother's recovery when Bailey approached. "Scarlett asked me to find you," she said to Claudette. "It's Coco's bedtime."

"Oh, thank you. Lukas and Scarlett are spending the night here tonight," she explained to Jack. "Scarlett asked me to help put Coco down, not that she actually needs help."

No, but she'd thought about her mother's comfort on this very difficult day. Some normalcy, and a slice of peace and quiet, were just the ticket. "It was a lovely service," Jack said, kissing her cheek again.

"It was, wasn't it? It was mostly Sasha's doing." They all glanced at the loveseat. Sasha had kicked off her ankle boots, and now sat curled in the corner, a brandy snifter in her hand. Chadden leaned close, as if to hear what she was saying. More likely, he wanted to gorge himself on her luscious, irresistible scent. "I'm so glad Chadden got her to eat something," Claudette murmured. "She's been running on fumes for days."

Booze and cake. Some fucking nourishment.

Claudette started walking away. "See you both at breakfast tomorrow morning," she called over her shoulder.

He looked at Bailey. "Breakfast?"

"A family breakfast, here, at nine a.m.," she confirmed.

Didn't Claudette know he and Sasha weren't dating anymore? That he wasn't family? Across the room, Chadden sat with his arm draped along the back of the loveseat, too close to Sasha's shoulders.

If Sasha sought comfort from Chadden tonight, his friendship with the vamp probably wouldn't survive it.

"Hey." Bailey nudged him with her hip. "How are you feeling? The service must have been challenging, given you couldn't take pheromone intoxication meds."

The siren choir, the speakers, and Sasha's tear-stained face had hit like body blows, but he'd shaken them off quickly, with no lasting impact. "I'm...okay."

"No hangover?"

"No."

What she saw in his face must have convinced her. "Good. It worked that way for me, too." Bailey tipped her head toward the loveseat. "So, what are you going to do about that?"

He shoved a clenched a fist into his pants pocket. "Sasha can sleep with whoever she wants to."

"She doesn't want to sleep with Chadden, you doofus. She wants to sleep with *you*."

Chadden had pulled Sasha's feet into his lap, working the kinks out of her soles with his thumbs. Sasha's expression was almost...carnal, her eyelids fluttering with pleasure and pain combined. He looked away. "It doesn't look like it to me."

"So, you're tapping out?"

"No," he quickly replied. "But I don't think this is the right time or place." He needed time to think, to strategize. To come up with his most convincing arguments.

"You want to mind-fuck it to death first."

She knew him too well.

"Keep acting like you don't care who she sleeps with, and she'll move on," Bailey warned.

"She's a succubus, for god's sake. She knows exactly how I feel."

"Do you?"

"Do I what?"

"Know how you feel?"

"I love her, of course."

"Good," she said, nodding. "There's hope for you yet."

Over on the love seat, Chadden continued his foot massage. Sasha had unbuttoned her suit coat, and leaned back against the cushions. "I need to apologize first," he murmured. "How can I begin to make amends for not trusting her when I should have?"

"Start there."

"What?"

"Start there. Say, 'Sasha, I'm sorry I didn't trust you when I should have,' and see how she responds."

"Do you really think that will be enough?"

"Hard to say, but you won't know until you try." She eyed him. "Let me pass along some advice Scarlett gave me when Rafe and I were having a similar problem: use your words."

"Use your words?"

"Yep. Incubi and succubi can read people's emotional vibes as easily as they breathe, and the

Sebastiani family's abilities are off the charts." She leaned closer, dropping her voice to a whisper. "But they have a blind spot."

"What is it?" He needed all the help he could get.

"They know *what* a person feels, but not *why*. They sometimes make assumptions or mistakes, just like everyone else. It helps when everyone uses their words."

He stared at her. "It can't be that simple."

"Oh, it's not simple at all. You wouldn't believe some of the fights Rafe and I have had, and over the stupidest things." Bailey paused, as if trying to find the right words. "It's really easy to fall into the trap of thinking they're all-seeing and all-knowing—that they have super powers, that humans are always at a disadvantage." She cocked a brow. "That's why you started taking too many pheromone intoxication meds in the first place, right? Been there, done that, have the surgical scars to prove it."

Yeah, she knew.

"But they *aren't* all-seeing and all-knowing. They're—" She laughed. "I was about to say 'they're human, too,' and of course they're not. But they need explanations, just like we do." She looked up at him. "Last I heard, lawyers are really good at explaining things."

"But—"

"Jack. Apologize, simply and directly, and see what she says." She turned toward the dining room, where Rafe sipped brandy with Flynn, Lorin, and Gabe. When Rafe looked back, his expression sizzled the air. Bailey blinked, then cleared her throat. "Pro tip from someone who has a sex demon for a bondmate? Clear your head before you apologize. Clarity helps reduce confusion."

"That makes sense." And right now, Bailey's emotions were crystal-clear. He waved a hand toward the dining room. "Go jump your bondmate."

"What a great idea," she said cheekily. "And look—Chadden's making his move."

Yep, Chadden was rising from the loveseat, saying something to Sasha. Whatever he said must have met with her approval. She nodded, touched his forearm, and gave him a tired-looking smile.

Ready or not, the time was now.

"Go for it." Rising on tip-toe, she kissed him on the cheek. "Pro tip number two? The make-up sex is—"

"Go away."

He was halfway to the loveseat before he realized Chadden was walking toward *him*.

"Hey, do you have a key to Sasha's apartment?" the vamp asked.

He had to give Chadden points for sheer balls. "If you want the key to Sasha's place, you're going to have to get it from her yourself."

"Dude, she forgot her key, and I can't find Antonia. Look at her, she's ready to drop."

Pushing past Chadden, he made his way to the loveseat. Sasha was on her feet, bending over to pick up her discarded boots. It was all he could do to keep his eyes off her ass.

"Hi," she said, straightening.

"Hi." Even pale and tired, she was so damn beautiful. "Chadden said you forgot your door key." He reached for his wallet. "I can let you into your apartment."

"Because you have a master key for the whole

damn building, right?"

"Yes." He had a master for the Sebastiani Building, and for all Sebastiani family properties and residences. He carried it at Lukas's request. He'd never abused the privilege, and he wasn't about to start now. "Do you want me to change the codes? Exclude your apartment?"

If she said yes, he'd know where they stood.

"No, you're Dudley Freaking Do-Right," she muttered. "You'd never sneak into my apartment, into my bed, like a thief in the night."

"Do you...want me to?" If his stiffening cock was any indication, the idea appealed.

She inhaled, cursed under her breath, then stalked toward the door.

He followed.

No one said goodbye. No one stopped them.

But everybody watched them leave.

He scanned the lobby that the elevator and both penthouse units shared, making sure it was clear before waving Sasha forward. Dozens of plants and flower arrangements had been delivered during the last few days, and the lobby smelled like a greenhouse. On the credenza, florist-wrapped flower arrangements fought for space with piles of mail, a good-sized lamp, and a multiple line desk phone. More plants sat on the carpeted floor, pushed back against the walls so people wouldn't trip.

He closed Claudette's door. There was a metallic click, then heavy silence.

Sasha had stopped in the middle of the lobby. "Thanks so much for helping lock up tonight. For your help with...everything."

So damn polite, as though she hadn't given him a

front-row seat into her sexual fantasies not thirty seconds ago. Frustration boiled over. *"That's* what you want to talk about?"

She tossed her boots toward the credenza, nearly knocking over a plant. "Are you ready to talk about more?"

The motion reminded him of a hockey player throwing their gloves, squaring off for a fight. He shouldn't find it so goddamn hot, but he did. He started to reach for her, but stopped. *Use your words.* Damn it, how was he supposed to follow Bailey's advice when his lizard brain was in the driver's seat? "First things first. I owe you an apology."

"What?"

It was nice to know he could still surprise her. "I owe you an apology."

"For what?"

He rolled his eyes. "Where do I start?"

"Could I offer a suggestion? How about…holding me?"

"Are you serious?"

When she reached for him, tendrils of her hot-house scent wound around his brain stem. "I know we need to talk, to clear the air," she said, looking into his eyes. "I need to apologize, too, but…could you please just hold me for a minute?"

The exhaustion in her voice just about killed him. "Oh, sweetheart, of course." He opened his arms. "Come here."

She didn't hesitate, just stepped into his embrace, sliding her hands under his suit coat so she could clasp them together at the back of his waist. She laid her cheek against his chest, nuzzling against his shirt.

It felt like a kiss.

Do not think about kisses, he thought, stroking her back, her shoulders, and her neck. She needed comfort, followed by a damn good massage. "Your muscles are all tied up in knots," he murmured, pressing the tense bundle where neck met shoulder.

"Yeah." Wincing, she leaned into his touch. "It's been...oh, God." Her eyelids drifted to half-mast. "*Mmm*, yeah. Right there."

The half-groan/half-purr grabbed him by the balls, but he continued his massage, wallowing in her heady scent. Jungle flowers, hair product, and pheromones...the combination was an elixir decanted especially for him, a balm that both relaxed and energized.

"Thanks, I needed that." She levered her upper body away, but kept her hands around his waist. "It's been...a really long day."

The position pressed their hips together in diabolical alignment. There was no disguising his hard cock, but she didn't move away. "A long day, a long week, a hell of a long month," he acknowledged. Had over a month passed since Elliott had died? Since he'd been shot? Yes. Elliott had died just before Thanksgiving. Tonight was New Year's Eve.

This was one holiday season he'd be happy to see in the rear view mirror...but it would never completely recede from view. Too much had changed, for too many people.

But tomorrow brought a new year, and he was lucky to be here. Sure, the bullet holes still twinged a bit, but he was alive to notice. His hand worked well enough to caress, to offer comfort. He was alive, and so was she. As long as they both lived and breathed, he had a chance to make things up to her, to make things right.

And speaking of breathing... Her scent had deepened, darkened, filling his nostrils with the inebriating musk he never thought he'd experience again. Her expression went carnal, and she went up on her tiptoes. Her hands, resting at the base of his spine, drifted south.

She wants me. She wants me, but—

"Kiss me, Jack."

He wanted nothing more, but... "Are you sure?"

"Always."

When she brought her lips to his, the world blurred around the edges. Plush lips, hot breath, soft tongues, a hint of chocolate... Her clever hands fought with his necktie, twisting and tugging. She muttered something. Tugged again. The tie slithered out from under his collar, then dropped to the floor.

He stepped on it as he lifted her, dancing them back toward the credenza. Her gorgeous purple suit was made from fine-napped suede, simultaneously rough and soft. When he set her down on the table's edge, he stroked his hand down her thigh.

The fabric stroked him back.

She wrapped her arms and legs around him. "Come here."

"I think I'm about to," he muttered.

With a giggle, she snaked her hand between their bodies. Down, down, gliding over his belt buckle then cupping his cock, assessing every steely inch. "I think you'll hold out for a while yet."

She was temptation incarnate, but good sense tapped him on the shoulder. If he wanted to tie more than two words together—if he wanted to apologize—he had to move her hand.

When he did—to his hip, not *too* far away—she blinked up at him, confused. "Why did you do that?"

"I need to say something." He cleared gravel out of his throat. "I need to say a lot of things, before we—"

"Lawyers." She squeezed his hip, stroking it with a diabolical thumb. "Try to cut to the chase, Dudley."

Get the most important words out first. "I'm sorry," he said. "I'm sorry I didn't prevent your father's death. I'm sorry I reacted so badly to the methods you used to stop Miranda DesJardins." He picked up her free hand, kissed her knuckles, then met her gaze. "I'm sorry I thought, for a single second, that you might purposely try to manipulate my emotions with your pheromones." Glancing at the ceiling, he sighed. "I'm sorry about so many things. You asked me to cut to the chase, but I seem to have verbal diarrhea."

Her smile was deadpan. "Occupational hazard."

"Always with the lawyer jokes." But if she was making jokes, things were going better than he had any right to expect. "I'm sorry I ran off to California without straightening things out with you first." He swallowed. "Please say something."

Her smile morphed, warming like the sun. "Apologies accepted."

"That's…it?"

"Do you want to fight a little more?"

"No, but..." Making amends shouldn't feel this easy. *Be* this easy. "I fucked up so badly."

"Oh, you weren't alone." Her expression turned wry. "Believe me, there were plenty of fuck-ups to go around."

He barreled on. "I'm sorry that we didn't have time to clear the air before your father's memorial service. That I wasn't sitting by your side today, holding your hand."

Tears welled, spilling onto her cheeks.

"Ah, shit. I didn't mean to make you cry."

"I wanted you there." She dashed the tears away. "It's…been a day."

The wobble in her voice was a stake through the heart. What was he thinking, doing this so soon after her father's memorial service? "I'm sorry—"

She put her hand over his mouth. "That's enough for now. The apologies can wait until tomorrow."

We have a tomorrow. We have a chance.

Her hand slid to the back of his neck, pulling his head—

"Hey, you two."

Spinning, he reached for his weapon—which he wasn't carrying, thank god, because otherwise he might be cleaning Bailey's brain matter off the walls. "Damn it," he breathed, shoving both shaky hands through his hair.

"Sorry to interrupt," she said, clearly not the least bit sorry. "We're leaving. The party's breaking up."

Rafe and Chadden were with her, and all three wore heavy winter coats. "You two should really get a room," Chadden said, waving his hand in front of his nose. "You're reeking the place up something fierce."

Pheromones. Instead of freaking out about it, he squeezed Sasha's hand.

Sasha slid off the credenza. "I happen to have a room, right over here. We're going there, together. And then we're going to have spectacular make-up sex."

His cheeks went hot.

Bailey glanced back and forth between them.

"Have you two made up?"

"Yes," Sasha answered, reaching for his hand.

Bailey did a little jig. "Victory!" At his inquiring look, she added, "You finally figured out that you love each other. It was taking forever and a day—hell, it was taking *years*—so we...um..." She exchanged a guilty-looking glance with Rafe and Chadden.

"So we what?" Jack asked.

"We gave you a teensy, tiny push."

"What do you mean?"

"I forced you and Sasha into close proximity during your recovery, and tonight, Chadden worked the jealousy angle."

Chadden was *still* working the jealousy angle, not making the slightest effort to hide how much he enjoyed Sasha's second-hand pheromones.

Asshole.

"Do you really think I couldn't have managed working from your place and taking care of you at the same time?" Bailey scoffed. "Puh-*leeze*."

Rafe just shook his head. "I'll call the elevator."

"Thanks." Bailey eyed his ass as he walked across the lobby. Blinking, she cleared her throat. "Thoughts of sexual deprivation might also have factored into my decision."

"You prioritized your sex life over helping me recover from gunshot wounds?" he asked. "Nice to know where I stand."

"Sasha was available, and you two definitely needed a nudge. Hashtag winning!"

He looked down at Sasha. "We're surrounded by manipulative assholes."

Chadden's smile was unrepentant. "But are you happy with the outcome?"

There was only one possible answer. "Yes." But he wasn't so sure he'd call the result final, not yet. He and Sasha still had so many things to talk about. They hadn't talked about anything beyond tomorrow.

They hadn't talked about love.

The elevator chimed. "Time for us to scoot." Bailey gave both him and Sasha a quick peck on the cheek, then joined Rafe at the elevator.

Chadden moved more deliberately, taking his time as he kissed Sasha on both cheeks. "Good night, sweetheart. Sweet dreams." When the vamp turned to him, his expression was deadly serious. "Take care, my friend."

Had Chadden's fangs dropped? *Shit.* Jack gave a slow nod, acknowledging the warning beneath the words. After several seconds, the vamp finally seemed satisfied. Chadden kissed his cheek—*ow!*—then sauntered to the elevator.

Bailey and Rafe waved goodbye as the doors slowly closed. Chadden flashed his fangs.

Jack waited until the elevator was on its way down before checking his stinging cheek. Sure enough, his finger came away smudged with blood. "Fucker bit me."

"Oh, it's just a scratch," Sasha said, waving her hand. "If he'd bitten you, you'd know it."

"How do you…" *I really don't want to know.* He glanced at Claudette's door, remembering Bailey's warning that the party was closing down. "Can we go someplace a little more private? Your apartment, maybe?" He touched her cheek. "There are so many things I want to say."

"And things you want to *do*, I hope."

"Yes." His imagination was on fire.

As he retrieved the keycard, she went over to the credenza to rescue the plant she'd tipped over. After setting it upright, she eyed her boots, the mail-order boxes, then her overflowing mail slot. "What a mess," she said, sighing. "The floral deliveries can wait until tomorrow, but…can you give me a hand with this?"

"Sure."

The stack of mail she plopped into his arm was heavier than it looked. As he juggled it, the top envelope slipped. He caught it before it fell, then froze.

There was a familiar logo in the upper left corner.

"What's wrong?" Sasha asked, picking up her boots.

Maybe nothing. Maybe everything. "Can you think of a reason why you'd receive mail from Kirkland & Kirkland?"

"Your family's law firm? No, my family uses Wyland, for everything." She eyed the crisp, white envelope. "Beautiful handwriting."

"My mother's."

"So that's why the ink looks like dried blood," she muttered. "Sorry, not sorry."

"No offense taken." He'd always thought his mother's signature red ink was creepy as hell.

"How did she get my home address?"

"K&K has an investigative division." It would have been child's play to verify Sasha lived above the store, in the building her family owned. "I don't have a good feeling about this."

"I can understand why you wouldn't." Dropping the boots again, Sasha set the packages back on the table. "Let's find out what we're dealing with."

Setting the mail down on the table, he handed her

the envelope. It was thin, not that thickness made a lick of difference. He'd seen first-hand how three paragraphs of legalese on a single piece of letterhead could change lives forever.

She opened the envelope, withdrawing a single, folded sheet. Something was paper-clipped to the top edge. "Hmm." Her blue eyes flicked as she read. When she finished, she looked at him. "Your mother's a piece of work, all right."

He couldn't read her expression. "What does it say?"

"First of all…" She slid a smaller piece of paper out from under the paper clip. "A check, signed by your mother, made out to me."

He didn't want to touch it—the check was a rattlesnake, ready to strike—but he took it, and read. "A million dollars." Yep, that was a one, followed by six zeroes, drawn against his mother's personal account.

"Apparently the money is mine if I convince you to marry me."

He clenched his jaw. "So much for that fucking contract."

"What contract?"

He told her about the oral contract he'd forced his mother to make, the one he'd hoped would stop her interference in his love life once and for all. "I'm so sorry," he said. "I honestly thought she—"

"Jack, this isn't your apology to make." Sasha set the letter on the table, then plucked the check from his hand. "And Cynthia doesn't realize it, but the terms she proposes are invalid."

"What do you mean?"

"Underworlders don't marry, we bond." She tore

the check in half, then into quarters. "As a lawyer familiar with our culture, I'm sure you can appreciate the distinction." She tore the check again, and again, and again, then held her hand over the recycling bin. Pale blue confetti fluttered like snow.

"I've never seen anyone tear up a million-dollar check before."

"I don't need it. We don't need it." She gave a one-shouldered shrug. "Here's where I'm supposed to come up with a 'priceless' joke, like in that credit card commercial, but..." A nervous huff of laughter as her gaze skittered away. "Shit, I'm horrible at this."

"At what?"

"Using words," she admitted. "Scarlett says we Sebastianis are pretty damn lazy about explaining our feelings. We take our emotional shorthand for granted, and sometimes we're wrong." Stepping closer, she took his hands. "You deserve words, Jack."

He loved her for realizing he needed them.

"I love you," she said. "I love you so much."

He could barely speak through the sudden lump in his throat. "I love you, too."

When he leaned down to kiss her, she stopped him with a hand against his chest. "Even if you can't take pheromone intoxication meds anymore?" She held his gaze, not letting it go. "Yeah, I found out about that."

"I'm sorry I didn't tell you myself."

"I can understand why you didn't," she admitted. "After what you saw me do to Miranda, can you trust that I won't manipulate *your* emotions that way?"

Do you trust me? It was a fundamental question, as important as any declaration of love.

"This is a deal breaker for me," she added. "No

matter how much I love you, I can't—*won't*—be in a relationship with someone who doesn't trust me." She gave him a bittersweet smile. "I'd rather let you go now than try to live like that."

She went silent, waiting, a warrior who'd survive whatever he said next—even if what he said dealt their relationship a death blow.

And she was right. Their relationship wouldn't survive the wrong answer. Thank god one of them was brave enough to confront this here and now. "Can't you tell?" he whispered, tapping the tip of her nose. "Yes, I trust you."

"That's good to know." But instead of looking relieved, she seemed…nervous. She stared at him, inhaling.

Shit. "Do my emotions not match my words?"

"Your emotions match your words just fine." She drew in a deep breath, then exhaled. "Can I ask you one more question?"

"Anything."

She eyed him. "You can say no."

Not likely, but… "Okay." What was up? Her nostrils were twitching up a storm.

Another deep breath. Then: "Jack Kirkland, would you be my bondmate?"

Shock rocked him, a sudden earthquake knocking him off-balance. "Um, wow," he blurted. In Sasha's culture, exclusive long-term partnerships—marriage proposals—were offered and accepted via oral contract. As a human, as an outsider, he never dreamed he'd ever hear such an offer, much less from *her*. He hadn't let himself think—*dream*—it was possible.

"You can say no—"

"Yes," he interrupted. "Of course I will." Yes, he was human, but he was no longer an outsider. Their culture was his, in all the ways that mattered.

He dropped to one knee, taking her hands in his. He didn't have a ring, but it seemed the thing to do. "Sasha Sebastiani, will you be my bondmate?"

She sat on his knee, clutching his shoulders. "Yes. Yes, I will."

Asked and answered; it was as simple as that.

He had a bondmate. He *was* a bondmate.

They grinned at each other.

"*Now* you can kiss me again," she said, giggling against his lips.

He slipped into the kiss, sipping at her mouth. Time ebbed and flowed, and her pheromones eddied around them. Each glide of his tongue was a promise, a promise he'd kill himself to keep.

Laughter crept into the lobby from the other side of Claudette's closed door. He reluctantly pulled back. "Let's go to your apartment."

"Good idea."

As Sasha collected her boots, he went to the credenza and picked up his mother's letter. Sasha had torn up the check, but it wouldn't hurt to keep the letter in case they needed it as ammunition someday. When he slipped the letter in its envelope, something caught his eye. "I can't believe this," he muttered, shaking his head. "Actually, I can."

"What?"

"Look at this." He pointed at the postage cancellation mark. "Mother sent the letter and the check two days *before* she and I entered into the oral contract." No wonder she'd been so specific about the contract's effectiveness date. "Legally, she didn't break the contract," he felt compelled to say.

"Legal, schmegal. You shouldn't have to enter into a legal contract with your own damn mother to enforce perfectly reasonable adult boundaries." She stroked his arm, as if trying to soothe. "Jack, I don't care how badly she wants a grandchild. What she did was—*is*—so damn *wrong*. It's a violation on so many levels I hardly know where to start." She pulled him into a hug. "You know what bothers me most?"

His bondmate's breath was warm against his shirt. "What?"

"She'd already violated the spirit of the contract when she agreed to the terms. She'd already written the check, had already mailed it. She could have told you then, but she didn't." She mumbled *bitch* under her breath. "She'll never hurt you like that again, not if I can help it."

Mother, I think you've met your match. "Are you sure you don't want to make a break for it?" he half-joked.

"Nope." The jut of her jaw was pugnacious. "Game on."

She looked ready to throw down, right then and there. "Later, Champ," he said, fighting a grin. "Right now, I have other plans for you."

Claudette's door snicked open. Antonia and Merrill tumbled into the lobby, giggling, mouths fused together. Antonia held what was left of Valerian's bottle of cognac in one hand, and clutched at Merrill's hair with the other. Merrill had both hands clamped on Antonia's ass.

Sasha shot him a look. "Speaking of getting a room…"

"Shit," Merrill gasped, jerking away from Antonia. "Sorry."

"No need to apologize," Sasha told her.

Antonia steadied her grip on the bottle. "Is everything okay out here?" She sniffed the air, then turned toward him, frowning. "What's the problem, Dudley?"

He goggled at Sasha. "You told her about…" Heat crawled up his neck. "Seriously?"

"There's no such thing as a secret in this family." Her blue eyes danced. "Sure *you* don't want to make a break for it?"

"Nope." He scooped her up, high in his arms, and headed for the door.

She squawked, slapping at his arms. "Put me down. You just got shot."

"You weigh as much as a gnat."

The opening notes of *Auld Lang Syne* suddenly blared into the room. Antonia reached for her phone, silencing it. "It's midnight," she said. "Happy New Year, everyone."

"Happy New Year." While Antonia and Merrill kissed, he juggled Sasha, and fumbled with the keycard.

Antonia laughed. "Smooth moves, Dudley. We're going to Merrill's place." She held out the bottle. "Need something to celebrate with?"

She couldn't know he and Sasha had just become bondmates, could she?

Sasha didn't confirm or deny, just looked at him. "Did you ever get a taste of Valerian's brandy?"

"No." He'd rather drink from her mouth, get drunk on her taste alone.

With one more clumsy swipe, the door finally opened. "Goodnight," he called out, ignoring Antonia's giggle. Stepping over the threshold, he closed the door with a bump of his shoulder, leaving them in silent, hushed darkness.

"Jack?"

"Yes?"

"Are you going to sneak into my bed like a thief in the night?"

Lust curled, rising like smoke.

Actions usually spoke louder than words, but as he swaggered toward her bedroom like a pirate carrying booty, he offered two more: "Game on."

The makeup-sex *was* going to be spectacular...for the rest of their lives.

EPILOGUE

Banner scowled at the clunky, handheld communication device. "Repeat that, please? I'm having difficulty hearing you."

"I said, I know you're disappointed," Kendra repeated, "but don't take it personally. Sometimes, despite our best efforts, our clients re-offend."

Miranda DesJardins had re-offended rather spectacularly, pulling a gun on two people Kendra had described as 'a local lawyer' and 'a nightclub manager' while at the lawyer's downtown Minneapolis residence. The people were Jack Kirkland and Sasha Sebastiani, of course. "Impersonating a police officer, you said?"

"Yes, and poorly at that." Kendra sighed. "She was taken into custody."

He pulled the device away from his ear then shook it, more out of annoyance than anything else. "When did this happen, and why wasn't I notified?"

"She was taken into custody." She paused. "Andrew, I think you should get your hearing checked."

Hearing, vision, joints, brain...some days, it was all he could do to form words. This body was breaking down, yes, but right now his hearing wasn't the problem. *Try a different question.* "When was DesJardins taken into custody?"

"She was taken into custody."

"Yes, I heard you. Who took her into custody?"

"She was taken into custody."

Vampire fugue. A vampire had sifted through Kendra's memories, leaving little behind—which meant Gideon Lupinsky's team had made the arrest, not the MPD. If he hadn't left a message for Kendra informing her that DesJardins had missed their most recent scheduled appointment, he probably wouldn't have found out about the arrest. "Where is she?"

"I said, she's in custody," Kendra repeated, loudly and slowly. "Andrew, seriously, get your hearing checked."

"I will."

"This coming week?" she pressed.

"Yes." The reassurance cost him nothing. He'd never see her again.

"Well, try to enjoy what's left of the weekend," Kendra chirped. "We'll start fresh on Monday."

"Yes." He ended the call. Kendra's words were more accurate than she realized. Within one day, maybe two, he'd have found a different host. Assumed another form.

His time impersonating Banner was at an end.

He glanced at the board he'd set up on the far wall of the human's home workspace, where images of Sebastiani Labs' board members surrounded a picture of Sebastiani Labs itself. Around each board member, smaller photographs—family, friends, lovers, work colleagues—orbited like satellites. DesJardins' decade-old mug shot was one of a half-dozen smaller photos surrounding Jack Kirkland's larger one.

One more source whisked out of reach, but it

mattered little. DesJardins had served her purpose.

On to the next line of inquiry.

Why was Lorcan so interested in Sebastiani Labs? Why had one of the galaxy's most successful and powerful entrepreneurs hired not one but *two* Morph Primes—transporting them to this archaic planet at exorbitant cost, insisting they separate—then provided them with so little information about their assignment? "Gather intelligence. Infiltrate if possible. Avoid discovery. Await further instructions," Lorcan's representative had said.

When would those instructions arrive? How? Lorcan's representative had insisted they use only their native abilities, that they leave all their tech behind on the ship. That meant no nanos, no implants, no devices of any kind.

No way to communicate, not even with each other.

Outside, across the street, three young humans and a canine played in the frozen precipitation humans called snow. Some days, he watched them for hours on end, when the loneliness became…when the loneliness became…

Turning his back on the window, he studied the board. *Focus on the task at hand.*

Did Lorcan realize Earth already had a small but thriving non-human population? That Sebastiani Labs seemed to be its nexus? Highly likely, he decided. But with the primitive planet already seeded and salvage rights legally claimed, what was Lorcan's interest?

Lorcan hadn't deemed that information necessary to their investigation.

Jack Kirkland, the sole human sitting on Sebastiani Labs' board of directors, had seemed an obvious place to start. It hadn't taken long to discover Kirkland's friendship with the felon Bailey Brown, then to infiltrate the human justice system. Assuming Banner's identity as Brown's corrections officer should have yielded useful information, but he'd underestimated the female's intelligence, and her fierce loyalty to her friend. Wyatt Cooper, the true perpetrator of the crime for which Brown had been convicted, had been arrested then whisked away before he could fully cultivate the man. He'd had high hopes for DesJardins, but her emotional state had rendered her a risky proposition at best.

One thing he'd confirmed from his interaction with Brown and DesJardins? Jack Kirkland was no weak link. Yes, it was time for another line of inquiry.

A low, thready moan crept up through the duct work.

Downstairs, chained to a bed in the basement, the real Andrew Banner was deteriorating. Every morph, every replication, drained the man, damaging his body and mind. After over two years in captivity, Banner's life force was nearly gone.

It was time to end the man's suffering. Time to end his own by finding a new, healthy host.

Up on the board, Wyatt Cooper smiled through a thick, black X, a mark he'd made after the incubus's arrest. Picking up the same writing implement, he scrawled a matching mark through Miranda DesJardins' photograph. Then, more slowly, through Elliott Sebastiani's.

Sebastiani Labs' charismatic leader was dead.

Did Lorcan know? Did the other Prime know?

Right now, the answer mattered not.

He set the pen on Banner's desk, then considered

the faces gazing back at him from the board. Yes, it was time to find another host—a healthy and robust organic form.

But whose?